BATTLE HYMN

To Zach's right he heard a cheer. He turned and saw it was Lincoln riding along the line, ignoring the enemy fire. Even as the tall general approached, Zach was unable to hear what he was yelling, but the meaning was clear. It was even clearer when General Lincoln turned his horse to face the enemy and gestured for them to charge.

The yell the 33rd let out would have done any Rebel unit proud. They followed Lincoln up the slope and over the fence. More from shock than fear, the Southern line recoiled. . . .

—from "Lincoln's Charge"

PLUS TWENTY-SEVEN OTHER GLIMPSES OF DIFFERENT AMERICAS . . . UNDER *ALTERNATE PRESIDENTS!*

Tor books by Mike Resnick

Santiago: A Myth of the Far Future
The Dark Lady: A Romance of the Far Future
Ivory: A Legend of Past and Future
Paradise: A Chronicle of a Distant World
Stalking the Unicorn: A Fable of Tonight
Second Contact
The Red Tape War (with Jack L. Chalker and George Alec Effinger)
Bwana/Bully! (a Tor Double)

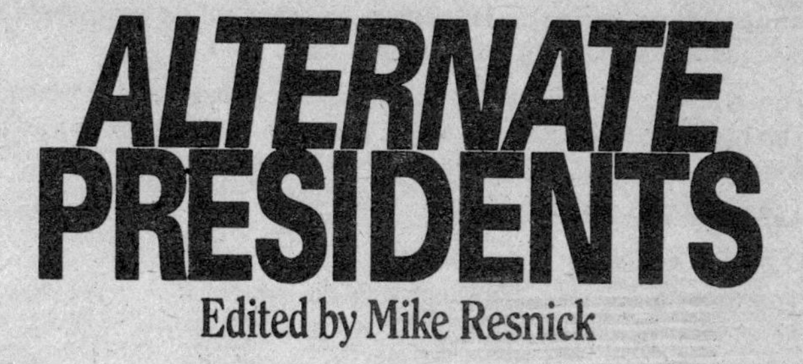

ALTERNATE PRESIDENTS

Edited by Mike Resnick

A TOM DOHERTY ASSOCIATES BOOK
NEW YORK

This is a work of fiction based on historical personages and incidents. The real people, places, and events portrayed in this book are used fictitiously; other people and events are purely fictitious.

ALTERNATE PRESIDENTS

A Tor Book
Published by Tom Doherty Associates, Inc.
49 West 24th Street
New York, N.Y. 10010

Cover art by Barclay Shaw

ISBN: 0-812-51192-1

First edition: February 1992

Printed in the United States of America

0 9 8 7 6 5 4 3 2 1

To Carol

And to all those defeated candidates
whose dreams had to wait until
the publication of this book

Contents

Introduction
Playing the Game of WHAT IF?

One of the joys of science fiction is that it gets to ask the question *What If?*

What if men can reach the stars? What if we find intelligent life there? What if Communism were to triumph over Capitalism? What if we run out of fossil fuels? What if the earth can no longer feed its starving billions? What if robots lobby for the right to vote?

Contrary to popular belief, science fiction does not necessarily have to look to the future to ask that question. A growing sub-genre of the field is the Alternate History story: what if Jesus had never lived, what if the Spanish Armada had destroyed the British fleet, what if the South had won the Civil War?

Nor do you have to be a professional science fiction writer to play the game—especially in an election year. Just walk into your local bar or supermarket or bowling alley or bookstore and keep your ears open, and you'll hear *everyone* asking *What If?* What if Gary Hart had not been caught womanizing? What if the Iranian hostages had been freed *before* Jimmy Carter ran for re-election? What if Bobby Kennedy had not been shot on the night he won the California primary? What if my defeated candidate had won?

Well, since this *is* an election year, I decided to put the question to the people who make their living by answering *What If?* I contacted a number of the best science fiction writers in the country, as well as a handful of very promising newcomers, asked them each to choose a presidential election, and told them to examine what might have happened if victory had gone to a different candidate.

Two best-selling authors who are simply too busy to write for original anthologies, Jack L. Chalker and David Gerrold, immediately agreed to appear in this one—*if* they could have 1856 and 1952, respectively. *1856 and 1952?* What in the world happened then? (Read "Now Falls the Cold, Cold Night" and "The Impeachment of Adlai Stevenson" and find out.)

That became the pattern: Almost every one of the writers I asked had some favorite, off-the-beaten-path historical era that they passionately wanted to explore in their stories.

Why, I wondered, did Michael P. Kube-McDowell and Martha Soukup instantly select 1880 and 1896? Did anything interesting actually occur in those years? Then "For I Shall Have a Flight to Glory" and "Plowshare" arrived in the mail, and I knew.

What if the first two women to run for the presidency had won? You'll find out in Laura Resnick's "We Are Not Amused" and Janet Kagan's "Love Our Lockwood".

What if Andrew Jackson's complicity in an 1819 scandal had not been covered up, or Zachary Taylor's vice president had died in 1848? Judith Moffett's "Chickasaw Slave" and Ralph Roberts's "How the South Preserved the Union" deliver the answers.

What if the bullets that were aimed at Theodore Roosevelt in 1912 and Huey Long in 1935 had been slightly off-target? My own "The Bull Moose at Bay" and Barry Malzberg's "Kingfish" show the courses our history might have taken.

What if the elections of 1968 and 1972, both of which

turned on the question of our involvement in Vietnam, had had different results? Pat Cadigan and Susan Shwartz offer you "Dispatches From the Revolution" and "Suppose They Gave a Peace . . ." a pair of brilliant novelettes that examine the consequences.

What if Jefferson and Lincoln had lost? If Dewey and Goldwater had won? If staid, unemotional Michael Dukakis had run into aliens his very first day in office?

The answers to more than two dozen alternate presidencies await you.

Read early and often.

—Mike Resnick

1789

Although he ran unopposed, George Washington was not everybody's choice to be our first president. There were some who preferred a man of international stature, such as Benjamin Franklin, to the military commander of a rebellion.

What if Franklin's supporters had gotten their way? What might his presidency have been like? Jody Lynn Nye, author of *Mythology Abroad, The Death of Sleep,* and several other fine novels and stories, provides the answer in a series of letters from Franklin's less-than-satisfied vice president, John Adams, to his wife, Abigail.

The Father of His Country

by Jody Lynn Nye

Letter from John Adams, Vice President–elect of the United States, to his wife, Abigail Adams, dated May 2, 1789:

Dear Madam,

We in Congress have elected a President to lead us, and not a King. I would have made a strong guess before this that General Washington would have been given the Supreme office. Cousin Sam Adams made a long Speech lauding the virtues of a man who could lead under such Adverse circumstances and come out the Victor. There was some approbation, but not as much as we thought.

The concept of having a military man in the Highest Office of the United States left an Ill Taste in many mouths. John Hancock said it himself to the full Assembly, "Generals should not rule countries," adding that it was a Bad Precedent to set. We cannot always be making War. The Quakers, most especially Secretary Thompson, agreed with him, as did numerous others.

Instead, it was felt that an infant country needed the best Parent it could have to win it acceptance in the civilized nations at large. The diplomat who has enjoyed the greatest entrée in society is Dr. Franklin. In spite of the Rumours (some of them are undoubtedly True) of his nude Air Baths while as an emissary to England, and his siring of numerous bastards on whatever French females took his fancy, he is well liked by foreign Heads of State friendly to the United States, had been prominent in matters of Diplomacy and Government at home and abroad, and had already proved that he had the best interests of his native Land at heart. It was felt that Franklin would provide a figurehead that would draw beneficent attention to our nation. His accomplishments are so many it took Thompson, who is an old Crony of his, the better part of an Hour to Enumerate them.

"Surely any child," Thompson had concluded, "would be grateful for such a wise Father?"

"Well, why don't we ask one of his?" Cousin Sam suggested waggishly. "There's enough of them around."

The room erupted into loud Debate, with both sides of the issue well represented, Franklinites and Washingtonians alike clamouring to be heard. I questioned whether a man with so many Irons in the Fire could have any time left for Governance, but I was outshouted. At last, the President of Congress banged on his desk for order, and the Secretary took a vote of the Electoral College. There was a clear Mandate for Dr. Franklin.

A party, I among those chosen, was despatched to approach the Candidate Elect, who was home nursing an at-

tack of the Gout. Franklin met the proposal with a simple reply. He bluntly refused.

We hastened to persuade him that it was the will of the People that he should ascend to the Supreme office as President. Hancock pointed out that the vote had been overwhelmingly in Franklin's favour.

Franklin twisted his lips to show his distaste, and protested that the idea was nonsense. In the good Doctor's opinion, America needed a young *man of Vigour and Understanding, not a meddlesome, Gout-afflicted grandfather set firmly in his ways.*

Irritatedly, I pointed out to him that it was not nonsense, and that we were quite serious. I begged him to reconsider accepting.

I thought he might have been dumbfounded at first by the conception that he, a son of the humble Trading class, should take his place beside Kings as an Equal Head of State, but he acceded at last.

There was some satisfied Handshaking all round, then I excused myself to go make preparations for his Coronation. I was arrested by an Imperious thump on the floor from Franklin's cane.

"I will not be made a King. This Government of the People which we have made, and God knows General Washington has defended, needs to be able to correct me if I'm wrong, and swiftly, too. You can't do that readily with a King. If a Brick drops from on high, it must be snatched quickly from a similar Height, or it will do all the greater damage when at last it strikes the ground. No, I never want any title greater than Mister."

As I made my way out, I was grateful for this example of his plain common sense. Though we of the Gifted classes shall rule wisely, all Americans in future shall be known by the same Rank.

A brief excerpt from President Franklin's memoirs, published as the *Autobiography*:

Modesty forbade me from accepting the position at first. The offer appealed greatly to my Vanity, but I would not allow it to cloud my Judgement. Like Caesar, I refused the Office three times, but unlike that August Statesman, I accepted in the end. It is Pleasing to be recognized as the first Caesar of the Americas.

Excerpt of a letter from Vice President Adams to Abigail Adams, dated September 17, 1789:

I regret not being at liberty to leave Philadelphia at this time to return home. The President, now duly installed in Office, has reverted to his tradesman antecedents and has insisted on organizing his government as if it were a business. As if Government could run with the same despatch and efficiency as a Printshop! The Notion, however, seems to have great popularity with the Citizenry at Large. Here in Philadelphia, Franklin is surrounded by his supporters, Friends, and former subscribers. They are accustomed to reading what he writes, and Agreeing with it.

I am fortunate to hold the second highest office in the Land. As time progresses, my role in the Senate cannot but mean that the Vice Presidency cannot but Eclipse the office of President in Importance and Prestige. Franklin is Popular on both sides of the House, but by no means all of the time. You will have read the copy of the Philadelphia Gazette *which I sent you, quoting his Speech decrying Ambitiousness and Avarice as the two Principal Sins besetting the United States. His position is popular with the small merchants and farmers, not to mention the Quaker brethren who hold similar Views, but does not carry well with the Landowners and Aristocrats who largely make up Congress. Fortunately the speech was considered whimsy, as it is unlikely any member of Congress would ever allow Avarice to interfere with his judgement.*

In an effort to promote the Dignity of the office of President, Congress had moved to insist that Franklin limit publication of his writings to only the most Serious of topics. The humourous Scrivenings of which he is fond were felt by Congress to be unbecoming the Office. Privately, I am made constantly aware that Franklin keeps writing his hoaxes and satires, which are published through others under a number of aliases. The most recent of these was a playful Satire on England's position regarding Trade with us, purported to have been written by a "Mr. Newly."

With the Paper in Hand, I made my way to Franklin's office to demand whether he had indeed written the Piece. He did not admit or deny it, but his eyes twinkled with Mischief. Losing patience with his coyness, I insisted that he accede to Congress's rule and cease publishing Nonsense. In this case, his playful Extemporanea might damage the Delicacy of our position. We have found a position of Strength from which to negotiate with Britain, and do not want it Jeopardized by Trivialization. The King-in-Parliament has hampered and delayed the Negotiations, it is believed, out of Anger at the treatment suffered by defeated Loyalists in this country, so the thought of establishing a working Relationship with England has not enjoyed much Currency.

To my annoyance, and that of many Like-Minded, the piece by Mr. Newly has become widely popular, encouraging the Man on the Street to support the Trade Negotiations with England. So the piece was useful to Government, although it sets a Precedent we do not wish to Establish, whereby the General Publick controls the Government's actions. We can only Admonish Franklin not to do it again. Who knows what would happen if the uneducated masses were to gain control of its Government?

Excerpt of a letter from Vice President Adams to Abigail Adams, dated March 5, 1791:

We have chained the Lightning, but cannot Control it. It continues to strike when and where it pleases, ignoring any Rods we set up to Catch it. In the following months since the Newly article, Franklin has suggested, in commentaries penned under a series of transparent Pseudonyms in the

Newspapers, that the Trade agreement with England should be reached with all Haste. Congress has allowed these to pass without comment since the Publick now agrees to the measure, but we are having trouble containing President Firebrand, who is Flush with his great Success. If we had wished for the people to actually run the government, we would have had them elect the President directly.

Franklin continues in Print to manipulate Opinion to suit himself, revealing Proposals to the general Readership before they have been presented to Congress. I and other Representatives are frustrated to learn any morning that our Servants may know more of the President's mind than we do Ourselves. Yesterday I was accosted by a Tavern owner who objected to the new duty on Rum. If this Trend continues, Statesmen will be forced to the indignity of consulting their Constituents before voting, an Absurdity that would likely delay all the dealings of government, and discourage the High Quality of man who would otherwise seek Government office.

From a letter from Benjamin Franklin to his son-in-law, April 29, 1792:

I am so busy with Projects dependent from my Office as President that I have Little time left for Writing. Every day brings a new Concern to which I must set my Hand or my Seal. It only remains to be Reveal'd whether the Rigours of this Job take away Years from my Life, or add to it.

Excerpt of a letter from Vice President Adams to Abigail Adams, April 29, 1792:

I cannot deny that the Institutions President Franklin proposes are good, but I wish we had believ'd him when he told us he was a Meddlesome old man. One comfort is that he won't be with us long. He complains always that he is about to Die. One day he will Oblige us, and do so. Then we will get on with the business of Governing this Nation, unhindered.

1800

Thomas Jefferson won the presidency in 1800, but because the election laws were different at that time, he and his vice presidential running mate, Aaron Burr, actually ended in a tie in the electoral college.

Burr was never known for his lack of ambition, and Jayge Carr, author of *Knight of a Thousand Eyes*, *The Woodscolt*, and numerous other well-received books and stories, asked herself what might have happened if Burr had taken advantage of his situation to wheel and deal for the presidency.

This is her answer.

The War of '07

by Jayge Carr

Alexander Hamilton:

"What? Who—*what are* you *doing here*?"

"But I am not 'here,' my dear chap. I am in Albany, preparing for my daughter's wedding. Since I am there and not here, this meeting is not occurring." Aaron Burr's black eyes flashed and sparkled, but as usual with Hamilton, the charisma was useless. Perhaps the two men were too much alike, perhaps instinctive antipathetic chemistry prevented anything but hostility, but with this one man, the charm did not work, had never worked.

Alexander Hamilton smiled wryly, leaning back in his chair, away from the man standing so casually where he should not have been. "If you say so. But there will be effects, nonetheless. Or did you come to ask me to throw what influence I have with the Federalists to your opponent?"

The smile broadened. "Not hardly." The man who wasn't officially there settled comfortably on the corner of the work-littered desk. "I'm here to tell you why you should leave off your distrust of me—"

Angrily: "You are a devil!"

Almost gentle: "A necessary devil. A devil you are going to support, or more accurately, urge your followers to support, when the inevitable balloting comes."

Hamilton's pale eyes glared at his visitor. "I was wavering. But your arrival, at this ungodly hour . . . How did you know I was working this late, anyway?"

"My dear Hamilton, when, lately, have you not been working late . . . against me?"

"Your arrival has firmed my decision. How like you, to come begging for votes—"

Aaron Burr laughed softly. "But I am not begging, my dear Hamilton. I merely wish to point out a few facts to you, and leave the rest up to your conscience. You do love your country, do you not? I am counting on that love of your country."

Alexander Hamilton almost soared out of his seat. "Surely you are not accusing Jefferson—Jefferson, the author of our Declaration of Independence—of being a traitor!"

"Did I accuse my fellow Republican-Democrat? No, I may disapprove of his preference for strong states' rights over the federal government"—Hamilton flinched; he was well known for his preference for a strong federal government—"but that's not what I was referring to. No, not in the slightest. Nor am I raising the specter of the almost inevitable threat of northern secession, if another Virginian accedes to the presidency." Hamilton flinched again, frowning.

"No," Aaron Burr went on smoothly. "I merely point with sadness to the fragility of our independence, not internally, but externally. As a country, we are no more than a few years old. The European powers look upon our government as not much more than the native Indian chieftains, and you know what havoc they have wreaked with those. We won our independence, mostly because England did not esteem us a sufficient enemy to throw her full might against us. But our country is young, and rich, with land and other resources. Europe is old, and crowded and envious. Once their internal quarrels cease, where will they look for expansion? Here we are, with the English to the north of us, the Spanish in the Floridas, Mexico, and the Californias, and France and Spain squabbling over the Louisiana Territory. Look on a map, man, and see our future. Unless we break the chain around us, we are vulnerable, surrounded by potential enemies."

"What has this to do—"

"You, a soldier, Washington's second-in-command not two years ago when the French crisis made it appear that we might have to go to war again to defend ourselves, can ask that? Do you truly want our country, in these perilous times, led by a philosopher, a thinker instead of a doer? I am a soldier, I know the value of preparedness, of a good offense—"

"This country can *not* afford war!"

Still gentle: "This country cannot afford peace. England controls the seas, she hovers at our northern border. Were I in command, I would increase our newly reestablished U.S. Marine Corps, I would stop the dismantling of our navy. I have Truxton in mind for Secretary of the Navy, and would have him build—"

Impressed in spite of his dislike: "How will you pay for all this?"

"I thought to have Morris or possibly Gallatin as Secretary of Treasury. The money must be raised. Perhaps via loans. Possibly we will sell some of the western lands. Possibly—" A sly smile. "An import tariff, or—" Hamilton himself had recommended such a tariff to protect the infant American industry. A shrug. "You know that managing money is not perhaps my strongest suit—"

Hamilton smothered a chuckle. That was an understatement. All his adult life, Aaron Burr had made immense monies quickly . . . and spent them even more quickly. "Build up our land forces and navy, yes . . . and then what?"

"The English first. If diplomacy accomplishes our wishes, well and good, but we must prepare ourselves to fight for our survival. I know you favored the English not long since, when the war between them and the French first broke out, but I am sure you will favor *our* country's advantage over either. The European powers will keep each other occupied for some time, one hopes. We have enemies on three fronts now, four if you count the sea. But eliminating the English on this continent will free us on that side, and give us an opportunity, also, at the riches of the fur trade."

"You've been listening to that fellow, what's his name, Adder."

"Astor. But that is a side point. The important issue is our boundaries, and our safety. How safe are our settlers in our Northwest Territory, for example, with the English north of them stirring up the savages?"

Hamilton was slowly nodding. "What if we lose, in our second war with the English?"

"With two soldiers like ourselves at the helm? Will we be in a better position if we wait until they have settled their battle with the French, and can concentrate on re-subjecting us? The choice is not war and peace, it is war now, soon, when we are equipped and ready, at a time of our choosing, or war later, when they are equipped and ready, at a time of their choosing."

It took quite a bit more arguing, but eventually Hamilton said, with a crisp nod, "All right, I agree. Yet if I do put my votes behind you, I want your promise: I do not trust you, Burr. I want to be in a position to counter you, if you go beyond the line."

Burr knew he had obtained what he wanted. "I can't make you vice president. If I win the presidency, Jefferson will get the vice presidency by default."

Hamilton waved away the vice presidency. "A powerless office. Secretary of State, now . . ."

"I said the two of us at the helm. I had you in mind for Secretary of War."

Sourly. "I'll think about it. The choice must be mine."

Knowing he had won: "Of course. My word of honor: if I accede to the presidency, you will be either my Secretary of State, or of War. The final choice will be yours."

Alexander Hamilton nodded.

The fate of a country was sealed . . . or changed.

Albert Gallatin, Republican-Democrat congressman from Pennsylvania:

Furious: "You promised me Treasury!"

"My dear chap," President Burr was laying on the famous charm. "You will get Treasury, but not yet. Let Morris have the inevitable blame; he will be a has-been when you are ascending."

"Our country needs a firm fiscal policy!"

"You will have your chance." A smile. "Remember this conversation, my dear Gallatin. There will come a day when I offer you Treasury, and you will not wish to take it."

"I want it now."

"I say again: Let Morris be the villain. Your turn will come. For now, patience. Timing is all important."

"I'll not forget this . . . *sir*."

President Burr shrugged. "Nonetheless, you will be my Secretary of Treasury. When the time is right. Though you will not thank me for the office."

"You're going to ruin our country."

"No." A slow head shake. "No, I'm going to glorify it."

* * *

Daniel Boone:

"Again and again lawyerly word-splittin' has deprived me of my rightful land. Now ye ask me now to trust another lawyer, even if he be the president of the Confederation?"

"It is because I *am* president that I can hope to untangle your problems. Which I will do, because you will be doing a good deed for your country as I am working to your benefit."

"Eh?" He had not dressed himself in the coonskin cap and buckskins he would have worn in the Cumberland, but in neat formal attire; not as fancy as President Burr, who was known for the elegance of his dress, but nonetheless, Daniel Boone's knee breeches and claw-tailed coat would not have looked out of place in Mayfair, London, though those seeing him there would have placed him as a clerk, not as a member of the *haut monde*.

"I wish to work, not just for the good of our country today, but for the good of our country tomorrow and all the tomorrows to come. Now north of us, the English loyalists of Canada may desire to stir up the natives between our territory and theirs. General Wayne's victory at Fallen Timbers was quite decisive, but some of those tribes . . . like that tribe that call themselves the Shining . . ."

"Ye mean the Shawnee."

"Yes. All those tribes with unpronounceable names. And especially some of the younger chiefs, the warlike ones. They could cause quite a bit of trouble, unless they are nullified. If you—"

"Ye doesn't mean to send me in and murder them, now!"

"No, no, never, my good man. I want them working *for* me and our country, not against me. Now, you have had such good experience with understanding the various native ways. I want you to travel up there, find out what they want—"

Sourly: "Likely, all the settlers to go back where they came from."

"And what we can do for them to satisfy them—short of all the settlers giving up what they have worked so hard for."

"What if I fail?"

"My dear fellow, you won't. Because if you do, I will be left with no choice at all. If so, I won't stop with a few rebellious savages. If the natives must be made innocuous, well, they are quite vulnerable to European diseases, are they not? I would not like to do so, but if supplies from a pest house or two were distributed to them, they would think an epidemic the wrath of God, and punishment for rebellion to their rightful rulers, would they not?"

Eyes bulging, a wad of tobacco caught half in, half out of his mouth: "Ye *wouldn't.*"

"My dear fellow, I wouldn't want to. But if I must, to defend my country, then I will." He was a short man, retaining much of the handsomeness of his youth; but his face was firm, he meant every word, and he wanted the man he was speaking with to know he meant every word. To believe him.

Which he did. "I'll do my best."

"My dear Mr. Boone, I never doubted you for a second."

When his visitor had left, President Burr smiled. "You just have to know how to twitch the reins," he said softly.

Captain Thomas Truxton:

"Secretary of the Navy? Me? But what would I do?"

"My dear Thomas, a country must be ready instantly to defend its peace, or it is vulnerable. Our military, land and sea, was much dismantled after the successful conclusion of our war for independence. A sad omission, and one which severely limited my predecessor's options. I don't intend to repeat his mistakes. Our country, if it is to survive, must be capable, always, to protect itself."

"Aye, but I'm no more than a captain. I've at most commanded a small flotilla. Surely you want someone with more experience in administration."

"From what I understand, England's navy has won its battles despite the Admiralty administrators. Why are men so reluctant to be pressed into the English navy? Because they are ill fed, disciplined with the cat, and poorly led. Too many of their officers purchase their promotions, with money or by connections, rather than earn them with merit. Worse, far too many of the men are pressed and resentful of it."

"Oh, aye, that's the way of it." He looked like what he had been, a rough privateer; but his eyes glowed with shrewd intelligence.

"Our navy will be a meritocracy. Well run and well commanded. So who better to establish such an effective force, one our country may well need to defend its shoreline, than a man already proven, the victor of the battle with the *L'Insurgente*?" The charismatic smile. "My one regret is that I am depriving our seas of their finest commander."

It took a while longer to get Truxton's agreement, but as they were shaking hands at the sailor's departure, President Burr added one final comment. "By the bye, don't I remember about some patriot, during our late war, attempting to design an underwater vessel?"

Truxton frowned. "Impossible."

Again that warm charisma: "Perhaps. But it behooves us to prove it. During the war we had little to spare for such long chances. But now . . . Once you are Secretary, I would hope you would find what happened to that man, Bushnell I believe his name was, and see if his ideas could be perhaps brought to fruition."

"Oh aye, but 'twill come to naught, I dare swear."

"Perhaps so. But there will be money for such experiments. Under the greatest secrecy, of course."

"Oh aye. Ye don't want folk thinking you've loaded your cannon without any balls."

"Of course not. Good luck—Secretary Truxton."

* * *

Edward Livingston, Secretary of State:

"I thought your plan was to oppose the European powers one by one, Aaron. Where does the Pasha of Tripoli come into this?"

"A declared war is a marvelous excuse to pump up our military prowess. Our warships will find it good practice."

Robert Morris, Secretary of the Treasury:

"The commission, specially appointed under the terms of the Jay Treaty with England, has found that in the settlement of the Revolutionary War claims of British citizens, the United States owes no less than $2,664,000."

A gentle smile: "So?"

Blunt: "We haven't got it. Even with the increase of internal taxation—and how long that will last without impelling another Whisky Rebellion, I can't say—our debt is increasing, thanks to your war expenditures. We simply cannot—"

"It doesn't matter. I have no intention of paying any such war claims. If the British government wants their citizens satisfied, *they* can pay the claims."

Almost choking: "But—the Jay Treaty—"

"I was not signatory to that, and I do not consider it binding. Don't worry, my good man, we'll just delay and obfuscate. I imagine we can do so with ease."

After Morris, frothing, had gone: "Besides, if the British are angry over the nonpayment of the claims, that will make them even less likely to appease us. Though I doubt they would even think of such." The smile fading, "We need an excuse . . ."

Essence of missive from Robert R. Livingston, minister in Paris: Spain has ceded the entire Louisiana Territory to France. What shall I do?

Essence of answer: Negotiate *immediately* for a tract of land at the lower end of the Mississippi suitable for a port. We *must* protect ourselves. As a secondary goal, obtain a permanent guarantee of free navigation and right of deposit in New Orleans. Third, see what else of the New World rights they are willing to sell. The more land and rights we can attain, the better.

Edmund Randolph, patriot and former Secretary of State:

"Greetings, President Burr. How may I serve our country?"

"Did you know that the Spanish in New Orleans, although Spain has ceded Louisiana to the French, have forbidden American traders the right to transship their goods in the port into ocean-going vessels?"

"But that's against the Treaty of Lorenzo!"

"Precisely. They haven't the right, anyway. I am appointing you as minister plenipotentiary to France. Livingston is already there, I won't replace him, but you will arrive with more recent instructions. Congress has approved two million for the purchase of New Orleans and West Florida. Try to get as much land as you can. As cheaply as possible, of course. Both Floridas as a minimum, and if you can . . . all of it." A sly wink. "Does Bonaparte truly want to remain enmeshed in the New World while he is in a death struggle with the English?"

"The Treaty of Amiens should—"

Burr snorted. "The Treaty of Amiens will last as long as Bonaparte wants, not an instant longer. I should not want to be a British citizen in France, either, when he breaks the treaty. I understand they have been pouring in, I suppose to gawk at the guillotines." Changing the subject: "I authorize you to go as high as ten million. But try not to. And bring me back the news that the Europeans are out of our south."

Albert Gallatin, head of the Republican-Democratic caucus:

"You are suggesting *who* as your next vice president?"

"Edmund Randolph of Virginia. Otherwise, Jefferson's

power in the south is sufficient to split the party. If our votes divide sufficiently evenly, the Federalists will get one last chance."

Gallatin glared and rubbed his chin. "You've not made many friends in your first term."

"This country is at war. Whether you agree with my policies or not, do we want to alter our leadership radically while fighting a war?"

Gallatin, who had several reasons to prefer Jefferson, sighed. "No."

"By the bye, Morris's health is failing. Were I to nominate you to take his place, should he retire for ill health—"

Gallatin flinched. "Your policies have all but ruined this country."

"I am not a gambler. My policies will pay handsomely in the long run."

"But we must survive in the short run."

"Yes. So I depend on you to supply our country with the necessary sinews of war."

Another sigh. "How can I refuse?"

"Precisely. As I once told you. I will offer and you will—with the utmost reluctance—accept."

Edmund Randolph, Vice President; Edward Livingston, Secretary of State; James Madison, Attorney General; and Alexander Hamilton, Secretary of War:

"We have the treaty with Tripoli. What's our next step, Mr. President?"

"Does anyone think England will not give us provocation?"

Four heads shake.

"With the help of Attorney General Madison, I am preparing a report to be given before Congress on the continuing British interference with our commercial shipping, especially their impressment of American sailors," informed Secretary Livingston.

President Burr nodded. "That should pave the way well."

The Secretary of War added, "America stands ready. Truxton is out overseeing the . . . ahhh . . ." He looked at the others, put a finger over his lips. "You know."

"How are they coming?"

"Benjamin Franklin would have been so enthusiastic. A pity he could not have seen this day. But our inventor Bushnell is a worthy successor. I do believe the whole will be successful."

"Excellent." The President nodded, satisfied. "And gentlemen, the news from the north continues good. We hear that a certain British general has been attempting to stir up the passions of the savages. But thanks to our Mr. Boone, he is too little and too late. If any passions are aroused, the British will find themselves on the receiving end."

Alexander Hamilton lingered after the other three had left: "I still cannot trust you, sir, but I cannot deny that your tactics are masterly. Sending Boone to the Indians, so far in advance, for example."

"We are getting reports from our explorers, too. It's a magnificent country. One day it will all be ours, from sea to sea, from north to south."

"A worthy ambition, sir."

After Hamilton, too had left, Burr added one comment: "But not my only ambition, sir. Not my only one at all."

In congress assembled, President Burr speaking:

"Gentlemen: On June 22, 1807, Britain perpetrated an act of war against our country. The H.M.S. *Leopold*, a frigate of fifty-two guns, stopped our own frigate, the U.S.S. *Chesapeake*, of thirty-nine guns, just outside the three-mile limit, and demanded the surrender of four men whom the British commander declared to be British subjects. Of course, to the British, anyone is a British subject at their proclamation."

The assembled congressmen roared.

"When our doughty Commodore James Barron refused to surrender any American sailors, the British opened fire.

Three loyal Americans died, simply for the crime of being American citizens. Eighteen others, hard-working men, going about their business, putting bread in the mouths of their wives and children, were wounded, some severely. The four alleged British subjects were then forcibly removed from our vessel; all are now under the threat of British law involving deserters. The British may even hang them. Gentlemen!" A raised fist.

"How long will we submit to Albion's might? How long will we bow the head and bend the knee to England's mad king? Have we not fought a Revolutionary War to free ourselves from just such tyranny? Shall we not now be ready and willing to pay the price, to lift this yoke from our necks once and for all? England must be made to respect our citizens, just as the Pasha of Tripoli was made to respect our citizens! The Redcoats will immediately promise to stop this harassment of American citizens, or we will teach them a lesson they will long remember!"

Another roar, filling the chamber. It became a chant. "War, now! War, now! War NOW!"

Sent by the heliographs set up by President Burr, to Generals Jacob Brown, Hull, Harrison, Jackson, Van Rensselaer, Wilkinson, and naval officers Bainbridge, Decatur, Lawrence, Perry: GO!

Alexander Hamilton, Secretary of War, and Edward Livingston, Secretary of State:

"They're falling like ninepins." Livingston frowned at the map spread out before all three men. "But how long will that last?"

Burr patted a small supply of tiny United States flags on little pins. "Perhaps I'd better ask my dear Theodosia to make me up a few more flags."

"The element of surprise served us well. I can almost feel it ungentlemanly to attack without warning. But we have used up that advantage now." Alexander Hamilton stared down at the map, more a relief map of the continent—as far as it was known. Fort Dearborn, Fort Meigs, York, Fort Erie, Montreal and several other sites sported American flags.

"The British will be too little, too late." Aaron Burr placed flags near several strategic spots, including Quebec. "Their generals will have to get orders, or wait for reinforcements to be sent from England. No, this is all going as planned. A quick, hard push . . . and we are successful." He smiled at his two companions. "Besides, our naval captains should be deploying the secret weapons about now."

"Do you truly think they will be successful?" Livingston had been kept up on the underwater warship experiments, but he still couldn't believe in their feasibility.

"They're useless against ships out at sea. But the British have only a few naval bases. The ships lie crowded together in each of them, some even waiting just outside the harbor for weeks to put in for repairs and refitting. My captains have their orders. The attacks will be as simultaneous as possible. We are almost sure that the ports will be unable to warn each other. As they will see it, all the ships in the harbor will sink mysteriously, with no one knowing who or why is responsible. If they suspect the small merchant ships, flying the flags of a neutral country and anchored well outside the harbors . . . well, that is the risk we take. At worst, the captains have strict orders to sink the underwater attack vessels if there is any chance the British will board, or seem to be on the verge, by any method, of discovering the vessels."

Hamilton nodded. "Stretched between us and Napoleonic Europe, this should be a devastating blow for England."

Aaron Burr picked up the flag near Quebec, put it down. "The only good war is a fast, planned one. England is on the ropes, and I intend to keep her there." He planted the flag, smiled. "Soon." Then: "Gentlemen, a toast. To America: long may her banner wave on high!"

"To America!"

* * *

Essence of report of an English spy, for the President's eyes only: . . . and they plan to send Lord Wesley, or Wellesley, as he now spells it, in a last desperate attempt to retake Canada . . . Also they plan an attack on the capital, in hopes of cutting off the heads of our country . . . They are desperate . . . Napoleon is winning in the Peninsula, and with their forces divided between the European and North American continentals . . .

Beware, they come to kill "by accident"!

Council of (political) war, with Albert Gallatin, again head of the Republican-Democratic caucus, Edward Livingston, Secretary of State, and several others, including Alexander Hamilton, Secretary of War:

"Why am I here?" Hamilton asked bluntly. "I work with you, President Burr, but I am still a Federalist."

"Perhaps we need a Federalist point of view." He sharpened a quill, laid it on a piece of plain paper. "The topic under discussion is my next vice president."

"I thought your whole campaign was based on not changing leadership in mid-crisis," Alexander Hamilton said, in some shock. "How do you explain replacing Randolph, then?"

President Burr laid a finger beside his nose. "We have no choice. That old scandal of accepting bribes during the negotiation of the Jay treaty has re-emerged. Randolph is now a political liability, not an asset. Besides, he has said several times that he had wanted to retire after his first term, by reason of ill health. So now, we will accept that retirement, and . . ."

Alexander Hamilton didn't say anything, but his thoughts were clearly written on his face: "Who started those rumors again, you old devil?"

"And," Burr continued, "I myself am finding the strains of responsibility . . . wearing. I would like to arrange my successor."

Complete silence, as the men chewed over what he was saying. John Adams, vice president under Washington, succeeded him. Thomas Jefferson, vice president under Adams, came within a hair of succeeding him. Now, Burr was saying he intended to name his heir.

When the silence was almost painful, Burr broke it. "Although the war seems to be going well, I deem it advisable to have a soldier in command of our great country. And who more suitable than he who was chosen second-in-command under our glorious General Washington?" He bowed toward Hamilton. "It will unite our parties, it will unite our country." He held out a hand. "You know I have made sure to make the office much less a sinecure, and I will pledge to make it a training ground, if such there could be, for the highest office, four years from now, when I am ready to lay down this burden."

Hamilton may have hesitated a second; if so, none of the other men present could swear to it. Then his hand reached out, and clasped Burr's.

"My chosen successor," Burr murmured, smiling.

Dispatch from General Andrew Jackson, the Northwest Front:

> Sir,
>
> It pleases me to report a stunning victory. The Redcoats have learned little about the use of terrain since the Revolutionary War. Our men were neatly sited behind ramparts on a slight rise. At first it seemed as if the Redcoats would decline the invitation, but one regiment broke ranks and charged, and then they all did.
>
> It was a slaughter.
>
> Our casualties were light, no more than a dozen deceased, and a score wounded. The British casualties mounted into the thousands. This breaks the back of the British effort here in Canada.

P.S. The English Commander, a General Wesley or Wellesley, was among the casualties. I can regret the loss of a worthy foeman. Had the fates permitted, he might have prevented the charge, perhaps won the day, or at least rallied his men to force an honorable retreat. But one of our native associates, seeing him moving openly among his troops, unlimbered his longbow and skewered him like a Christmas turkey. We buried him in the mass grave.

Vice President Hamilton, Secretary of State Livingston, Secretary of War Henry "Light-Horse Harry" Lee, Treasury Secretary Gallatin, Attorney General Madison, Secretary of Commerce Joseph Alston:

"Marry *who*?" Joseph Alston, son-in-law to Aaron Burr, sputtered.

"The Princess Pauline Bonaparte."

General Lee burst into rude laughter.

"If you mean La Borghese, I thought she was married to that Italian prince." James Madison spoke as soon as he could be heard.

"She is." Aaron Burr sighed. "But the marriage is unsatisfactory, and she has long been separated from him." He ran a hand over his black hair, still thick and dark, though receding a trifle at the forehead. "There's precedent for a divorce."

"But why would you want to? You've never even met her!" Joseph Alston could barely get the words out.

"I don't." Burr was for once almost blunt. "But it's a choice of marriage, or paying through the nose for the Floridas. The Bonaparte King of Spain has made us an offer. The ostensible price is eight million dollars."

"We can't afford it!" snapped Albert Gallatin.

"You always say that, my dear fellow"—Burr was still smiling—"and yet you always manage to find the money somewhere. However, in this case, part of the price is to be remitted to our country as the lady's dowry. As you know, France and England are still locked in their to-the-death struggle, which we have been taking advantage of. France wants to ensure our favor, or at least our neutrality after England formally surrenders Canada to us. The war on the sea is winding down, thanks to Bushnell's Undersea Turtles. France is looking ahead."

"I thought you said the King of Spain," mumbled Alston, who was there mostly as Burr's son-in-law. "I thought Spain and France were enemies."

"They were. But the Bonaparte invaded Spain after Godoy and King Ferdinand fled, conquered as is his wont, and left his brother Joseph on the throne. This offer, while ostensibly from 'King' Joseph, is in truth Bonaparte sensibly making sure to cover his back."

"But marriage—" Even Livingston, who knew much of the politics behind the offer, didn't like it.

"A dynastic marriage, dear chap, just as they employ in Europe. Not my choice, by far. The lady has a reputation—"

Hamilton hid a smile. Burr, too, had quite a reputation for his successes with the fair sex.

"And half of eight million dollars, chaps . . ."

"The Floridas for a dowry." Hamilton didn't like it either. Then, smiling openly, "Better you than me, Burr."

"Bigamy, dear chap, in your case." Burr smiled back. "Unless you want to consider a divorce—" It hung in the balance; Hamilton loved his wife deeply, and resented even the implication of insult.

Then the slightly older man chuckled. "No, Mr. President, I pass. This loathsome, difficult—I do hear she is rather lovely—duty is yours, all yours."

Popular song of the '07 War:

In eighteen-seven, we took a little jaunt,
Long with Gen'ral Jackson down the frothin'
St. Laurent.
We took a little bacon and we took a little corn,

And we fought the bloody British near the tow'rin' Fort Dearborn.

Chorus: *Fired our guns, and the British kept a-comin',*
'Twan't nigh as many as they was a while before.
Fired once more and they began a-runnin',
Down the St. Laurenty to the gray Atlantic shore!"

An assortment of high officials; also Burr's only living child, his daughter Theodosia:

"But, Papa, if you must marry her, why must it be in New York?"

"Because she's a product of the Old World, my dear. A civilized woman. While I can command her to live here with me, while I am still president, I cannot expect her to marry from here, to try to find her bridesclothes here; in short, for a wedding of this magnitude, she must have the finest of resources our country can offer. Which means New York, with side trips to Boston or perhaps Philadelphia."

"But why must I go and greet her?"

"Because I should but cannot, my dear. Have I asked so much of you, that you gibe at this small favor?"

"No, Papa." A small voice: "I shall miss little Aaron."

"Take the lad with you, by all means. I know women, and this one, especially, has a reputation for finery. It will take time. I will join you as soon as I feel secure leaving the affairs of state, even temporarily. The wedding of its president must not embarrass our country."

"Oh, no, Papa." (The men have been shifting uncomfortably.)

Burr chucked her under the chin. "Thank you, my dear. I knew you wouldn't let me down. I don't know exactly when she will arrive, but I trust you to have as much as possible ready for her." Joseph Alston, thinking no one could see, rolled his eyes skyward.

"As for the rest of you"—Burr's voice was still jovial, but with an undernote of command—"we have already decided who must stay to keep the country running, but I will hear no excuses from the rest of you. This is the face our country presents to the world, and it will be as elaborate and ostentatious as we can afford."

Gallatin sniffed. "In that case, Mr. President, I suggest an elopement." The other men roared, and even Theodosia giggled softly.

"Even now, you don't understand, any of you. Our safety depends on our enemies' perceptions of us. At all costs, we must appear strong. Strength includes ability to pay for the sinews of war, even to the extent of being able to waste those sinews on a lavish display. All the ambassadors will be invited. They will then write home to their governments that we are strong. Thus, we will not need to test that strength."

Essence of report of an English spy, for the President's eyes only: The invasion force will be leaving within the sennight. Protect our government!

All the upper-level officials residing in the District of Columbia, being addressed by President Burr:

"Gentlemen, my darling Theodosia writes me that all is in train for my wedding. It has taken some time and rearranging of my schedule, but I will be starting north tomorrow. Those who are accompanying me, I do hope you have your clothes selected for the great day. The rest of you, I have ordered champagne sent down. I wish you to drink a toast to my nuptials while I'm gone."

Major Zebulon Montgomery Pike, after riding hell for leather from the District of Columbia to Philadelphia, the final choice for the site of The Wedding:

"Sir!" Skidding to a stop, he saluted briskly.

"Major?" Burr, seated next to his bride at the formal dinner, rose slowly and with some dignity from the elaborate chair, almost a throne.

"Sir, I regret to inform you . . . the enemy attacked the capital."

"What!" After a single indrawn breath, he rapped out questions: "How many? How did they arrive? Were they driven off? What forces are available for a counterattack?"

"At least five thousand Redcoats. From ships. They were still in possession when I left. Except—" He swallowed loudly. "They were burning the capital, sir. Mrs. Hamilton, sir, she went in for the Declaration of Independence, but I don't think she got out. Vice President Hamilton was organizing the defense, but—"

"Dear God!" Turning to General Lee, seated only three seats down from him. "General, gather what forces you can. We ride tonight!"

"Sir!" General Lee leaped to his feet, and snapped out a salute. "Major," to Pike, "how many men do they have, how many men do we have?"

"Their forces? Out of at least five thousand? I can't know, sir. But Vice President Hamilton, he was going to make them pay, and pay dear!"

"My husband!" Theodosia suddenly realized that all left in Washington were vulnerable.

"Ma'am?" Pike nodded to her.

"Alston, Joseph Alston. Is he—?"

"I believe he was part of the defense force, ma'am. The vice president, he was setting up ramparts."

"We'll have to reinforce him immediately." Burr's gaze flicked around, and he began snapping off names, finishing, "All of you, a council of war in my private suite, and then we ride! Our capital is at stake! We will save her . . . or avenge her!" Even louder: "Citizens of the United States! Our country has been betrayed and insulted! Revenge will be ours! Pass the word to your friends and fellow patriots! We assemble at dawn! Victory and vengeance!"

As he stalked out of the hall, a roar of approval followed him. But as he went through the door, General Lee and the others following closely, no one could see his face. With its sly smug expression of a successful conspirator.

1812. Edward Livingston, Vice President:

"Of course, there will be no problem re-electing the Victor of Washington, Aaron. But I thought you wanted to lay down the burden of leadership."

"One more term, Edward. Just one. So many affairs are at a critical stage. Also, I promised myself I would see the Europeans off the stage of our lovely continent, and that is well along, also, but—" A sigh. "I wish I had more time for my beloved grandson, Aaron, to say nothing of my son Paul, but— You will serve again as my vice president and right hand, Edward?"

"Of course, Aaron." A snort. "Try to pry our Theodosia out of Washington." Both men laughed, and it was settled. Aaron Burr would run again for president, with Edward Livingston as his vice president.

1816. Headline from *Washington National Intelligencer*:

VICTOR OF WASHINGTON DRAFTED FOR FIFTH TERM.

1830. Headline from *Washington National Intelligencer*:

GRANDSON OF REVERED BURR TO RUN WITH HIM
AS VICE PRESIDENT.

1836. Headline from *Washington National Intelligencer*:

OUR BELOVED BURR HAS PASSED TO HIS ETERNAL REWARD.
VICE PRESIDENT AARON BURR ALSTON CROWNED SUCCESSOR.
PAUL AARON BURR ANOINTED VICE PRESIDENT.

1824

Andrew Jackson, who won the presidency in 1828 and 1832, actually had the greatest popular and electoral vote total in 1824, but as he lacked an overall majority, backroom manipulations gave the office to John Quincy Adams.

Would it have made any difference if Jackson had started serving as president four years earlier? More specifically, would it have had an effect, some seven decades later, on the great black botanist, George Washington Carver? Thomas A. Easton, author of *Sparrowhawk, Honeysuckle Wine*, and long-time book reviewer for *Analog*, thinks so.

Black Earth and Destiny

by Thomas A. Easton

"Come outside, young Henry." The tall black man set aside the new journal he had been perusing and stood up from his desk and the small bundle of mail that awaited his attention. "This just came," he said. "But . . ." His voice was thin and piping, the result of childhood illnesses that had damaged his vocal cords. The boy was the son of Henry Cantwell Wallace, the assistant to the Iowa State College of Agriculture and Mechanical Arts. The older Wallace was also the director of the experiment station where George Carver ran the greenhouse.

Carver and young Henry had met two years before when the boy, then only six, had come across the lanky botanist on one of his frequent tramps along the muddy verge of the Skunk River. Carver had explained that he was hunting for fungi, plant diseases, and the boy had been fascinated. Despite the difference in their ages and their races, they had become fast friends. Now, hand in hand, they left the greenhouse and its ranks of crops and roses, of hybrids and Mendelian adoptions.

Before them now stretched endless acres of Iowa's dark soil, divided into squares covered with new corn, barely begun to spread its blades to the life-giving sun, and other squares, in contrasting shades, with legumes and other crops. The more varied greens of wild vegetation marked the watercourses that bordered the fields. And all of it—the green, the vibrant blue of the arched bowl of sky above, the very tension in the air, as if a thunderstorm were marching, with golden lightning crashes for its strides, in their direction, seemed to presage events of great moment. Carver had felt it that morning, when he rolled from his narrow bed. He felt it more sharply now, as if those presaged events were almost upon them.

Carver took a deep breath. "You know," he said, "that the soil cares for the plants, and the plants care for the soil. What one plant takes from the soil, another returns."

"Corn," said young Henry. "And beans and chick-peas. Crop rotation." His voice, though it was of course a boyish treble, was yet not as high as Carver's.

The man nodded. "Exactly," he said. "God's plan is a marvelous thing to behold, and we have a duty to help it along as best we can. To learn about things like crop rotation and fallowing and fertilizers."

"If we don't, sir, the soil dies, doesn't it?"

"Exactly right, young Henry. If we fail to help God's plan, well, God will shrug us off. He will, let's say, decide that we are just too stone-dumb to catch on, and He will concern Himself with other matters."

The boy looked at the man skeptically. "That isn't what the Reverend says."

"Ah, well," said Carver. "Ah, well. But the truth remains. The poor farmers of the south need not be poor, if only they understood what you know so well about crop rotation. But there is more. Consider the earthworms." They had come to a pair of wooden bins, each one half-full of dark, black soil in which grew young tomato plants. The plants in one bin, however, were twice the size of those in the other.

"Earthworms, sir?" The boy was still skeptical, but he knew better than to walk away from George Carver. Time and again, the man had surprised the boy, as he surprised adults of every kind and race, with the ideas that sprang from his brain.

But now Carver simply bent and dug his fingers deep into the soil of one bin, and then of the other. Each time, he churned to the surface several large worms of the sort one might use when fishing. Those from the soil that fostered the larger plants were a trifle grayer in hue. "They till the soil," he said. "Their tunnels let air and water reach the roots, and their casts bring deeper soil to the surface. But these . . ." He pointed at the grayer worms. "These do something else as well."

After a pause, he continued. "The legumes do what they do," he said, "because the bacteria that live in the little knots upon their roots take nitrogen from the air and put it in the soil. Fertilizer, my boy. And Morgan learned two years ago that it is possible to soak one kind of bacterium in the juices of another and so transfer the Mendelian particles that make that other what it is."

The boy's eyes were wide. "Is that what you did?"

"In a way, young Henry. In a way. I ground up nodules I collected from pea roots to prepare the juice. I added some juice from a fungus that seems to help when I want to persuade a cutting of one plant to adopt the particles from a different plant. Then I soaked the eggs of earthworms in the resulting mixture."

"And the adoption worked!"

"Exactly. These earthworms . . ." He held a gray one in the palm of his hand. "Their soil is richer because they enrich it not only with tunnels and casts, but also with fertilizer."

"Have you published?" Carver had told the boy many times that it was essential to share whatever one learned with those who might benefit.

"Of course. I was looking at the paper when you came in." He smiled gently. "They were kind enough to put my offer of samples of the worms on the very first page."

Later, after Carver and the boy had inspected the plantings outside the greenhouse, including young Henry's own plot of hybrid potatoes, the man sniffed the air. Thunder coming? he asked himself. Lightning? *Something*, and he wished he knew *what*. Then he returned to his desk. It stood toward one end of the greenhouse, where he could keep an eye on his beloved greenery, looking up from his paperwork to spot the merest hint of smut or rust, of insect infestation or nutrient deficiency. To one side of the desk stretched the broad workbench where he performed his experiments.

But he had hardly laid a hand on the stack of his mail before the creak of the greenhouse door struck him with all the import of the storm he had been awaiting all the morning. He jerked his head up abruptly, and two figures were stepping through the doorway. These were no boys, but full-grown men wrapped in long overcoats. Their boots were shiny beneath the mud they had acquired on the grounds of the experiment station, and their shirt-fronts were snowy white. One, a little taller than the other, wore an open, cheerful expression on his face. The other's lips were pursed, and his gaze roamed the greenhouse as if he suspected attack.

"Where's Dr. Carver, boy?" asked the latter brusquely. "We're in a hurry."

Carver suppressed the stiffening of his face that came

to him far too often when whites realized that his skin, for all his growing reputation as a plant scientist and Mendelian engineer, was black. "Not doctor," he said. "Just George Carver."

"Well, where is he?"

"I am he."

"You? A nigger?" The other gave him a long and hostile stare. Then he turned to his companion and said, "Let's go, Alvin. We've got enough niggers in Nashville. There's no point in importing any more."

The taller man looked pained, but he held out a broad hand with no trace of hesitation or revulsion. "Mr. Carver?" he said. "I'm pleased to meet you."

He accepted the hand with a quiet sense of relief that not every white was like the other, and even gratitude for the simple fact of being called "Mr." That was, almost everywhere in this year of 1896, a title reserved for whites. The gratitude was undiminished by the awareness that it might well be just what he was intended to feel. He said simply, "Yes, sir?"

"I'm Alvin Bryant. From the Hermitage." Shortly after the War Between the States, when Carver was still the child known as Carver's George, the Hermitage Federal Research Institute in Nashville, Tennessee, had become the locus for the nation's most advanced biological research.

Carver stole a glance at his mail. The envelope on the top of the stack bore the postmark of Tuskegee, Alabama. That made him curious, for he could think of no one there whom he knew.

Beside the mail was the well-thumbed Bible Aunt Mariah Watkins had given him one Christmas years before. She had also told him that he had a responsibility to give his learning back to his people. She had meant their fellow blacks; he himself had never felt that the return of his gift should be so restricted.

The visitor continued: "Dr. Burbank has instructed us

to tell you that in his opinion your earthworm paper represents a marvelous piece of work."

"Ah," said Carver, looking up again. "I have hopes for my worms. If I can just get them into the hands of the small farmer, they should do a great deal to lift him out of poverty. I've thought of taking a wagon . . ."

"Just so, of course. But Dr. Burbank thinks you have a great deal more to offer. Especially if you can get the proper equipment. And we're supposed to invite you to come back to Nashville with us."

"They don't know he's a nigger, Alvin. And when they find out . . ."

Alvin Bryant sighed. "Shut up, Timothy. You know as well as I, it's the man's brain that matters, not the color of his skin."

"I do not. *You* know as well as I, niggers are dumb, filthy, good for nothing but stoop labor. They wouldn't even know what to do with a potato if they couldn't watch an Irishman sniffing at one."

Another sigh. "If you can't shut up, then leave. Go home. I'll follow later, with Mr. Carver if he'll come."

"Good-bye, then. But don't complain to me if you wind up with fleas." He turned on his heel and left, slamming the door so that the greenhouse's panes shivered in their frames.

"I'm sorry, sir," said Alvin Bryant. "But I do hope you'll come. They've already set a laboratory aside for you."

Carver stared at his visitor. Even a "sir"! "You take me aback, sir," he said in his piping voice. "I am nonplussed. I am." He paused for a moment before adding, "I will have to think about your kind offer for a moment or two before I can even discuss it properly. Have a seat." He gestured toward a cane-bottomed stool that stood before the workbench. "And at any rate, I must finish looking at my mail before I could possibly leave."

For some reason, he did not wish to open the Tuskegee letter immediately. He set it aside while he opened envelopes from other towns and states. One held praise for the paintings the botanist had lately exhibited at an art fair in Cedar Rapids and invited him to consider sending his No. 99, *Yucca gloriosa*, to another exhibit in Indianapolis. He smiled at the praise but only shook his head at the invitation; then he hastily took pen in hand to put his response into words. Other letters held requests for earthworms, and these made him speak aloud. "Already!" he said to his visitor from the Hermitage. "See? The people want what I can give them."

"And so do we at the Hermitage," said Alvin Bryant. "Those requests only prove your value to humanity, and the nation, and us."

Only the letter from Tuskegee remained. Carver opened it at last and finally read the invitation to come and create a department, a school, of agriculture: "I cannot offer you money, position, or fame. The first two you have. The last, from the place you now occupy, you will no doubt achieve. These things I now ask you to give up. I offer you in their place work—hard, hard work—the task of bringing a people from degradation, poverty and waste to full manhood." The signature was that of a man who called himself Booker T. Washington.

Wordlessly, the botanist held the letter toward the man from the Hermitage. As wordlessly, Bryant took it and read. When he was done, he said, "I know of this man. He wants to build a school for your race. He wants to teach 'the man farthest down' how to read and write and build and make and thus to move him, and all Negroes, toward equality with whites."

"To do that, then," said Carver, "he must also give them food." No one could know the grinding poverty of the poor southern farmer—most truly "the man farthest down"—better than he. He had grown up with it all around him. He had spent all his boyhood and young adulthood wandering through a human landscape scarred by it. "He needs me."

"He can have you just as well if you come to work with

us. And with us, I dare to say, you will be able to produce many more such marvels as your earthworms."

"But would I be free, sir, to pursue those marvels? You have a reputation for seeking weapons."

"The alligator cannons?" Bryant snorted. "When Jackson won in '24, that legend still obsessed him. He was there, at the Battle of New Orleans, and he saw no one stuffing alligators with cannonballs and powder. But the scholars say that he was jubilant after turning Clay around, and that the mythmakers were able to convince him the possibility was worth pursuing. He put federal money into our science, and when Mendel discovered his particles, we were prepared to grasp that banner and carry it forward. The rest you know. Alligator cannons are a matter for the distant future."

"But still . . ."

"Would you rather we knew nothing of genetics? It was a near thing, you know. Clay hated Old Hickory, and even though he had his orders from his Kentucky home, he was not about to vote for Jackson. John Quincy Adams was his man."

Carver let himself be sidetracked for a moment. "Then how did Jackson win?"

Bryant shrugged. "I've heard a hundred stories. Many of them agree that Jackson found something shameful in Clay's past and threatened to reveal it. But no two agree on what that something was. And no one seems likely ever to learn the truth. It was seventy years ago, after all."

"It doesn't really matter, does it?" Carver's high voice turned soft and thoughtful. "The result's the thing."

Bryant nodded. "Of course. If the election had gone the other way, if Clay had succeeded in his spiteful aim, if Jackson had lost, perhaps to try again in '28 or '32 . . . he would surely have been a bitter man, far less inclined to think of the future. The money would have gone to other things, Mendel would have been ignored, and we . . ." He paused and gestured as if to indicate that some things could not be known, and not just because the truth was lost among the mists of the past. "God only knows what our lives would be."

Carver bowed his head for just a moment. "I still do not believe I could work on weapons."

"He was a war hawk. And yes, we did find a gas that can kill soldiers on the battlefield. But Burbank himself developed the whiffle-tree, which removes that gas, and other noxious vapors, from the air. For every weapon, there is a defense, and to those defenses we pay far more attention. Often enough, they have great value in times of peace as well. That whiffle-tree, for instance, is doing much to make the air of our cities sweet again."

Carver nodded slowly. "But the best defense of all," he said, "it must be a strong people, well fed, free of tyranny."

"Even the tyranny of hatred, sir."

He nodded again. "You make your point well. But still, I will have to think on it. You tempt me. But so does Washington."

That afternoon, Carver and young Henry Wallace were walking near the river. "He has taken a room with Dr. Pammell," he told the boy. He halted the motion of his long legs and bent over a weed. "What is that?" he asked, pointing at a spatter of dark spots on a leaf.

"A mold. It will eat into the plant and make it sick," said the boy. He had learned well.

"Yes," said Carver. "And I am afraid there is a mold in the Hermitage as well. It is that interest in those weapons of destruction that our science might yield." He looked upward. To the southwest, the thunderstorm whose promise he had felt all day was finally visible, its towering anvils rising against the sky.

"But you said they work on defenses too."

The man nodded. "Yet the weapons must always come first. You cannot design a defense before you know what you must defend against."

"Can't the weapons come second?" asked the boy. "Your earthworms . . ."

"Yes?"

"Couldn't you make them to produce a poison?"

Carver looked thoughtful for a long moment. "Perhaps," he said at last. "Though I would think the poison should kill the worms before much damage was done."

They walked on in companionable silence, man and boy. Eventually, the man halted to stare out over the river, southward. The thunderheads were already higher above the horizon, and the water, in reflection of the sky, was shifting its color from blue to stormy gray. "There is mold in Tuskegee too," he said quietly. "And more than one."

Young Henry said nothing, though he rummaged in a pocket and found a single flat stone. Swinging his arm, he sent it skipping over the water. Fifty feet from shore, it sank, leaving a chain of ripples spreading from its path.

"Washington has nothing but energy and high intentions," said Carver at last. "And a crying need for what he wishes to do. All that may not be enough. And if it is . . ." He paused. "The whites in Tuskegee may not be pleased to see blacks improving themselves."

"Then he needs all the help he can get, doesn't he?"

"Heennrryyy!" The voice echoed from the yellow house on the hill behind them.

"That's my mother," said the boy. "I've got to go."

Carver stared after the small figure as it ran, thinking that if he were married, he might have a son like that, only black, of course. Yet he was alone. Surely, he would remain so, for he was sure God had a plan for him that would leave no room for a wife and children. Already, his work consumed all his time and interest. When he learned what God's plan was, he thought, he would be even less able to spare the time and devotion a family would require, and deserve.

What were his choices? He could, he supposed, stay where he was. He was valued, he was doing good work, useful work, work that would benefit everyone when in due time it reached those who needed it. If he went to Tuskegee, well, Booker T. Washington did need help, didn't he? He needed it desperately. And if there he could develop fewer novelties such as his earthworms, whatever novelties he did find, whether they were his own or someone else's, he would be able to take directly to the farmers who needed them most. He would be free to take those farmers in hand and show them how to repair their soil and improve their diet and broaden their choice of crops. He would . . . He realized he was smiling. What he saw in Tuskegee would be a colossal pile of work, just as Washington's letter had promised, but work had never scared him. Why, how could it? He had worked his way from town to town as a laundryman and harvester and cook and *everything* until he could graduate from high school. And then college, though the principal of the first, when he had seen the color of his skin, had said, "You didn't tell me you were Negro. Highland College does not take Negroes."

That memory still hurt, though it had been buried beneath more recent memories of kinder days in Iowa. In Tuskegee, surely, it would stay buried, for he would be among his own kind. In Nashville, there were men like Timothy. There were as well men like Alvin Bryant and Luther Burbank, who had come from California to direct the Hermitage, and Thomas Hunt Morgan, the biologist who had discovered the technique of transduction. There were also the towers of the Hermitage's laboratories, gleaming like ivory though they were made of simple limestone.

Thunder rolled. Distant lightning flashed. Raindrops pocked the river's surface and struck at his head. He felt his face. Yes, his smile was less, just as he had suspected. They wanted Mendelian adoptions. They wanted to put him in a laboratory. If he agreed, he would be far from the soil he loved and farther from the people—his people—whose problems he ached to solve, whether they required his ability to induce Mendelian adoptions or a more plebeian insight into the value of a compost heap.

God's plan. Not money. That was, for him, only a means to an end, to schooling, to food, to helping others. Any more than that was a nuisance. Not fame. That was irrelevant. It meant nothing, less than nothing, to him. But service. And Tuskegee was where his service was needed most.

When Carver returned to the greenhouse, he was soaked through and through, and the wave of heat that greeted him was welcome. "I saw you coming," said Alvin Bryant. "I lit the stove. And the lights."

"Thank you," said Carver as he removed his jacket and positioned a chair to hold it near the heat. "I was not expecting to see you here."

The other shrugged. "There is not much to do," he said. "I'm supposed to bring your decision, if not you yourself, back to Nashville with me, and I must wait. In the meantime, perhaps I can help by answering your questions."

Carver shook his head. "I have made my decision," he said. "God has a plan for me. I've always thought so. A destiny, if you will, though I never knew what it was until this day of your arrival."

"Ah!" Bryant's eyes opened wide with expectancy.

"No," said Carver, and the visitor's face fell. "Something else came today as well."

"Washington's letter."

"Exactly so. Whether you had come or no, indeed whether or no there were such things as Mendelian engineering and Hermitages, my destiny would be the same."

"You'll go to Tuskegee."

"My science is for the people." Carver nodded gravely, though his face seemed illuminated from within.

Carver's clothing steamed in the heat given off by the stove. The two men stared through the greenhouse's panels at the storm outside. The silence stretched and stretched, neither man willing to break it, until a lightning bolt forked toward the ground not far away and the lights in the greenhouse office winked out.

The crash of thunder came so promptly on the lightning's heels that Carver thought of the river and the trees upon its banks, at the mercy of whatever storms might rage.

So too, he thought, were his people. Unless, at Tuskegee . . .

1828

It is an historical fact that Andrew Jackson's part in an 1819 land speculation scheme was covered up, and that nine years later he won the first of his two terms as president and ushered in what is now known as the era of Jacksonian democracy.

But Judith Moffett, winner of the Campbell Award, Nebula and Hugo nominee, and author of *The Ragged World* and *Two that Came True*, wonders what might have happened had the scandal not been buried. More to the point, could an alternate president have changed the course of the Civil War?

Or, if not an alternate president, then how about two young boys?

Chickasaw Slave

by Judith Moffett

Lexington, Kentucky
July 17, 1852

Madam:

I regret to inform you that your fiancé, Sgt. Levi Colbert, was killed in action on the 13th of July, while attempting to storm the heights of the north bluff of the Kentucky River, which were held by the troops of Genl. Winfield Scott. He was shot in the head and died instantly. He served bravely in this regiment and was liked and admired by all. Sgt. Colbert is the only Indian I ever knew personally. He was a fine man, and I feel privileged to have been his commanding officer.

Sgt. Colbert's effects will be forwarded in due course. An envelope, addressed to you, was found on his body; I take the liberty of enclosing it herewith. The blood that stains it is his own.

May it comfort you in your great sorrow to know, that our victory over the enemy at Lawrenceburg, in the attaining of which your fiancé and so many others made the ultimate sacrifice, ensures that our sovereign Confederacy will take its rightful place among the nations of the world. This morning in Lexington General Scott surrendered to General Lee. The War is over.

My deepest sympathy to you.

I remain, Madam,

Yours faithfully,
George Pickett, Capt.,
"B" Company,
Seventh Tennessee Volunteers

Inside the bloodstained envelope:

Lawrenceburg, Kentucky
12 July 1852

My Dearest Rachel,

It is now long past midnight, and I am very tired. We marched all day yesterday and today, from near a little village called Simpsonville, east of Louisville, here to Lawrenceburg in Anderson County—a distance of some fifty or sixty miles—sleeping rough in a pasture last night and pushing on this morning at first light. About all I'm able to recall clearly of yesterday is *mud* and *rain*. Today was mostly fine weather, but we had our work cut out for us finding a place to camp that wasn't a quagmire from all the rain that fell yesterday and the day before.

Lawrenceburg is a Kentucky River town—high bluffs—

a blown-up railroad bridge—and about a million Yanks across the river; I can see their fires, just as I know they can see the one by whose light I write this, and know they are thinking about the battle to come, just as I am. The high bluffs on both sides of the river make admirable defensive positions, we can keep the big guns booming back and forth for a time, but sooner or later one side will have to try to cross over and charge the other, straight up into those guns. If my regiment is ordered into such a charge, this letter may well be the last I am ever able to write. God knows whether you will receive it.

It begins to seem as if the War may about be over, and that the Confederate States of America may soon be a reality. General Lee is said to believe that one more decisive victory is all that is needed. God grant the morrow will give us that victory. We outnumber the Yankees this time, and we all know Marse Robert can outfox Genl. Scott with one hand tied behind him. So I may see you all again very soon.

Yet tonight I feel compelled to address you, not only—as ever—to address that which is most dear to me upon the eve of battle, but because I wish to entrust now to your keeping an account, herewith enclosed, of something both extraordinary and of far-reaching consequence—something scarcely thought of for years, yet lately called back to mind, that occurred when I was but a boy.

The account I speak of was written for you, it was of you I thought as I set it down—yet I wish and request that you may keep it for me with the seal unbroken until my return. Or should it not be granted to me to survive this War, then I desire you to read and dispose of it as you think best. I believe you will find it a remarkable tale; but whether better published or concealed you must determine for yourself. I trust entirely to your judgment in the matter.

Rachel, you and I have been too briefly acquainted, and our circumstances throughout that little time too trying, for you to know much more about me than the obvious fact that the biggest number of my ancestors were Indians—a fact stamped upon my countenance where all may see it. I fear—nay, I am certain—that the story told herein will reveal to you certain elements of my family and personal history which can scarcely fail to distress you. Not for worlds would I injure you; yet I have told the tale after all, albeit with much agitation of mind. The reason is this: that the turmoil which has accompanied me since Cincinnati, together with the sense of the nearness of death which is with me always now, have impelled me to it. And I count on your good sense, and your regard for me, to bear you up, whatever fate befalls us.

God bless you, my darling. I long to see you. My fondest love to you. Pray convey my kind regards to your mother and sisters.

Levi Colbert.

The document which follows was found folded about the letter:

My mother was a Chickasaw full-blood called Ish-te-cho-cultha. She was a kind woman, and made for another sort of life than the life my father chose for them both, namely that of keeping hogs and raising cotton, but she never complained, unless her refusal to learn English was a sort of indirect complaint. My father talked good English; he was a mixed-blood, though I never knew much about his parentage, owing to the circumstance that his father and mother had both been dead for years at the time he married my mother. I do know that he was in some fashion related to the Colberts, a large and powerful family of mixed-bloods all descended from James Colbert, a Scot, who had married into the tribe sometime in the last century. The Colberts managed our tribal affairs, and were said to be fabulously wealthy, but so far as I know I never met any of them.

Pa used the name of Colbert, whether strictly entitled to it or not. He named me Levi, after the great Levi Colbert, and often exhorted me to live up to the name. As well as I can make out, the first Levi Colbert was a fellow who knew how to look after his own interests, yet bore himself honorably toward our people. He married three or four different wives, that I *do* know—it was the custom in the old days, and he followed the old customs pretty regular—and that's one way I *don't* intend to profit by his example! For the rest, I don't reckon I've done the name much honor, but perhaps I've done it little harm—though I own I'm less sure of both harm and honor now than I was a month ago.

I was born down in the Chickasaw Homelands in northern Mississippi. My father and his brothers farmed a small acreage there, but my earliest memories are of village life, the cabin, my mother and my two little sisters, pounding corn to make Tom Fuller or *pulaska*, or hoeing the small patch of garden, and Cal and Watty always somewhere about. But I was only a lad of five in 1828, when the Tennessee Vacant Land Bill was put into effect, and soon after that my father moved the family north, and settled on the Obion River in western Tennessee.

The way it come about was this. The Chickasaw chiefs, meaning mostly my Colbert relations, made treaties with the Government in 1816 and 1818, ceding what was left of our ancient tribal hunting grounds—that is, a little piece of western Kentucky bounded by the Ohio and Mississippi Rivers, and the whole of the western portion of Tennessee—to the United States.

For many years before, the tribe had been pressured and harassed relentlessly by white intruders, greedy for land, who could see that the Tennessee canebrakes was prime cotton-growing country. They could not be kept out. By the time the chiefs made up their minds to sell, that country was already plentifully salted with white settlers, and the Indians had by and large given up hunting there. Those of the tribe, mostly the remaining full-bloods, who wished to pursue a traditional way of life, were at that time already moving beyond the Mississippi, where game was still plentiful and where living in the traditional way, in a central village surrounded by many miles of wild and uncultivated land, was still possible. Those who stayed—most of them mixed-bloods—did so because they had to a large extent abandoned the old ways and adopted the white style of farming, scattered out thin, with fenced fields and livestock; and my father, Charlie Colbert, was one of these.

Well, after the land had been purchased, there was considerable to-do in the Congress about how it should be disposed of. General Jackson was known to favor a scheme whereby the Tennessee vacant land—"vacant" because the Chickasaws and Cherokees had been harassed into selling it—should be sold off by the section at auction to the highest bidder, and the proceeds given to the state for educational purposes. And Jackson, though holding no office at that time, was right up next to God with the Tennessee politicians.

But Davy Crockett had just come up to Washington fresh from the canebrake country, and he presented them with a different scheme. It was his first term, he having been elected to Congress only the year before, and properly speaking he'd no business challenging the mighty Jackson party. But he had little personal love for Jackson's people, having butted heads with some of them back home, and he genuinely disagreed with the position on the vacant lands. According to his thinking, the land should be offered cheap to the people already living on it—the people who had pushed in while it still belonged to the Chickasaws, and built their cabins and dug their wells and cleared and planted. They were Davy's kind of people, and he stuck up for them. If he had his way, every squatter should be offered a chance to buy 160 acres, a half section, including his own improvements, at a price he could afford.

Well, the debate went back and forth. Like I say, the Tennesseans, except for Davy and one or two others, mostly thought a heap of Old Hickory, they still called him the Hero down there; but he'd been involved in some very shady land speculation at the time of the 1816 Chickasaw treaty, and when the scandal broke it hurt him considerable with the politicians from outside the state. The House wasn't going to let him have what he wanted without an argument, like it might've if word about the land deals hadn't got around.

And Davy Crockett was popular! He was a *real* frontiersman, the genuine article—more of a frontiersman by a mile than Old Hickory, who was from a higher and softer class of society altogether. Davy'd killed pretty near as many Indians as Jackson but he never swindled the Government out of twenty thousand dollars to line his own pockets with, and lied about it afterwards, like the General had done. And he'd fought bears hand to hand, and hewed out his own clearing in the wilderness with his own hands . . . well, everybody knows the stories. Even people that thought Davy nothing more than a backwoods clown respected his personal integrity; and his natural eloquence in defense of his land bill ought to have made them all stop and think. He may have let people use him, but he was no fool, and a great deal more than a clown.

So the Congressmen from the other states let the Tennesseans fight it out on the House floor, Davy Crockett and the poor squatters against Old Hickory and the landed gentry, then they supported Davy. Back home they used to say that Davy's way of putting that land bill before Congress—a manner and style that made it look like he just might be able to get it passed, too—was the thing that caused the bankers and the Quakers and the Whigs back east—and some anti-Jackson Democrats too—to blink a couple of times and see a presidential alternative to Jackson the Indian Hater *and* Jackson the Bank Hater, wearing the same buckskin shirt.

As I said, Davy and Old Hickory had been enemies for years; there was a time Davy didn't back a Jackson man for some state office, and the General never forgot nor forgave. It weren't no skin off Davy's nose if he and Jackson became opponents on a bigger stage than the one down home. So when the Easterners that saw their chance during the debate over the Tennessee Vacant Land Bill, and started courting Davy, needed him to distance himself from Jackson in a more decisive way, he had no objection.

Now, Davy really *believed* in cheap land for white squatters. I don't think for a minute that he believed in free land for defrauded Chickasaws, but maybe I'm wrong about that; at least he did defend some Cherokees who were trying to get *their* land claims upheld, based on a treaty that said any Cherokee agreeing to become a citizen, and to abide by the laws of North Carolina and Georgia, could have 640 acres of his own ancestral lands free gratis for nothing.

However that may be, everybody knew that if Andrew Jackson became President he would make war on the Second Bank of the U.S. The Whigs, who supported the bank, were all in a sweat for Davy to run against Jackson. Which meant they wanted Davy to be not only their pet frontiersman and Indian fighter, and champion of the poor settler, but also their pet defender of the rights of the Red Man! You might wonder just how a fellow who fought as hard in the Creek Wars as Davy did could be dressed up to look like an Indian Lover, without losing any of the only-good-Indian-is-a-dead-Indian vote; but they had to try. There was a lot of sympathy for the Red Man in the East just then, from Pennsylvania on up north, and the Whigs knew that that sympathy could all be translated into votes, if Davy would come out against Indian Removal too, which was an idea that was picking up steam in the South and West along about then.

So the long and the short of it was, they put it to him: our men in the Congress will bring your vacant lands bill to a vote, and get it passed, if you'll introduce another bill granting land rights to the Indians whose ancestral hunting grounds that same land used to be. There's the

Cherokee precedent, you won't have to sell them anything new. And if *that* goes through, they said, it'll be time for some very serious talk.

And Davy agreed. I guess the notion of being President appealed to him even then, when it looked like such a preposterous idea. He fixed it so that the white squatters in the canebrake country could afford to buy a half-section of the land they were living on illegally already, and then, riding on the coattails of that success, he fixed it that any head of a Chickasaw family that would become a citizen—a citizen, incidentally, with a vote—and abide by the laws of the state of Tennessee, could trade his legal allotment in the Mississippi Homelands for a half-section in the canebrakes.

The white squatters hadn't hardly got through celebrating the passage of the Vacant Lands Bill when they started meeting to vilify the passage of the Chickasaw Tenancy Bill, but Davy put it to them straight. He made a trip back there to his place in Rutherford and he told those squatters, "Fellows, I got you your farms, and the only way I could do it was to get farms for the Injuns too. Now, there's a lot more of you than there is of them, so you all settle down together here and learn to get along. I got to do it with all them savages up in Washington, and they ain't nothing happened in the Creek Wars that's a patch on what them cutthroat varmints up there will do a man."

And do you know, they bought it. They knew Davy was one of them, not a middle-Tennessee aristocrat like the Hero, and that they owed their farms to him and he had never let them down; but the truth is, he purely charmed those men, same as he charmed the whole country later on. People always underestimated Davy, and they always got fooled. Old Hickory looked unbeatable till the middle of that election year of 1828, with the country so ripe to be led by a tough backwoods Indian fighter who defended the rights of the little man. Nobody expected a half-baked greenhorn like Davy from Jackson's own state to beat the old man at his own game, even with all the power and influence of the Second Bank of the United States behind him; but by November Jackson was down and Crockett was up, and what happened after that, as they say, is history.

Well, my pa had often been hunting up in the canebrakes as a boy with his uncles, and he remembered that country as a mighty fine place. So when the chance came, he took it. Though not a full-blood, he had rights in the tribal lands and no wish to live according to the old ways. He moved us up onto the North Fork of the Obion River in Obion County, not twenty miles from Davy Crockett's own farm, and had his half-section surveyed, and filed his claim, and cleared and planted. And a few years later, when the road from the Natchez Trace came through, he built a ferry over the river.

Watty and me grew up together there. My family traded a purebred boar for his mother, Callie, when Watty was just a baby. Callie always said her pa was a Cherokee chief, it was something her own ma had told her and I guess it might have been true. And Watty's pa was a mixed-blood from Muscle Shoals down in the Chickasaw Homelands, so Watty was even more of a mixup than me, and I was one-quarter white myself, more or less. That purebred boar had clearer blood than any of us. But I looked plain Indian, only with a little bit paler skin; and Watty looked plain African, only light brown colored with brown kinky hair, done up like Callie's in lots of knotty little braids bound with strings, the way all the Chickasaw slaves used to dress their hair.

Like I said, we grew up together. Slavery among my people is a different thing than you've ever seen among your own, and I've heard white people say they wouldn't have Indian Negroes, as they were too difficult to control, and too accustomed to our lenient ways. Except for me going to school, Watty and me was always together. We chopped cotton and corn, and helped Pa run the ferry, me working just as hard as Watty and him just as hard as me, but then we'd go off hunting for a week at a time, or fishing, or just fooling around. Pa used to take us possum hunting at night sometimes; I remember the big full moon and the lantern and the hound dog, Piomingo, baying till he scared the possum into playing dead and falling out of the tree, and Pa joking and laughing with us, treating me and Watty just the same. Those were the best times with Pa. He was a likable, hard-working man when he was sober, but a mean drunk, and he always kept a bottle in the barn. And as the years went by there was more of the drunk in evidence, and less of the likable fellow.

We boys was the same age, near as anybody could figure. Chickasaws don't keep track of birthdays, but my ma knew what year it was I was born in, 1823, and Watty was just a little bitty thing the size of me when we got Callie, and him too, from Esh-ma-tubba before we came up north to Obion County.

What I'm going to tell you about now happened in March or April of 1836. I made sure of the date, because it happened the day after we got the news about General Santa Anna killing all the Americans at the Alamo. Watty and me was thirteen or thereabouts. He was bigger than me, he could beat me at running and wrestling. I was still scrawny. But Watty never pressed his advantage of size; he was remarkably gentle, for such a strong boy. "What if you grow up bigger than me and pay me back later?" he used to say, and smile his sleepy smile. "I ain't no dumb Indian." Another thing about him was, he was a Christian like his ma. I was converted at a school I went to, after leaving home; but Watty grew up Christian. Something else: he spoke no English, though he could understand it some. We always talked Chickasaw at home, because of Ma. Callie had talked English when she was a girl, but had forgot it from lack of use, though she understood people fairly well.

Well, the day after we heard about what happened at the Alamo, Pa came down to breakfast all sick and rheumy-eyed and said to me in English, so my ma wouldn't understand, "Levi, I done a terrible thing."

I knew Pa'd been out drinking the night before, but that was most nights by that time. I waited for him to tell me what he'd done, and my two little sisters froze in their chairs with their spoonfuls of mush halfway to their mouths.

"Levi," said Pa, kind of whining, "I lost Watty to Bill Bertram in a crapshoot last night. He's coming to fetch him away this afternoon. I can't tell Callie or your ma. I don't know what to do."

The news skewered through me exactly like a bullet, or a lightning bolt, but my mind couldn't seem to take it in. All I could think of to say to him was, "But we was going fishin' this afternoon."

"Then you'd best fish quick," said Pa, " 'cause Bill Bertram will be here at four o'clock and Watty needs to be ready."

My youngest sister, Mary, commenced to cry. "Buy him back, Pa," she sobbed. "I don't want Watty to go away."

Pa said dolefully, "I wouldn't'a lost him in the first place if I had any money to buy him back with. He's going, and that's all there is to it. But I swear I don't know how I'm going to tell Callie. I wisht I'd fell in the river and drownded before I gambled that boy away, but it's over and done with now." He wiped his red eyes on his sleeve. "Levi, you best go tell him to get his things together. Then you boys take the day off. Have a last day together. But you be back here by mid-afternoon, you hear? Old Man Bertram'll have the law on me if I can't produce his property when he comes to collect it." He put his head between his hands and groaned.

Old Man Bertram was a drunk like Pa, only older and worse—mean when he was sober, mean as a rattlesnake when he'd been drinking. I knew what Pa said was true, and for a minute I hated him so much for losing Watty to such a man that I saw a picture in my head of me picking up a piece of stove wood and bashing his brains in.

But instead I stumbled out of the house and across the

barnyard, scattering chickens. Watty and Callie were still in the barn, seeing to the milking. Callie smiled when I came in, the same slow, sleepy smile Watty had. I remember she was wearing a bright green dress under her shawl, and shiny brass rings in her ears, like the ones in Watty's, only three times as big. She said, "I put you boys up some dinner. Bring us back a nice mess of fish now."

When she said that, I felt like puking. But I had just enough wit not to say anything till she'd gone on back to the house, pulled sideways by the weight of the full wooden pail, and Watty and me were alone.

When I told him, Watty went pale as a ghost and dropped his bucket; milk sloshed into the straw and all of a sudden we were ankle-deep in cats. I remember how he shook, and I saw, though I didn't think about it then, that this news had struck him different than it had struck me. What was to me a brand-new, utterly unthinkable thought, wasn't at all new or unthinkable to him. The idea that Watty could be handed over to some other person, just like a blanket or a bucket of lard, bewildered me; for him it was more like hearing that his worst nightmare had come true. He believed me at once. "Marse Charlie was drunk," he said, not asking, stating a fact.

"You know he was. He'd never have done it sober." Then we stood and stared at each other, and I never saw terror like that on a human face in my life, not even on the battlefield. Looking at Watty's face, that I'd known all my life, transfigured with terror, I said without knowing I was going to: "We got to get away from here."

Rachel, you must understand that the idea of helping a slave escape had been for me, till that moment, like the idea of robbing a bank: something I knew of as possible, but nothing I'd ever connected my own self with. In all my wild imaginings I had never imagined myself as a fugitive from justice. But the prospect presented itself to me in the same light as if Watty had fallen off the ferry in mid-crossing: he was in trouble, I would do all I could to save him. That's how I felt, and what I intended, and that is what I did.

As soon as I knew we were going to run away together, my brain commenced to work again. "Callie said she put us up some dinner. I'm going to fetch it now; you get the blankets off your bed and a good knife and whatever you can find in the cellar, maybe some spuds and onions and a poke to tote them in. And your boots," because we was both wearing moccasins, and the land all about was under water. "We can light out soon as we get ready. Pa said we was to have the whole day off to go fishing and that's what I'll tell 'em back at the house."

Watty didn't argue. He just said, "Levi, where we going to go? We can't hide out in no cypress swamp waiting for the mosquitoes to suck us dry. We got to have someplace to go."

Just like I'd planned the whole thing to perfection I answered him right back: "We'll go to Davy Crockett's place. He's there himself, home for a visit, I heard a man on the ferry say so. He could help us, he's the President, ain't he? He can do whatever he likes."

A little color had come back into Watty's face, and he said hotly that he didn't put no stock at'all in Davy Crockett's helping him out. "They all call him Indian Lover around these parts, and grumble about how Old Hickory wouldn't never'a let a fine farm like this one here be owned by no murderin' redskin"—he said "Indian Lover" and "murderin' redskin" in English, which startled me—"but they ain't never said he was unreliable on slavery, Levi, so what makes you think for one minute he's going to go out of his way to help *me*?"

Watty had *never* talked this way before. Until that morning the idea that he minded being our slave had never crossed my mind. Hearing him say such things frightened me almost as much as Pa's announcement had; but I shouted that he was wasting time talking, we could worry about all that once we were well away from the farm. I said, rather wildly, "Davy vetoed the Indian Removal Bill, didn't he? Ain't that the only reason we ain't all living over in the Territories right now? We'll tell the President you're one-quarter Cherokee and one-quarter Chickasaw, and one quarter *white*! But come on, Watty, come *on*! We got to get away from here!"

He snapped out of it then, and did what I told him. An hour later the two of us had crossed the North Fork and were scurrying through the big stand of cypress east of our place, heading south, over towards Rutherford and the Crockett farm.

Getting away from the house was surprisingly easy. Nobody could bear to look at Watty, though everybody but Callie now knew of the calamity. They all skulked and hid from the sight of him. Pa had sent Callie to fetch a couple of spring lambs from a neighbor, to keep her out of the way. So Watty never said good-bye to his ma; but it was the only way to keep the secret and I thought things had worked out pretty well, considering what a disaster had befallen us.

Once away, we went fast. We had ranged all over this country together, we knew every cottonfield and swampy brake and farmstead for miles around. We kept to the cypress groves and boggy places and avoided people, but even so we made good headway, crossing invisible streams on invisible logs in a featureless sea of floodwater and trompling down the wild berry canes with our heavy boots. Aboveground, the weather held dry. We pressed forward all day, not stopping and not talking much, till it got dark, and then we pushed through the brambles to a high dry island where we'd often camped before. It was a long way from the nearest farm or town, and we were soaked and exhausted; we decided to chance a fire, and Watty built one and struck a spark while I plastered mud on three or four of the potatoes he'd been humping all day in a gunnysack. When the fire'd died down some, we scraped it away and buried the spuds in the coals to roast.

I don't recall that we talked much that night, tired and scared as we were, aware that they all knew by then that we'd run away, and would be hunting for us soon. I do remember Watty saying passionately that he wasn't going to live on Old Man Bertram's farm if they killed him for it. It wasn't just the drinking; there was something unclean about that old white man. Watty said he absolutely would not do it. Old Man Bertram's house and barn, on the hundred and sixty acres he'd built on and "improved" back when all this land was still supposed to belong to us Chickasaws, were falling to pieces. He'd found a young wife somewheres, but she was slatternly and unkempt and looked about sixty, all worn out with childbearing and abuse. The six slaves he already owned always looked wretched, and more than half-starved. Thinking of them, I was flooded once again with a blinding rage at my father, that he could have risked having to hand Watty over to such a man. And I remember knowing then, clearly, that I hated Pa, and deciding to go away with Watty, and never come home no more.

It was cold that night, but we rolled up together in Watty's blankets and slept hard in spite of everything, we were that done in.

Next morning, the first thing that happened was that we blundered onto a bear, just woke up and bad-tempered, prowling through the cane looking for something to eat. A she-bear with cubs would have been bad trouble; luckily for us, this was a young he-bear, glad enough to go crashing off as fast as he could. But it scared us. We hadn't been keeping a lookout for bear, a month before their usual wake-up time, but it was an early spring that year. I hadn't brought my musket, and the canebrakes was full of bear. But you don't carry a musket, going fishing.

But we had to go on. It came on a mild spring day, birds singing their heads off, squirrels leaping about, deer trotting away through the thickets and stopping to look back at us. Watty and me marched along all day, except—like on the first day—and like some I've been doing just lately!—a lot of the marching was *wading*. The land lay all under water a good mile back from the channels on both sides. Avoiding roads and towns like we had to, we had no choice but to swim the Middle and South Forks of the Obion, which were in flood from the spring melt, and the current both swift and cold, pulling our feet out from under us. What with one thing and another, it was twilight before we came to the edge of the woods and saw lamplight glowing in the windows of President Crockett's house.

Watty sat down on the ground, telling me plainer than words that it was my plan and what happened next was up to me. The truth was, I hadn't thought beyond getting us this far; but I spoke as if I had. "You wait here. I'll go on up to the house and ask to talk to the President. If I don't come back in an hour, better lay low till morning, then—" Then what? What could Watty do on his own, a fugitive slave everybody was out looking for, that didn't even talk English? Those twenty cold, wet, dangerous miles had made me see things in a different light; suddenly I appreciated the recklessness of what we had done, and the thought in my mind was that if I couldn't persuade the President to help us, Watty might best think about giving himself up. But I knew better by then than to say any such thing to him.

So instead I squared my shoulders and trudged across the field to the house.

There was a soldier in a blue uniform, with a musket, guarding the front door. He watched me coming. I walked up to him and said, "I need to see the President."

"That a fact," said the soldier in a bored voice, and shook his head. "Now, it may surprise you to hear this, but the President of the United States didn't come all this way just so he could talk to no little shirttail Indian brat. You run along home. Go on now."

"Please tell him I want to see him," I said. He told me again to get along home. I thought we might go on like that all night, but then the soldier opened the door, put his head inside, and called, and another soldier came out.

"Do me a favor, Ned," the first one said. "Dust this boy's britches and send him home."

When the second one started for me, all I could think of to do was raise a hullabaloo. I backed off and shouted and yelled—I don't know what all—and at that the first soldier put down his musket and they both went for me. One chased me into the arms of the other, who began to drag me away from the house; I flailed and kicked, making as much noise as possible, and helped considerably in this by the swearing of the soldier who had hold of me.

Then a new voice said, "Boys, what's all the commotion about?"

The soldier dropped me on the ground like a sack of meal and stood at attention. "This here little Injun come up here bold as brass and demanded to see you, *sir*."

"Well, boy," said Davy Crockett, "now you see me. What in thunderation did you want to see me *about*?"

I looked up and there he was, a black silhouette in the light from the open door, though I could tell he was wearing formal clothes, a frock coat, and carrying a napkin; he'd been at his dinner. I spoke up and said I needed to talk with him private. This amused the President as much as it exasperated and embarrassed the two soldiers; he laughed, and said I might have ten minutes by his big watch of the presidential time, and then he would have to rejoin his guests. And he told me to come in. I picked myself up and did as he said.

The house wasn't so different from ours, plastered logs inside and a big fireplace, two largish rooms down and a loft above. As I entered, my knees went weak from the good smell of cooking. In the second room three well-dressed gentlemen were seated around a table spread with a white cloth and covered with dishes. They turned to stare at me, no doubt curious about the interruption—leading citizens of Rutherford and Union City, most likely. I didn't recognize anyone but ducked back in alarm for fear one of them might recognize me, or at least get a good look at me and put two and two together. But no one did.

The President indicated I was to climb up into the loft, and he climbed up after me. He asked me my name and age and I told him, Levi Colbert, thirteen. His eyebrows went up. "I knew the first Levi Colbert. Any relation?" And then, "It's a hard name to live up to." Then he remarked that I was soaking wet and shaking with cold, which was true, and bade me hunker down and hug the chimney to get warm. He saw that my face and hands were criss-crossed with bleeding scratches and asked the reason, and I explained that I'd been crawling through the canebrakes for two whole days.

Then the President sat himself down on a stool and listened to me tell my tale from start to finish, which I did in the most unadorned fashion imaginable, being so tuckered out and in such anxiety of mind, and unmanned to boot by his kind manner. His face changed from humorous to grave while I talked, and when I was done he didn't say anything for a spell. Then he told me it was a very serious crime to help a slave run away. He said that as President it was his duty to uphold the law, and other things of the sort, and partway through this speech I started to cry—I couldn't help it, everything seemed so bleak and hopeless, and I couldn't think what to do now except give up. When he finished I blubbered that Watty was one-quarter Cherokee and one-quarter Chickasaw and one-quarter white, and everybody knew Davy Crockett was a friend to the Indians nowadays; but I didn't need nobody to tell me how pointless all that was, since the one-quarter of Watty that was black condemned all the rest, and so I figured we were both goners.

Then the President surprised me. He got down off his stool and sat on the floor of the loft next to me in his good trousers, with his back to the chimney, and said something like this: "Levi, when I was a boy of thirteen, the same as you are now, I got myself in trouble with the schoolmaster, and my pa was looking to lick me with a hickory switch for missing school, and for pure terror of the two of them I lit out and run away from home. I was gone a couple of years altogether, and had a sight of adventures, and many a time was cold and hungry and friendless—and I never would have come through it all if it hadn't been for the kindness of strangers who took pity on a poor homeless lad and gave me a ride, or a little money, to buy a bit of food and keep my courage up. And after all that I came home again in the end. But I was my own man, or boy. Even then I could never bear to wear any man's collar, I had to be free."

I'd often heard people say how Davy broke with Old Hickory because the Jackson party wanted him to knuckle under and wear a collar engraved *"MY DOG. Andrew Jackson,"* so I nodded.

Then he rubbed his face and thought a bit, and looked at me over that big hook nose he had, and finally he told me to wait there, and climbed down the ladder. And a minute later he climbed back up, followed by a portly gentleman who puffed a good deal. The President said that this was Mr. Barclay, from Philadelphia, and he thought I'd best tell this Mr. Barclay my story, but he didn't want to know any more about it himself. And then he climbed back down and left us alone—but reappeared yet again with a plate of meat and bread for me, and a cup half full of whiskey "to warm my insides."

If you have guessed already that this Mr. Barclay—which was not his real name—had connections with what is called the Underground Railway, you would be correct. It appeared that the gentlemen dining with the President that evening were guests of his from the East, and not the local bigwigs I had taken them for.

Now I know for a sure and certain fact that Davy Crockett was no Abolitionist. He'd owned slaves himself in former times. But neither was he a convinced and committed pro-slavery man. And many of his Eastern supporters purely hated slavery. Davy had to juggle his peculiar coalition of poor farmers and bankers, Indian

Lovers and Indian Haters and Abolitionists, as best he could, so it was not after all so very surprising to find such a guest as Mr. Barclay from Philadelphia tucking in at the President's table in Rutherford, Tennessee.

This same Mr. Barclay took Watty away with him that very night. But the adventure was by no means over for me. There was a bodacious to-do to be faced when I came straggling home two days later: Callie in hysterics, Pa humiliated and furious, and—worst of all—me getting indentured to Old Man Bertram in Watty's place, as punishment for helping him escape.

Rachel, I was obliged to work for that old man three years without wages, to keep him from setting the law on me and Pa. And I tell you, I was mighty glad Watty had got away. Bad as he treated me, his slaves got treated worse. I don't know how long I could have stood it; but about the time I turned sixteen the old sot fell out of his wagon, coming home drunk one winter night, and froze to death; and the term of my indenture ended with his demise.

Soon after I was offered a chance to ride with a drover to convey some horses to Nashville, and took it. And when I got to Nashville, and the drover paid me off, I went on east instead of west, and didn't see my home again for many years.

From the foregoing, you will have realized that I had abandoned my intention to run away North with Watty and Mr. Barclay. Trying to smuggle a brown-skinned African-featured boy and an Indian boy both into free territory would surely have made Mr. Barclay's job harder by making him more conspicuous, and he might well have refused to take me; but the fact is, I never asked to go. President Crockett's tale of running away for fear of his father and the schoolmaster had impressed me deeply. At the end of two whole years' hardship and knocking about the world, *he* had ended up at home again after all. I figured I'd had enough of being on the move to last me quite a while, and if I was likely to wind up back home again in the end, I might as well go there now, and spare myself the hardships of the road.

I don't know how the hardships of the road could have been any worse than those I endured in the service of Old Man Bertram, but I couldn't foresee that as I made my way back through the flooded country, going slow to give Watty and Mr. Barclay a good start, crying because I missed Watty already and felt certain I would never see him again, and because I knew everybody would come down on me when I got back and try to make me tell where he was, and also because I was only thirteen years old, a Chickasaw boy in a country full of people who had shot Chickasaws like dogs not so very long before, and hadn't forgot the knack of it neither, and because all these dreadful events had been too much for me.

I made a plan as I went along. I decided to say that Watty had drowned while we were swimming the Middle Fork, and that was near enough to the truth that I could make a good story of it. I almost drowned myself, going back. Then later, when I judged it safe, I'd tell Callie what had really happened.

All this came about the way I planned it; but I never looked to bind myself for seven years to that foul old drunkard. If he hadn't died when he did, I believe the choking sensation of wearing a collar engraved "*MY DOG. Wm. Bertram*" would have surely forced me to run away, though I had no desire to be a fugitive a second time.

Well, Rachel, that is my story. I know you can scarcely help but feel that my part in it, and President Crockett's part, were best left untold even to you, however warmly you may sympathize with my feelings and deplore my father's actions. I had no expectation of revealing any of these events to you or to anyone, and but for a most remarkable occurrence would very likely have carried them with me to my grave.

What altered my intention, after much agitated considering, was this. You know that after receiving my shoulder wound at Cincinnati I lingered on a month there, at a Methodist Church which had been turned into a hospital. As I began to regain my strength I used to walk about the place for exercise, and to be of use to those more grievously wounded than myself. One day I wandered into a room where some wounded Yankee prisoners lay. To my surprise I saw several Negroes, swathed in bandages, lying among the white men. I knew that companies of freedmen and freeborn Negroes had been formed under white officers, but had never met with these on any battlefield. But obviously they had been at Cincinnati, for here was the evidence.

Wandering nearer, and peering curiously at these black soldiers, I saw with a shock that one had copper rings run through his earlobes. The only place I ever saw these large rings in the ears of a male Negro was among the Chickasaw slaves, where it is the common practice of both men and women to decorate themselves in that way. My curiosity was roused further. I went up to the cot where the man lay—and knew at once, despite the swathings of bandages around his head, that this was my long-lost Watty, grown to manhood, not safe and sound by any means but found at last.

I wonder whether you can possibly imagine my feelings upon discovering that here was the childhood companion I had never thought to set eyes on again in this world—but gravely wounded, no longer free, and my sworn enemy into the bargain!

That his wound was grave, I ascertained from the surgeon. He lay in a coma; they were doubtful of his recovery. Upon learning that I had known Watty as a child, the surgeon urged me strongly to sit by his bedside and talk to him, as a well-known voice has often succeeded in bringing a patient out of a comatose state when all else fails. I was happy to accede to this suggestion. For several days I sat beside Watty's sickbed and spoke to him, in the Chickasaw language, of our life in the canebrakes, of the Obion River and my father's ferry, of hunting and fishing, of the farm work—anything and everything that came to mind. The memories flooded back, though many a year had passed since I had cared to think of that life.

And not to leave you in suspense of the outcome I will tell you at once that my efforts were successful; for on the fourth day Watty's eyes flickered and rolled, and he spoke to me, and after several more days he was fully conscious (though in considerable pain), able to take nourishment, recovering from the astonishment of my having found him (and perhaps saved him once again!—a thought which I own affects me very strangely) and ready to say what had become of him since that night when he had embraced me for one quick tearful instant, before being led away into the darkness by Mr. Barclay.

Briefly then: Mr. Barclay had friends all along the route north, who were ready to swear to all and sundry that Watty was Mr. Barclay's slave and always had been. He swiftly obtained some papers to prove it, as well as some less exotic clothes for Watty, whose gaudy but thorn-ripped garments were at once too tattered and too unusual to pass muster as the traveling outfit of a wealthy man's servant. As they could not undo the knots in his hair, they cut it, close to his scalp.

Watty's inability to speak English was a problem at first, but he applied himself and learned enough to get by on in a very short time. (It turned out he knew more English than he realized, having heard it spoken all his life.) His Chickasaw accent was another problem. I gathered that they solved both problems by agreeing that Watty should not speak at all where anybody could hear him. Watty said that as for his rescuer, once they began their journey Mr. Barclay's own Eastern accent turned to pure Virginia Planter.

Mr. Barclay brought Watty all the way back to Philadelphia with him. They took passage on a steamboat at Paducah and traveled up the Ohio all the way to Pittsburgh. The rest of the journey was made by rail—by Aboveground Railway, as you might say.

Watty lived in Mr. Barclay's house for a time—and was

very kindly treated by the family—but the Underground Railway people decided that Philadelphia was too far south to be safe. Even though it seemed unlikely that anybody would consider Watty valuable enough to chase him so far, things had happened to make Mr. Barclay and his friends uneasy. At first there was some talk of sending Watty to Canada, but in the end it was decided he would be better off placed with a family of free Negroes in Boston. So they sent him there.

And this is the part of the tale that has impelled me to break silence after keeping the secret so long. In Boston it was at once imcumbent upon Watty to find a way to earn his keep. As he had grown up on a farm, they naturally looked about for a trustworthy farmer to take him on as a hired hand—and in this way a place was found for him on a good-sized farm southeast of Boston, near a town called Marshfield. And who should own this farm but Daniel Webster!

Does it not seem to you a strange destiny for a former slave boy, to have crossed paths with such an uncommon number of great men?

Watty attempted to describe his feelings upon arriving at last in the situation that had been arranged for him, but I doubt that I can appreciate them fully. The sort of farming he was used to was not much like the New England sort, the weather and country being both so different. He suffered a good deal from the cold, especially at first, and sorely missed his mother and me. But he got used to it all in time. His English quickly improved. (We were speaking Chickasaw together, but at this point he switched over temporarily to demonstrate his perfect fluency in English, as well as to amuse me with his Yankee pronunciation.) He also had his liberty, and a thoroughgoing determination that he would do anything rather than lose it.

The men over him were prejudiced against colored people, but his work gave satisfaction and this brought increased responsibility, and in time Watty came to the attention of Daniel Webster himself, who (though away a good deal) was sometimes at home. Mr. Webster became interested in Watty and took a notion to provide him with a basic education, in case he should later wish to follow a trade, and lessons in reading and writing were accordingly arranged. Watty appears to have astonished his employer with his quickness and readiness to learn. More lessons ensued—history, the natural sciences.

By this time Watty had attained the age of twenty, Daniel Webster had attained a place in the Cabinet, and the whole country, North and South, was in a ferment over slavery and the question of secession. And one fateful day, his benefactor said to Watty that he believed peaceful secession to be impossible, and for this reason had reluctantly been ready to accept the principle, that runaway slaves must be returned to their owners, as the only means by which the Union could be preserved. But having known Watty—heard his story—imagined the horror of his being thrown back into the clutches of such as Old Man Bertram—Mr. Webster now understood that slavery was too high a price to pay, even to preserve the Union.

Rachel, you may guess what terrible thoughts have been whirling in my brain since the day I had this from Watty. Again and again I ask myself, did Mr. Clay's Compromise fail, and the South secede, and the War, which has cost so many lives and so much suffering, begin—because an Indian boy helped a slave boy to run away, all those long years ago? Can it be that all unwittingly I have participated in events which, though seeming small, have had so mighty an effect? There are moments when my oppression and agitation of mind can scarcely be described, and I begin even to imagine how one day the United States—our future Confederacy's great neighbor—may have a Commander in Chief called President Watty Colbert: it would astonish me no more than any of these other great oaks from little acorns grown.

Stumbling in the dark we make our choices, the consequences of which are beyond our understanding; but as God is my witness I acted for the right as I saw it then. May God forgive me—and may you, my darling Rachel, forgive me too—if I was wrong. Wrong perhaps also in sharing my story with you, though the burden seemed too heavy to bear alone. I cannot know. Yet how desperately, and how hopelessly, have I wished for reassurance, that all that I have done will finally seem to have been for the best!

1848

Zachary Taylor was elected to the presidency in 1848, and after dying in office was succeeded by his vice president, Millard Fillmore.

But what if *both* men had died in office? The president, under the law at that time, would have been President Pro Tem of the Senate David R. Atchison. (He actually *was* president for twenty-four hours, as the religious Taylor refused to take the oath of office on the Sabbath.)

Ralph Roberts, author of more than twenty nonfiction books, once again turns his hand to fiction with this story, which shows that the Civil War might have taken a strikingly different form under President Atchison.

How the South Preserved the Union

by Ralph Roberts

On the train through Nebraska and Kansas last week, I picked up a tawdry dime novel. Abandoned on the next seat by some fellow passenger, the book was by one of those notorious literary hacks—not Ned Buntline, but one of his scandalous ilk.

Normally I'd rather be attacked by Red Indians than be

seen reading something so trashy, yet the trip was long and I was bored. It helped me forget the jolting of the train and the aching of my old bones that, even after forty years of faithful service to the Whig party, were still called on to make sacrifices in the cause of politics. So, as we rattled across the endless prairie, I ignored the smoke and cinders coming through the rocking coach's open window, the smell of the gent across from me, and immersed myself in the book.

This hack writer was amusing. His contentions of fantasy were that the Civil War had not started until 1861, that Abraham Lincoln had been president and, if you can believe *this*, it was the South that seceded from the Union and not the North.

Such literary devices are a momentary diversion at best. I'm not sure that this new so-called "scientific fiction" will ever really catch on. Can you imagine that? Abraham Lincoln as president? I knew Lincoln during my many years in Washington. He never rose higher than a seedy backwoods congressman from Illinois. A vulgar, incompetent man who amounted to little and accomplished less. He was shot in a tavern brawl—sometime in 1865, I think. A silly dispute over theater tickets with an actor named Booth.

Literary fantasy aside, we all know that the Civil War started in 1849 with the secession of Massachusetts from the Union and the Second Battle of Lexington and Concord, which the New Minutemen, abolitionists all, again won. New Hampshire and Vermont quickly followed, as did the rest of New England, New York, New Jersey, and Pennsylvania, all to the rabble-rousing strains of "Yankee Doodle." To say otherwise, even in a dime novel, is as laughable as saying General George Armstrong Custer never won at the Little Big Horn and became president in his own turn.

Forty years ago, I was there during it all—a young man of but twenty years, serving as aide to President Atchison. It was a hard-fought war. Brother against brother on the blood-soaked battlefields of New England, New York, and Pennsylvania.

The election of 1848 had started out ordinarily enough. General Zachary Taylor—fresh from his heroic victories in the Mexican War—and his running mate, Millard Fillmore, had won handily. His opponent, Democrat Lewis Cass, never really stood a chance against the public's love affair with the hero of Buena Vista—where General Santa Anna had 20,000 troops to Taylor's 5,000 and still went down to defeat.

The Whigs were just as victorious and, once again, the party of Henry Clay, Daniel Webster, and even of Taylor's military rival, General Winfield Scott, had won the White House. Or so it seemed in those heady days leading up to the Inauguration in March, 1849.

The initial Inauguration had fallen on a Sunday. President-elect Taylor had refused to be sworn in on the Sabbath and, as President *pro tem* of the Senate, Senator David R. Atchison of Missouri had been acting president for the day. He later told me he had never known it, and had slept through most of that Sunday afternoon.

Taylor was sworn in on Monday, and all seemed to be proceeding as normal. Until, that is, the new president and Vice President Millard Fillmore had gone for a carriage ride in the country. No one knows why, or what they wanted to discuss out there all alone, except for a driver. We will never know. On the way back to Washington, the carriage careened down a small hill and overturned in an icy creek. All three men died.

This time, the Senator *knew* he was president of the United States, given the office not by election but by rightful law of succession.

I had been back home to Missouri, running political errands for my boss, a hard but fair man. I had come to Washington with the newly appointed Senator, and stayed with him through election in his own right. Liking my abilities, he had given me more and more responsibility until I had become his chief aide.

An urgent summons to return to the capital reached me the last of January and I arrived back in Washington on the evening of the 9th of February, 1849—alighting stiffly from the stagecoach and retrieving my own horse from a nearby livery for the short ride to the White House. Senator Atchison had by that time been *President* Atchison for the better part of three weeks.

I wearily guided the horse through the frigid night air and onto the grounds of the White House, riding carefully in the dark streets whose mystery was broken only occasionally by fitful candle or lamp light from some uncurtained window.

A black servant took the reins as I dismounted and he led the horse away. I leaned against a column for a moment as my back muscles twinged in pain, then let another black servant lead me inside, take my coat, and usher me into the president's office.

"Ah, there you are, Garrison," Atchison said, then turned to the other distinguished-looking gentlemen in the room, their hands comfortably gripping snifters of brandy and cigars. A delightful pungent haze filled the room. "All of you know Sam, I think?"

"Yes, indeed, Mr. President," General Winfield Scott said, rising to grip my hand. "And how are you, Samuel? A good trip, I hope? And a little surprised to find your boss promoted from senator to president, I'll wager."

Henry Clay also rose. "And yet more to find him now a Whig instead of a Democrat, eh?" He reached out and also shook my hand.

"It was the obvious political move," I said, taking a chair near the fire and accepting a snifter of brandy from General Scott. "And congratulations to you, Mr. Secretary Clay."

"Tell me, Sam," the President said, hitching his chair closer to mine. "How's all this playing out there?"

I nodded seriously, recalling my many conversations

on the long trip from Missouri to Washington. "Pretty well, Mr. President. Everyone accepts that since the Whigs won the White House legitimately, it was only right that you would switch parties. People felt that Mr. Clay was a good choice for Secretary of War also."

General Winfield Scott smiled. "Except perhaps for Webster, eh? So you found that people in general didn't mind the President's change of parties?"

"That's right, sir. At which time I also admitted to now being a Whig."

The three men laughed in delight.

"You see, gentlemen," President Atchison said, "I told you young Garrison was smart." He relaxed back into his chair. "And what do you see as our biggest problem here, Sam? The new British demands on the Oregon Territory?"

"Fifty-four forty or fight," Scott said with some vigor. "When will those lobsterbacks ever learn? We taught the Mexicans and we can teach them just as well."

"No, Mr. President," I said. "John Brown is obviously your biggest problem."

"Hmpf," Scott said. "That damn farmer? Granted, he's a thorn in the side, but surely not a threat? His sum total of military experience is tilling the fields at his farm in New York . . . in . . ."

"North Elba, General," the President said.

"Exactly, *North* Elba, and now he thinks of himself as some sort of Yankee Napoleon, eh? New Minutemen, indeed! Why, those greenhorns would not have lasted a day with me in Mexico!"

"They are only state militias," Clay said.

President Atchison rubbed his chin. "That's all they are now, but the abolitionist sentiment is spreading like wildfire in New England and New York. Even as far south as Pennsylvania. Samuel's right. It's a serious problem. Especially now that Daniel Webster has allied himself with the movement."

Scott, the gruff, straightforward military hero of the recently concluded Mexican War, shook his head in bafflement.

"I don't understand their rabid objections to your taking office. Zachary Taylor supported slavery as well—he owned that huge plantation down in Baton Rouge and employed slaves in the fields. What's the difference? So what if you support slavery as well?"

"Well," I said, forgetting my place as the youngest and most inexperienced man present, "wars often have a popular justification, such as the abhorrence of slavery, but the real reason is always the same as that for every war throughout history—economics. The South and the new West given to us by General Scott's success in defeating Mexico are full of raw materials. The greedy industrialists in New England intend to make sure their control is complete. They fear Southern and Western factories full of cheap slave labor will put them out of business."

The President nodded, smiling. "As, indeed, they probably will. See, gentlemen, I *told* you he was smart."

Mr. Clay waved his hand in reluctant agreement. "Yes, yes. Precisely as we've been discussing. But surely it will not come to war? We are, after all, one country."

"No," the President said sadly, "the rabble-rousers shout of secession, or of coming down here to Washington and replacing the government by force. This fiery-eyed John Brown has captured their imagination. Gentlemen, the problem is serious."

"Yes," I said, "especially now that they have the respectability of Daniel Webster on their side. There is talk that he will be made president, and that John Brown will be his chief general."

General Scott snorted again. "My God, the man has no military training! My troops will chew up his like a biscuit soaked in water!"

"Maybe not so easily," I said, again forgetting my place and disagreeing with the general. "They have quite a few veteran officers who fought with you or General Taylor in the Mexican campaigns so recently concluded. And they have most of the gun and other munitions factories. Their resources outmatch ours."

"Wait," Henry Clay said. "We are talking as if there already *is* a civil war. It's our job to prevent it! We must talk the North out of seceding, and effect a compromise of some sort."

President Atchison grunted in the affirmative and stood up. He walked over to the fire and rubbed his hands in its heat.

"But . . . Mr. President," I said, looking at his broad back, now bowed slightly as if his new and vast responsibilities were weighting him down. "Mr. President, it would take a negotiator with the patience of Job, the wisdom of Solomon, and the bravery of a fool to get anywhere with a fanatic like John Brown."

The President turned and smiled at me. "Exactly right, Samuel, and that's why I'm sending you. Not that I believe the fool part. After consulting with me, you'll leave tomorrow, and may God be with you. Events are pressing and we may only have days to solve this problem and preserve the very Union itself!"

"Thank you, sir," I said. "I'm glad you still want me as your aide."

"Oh, right. Sam, in view of the magnitude of this problem, I've created a new office. We're calling it, er . . ."

"National Security Adviser," Henry Clay prompted.

"Yes, and that's what you are now, Sam. Should tell them just how serious we consider this meeting to be."

I nodded. "Then you think the national security is threatened by this movement?"

"It could very well give us a nation divided," Secretary Clay said.

The President shook his head sadly. "If the North secedes, Henry, we may be that—and soon."

North Elba was a small farming community in 1849, located southwest of Plattsburg in upstate New York, only a few miles west of the Vermont border. In today's fast-paced world of the 1880s, such a trip would have been nothing. Speedy trains and the convenience of telegraph wires have spoiled us. Then, it was just as fast to go there in person as to send a letter.

Riding from Washington to North Elba, a portion of the trip through a three-day midwinter blizzard, took me almost two weeks. It was a cold, exhausting horseback journey, and seemed endless. All of which give me considerable time for reflection and to absorb my president's instructions on approaching John Brown.

The hamlet of North Elba, for it was no more than that, had no hotel, no inn. There was a small store, at which I stopped to inquire directions to the Brown farm.

In the crowded, overheated interior of the small store, I was at first surprised to see Negroes or—as they prefer to be called since the great Civil Rights Act of President Stephen A. Douglas in 1861, which ended slavery for all time—African Americans. At that time, all men and (just a few years later) all women were declared equal and given the right to vote, although certain veterans already had enjoyed voting privileges for several years.

Which reminds me, in that book by the hack writer I mentioned at the first of this article, if the Civil War had occurred in the 1860s, these civil rights might not have been granted for decades more. So, perhaps, a few years can make a big difference.

A white-haired African American gent, who answered to the name of Josh Washington, lit up when I mentioned Brown. He gave me directions to the abolitionist's farm, and went on to enthusiastically talk about both Brown and Mr. Gerrit Smith. He slapped his rough work clothes and laughed in glee as he went on about how the great John Brown was defying those pointy-heads down in Washington. I smiled and nodded politely, deciding that now was not the time to speak of my connection with the government.

Gerrit Smith, as I learned, owned extensive land in the area and was donating small farming plots to former slaves. To John Brown, he had just this year granted a large tract of land out of admiration for the man and his cause. Brown had just moved here recently from Ohio, where he had gone bankrupt in the wool business.

Josh Washington, of course, did not mention Brown's failed business, nor that the man had spent twenty years before that as a tanner and a sheep farmer. His words, and those of the others present, were all the most effusive of praise for John Brown. The man, so it seemed, was a saint who could do no wrong. The messenger of God who would lead them all across the river Jordan and to the Promised Land. In other words, as today's popular politicians like Custer and Buffalo Bill Cody would put it, Brown had a high approval rating.

I thanked Washington and rode the three miles through the snow and gathering winter darkness to Brown's farm. A small house, no more than a shack, greeted my eyes with a plume of wood smoke and the welcome glow of lamplight pushing back the dusk. Several barns were nearby—all with lamplight spilling from their windows as well. It looked like a busy place.

The young man with a rifle who stepped from behind a tree was not so welcoming. I heard the rifle's *click* as he cocked it, the sound seeming to shatter the winter's silent stillness.

"Halt! Identify yourself."

He couldn't have been more than seventeen or eighteen. Obviously scrawny and underfed, even bundled against the cold as he was in some sort of military-looking great coat.

"My name's Sam Garrison," I said politely, looking into the maw of that rifle pointing at me. It looked to be brand-new and of the latest model. "And who may you be?"

"Private Absalom Harris, New York State Militia," he said proudly. "Get off that horse and state your business. Smartly now. This here's a restricted area." His cold-reddened hands gripped the rifle tightly and he looked determined.

I sighed and stiffly dismounted. "Would you inform Mr. Brown—"

"That's General Brown," he said.

"Yes, well, tell General Brown that a representative of President Atchison is here to consult with him."

The kid was impressed in spite of himself. Forgetting to ask for any sort of identification, he motioned for me to follow and led the way to the house. We entered, and the young soldier pushed his way through the crowded, noisy room and whispered something into the ear of a tall, bearded man by the fireplace. The man clapped the boy on the shoulder and came to me, extending his hand.

"I'm John Brown, brother. How may I serve you?"

I shook his hand. "I'm Samuel Garrison, National Security Adviser to President Atchison."

Brown raised his eyebrows, but otherwise waited politely for me to continue. At this time, in 1849, he was fifty years of age and—with his bushy beard and unkempt hair—looked very much the fiery-eyed fanatic we would hang for treason a few years later.

Interestingly enough, the hack writer I told you about predicted this same end for Brown—hanged for insurrection—but not until 1859 at some place called Harpers Ferry way down in Virginia. I suppose a few people, even in alternate universes, meet the same end.

I explained to Brown that we must have an urgent meeting. He shrugged and led me into the house's tiny kitchen. He gestured to a table laden with food and invited me to help myself. The real surprise was the sleek, well-fed elderly man of around seventy years already seated at the table.

"Senator Webster," I said, acknowledging his offhand greeting of a waved chicken leg.

"So, Atchison called you back from Missouri, I see," Daniel Webster said, passing me a platter of cornbread.

Famished, I heaped a plate and stuffed my mouth, only able to nod for the moment.

John Brown seated himself and gazed steadily at me, but his tones seemed casual enough.

"Missouri," he mused. "I've thought of moving there, or perhaps to Kansas Territory. That would seem to be a good place to stop the spread of this godless practice of slavery."

Daniel Webster put down what was left of the chicken leg. "Well, that won't be necessary now, will it, General Brown?"

Brown seemed to change focus to Webster—you got the impression that he was that intent, a very narrow-minded man.

"No, not now," he agreed. "The Lord's work can be done just as well out of the North as it can the West."

"Ummm," I said, finishing off a mug of buttermilk, "there are those who would dispute that you do the work of the Lord. I believe a number of Southerners mention another being in connection with your name."

"Satan and the South both start with an 'S,' " Brown said, and began noisily worrying a chicken wing, causing me to unhappily take note of the congealed grease on his beard from earlier snacks. "God is with our legions and we shall soon smite the slaveowners a mighty blow."

Daniel Webster had the grace to look uncomfortable, but he still defended Brown. "General Brown expresses a widely held sentiment. In the last several months I've traveled widely in New England, New York, and Pennsylvania. The people are demanding an immediate end to slavery. We feel the government is now in the hands of Southerners and that our interests are not best served by those in Washington. It seems to be the time either that our national government is restructured, or to go our own way."

I reached for more cornbread. "What kind of support?" I asked.

"The same kind the Sons of Liberty had in 1776—*armed* support," Webster said, leaning back in satisfaction. "Two weeks ago in Boston we had a meeting. Delegates from the states of New Hampshire, Vermont, Maine, Connecticut, Rhode Island, New York, and Pennsylvania all voted to put the militias we are raising and training under the command of General John Brown. Two days ago, New Jersey also agreed, and only today I received correspondence from Ohio indicating the same. Michigan and Indiana will not be far behind."

"It is God's will," said John Brown, showing agility in beating me to the last piece of chicken.

"That all sounds very bellicose," I said. "I don't remember the federal government threatening its own states militarily."

"It will come to that," Webster said. "After months of debate, the consensus is that we should arm ourselves and, if possible, enforce our will on Washington. Failing that, we'll defend our right to exist as a separate nation—the Confederacy of North America. If it does come to that," he added smugly, "I am already designated to be its first president."

"But, Senator Webster," I said reasonably. "The U.S. Army has just concluded a victorious war against Mexico. We have many regiments of battle-hardened troops. What do you have to match that? Surely not that hayseed private that you have on guard duty outside?"

"Absalom is a believer, like so many others," Brown said. "He'll do what's needed, even if it means dying for the cause."

Daniel Webster shrugged. "It is true that many of our troops need training, but some of those veteran regiments you speak of will come over to our side if we are forced to secede. Some already have. Not to mention that almost all of the arms factories are in our states and in our hands. No matter how hardened the combat veteran, he'll do little effective fighting without weapons or powder for his shot, I'll wager."

I sighed. We were indeed becoming a nation divided, but I followed my instructions from President Atchison. "Gentlemen," I said, taking documents wrapped in oilcloth from inside my coat. "I have here correspondence from President Atchison. He's offering a compromise."

I unwrapped the package and held out the presidential correspondence. John Brown showed little interest and ignored the documents. Webster sighed in his own turn and took them, perched a pair of spectacles on his nose, and busied himself for several minutes reading.

John Brown seemed indisposed for further conversation, so we both continued to eat while Webster studied what I had brought.

Finally Webster grunted and looked up. "Do you know what's written here?"

"Yes, sir," I said. "I helped the President write it. We feel it's a fair compromise that will preserve the union."

"Too late for that," Brown said. "Not so long as one slave remains under the yoke of ownership. We shall sing our mighty battle hymn and not quit until all our bodies lie a-moldering in the grave!"

Once more Daniel Webster shrugged and smiled at me as if to say, "One has to work with what one has."

"It *is* too late, I'm afraid," Webster said. "What you are offering here is just a compromise—not a solution. No more new slave states, but those already allowing slavery to remain as they are. This is not at all acceptable. We want an *end* to slavery, not to simply to halt its spread."

He dropped the documents onto the table with a sad finality.

I didn't give up, of course. Daniel Webster and I argued far into the night, and others joined us. Many of the other men there I knew, for they had at one time been high in the halls of government down in Washington. Now they had cast their lot with the Northern states, and turned their back on the federal establishment that they had once served.

Even John Brown, in among his many platitudes, made occasional sense. The people, these abolitionists who were dragging the rest of the North with them, truly believed that slavery was evil, and they intended to end it at all costs, even if it drove the nation asunder. There was no give, no willingness any more to look at the other side, the side of the South. Webster assured me that this view was strongly and unbreakably held all across the Northern tier of states.

They all held forth at length against the evil institution of slavery, but I noticed that only Daniel Webster said much about economics, although he railed mightily about how factories in the South, manned by that cheapest possible of labor—slaves—would drain the very lifeblood from Northern industries.

Webster, so I knew from his years as a senator in Washington, was fond of high living. I had a feeling his sudden and complete espousal of the Northern cause had not a little to do with the gold of those industrialists whose interests he was so verbosely and elegantly defending. Being passed over by the Whigs for president of the United States most likely rankled in his mind as well. It had been obvious that he desperately wanted the nomination, the one Zachary Taylor had acquired with so little effort.

It was all so hopeless back then. Today I cannot help but reflect on that hack writer's contention of fantasy. He wrote that the Civil War had not occurred until 1861 because of various compromises which had prolonged the peace. There was something called the Missouri Compromise and the Dred Scott Decision—he was very good at making up believable-sounding names.

But I can tell you this: that cold winter night in 1849, there was no compromise in North Elba, New York. No compromise and no give in the heart of the North. That's the message I would have to carry back to Washington.

Finally I was given a blanket and allowed to sleep on the floor of the living room, lit by the blazing fire. Nor was I alone; there were congressmen and senators, and ranking military officers who were glad to share that hard floor of John Brown's shack. A couple of blanket-covered figures from me, Daniel Webster—the soon-to-be president of the Confederacy of North America—snored in self-satisfied lustiness.

Washington in June of 1852 was beautiful—all green and blooming. Gentle breezes made the days pleasant and the nights great for sleeping—a wonderful time before the hellishness of July and August. Unless, of course, you were in the government and involved in futilely fighting the three-year-old armed insurrection of the Northern states.

Compromise had indeed proved impossible. The speed with which the Confederacy of North America had fielded a well-equipped, well-provisioned army showed long prior planning, and the fact that compromise had not truly been an option after all. Their naval forces, many ships converted from the China trade to be men-o'-war, soon ruled the Atlantic coastline from Maine to Georgia.

President David R. Atchison looked gaunt, haggard—it was if the cares of the office were aging him far faster than the rest of us. We were gathered in the White House's cabinet meeting room—leading generals, congressmen, cabinet officers, and the President and Vice President.

General Winfield Scott was treating us to a lengthy discourse on the federal forces' consistent lack of success on land and water. A large map of the Eastern seaboard was tacked to one wall, and Scott now stood by the map, tapping it occasionally to show the area he was discussing. Flies droned in through the open windows, the buzz of their wings not far different from the general's tones.

". . . and our forces are pulling back into Maryland to regroup while—"

"Retreating, in disorder, you mean," Secretary Henry Clay said unkindly. "They were soundly whipped at that little village in Pennsylvania, what was its name?"

"Gettysburg," General Scott said softly, his eyes distant, perhaps seeing fallen comrades, fire, and destruction. "They were just too many for us."

I knew he had been there personally, and was only recently returned from the front. One couldn't fault him for bravery, just for results.

His manner firmed and he whacked the map with his hand. "Our artillery was out of powder an hour into the battle. The Yankee guns kept pounding us for the better part of two days! There was no way we could prevail against those odds. I withdrew with what forces I could salvage. Be thankful for them, gentlemen—they are all that is keeping John Brown from sitting in this very room and putting his blood-soaked boots on this table in triumph!"

He walked over and slammed the conference table to make sure we understood exactly which table.

President Atchison put up a placating hand. "We understand your problems, General Scott. Believe me, we understand them all too well." He turned and looked at me. "Sam, refresh us on the course of the war and the situation today, and give the general a breather. Don't hesitate to add your viewpoint. Lord knows we need all the help we can get right now, if we are to survive the year."

I nodded, rose to my feet, and approached the map. General Scott sat down, sighing gratefully to be out of the spotlight for the moment.

"Gentlemen," I said, placing my hand on Massachusetts, "on April 17th, 1849, a small militia force calling itself the New Minutemen attacked an equally small federal force near Lexington and Concord. They easily routed the federals.

"This was followed by quick captures of Camp Devins, the Brooklyn Navy Yard and, indeed, virtually all other federal facilities north of the Mason-Dixon Line.

"By July of 1849, General Scott had moved into New Jersey with a large force of regulars and was marching on New York City. Just outside of Trenton, he was opposed by John Brown and the massed state militias of the Confederacy of North America—an army which outnumbered ours by some two to one."

"Damned amateur," Scott muttered.

I ignored him and continued addressing notables present. "The battle, due mostly to Brown's inexperience, was inconclusive. General Scott had to withdraw, but Brown failed to capitalize and achieve what could have been a decisive victory for him—one which could have ended the war right there."

The President took a deep breath. "We were lucky, and at least a few people believe that God is not totally on the side of John Brown after all."

I continued. "The Northern forces grow in strength, but have been very cautious in pressing South. They waited until their naval forces could mount an effective blockade, and it is only with the coming of warmer weather this year that they have resumed the offensive. Gettysburg is the largest battle since Trenton. And the bloodiest, and the most successful for us."

"How so?" Zebulon Vance, a congressman from North Carolina asked.

"Give General Scott credit," I said. "He was vastly outnumbered and outgunned, but he fought Brown to a standstill. They're very cautious and it has gained us valuable time. Perhaps several months even. Other than that, military action has been sparse."

"What about Atlanta in April?" Henry Clay asked.

"The burning of Atlanta," I said, "was not much of a battle. They landed troops on the coast, who marched inland, burned the town, and marched out again. It was simply a raid, albeit one totally unforeseen. I don't think it significant."

General Scott's hand hit the table again, causing several of us to jump in alarm. "Well, I *do* consider it serious! Exceptionally so! We are failing miserably due to lack of munitions and manpower to maintain a one-front war. Now the damn Yankees have found out they can land in Georgia at will. How long do you think it will be before we have Northern beachheads over in Alabama, the Mississippi Delta, and even our newest state of Texas? Not long, my boy, not long. And we simply ... cannot ... fight ... them ... all."

He lapsed into silence and sat very still, staring blankly at the wall.

There was dead silence for awhile, broken finally by the President.

"What General Scott says is obviously true. The North's factories are turning out weapons even faster than they can train troops, which is pretty quick the way John Brown brainwashes them. We are going to be overrun in very short order. Would have been by now if those cautious ninnies like Webster were not holding Brown back. We need a solution, and we need it *now*."

Henry Clay suddenly sat up straight.

"Mr. President, I have it!"

All eyes turned to the Kentuckian.

"The answer has been staring us in the face all along. What's the real reason the North is attacking the rest of the country?"

Again there was silence but, despite being very junior in this august company, I essayed an answer.

"Because, sir, the Northern industrialists are worried that we will use slave labor and our abundant raw materials to put them out of business."

Clay beamed. "Exactly, Samuel, exactly. So that's what we do: Immediately start a massive program. As you said, Gettysburg has given us a few months. The North is not aware of just how weak we are. Throw up factories. Put the slaves in the factories. We'll soon be outstripping the Yankees in producing munitions!"

"That's fine," General Scott said, "but what about additional troops?"

John Calhoun of South Carolina suddenly slapped the table in his own right. "Slaves—we put the slaves in uniform, too! In a year, we'll roll up the North like a carpet going out for spring cleaning."

"But—" I started to voice my belief that this course of action would not work; however, President Atchison had once more taken control of the meeting.

"I see no other choice at the moment. We will begin immediately a massive and total mobilization of all slaves —and everyone else, for that matter. No planter is going to complain about his slaves being sent to the factories or front lines if that's where he's headed himself." He stood up. "Gentlemen, we have a lot of planning to do. Let's get at it!"

In June of the next year, 1853, almost the same group was meeting in Richmond, Virginia—the capital having been occupied by John Brown's forces in late Spring. Missing only was Henry Clay, who had passed away the previous year. John C. Calhoun now sat in his place.

We were not a happy group. The country was in danger of crumbling around us. The Yankees had taken New Orleans and were pressing west into Texas and north toward Arkansas. Vicksburg was holding out, and Natchez, but it seemed a matter of just weeks before we would be cut off from the rest of the country and the Mississippi would be our Western border.

Delaware, Maryland, and most of northern Virginia were now under Brown's control. Times were dark, indeed.

General Scott once again stood before a map on the wall. Colored pins indicated our shattered position. I wondered where would we be meeting next year? In North Carolina? Or in some Northern prison?

"We are being pushed back faster and faster, gentlemen. Production of munitions drags on, our troops are lackluster even when they stand and fight, and our lines are collapsing all along the various fronts. I cannot guarantee protecting Richmond much longer. I suggest you remove the capital farther South. Raleigh might be safe for a few months."

"It's not working," President Atchison said, his face so worn and haggard now that my heart ached for him. "The idea of using slaves in the factories and as soldiers was not the salvation we had hoped."

"They are people, too," I said. "It's hard to be enthused about either making guns or shooting guns if you're a slave. What's in it for you? Especially if it's the *other* side that wants to free you."

Several of those present screwed up their faces in thought as they pondered this novel viewpoint.

"Weeks," Secretary Calhoun said. "At best, that's all we have left. What do we do?"

"It is time for a radical solution," I said. "A last-ditch, valiant effort that will win or lose the war for us. Something no one would ever even *think* we would have the guts to do."

All heads turned to watch me intently. I wish I could now say that I then stated the idea which saved the Union. Certainly I've outlived both friends and enemies who were present that day—there are none alive who could challenge my version. But it wasn't me, it was President David R. Atchison who stood wearily and announced his decision.

"Today, gentlemen, I am issuing a proclamation. Any slave working in a factory who performs satisfactorily will be granted his or her freedom at the end of the war, and they will be *paid* for that work from this time forward. Any slave that fights in our armed services will be granted his freedom at the end of the war. There will be other incentives offered as well. Land in the West—other things that the North can't match."

I thought John C. Calhoun, that South Carolina gentleman, was going to have a heart attack. "But Mr. President," he protested, "that will give the North exactly what they want—an end to slavery."

Both the President and I looked at him impatiently.

The others in the room had already seemingly grasped the idea. I took it on myself to correct the secretary, so as to leave my boss's hands clean.

"No sir. What the North really wants is to control the South. They were afraid of slave labor in the factories competing with them. Well, they're going to find that they are no match for a large, free work force and a government that controls most of the raw products in the country. Already their factories are having to slow down gun production due to lack of iron ore. The tide for the North is ebbing."

"It will never work," Calhoun said. "Africans the equal of whites? This will never be accepted."

"Of course it will," President Atchison said. "I should have done this sooner. That's all, gentlemen. Sam? Would you come help me prepare this proclamation, please?"

It did work, but not overnight, and not much change was immediately detectable. But it was a spark that ignited us just enough to first hold our own, then to slowly push the Northern forces back with the increased fighting spirit of our men. As the vastly increased output of the factories began reaching the front lines, the push became faster and faster.

The great battles that followed—Baltimore, Harrisburg, the Second Battle of Trenton, Albany—those were all victories for General Scott. His scores of brand-new artillery pieces poured a continuous hail of death onto the enemy. His men gallantly charged, their new repeating rifles—invented by a former slave who just happened to also be a mechanical genius—spit lead in a solid roar. Overhead, the hot-air balloons of the new Air Corps rained down bombs.

Within two years, the last of the Yankee forces had surrendered. Webster was already dead, but we hanged John Brown and a few others, then began the massive reconstruction of the North. A lot of lives had been lost, but the Union was again sound.

I served as Secretary of State for President Atchison in his second term, then was elected Senator from Missouri in my own right in 1860—a seat I've protected for the Whig Party ever since by the dint of hard work and constant campaigning.

That's the way it really happened, not the way that hack said. Abraham Lincoln president, indeed! It's hard to believe that people really get paid for writing such foolishness.

1856

Millard Fillmore was elected vice president in 1848 and became president upon Zachary Taylor's death, at which time he presided over the Compromise of 1850. He was denied the 1852 nomination by his own party, and in 1856 ran as an independent, the candidate of the so-called "Know-Nothing Party," losing to James Buchanan.

But what if fate and circumstance had contrived for him to win in 1856?

Jack L. Chalker, a former history teacher and the author of more than two dozen science fiction best-sellers, including the now-classic *Midnight at the Well of Souls*, offers an intriguing speculation concerning the course history might have taken had the president just prior to Lincoln been both pro-Union and pro-slavery

Now Falls the Cold, Cold Night

by Jack L. Chalker

He was giving, by all accounts, the finest—his enemies said his most coherent—speech of his life, when he suddenly stiffened, a look of complete and utter surprise on his face, then crumpled to the podium, his right hand still outstretched as

if making a point. Aides rushed through the suddenly alarmed gathering and reached his side, finding him still alive but unconscious. Carefully they found some tenting and flagpoles to rig up as a stretcher and moved him with great care across the street to the home of Robert Guiness, a major supporter, and summoned the doctors. Within a week the doctors completed what the stroke had started; on October 27, 1856, Ambassador James Buchanan of Pennsylvania, Democratic candidate and certain winner for the office of President of the United States, was dead, leaving his southern vice presidential candidate, Senator John C. Breckinridge, as the only candidate possible for the party with so short a time before the elections, to face the candidate of the new party of the west, Captain John. C. Frémont of the Republicans. The South would not vote for a Republican; Frémont received a mere fourteen hundred Southern votes. The North could not vote for Breckinridge, inheritor of the mantle of John C. Calhoun, arguing for the reopening and relegalization of the slave trade and for slavery to be legal in all new territories. Thus did those of the Democratic Party, who feared polarization and division within their party and country, perhaps even civil war, if Breckinridge won, turn to the third-party candidate, former President Millard Fillmore, running for revenge and vindication on the American Party, or "Know-Nothing" banner, because he was safe, a known quantity, and would offend the least number of people. Or so it was thought. . . .

Morgan was the first man into the dining room at Mary Murphy's boarding house; he always was, ever since he'd come in for the special session of the New York legislature. He was a handsome devil, young, with a big, thick mustache and slicked-back hair and flashing blue eyes. A real charmer, the kind her mother had warned her about back in Ireland, that's for sure, but he charmed her anyway.

"Ah! Mary Murphy!" he almost sighed in a put-on Irish brogue, sniffing the air. "Nobody but nobody cooks like you. I could gain forty pounds just standing here!"

"Sure and you've used that line once too often, Rafer

Morgan!" she retorted playfully. "And you'll still have to be content with the smellin' 'til the rest get here."

He looked around and saw that the table was set for seven. "So, is this just wishful thinking, or is our mysterious Mister Green actually going to join us tonight?"

She shrugged. "He said he'd be down. Goodness knows *he* must find somebody else's cookin' better, for all he's sampled mine to date." She went up to him and lowered her voice. "He was prayin' again in that loud voice o' his when I was by. I don't even know how he heard me, but he said he'd be in for supper and that's that."

The others were coming down now; LaGrange and O'Rourke, the two old burly lobbyists from New York City; Father Flaherity, the Archbishop's man in Albany, dressed as usual in his priest's garb; Harold Schumaker, the sweatshop owner so cheap he did his own lobbying; and Frank Farmer, the paid lobbyist for the Anti-Slavery Society of Greater New York. All of them, except Morgan and the still-absent Green, had two common bonds: politics, and the fact that all of them were Catholics. They assumed Morgan was also Catholic, and he'd done nothing to dissuade them, since this was one of the usual bases used by lobbyists of and from that church during unexpected emergency sessions of the legislature in Albany. There was no question that Green wasn't a Catholic, although he seemed to bear them no special ill will, but comfortable spaces were at a premium right now and Mary Murphy could not afford to turn anybody out who had good cash to pay, particularly when she could safely double her rates during such times as these to two dollars a day without complaints.

They all stood around awkwardly for a moment, then Schumaker growled, "Well, I'm not about to eat cold food because one of us might or might not come down," and, with that, he took his place—and the others, grateful for the first move, did the same. Mary started the service, also relieved, and it was feeding time at the zoo, as she called it to herself.

"Morgan—you're from Boston, I believe?" young Farmer said between chews. "What do you think of the riot there yesterday?"

It was all over the day's papers; although President Pierce had never tried to enforce the Fugitive Slave Act in New England since rioting mobs had caused terrible scenes there years earlier, now one of the authors of that act was President once more and had ordered federal marshals to assist in enforcement. Bounty hunters had taken several in Boston, and when mobs had formed as expected to block them being taken out by ship, overland being out of the question, the marshals had called upon an executive order they had in hand and called in troops to protect the slave hunters. In the resulting melee, shots had been fired, two marshals, a private, and sixteen Bostonians had been killed or wounded, and the whole of New England was in flames and threatened with martial law.

"To be expected," Morgan responded carefully. "They *wanted* an incident. That's why they picked Boston instead of some safer or easier place."

"It's this Dred Scott business," O'Rourke growled.

"Dreadful Scott, you mean," Farmer responded. "Horrible. Horrible. I can't believe this is happening under Fillmore. I mean, the man's from *Buffalo*, for heaven's sake!"

Morgan stared at the young abolitionist. "You're a New Yorker. All of you are. Is Fillmore really another Pierce? A northern slave man?"

"Well, he's always said he detested slavery," Farmer responded. "But he sure hasn't acted like it."

"He doesn't give a *damn* about slavery!" LaGrange thundered, then caught himself. "Sorry, Father."

"Don't mind me," the priest responded, somewhat amused. "But I do think you should watch yourself in the presence of a lady."

LaGrange gave a sort of embarrassed *harumph!* but got back to the subject. "We—all of us sitting here—know what the issue is. Fillmore's only President again by a back-room deal in the Electoral College and the devil's stroke. It's Breckinridge who's as much or more President than Fillmore, calling the shots from the Senate. The Scott decision was a put-up job—we all know that."

"Fillmore could have stopped it," Farmer pointed out. "He knows he's only in for this one term."

"Aye, but what's in it for him?" O'Rourke countered. "Isn't that the reason most of us are here now? Give the southern Democrats what they want on slavery and what's he get in return? His cursed Immigration Bill, that's what! If that abomination passes, there'll be riots in New York City that'll make this Boston thing look like a tea party, I'll tell you! They say they changed, but that anti-immigrant—anti-Catholic it really means—secret Know-Nothing society of thugs with their plug-uglies has but one leader and his name is Fillmore. He was with them from the Forties, gentlemen, and he refused to even condemn their thuggery at the polls just two years ago! We all know how the plug-uglies got their name—from those carpenter's awls with which they'd drill anybody who didn't vote their way! Fillmore is selling out the slaves, who can't vote, and the abolitionists, who voted for Frémont, and in exchange he'll shut the doors to this country!"

"Yes, and then his thugs will be after everyone already here with any sort of accent, even our poor Mary, here," LaGrange added. He looked over at Morgan and noted what seemed to be a slight smile on the New Englander's face. "Something funny about that, Morgan?"

"Huh? No, no! I was just wondering how far such logic would go if they had any sense to think it through. Will Pontiac's descendants demand Ohio and Michigan back? Will the last of the Mohicans emerge at last from the Catskills and dump fifty guilders worth of cheap jewelry at the New York City Hall and repossess the state, throwing immigrants like Millard Fillmore out?"

They all laughed at that one. "That's very good," O'Rourke

approved. "I'm going to have to steal that one from you when I meet with the Speaker tomorrow!" He continued to chuckle. "Throw the immigrant Fillmore out!" he muttered lightly, and started laughing all over again. His eyes went up, past the gathering to the hall, and the humor suddenly went out of him. The others turned or looked where he was looking, and a sudden hush descended over them.

Mr. Green was a tall, gaunt man, possibly in his fifties although he looked older, his face weathered and worn, his long, scraggly beard and equally long hair almost white, but his bearing and movements were of a younger, more athletic sort of man than he seemed to be. But it was the eyes that made everything else irrelevant; as blue as Morgan's, but mean, cold, and threatening, darting back and forth as if the mind in back of them were some military commander choosing which of the enemy to hang first. They were scary, fanatic's eyes, reinforced by the chiseled and worn features and stern, frozen expression on his rugged face.

"I'm glad you did not wait for me, gentlemen," he said in a rich, deep baritone that commanded attention. "I apologize for being tardy, but I had much paperwork to do. Please carry on with your conversation, which I could not help overhearing. I share your sentiments, if not your levity. I have seen too much of the suffering of those captive people to be able to laugh much anymore."

He took his seat, the others resuming their eating if not their conversation, and began to take as much of the stew as the others, particularly the portly O'Rourke, had left him.

"This is quite excellent stew, Mrs. Murphy," Green said approvingly. "Many's the time I have dreamed of a good, filling meal like this."

"You are a westerner, are you not?" LaGrange asked politely. Seeing Green tense, he added, "I could not help but notice your boots and belt, which are not that common in the East."

Green relaxed a bit, although none believed that the tall man ever relaxed more than a bit. "I have spent a good deal of time in the West, yes," he admitted after a moment, "although that word has new meaning with California a state and Oregon certain to be any time now. 'West' to me means Nebraska and Kansas, the flat plains region."

"You are a farmer, then? Or a cattleman?" O'Rourke asked.

Green's eyes darted around once more, as he tried to decide just what to answer and, perhaps, seek a motive in the questioning, although this was common boarding-house talk.

"I was briefly in and out of the cattle business, you might say," he answered warily. "But my primary occupation was doing God's business."

"You are a minister, then?" the priest put in.

"Not in your sense of that word, Father," he responded. "I am more a layman than a preacher, although I believe my calling to be from the same source as your own."

Farmer jumped in. "Uh, I assume that you are here for the legislative session as well, Mr. Green?"

Very slick, Morgan thought approvingly. *Somehow I could see Flaherity's mind jumping to Oliver Cromwell, and Cromwell was no friend of Ireland's.*

Green nodded. "I have a number of letters from friends in New England that I am to deliver to various key members here," he explained. "That is what took me so long. Many of the key letters only arrived this very day, and others I could not produce until such an incident as happened in Boston last week actually occurred."

"You expected it, then?" LaGrange asked.

"From the moment of the Scott decision, yes. It was only a matter of when, and I had faith that God would make it occur when I was here."

That one bothered Father Flaherity a bit. "Indeed, sir? You believe that God arranges deaths and incidents to your schedule?"

"I believe that I am one of His instruments, yes, sir. Is not the Bible full of such violence in the service of God? From Sodom and Gomorrah through the execution of the Apostles, it's the way He works much of the time. Crucifixion of His own Son was a particularly ugly way to do things, but it made its point as few other methods could, did it not?"

"I am not too certain that a rioting mob in Boston is in any way equivalent," the priest responded.

"Indeed, sir? Have you ever been in the South? Have you ever truly *seen* slavery? The chainings, the beatings, the keeping of men, women, even *children* in miserable hovels, often eating the dregs of food they are allowed, forbidden on pain of death to even learn to read and write? Wives sold away from their husbands, children sold away from their parents. . . . Human beings actually *bred* like cattle, and liberties taken by their masters without recourse or reproach?"

"Please, sir! There is a lady present!" O'Rourke exclaimed, shocked.

"The truth can not be shut up for politeness' sake," Green retorted. "It is time all men and all women knew just what that despicable institution is really like. Millions of human beings are being treated like animals in our so-called free and democratic nation and the law and the courts support it! We may dispute the fine points of the Bible, Father, but I have seen Hell with my own eyes. When they created this country and left the slavery intact they took upon themselves the mark of Cain. Satan moves through this land, while those of the North and West mostly look the other way, and unless he is purged from the soul of this continent then some election down the road you will all be cheering the election of Antichrist!"

"Is it really that bad?" Flaherity pressed. "My own father came here, near starvation, after spending much of his good years as a dirt-poor tenant farmer for some English lord who never even saw the property, no different except in the words they used than a serf of the middle ages."

"Far worse," Green assured him.

"Aye, I think you're right, Green," O'Rourke put in. "And, beg pardon, Father, but I myself came from one of those Killarney dirt farms more than thirty years ago, but I had someplace to go. Someplace with no English landlords where I could make a name for myself if I was able and become the equal of any man. That's the sense of the Boston mess. Where do *those* poor devils go now, even if they escape their bonds? They're more removed from Africa than I, or even you, are from Ireland. Still and all, Mister Green, I do not fully accept your position. The *first* revolution was folk such as we trying to break free of the absent English landlords and provide a place for those left behind to come as well, and that was a good thing. Don't throw the baby out with the garbage! We need to *perfect* what they created, not discard the whole fruit because a part of it is rotten."

"I see little hope of that," Green replied. "First such abominations as the Compromise of 1850, Fillmore's compromise as much as any; then the fight to keep it from the territories, won only with blood; now Dred Scott and the Breckinridge agenda. If a body is gangrenous then the limb must be removed; otherwise the corruption spreads and the body dies. You are here to see what New York can do to circumvent the new Immigration Act that is certain to pass—an act reversing that *first* revolution you seem to revere so much, so that now the corruption that was left in 1776 has grown to infect what was still good tissue. Shut down immigration and you shut down the northern labor pool. Mister Schumaker, here, runs out of seamstresses, and the mills and industrial might of New England grind to a halt as well. No one to build the railroads to the West or mine its riches. And what will the answer be coming from the South, gentlemen? Slavery."

"New England would never accept slavery," Morgan noted.

"Nor New York, either!" O'Rourke added emphatically.

"Gentlemen, with economic pressures and a shrinking labor pool, the people that count will look the other way and accept it, even justify it to themselves," Green maintained. "It's either that or see industry shut down or go bankrupt in the North and reopen in Atlanta and Birmingham. Pierce was a New Hampshire man, but he might as well have been Breckinridge. Fillmore and his ilk *say* the right things, but would never stand in the way if a few dollars were involved. With federal troops—*Southern* troops—and judges appointed by the Pierces and the Fillmores of this land, the committed abolitionists will either have to spill their blood or leave the country. Every day millions of slaves suffer horribly. If blood must bespilled, why prolong their suffering? And why wait until immigration is a word one must look up in the dictionary and the North and West are thereby so weakened and disconnected as to be unable to resist?"

"What are you advocating, Green? Some sort of civil war?"

"Why not? Better now, when the North is so powerful, than later, when it is anemic and bled dry. Half our history has been one of compromises with this evil, and look where it's gotten us!"

"All well and good, sir," Morgan commented, "but the Immigration Act will be a federal law, as you note, supported by the government and its army, and even Dred Scott is a decision of the highest court, from which there is no appeal save to God. For eighty years we've worked to keep the South from walking away. Now that they, as you note, hold the whip hand, why should they do so?"

"I was not thinking along those lines," said Mr. Green evenly. "The only secession movement in this nation's history was during the War of 1812. At that time New England was so adamantly against the war its states formed the New England Confederacy and threatened to leave the Union. Perhaps it is time we think that way again."

They were all shocked. All, Morgan couldn't help noting, but Farmer.

"Leave the Union? The whole of New England?" LaGrange almost gasped. "You can't be serious! Besides, if there's anything Fillmore really believes in, it's the sacredness of the Union. That more than slavery was behind his decision to use federal troops and marshals in Boston, of that I am convinced. The mere suggestion of it would drive him wild! The industrial base, the population—he wouldn't stand for it!"

"What if it went beyond New England?" Farmer asked, sounding very interested. "New York, perhaps? Perhaps further? Such a huge population base would be formidable."

"New York? Leave the Union?" LaGrange could hardly believe what he was hearing.

Farmer stared at him as Green looked on approvingly. "Is it that absurd? No Dred Scott. No slavery. *No Immigration Act!*"

LaGrange seemed caught off guard by the argument. "What?"

"No Immigration Act. Put the Know-Nothings back where they belong, in the shadows and sewers."

"And no cotton for my seamstresses or New England's mills," Schumaker pointed out. "They could easily sell all their output to England, which would have a stake in putting me out of business. Didn't think of *that*, did you, Mister Abolitionist?"

Green sat back in his chair, the trace of a wry smile on his lips. "If they will not sell to you, then I suggest we shall have to make them, won't we?"

"So we are back to war once again," Morgan noted. "Have you considered the cost in blood?"

"Or the treasury," Schumaker added.

"Hang the cost! Blood or money!" Green stormed. "What price would you place on your own life, sirs? Come, come! Give me a dollar figure! What is the worth of your life?"

"The question has no meaning," O'Rourke commented dryly.

"It has *every* bit of meaning, sir! People are doing that to other human beings every single day! Ten dollars, fifty, a hundred, more? Times thousands upon thousands, gentlemen! You who sit here fat and away from its sight in the North can convince yourselves that it has nothing to do with you, that it's not your problem, that Alabama and Virginia are as distant and as exotic as Arabia or the docks of Canton. But they are not in Arabia or China, sirs—they are here, in what we call our country, and some of them make our laws in a city filled with their slaves and have tea parties in urban equivalents of plantation houses—and the largest plantation of all is the White House."

"I note, sir, that *you* are here in Albany," Father Flaherity said icily.

"For the cause, yes. But I am no less willing to hang my body and give my blood to wipe out that abomination when this is over. Mark my words, gentlemen—the moment a northern army, a *free* army, steps across the Potomac, the slaves of the South will rejoice as the Israelites did when they entered the Promised Land, and they will rise up, kill their masters, destroy the southern economy, and flock to us! There will be blood, yes, but southern blood more than northern, and those of us who die in this cause will be blessed of God. All that I have is pledged to it. We have but to try it."

"Perhaps someone should, just to see," Morgan suggested, goading a bit.

"I was thinking along those very lines," Green answered, taking no offense. "But if we can be not a vanguard but a mighty army of a sovereign and committed nation, then it will be over all the quicker and with far less blood. Mark my words, gentlemen—the Union is coming unstuck. The crude carpenters of compromise can hold it off no longer. Buchanan might well have managed to just look the other way on all this, forcing direct action, but the hand of God slew him and put in his place this apostle of hate, fear, and Union, bloody Union, above all else. Already he has precipitated a second Boston Massacre, and lit the fires of liberty where they first burned." He suddenly yawned and stretched, and his tone changed radically from that of a fanatical proselytizer to merely that of a tired old man.

"It is out of our hands now, in any event, gentlemen," he continued. "I am quite tired, and tomorrow I have a very busy day." He got up and pushed his chair back from the table. "Good night, gentlemen. Mrs. Murphy, it was an excellent meal. I shall be down for breakfast tomorrow morning as well." And, with that, he walked out and they sat in silence listening to his footsteps on the stairs as he went to his room.

O'Rourke pulled out a cigar, bit off the end, and lit it. "That, gentlemen, is the strangest man I believe I ever met."

"The most dangerous, certainly," agreed the priest.

Young Farmer, the abolitionist, shook his head. "I don't know. He may sound extreme, but he has truth in what he says. I fear that if we do not find a way to abolish this scourge, at least the first part of his prophecy, the separation of the Union, may be inevitable."

One by one they drifted out, either to the sitting room or porch for a smoke, although it was a chilly night, or to their rooms. Finally, the first to arrive was the last still there.

Mary Murphy came back in to get the last of the dishes, which were even then being attacked by her two daughters in the kitchen.

"What did you think of the conversation?" Morgan asked her, curious, knowing that she'd heard it all even though she'd spent most of her time in the kitchen or going to and from it.

"Blood, rebellion, and God's sword," she muttered. " 'Tis glad I am that I am a woman with only daughters, for all you men seem to think about is killing one another."

"I fear that Mister Green is actually a darker color," Morgan responded. "I must go out for a bit tonight, so I will probably miss breakfast tomorrow."

"Very well, if you'd rather sleep than eat my cookin' after all, that's up to you," she responded playfully.

"For once," he responded, "I think I'd rather not be here at all." And with that cryptic comment he got up and walked to the front door and out of the boarding house, then down the several blocks to the horse-car line into the city proper.

The car came in a few minutes, and he boarded and took a seat, and it lurched off toward the lights beyond. From the darkness, another, smaller shape ran out in a crouching position and jumped on the rear apron of the car, keeping low so as not to be seen either by those inside or by the conductor.

Downtown, Morgan headed for the train station and found the telegraph office. The unseen shadow, who had managed concealment, slipped off a block before, assuming the other man's destination.

The follower remained in the shadows of the station for some time, watching Morgan pick up some telegrams, read them, then write out others to send. Morgan began to leave, but before he got outside he spotted a spittoon and stopped at it, striking a match and then setting fire to the telegrams in his hand. When he could hold them no longer, he let the still-flaming remnants drop into the spittoon, then left the station.

The other man now emerged and boldly walked up to the telegrapher's office himself.

"Yes, sir?"

"The gentleman who was just here. He sent some telegrams?"

"Yes, sir. Just about to put them on the wire. Why?"

The man took some money out of his pocket and held it so that the clerk could see it.

"I ain't goin' to lose my job over a bribe!" the clerk huffed.

"Come, come! This is *Albany*, where men do not lose their jobs over bribes, they enhance themselves by them." He unfolded a bill so that the clerk could see the denomination and the little man's eyes bulged.

"If I were to send my own telegram," the stranger said softly, "and stand while writing it where I might just happen to read the two slips the first gentleman handed to you, I might well forget to ask for change. Now, that's not a bribe, is it? Whether you turn in the overage or pocket it is between you and your conscience."

The bill was ten weeks' salary for the little clerk easily. He'd handled them now and then, but never had one of his very own, of that the stranger was certain.

The clerk thought a moment, then turned, picked up a blank form, and said, "Certainly, sir." When the stranger moved to see the two slips, the clerk held up his hand. "Ah—sir?"

The stranger smiled and placed the bill on the counter.

"I believe the gentleman here before you said the inkwell was dry at the desk there, sir," the clerk commented in his normal businesslike voice. "Why don't you just come around the counter and use my pen and desk, there?"

"Thank you, I believe I will do just that," responded the stranger.

They were all downstairs at breakfast, all except Morgan, and the sounds of a more convivial meal than the night before drifted upstairs.

Satisfied at seeing all of them go down, one by one, through his keyhole, Morgan, fully dressed but wearing only his socks, eased out of his room and down to Green's. As he expected, the door was locked, but he hadn't been spending all that time with the widow Murphy just because of her red hair and good looks; the master key had been simple to borrow and simpler to duplicate.

He opened the door as quietly as possible, went in,

then immediately closed and locked it again. If Green should come back early, the need to unlock it once again would allow a precious couple of seconds of warning.

Still, he took the time to go over to the window, unlatch it, and lift it slightly. It was a fair leap, but he'd done worse in his time, and if it were a choice of facing Mr. Green now and trying it, there wasn't much question as to which was the preferable alternative.

With the moves of long experience and the aid of a keyring full of lock-picking devices, he had no trouble rifling Green's small carpet-bag suitcase, as well as the drawers and even under the bed. Nothing! Not so much as a postal card of the state capitol building!

He turned and lifted the mattress, wondering if he would have to shred it and the pillows, too, and felt joy and relief when he spotted a carefully written folded sheet of paper there. He plucked it out, opened it, and started to read.

> My dear Mr. Morgan (or should I call you Mr. Baird?):
>
> I fondly hope that you enjoyed rooting through my dirty laundry this morning while I enjoyed a fine breakfast. I tried to make it particularly rancid just for you. I will spare you further efforts, as your incompetence continues to delight me and serve my ends. You did not come close to me in Kansas, and your eagerness to get at the documents I so freely told you I had received made you too cocky, as usual, so that I know that you have not put out an alarm for me as yet, and by the time you can do so I shall be, I assure you, difficult to locate. Please inform the lovely Mrs. Murphy that she may donate the clothing here to any worthy charity, Irish Relief or whatever, and retain the bag if she likes for herself.
>
> As for the documents, I assure you they do in-

deed exist, and, thanks to my youngest son's efforts of last night in tracking you down and revealing you, I assure you that they are already in the hands of the Assembly pages and will be in the hands of those key gentlemen before you could get to the capitol. You see, I neglected to mention that those documents were in Mr. Farmer's possession, not mine, and I fear he, too, skipped breakfast this morning.

You may come down and join us if you wish. I would like to see your expression. It is often said that I am humorless, but I assure you that this is not the case. Any attempt to take me there, however, will be fruitless, I assure you, as some of my men have been covering this house, front and rear, since I arrived, and would not hesitate to do violence to you should we, say, emerge together, or, on this morning, if you emerge from the house first. I should not like to see you dead. They might send someone less known and more competent after.

Resign yourself. You are playing not merely against me but against God Almighty here, serving a Satanic cause, yet you are a Boston man. It will not be very long when you will be forced to choose between betraying and killing your own or joining us, and I sincerely doubt if Mr. Pinkerton is paying you what thirty pieces of silver can buy these days.

King Canute marched to the sea and commanded it to stop, but it kept rolling in and engulfed him anyway. Now comes the cold, cold night over this nation, and only Mars commands its sky, and neither you nor Fillmore nor Breckinridge nor all the forces of Hell can stay it, and this nation can only be bright and green once again if bathed in the sunrise of blood and the cleansing fire of the sun.

With my very best regards for you and for your immortal soul, I remain,

Sincerely yours,
John Brown.

"*DAMN!*" Morgan swore, then he stopped and read the last part of the letter again.

"*Now comes the cold, cold night . . .*"

Brown's sort of night? he wondered. The kind of terror he'd spread in Kansas, slaughtering men, women, and children based upon whether they were for or against slavery? It was that sight which had convinced him that no crusade of Brown's could be *his* cause, no matter whether he abhorred slavery or not. A man who could justify the butchery, those innocent kids who just picked the wrong parents . . . this was not a crusader but a maniac.

He would still have no problem seeing the Browns and their gang hang, of that he was certain. And yet, if the man proved a better prophet than avenger, could he fight alongside the Browns if it meant fighting with New England against the South?

Angrily, he crumpled up the letter and started to toss it on the floor, but his hand stayed, and instead stuffed it into his outside jacket pocket.

By the time he unlocked the door, got his boots, and came downstairs, Brown and, indeed, most of the others were gone.

"Oh, Mister Morgan, did ye hear the news?" Mary Murphy called to him.

"Huh? No. What?"

"It was the talk all this mornin'. They been runnin' all about town with 'extras' all over." She reached down and picked up a crumpled newspaper and handed it to him. The headlines were hard to miss.

NEW RIOTING IN BOSTON OVER SLAVE CAPTURE CAUSES
PRESIDENT TO DECLARE MARTIAL LAW IN NEW ENGLAND!
Sporadic Rioting By Immigrant Groups in New York City
Draws Threat of Same Treatment.
President Declares State of National Emergency.

He read the words over and over, then put the paper back on the table.

Morgan looked over at the slender form of Mary Murphy and thought for a moment that his fanciful romantics to her about packing it all up and moving to California seemed suddenly very tempting and very real at this moment.

But how far must one go to flee the cold and night? How do you run to the warmth of the sun when the cold darkness is inside your soul?

Five days after the declaration of martial law, the governors of Massachusetts, Connecticut, Rhode Island, New Hampshire, and Vermont, meeting with their legislators outside of their normal capitols, passed resolutions nullifying the Dred Scott decision and refusing the Presidential order and proclaiming the creation of the New England Confederacy. State militias were called to duty, and many officers and men from the region who were in the regular army flocked to their defense.

Two days after that the Battle of Cambridge was fought, in which the small and thinly spread federal troops put up a token fight before surrendering to the state militia.

Three days after that, sparked by massive rioting by immigrant groups in New York City that put a portion of it in flames, the New York legislature followed suit and joined what then became the Northern Confederacy.

One week later, after emissaries from Washington reported that there was no single body as yet even to deliver ultimatums to in this new creation, President Fillmore went before Congress—minus the New York and New England delegations, who had walked out and returned home—giving the most impassioned speech of his career in support of Union, Manifest Destiny, and calling upon all loyal Americans to join him in putting down this insufferable and dangerous rebellion. Many of the Midwestern and Western states abstained, but the motion was carried by a united South.

The next day, the Army of the United States was formed under newly promoted General Robert E. Lee, who pledged to restore the Union within a year. In the meantime, the Northern Confederacy moved to establish a shadow government. John C. Frémont accepted the presidency, hoping that it would pull California and the rest of the West to their cause or at least to neutrality, appointing a little-known officer named William Sherman to organize the militias into a national army for defense. Frémont, feeling washed up and disconsolate after his prior loss, was suddenly a new man, back in his element as if reborn. Herbert Baird organized the new President's security.

John Brown, upset that Frémont and Sherman organized for defense, attempted to precipitate action by attacking the arsenal at Harpers Ferry, Virginia, on his own. Lee made short work of him, but the action infuriated Washington and caused volunteers to flock to the Army. At his hanging, Lee said, "Thus die all traitors to the Union."

The rest, of course, is history.

1860

Abraham Lincoln defeated Stephen A. Douglas for the presidency after a series of stirring debates, and was at the nation's helm for the duration of the Civil War.

But what would the tall man from Illinois have done had he not debated Douglas, and hence lost the election? Given his passionate belief in the Union, might he have obtained a commission and fought for the North? Bill Fawcett, co-editor of *The Fleet* and *War Years* series, and co-author of *Lord of Cragsclaw*, offers this vision of General Lincoln.

Lincoln's Charge

By Bill Fawcett

"Damned militia officers," Grant muttered as he glanced up from his map. Outside, the rumble of distant cannon rose and then ebbed as if to emphasize their commander's annoyance.

"Courier arriving," the aide to the commander of the Army of the Western United States announced, with some relief. Perhaps the dispatches would help dispel his superior's foul mood. It was a vain hope. Brigadier General Ulysses Grant was always in a bad mood when he had been drinking the night before, and lately that had been every night.

Not that his aide blamed him, what with the way the war was going, and all.

"It's from President Douglas," Grant summarized for the benefit of the half-dozen staff officers gathered in the command tent. "Things have been very quiet in the siege lines south of the capital. Lee hasn't attacked in almost two weeks, and the bombardment is less severe. Something has to be happening, something that bodes ill for the Union. Burnside refuses to commit to an attack, but Hooker's probes show some weakening in the Confederate positions. The president suspects some of the Army of Virginia has been withdrawn."

After taking a moment to reread the short telegram, Grant glanced out in the direction of the Confederate lines. "Damn, I wish I could get some decent intelligence."

But he couldn't. Not with the Ohio closed and Rebel cavalry constantly cutting the telegraph and rail lines as far north as Dayton. No one answered; no need to repeat the obvious. The blue-clad officers stared silently at maps spread on the table in the center of the tent.

The arrival of General Abraham Lincoln of the Illinois Militia was greeted with obvious relief. It not only ended the uncomfortable silence, but gave Grant a new target at which to vent his frustration.

"I expected you at dawn." The commander's tone was challenging.

Surprisingly, the tall, gaunt Illinois general just smiled. "Thought it was better to get the regiments moving than be here early." He paused for effect, then added, "We will be in a position to reinforce the left or center of your line by noon."

"I want your men here, and here." Grant stabbed his finger at the map. "Hove's men have been chewed up badly and it will take hours to reform them."

Hove's men were mostly conscripts, city boys drafted after the disaster at Huntington. There had hardly been enough time to train them to shoot, much less to harden them for battle. What Grant meant was that they needed time to gather up enough of the raw recruits from behind the lines, get them into some order, and push them back into the fight.

The Union army's position was clear after one glance at the map. After a few seconds scrutinizing the yellowing charts, Lincoln began nodding. Even so, Grant began to brief Lincoln in some detail. He couldn't forget that the man was also a politician, and not really a soldier. He had little use for bad whiskey or inexperienced civilians. Even though Lincoln had been elected by the Illinois men as their commander, it would be his first battle.

"Eight weeks ago Johnston's Rebs took control of the Ohio as far north as Wheeling while the Army of the Potomac danced with Lee in Maryland. Last month we met John Pemberton's Army of Tennessee and Kentucky in Illinois and drove them out of Centralia, but were not able to crack the Reb fort at Cairo."

Grant hesitated then, checking to see if Lincoln reacted. Lincoln's Illinois regiments had been mustering at the state capital, Springfield, and had arrived too late to take any part in the battle that drove the Confederate forces from all but the southern tip of Illinois. Lincoln did meet the shorter general's eyes, but his expression was unreadable.

"Pemberton kept withdrawing past Cairo and joined with Johnston near Louisville two weeks ago," Grant went on. "Four days ago their combined army pushed over the Ohio near Bloomington. It is my best guess that they intend to push north and cut the Union in half. There are less than three hundred miles from here to Lake Erie, and we're the only intact Union army left west of Pittsburgh. Without western crops, the Seaboard will begin to starve and lose heart. Worse yet, we'll lose our last Ohio crossing. That could mean another year before we could hope to take the war to the Rebs. We have to stop them here, make them bleed until they go back to Tennessee."

"I can't but agree with you on that, sir," the rangy Illinois officer commented as he bent his long frame further to study the armies' dispositions. "I have spoken for years about the sanctity of the Union and the evils of slavery." With his finger, the militia general traced the route the Rebels had taken to reach their current positions.

The Confederate force had pushed along the north bank of the Ohio. They had probably drawn most of their supplies from across the river. Grant had sent what forces he could spare by railroad and fortified Cincinnati. The thick fortifications had held up the hard-marching Confederates until Grant's Union force could hurry south to join the battle.

Yesterday, in a surprise move, Pemberton had ended his siege at Cincinnati and turned to face the slightly larger Union army rushing south through Indiana. Grant's first units had found the entire Rebel force drawn up on the bluffs outside Carrollton. Now the Union army was in a line facing the bluffs. The Ohio River flowed less than twenty miles behind Pemberton's force. A shattering victory, one that drove the Confederates back against the river, would be decisive. Most of the Confederates would be unable to retreat across the Ohio on the few ferries available and would be forced to surrender in mass. With the war stalemated in the east, such a victory would regain the initiative for the Union. A Confederate victory would leave Pemberton in a position to threaten everything from Dayton to St. Louis. Both sides were risking much. If the Midwest was subject to another invasion there was little doubt the Whig Party's peace platform would give them next year's election—if Douglas's government lasted that long.

The Confederate position was also a clear statement of how much faith Pemberton had in his slightly smaller force. They had been defeated only once, and that a near thing in the battle of Centralia a month earlier. There was no doubt every Confederate soldier had been anxious to revenge that setback. Pemberton had challenged Grant to a battle, winner take all.

The first day had been indecisive. Both sides had been more concerned with bringing up troops and securing their flanks than fighting. Just before sunset, Pickett had led his division on a valiant charge against the Union line. Costly counterattacks had regained the position, but at a high price. The brigade Lincoln was replacing was near collapse: most of its battalions had less than half-strength remaining.

Since dawn, the Confederates had brought up several batteries and were punishing the entire Union line. What Grant didn't say, but Lincoln and the others could clearly see on the map, was that there were no more Union reserves. A year of lost battles and near disasters had drained the manpower of the Union. They had to win or lose with the men already in the line.

Zachary Bolton, private, 2nd battalion, 33rd Illinois, Jones's brigade, Geary's division, also was worried about the upcoming confrontation. Most of the men with him had at least been in a battle. He had enlisted less than two months earlier and had joined up with the battalion only two weeks ago. When he had enlisted, all this had sounded like high adventure: wearing a uniform and shooting one of the new breech-loading muskets. Having just turned eighteen, he'd been anxious to heed President Douglas's eloquent call to save the Union.

Now he was marching to his first battle. Was he a coward? Would he run? Some of the veterans had kiddingly suggested he would. The anticipation made the young recruit's stomach churn.

Worse yet, Zach's feet hurt. He had been marching for almost a week without rest. He wasn't used to this kind of exertion. And the breeches he had been given to replace the pair ruined in training were made of wool: they chafed. It was a kind of pain different from anything Zach had known in Chicago.

The rumble of the guns was getting louder. Wounded began to stream back along the edges of the road, around the marching ranks. Their blood seemed so bright, their pain so evident. One collapsed just as he approached. Zach tried to stop to help him, but the sergeant rushed over and yelled for him to get back into the formation, inferring that Zach might be a coward but that to avoid the battle he'd need a better reason than helping some stray casualty.

Zach stumbled back into the column and tried to ignore the grins of the men marching near him.

"This one's going to be bad," the veteran captain commented as they left Lincoln's briefing. "I'm still not sure your Honest Abe's up to it."

"He was nearly elected president, Arthur," the major, Phillip Holland, objected.

"And that makes him a general?"

"He's *our* general," the major pointed out, looking around to see if anyone overhead the other officer's mutinous comments. Phillip's father's Republican political connections had gotten him his command. He was proud of his men, but worried how they would perform. Neither he, nor most of them, had ever been in a battle. The few who had were mostly men who had been recovering from disabilities when Douglas had called to the colors all able-bodied men not needed to grow food. Holland's insecurity made him even more adamant; he had to believe they were going to win. How else could he order his men to fight?

The argument itself was an ongoing one. It had begun when Lincoln had ordered an early halt to rest his exhausted regiments and caused them to miss Centralia. The captain was from Vermont and had a schooled disdain for the "log cabin general." He had supported Douglas—the Great Compromiser—in the last election.

The major had worked for Lincoln's election, even after the candidate's illness had caused him to miss the debates and lose almost two months' campaigning time. Holland had still supported Honest Abe, even after the strain had caused Mary Todd Lincoln to run off the podium, literally frothing at the mouth, during her husband's disastrous St. Louis rally.

"He's not only a loser, but completely inexperienced at command in a battle situation," the captain reiterated, enlarging on his theme. "You can't afford to be too concerned with the welfare of each individual man. We're fighting a war! Our entire Union's at stake." He was a recent West Point graduate and liked to quote Napoleon about casualties being the price of victory.

The veteran officer went on at length in the same vein. Thoroughly irritated, Holland waited for an opportunity to interrupt, but the captain wasn't about to relinquish the floor. By the time he had finished they were walking through the stacked muskets of the 33rd Illinois and unable to argue further.

When the first eleven Southern states had seceded, the Union navy had placed a haphazard blockade on the ports north of Savannah. As negotiations on the South's return to the Union dragged on, England and the European powers forced the ports open to allow for the cotton trade, which was vital to their textile industries. Within months the cotton and tobacco that left those ports returned in the form of cannon and muskets. It also gained the Confederacy four more members—Tennessee, Florida, Kentucky and Missouri. Among the most common of the British guns was a new style of British rifled cannon with exceptional range and accuracy—the "cotton gun."

The Rebs had brought up a battery of cotton guns just after Zachary and his company had taken their place in the line. Before he had even settled in the shallow ditch behind a rail fence, the guns began to drop shot and shell among the battalion. The worst part was that all you could do was cower. Twice dirt splattered onto Zach from near-misses. Soon the shrieks of the wounded filled the occasional lull in the barrage.

"Good Alabama powder!" Corporal Henderson, cowering fervently in the trench, yelled in an obvious effort to act casual. Henderson considered himself a veteran; he'd fought at Centralia and Cairo. The effect of his bravado was lost when a shell exploded just beyond the fence, and both men forced themselves even harder into the ground as grass and dirt showered down on them. Not to be outdone, when they raised their heads a few seconds later, Zach smiled back.

Then the cannon stopped. Tentatively, glancing nervously around as if they couldn't believe the barrage had ended, more men began to stagger to their feet. The surreal mood was broken as men began tending to the wounded, and the sergeants began driving them all back into line.

From his position on a hill a few hundred feet behind his men, Major Holland felt ill. Where shell or shot had landed in the line, bodies were scattered in circles around the blast area like malign flowers. It seemed so senseless. He was glad he stood alone, but suddenly felt lost. This was so different, so much more horrible than he had ever imagined, yet it had just begun.

Holland was still in a daze when the front of the Rebel line emerged from the cloud of powder smoke. The first thing visible was the scarlet and yellow of the Stars and Bars. Then the vague blotches formed themselves into groups of men. The major was still so dazed from his first taste of battle that he just stood there and watched as the approaching graycoats let loose one of their Rebel yells and charged.

"My god, Major, see to your ranks!" The voice was both insistent and gentle. Still, it shocked Holland, who had thought himself alone.

His shock turned to amazement when he turned and saw that the speaker was General Lincoln himself. Embarrassed, certain he was in disgrace, the newly commissioned officer mumbled some sort of reply as he stumbled down the slope toward his command. Within minutes

Major Holland had recovered and was dashing behind the ranks, exhorting his men to choose a target and fire carefully. Phillip Holland would have been reassured by the smile and nod this earned from his commander, but by the time he dared risk a look back, the hilltop was empty.

The Rebel charge broke short of their line, as did the next three charges, though each exacted its cost in blood. At sunset, to their own amazement, the 33rd still held the fence line and the Union center was steady.

In his tent, alone and unseen, Lincoln wept. The images of death and ruination haunted him. He had watched good men die terrible deaths today. Men he had known, friends, fathers, good men. Abe's family was from Tennessee; some of those dark mounds sprawled in front of his Brigade were likely to be his own cousins. For the hundredth time the gaunt, haunted man tried to tell himself that other men had caused this war. *He* had never wanted it. But this did not prevent him from feeling responsible for each man lost on either side. He had campaigned against slavery. It was his rhetoric that had inspired his fellow Republicans to see the Southern representatives as the enemy. If he had been a better man, if his body had not failed him . . . He would have been the kind of president who led the nation with a strong hand. With a strong man guiding the Union, this fratricidal war would not have happened.

If he had had the courage to admit to himself that his beloved Mary was ill. If his speeches had been less inflammatory during those last frantic weeks when they knew he would lose the election. Then things might now be different. The death of so many thousands, Jackson's burning of Baltimore, all of this slaughter and ruin could have been prevented.

But he had lost the election and emotions had risen to a fever pitch. Within weeks of his defeat the senators of his own party had driven their Southern counterparts from the Congress. The Manumission Act of 1862 had not been meant to destroy the Union. It would have freed the slaves over a period of ten years, allowing everyone time to adjust. Douglas had foolishly heralded the law as yet another great compromise and called upon the Southern representatives to return. Instead they had formed the Confederacy and begun arming for war.

The crash of a caisson rushing past his tent broke through Lincoln's melancholy reverie. The tall general shifted uncomfortably on the cot and held his head in his hands. He realized he could smell smoke, and hoped it was from campfires. They said two thousand wounded who were too badly hurt to crawl to safety had been roasted alive when the forest at Tappahannock caught fire. Lincoln tried to rise from the cot, but his body just wouldn't move. He felt tired, knowing that even if the fields were on fire there was nothing he could do. Soon he drifted back to condemning himself.

Lincoln wasn't sure what he would have done differently. Act sooner with the full might of the Union army, perhaps. But it would have been something. He would have at least called for a draft and built a real army. Douglas's fear of further provoking the South had meant that the much smaller, though professional, Union army had been overwhelmed and nearly destroyed at Manassas Creek. It had taken them over a year to recover from that disaster. At first everyone in the North had welcomed the lull, false peace that it was, existing only to allow both sides to arm better, and to allow the British to decide to back the Confederacy with the full power of their diplomacy and trade. That false peace had lasted over a year, with negotiations filling the papers every day. Douglas had thought in terms of compromise and peace, and had ignored Lincoln's warnings. He had not understood that every day lost was a victory for the South.

If only he had been strong enough to become president, Lincoln was sure that all of these deaths could have been prevented. It ate at him, punished him every day, with every death, that all this was happening just because his own body had been weak and Douglas was president.

It was all so unnecessary. This war could have been so different. Knowing they would have faced a strong and determined enemy, the South would never have seceded. If they had, he would have acted decisively, just as he had advised Douglas to do, and the Confederacy would have been crushed before it had time to raise and train an army.

When the colonel burst into General Lincoln's tent, the former candidate had fallen into an exhausted sleep while still wearing his rumpled uniform. It was three in the morning and most men slept as well they could. The guard had protested, but such was the urgency of his message that the staff officer risked being shot rather than lose even a minute.

"General!" The West Point graduate had snapped to attention in front of the sleeping figure. "I have an urgent message from General Grant to come to his tent as soon as is possible."

Looking around the tent, the colonel was surprised at how austere, almost sterile, the interior was. Where most general officers used the wagon assigned them to furnish their sleeping tent with at least a few pieces of furniture or some other comfort, such as Geary's canvas bath or Meade's fifty changes of uniform, there was nothing here to distinguish this tent from that of a lowly lieutenant. Except for the cot on which the long figure was now stirring slowly, the only other furnishings were a map-covered table and an issue chest. Even the blanket covering Lincoln was army issue and threadbare.

"Who? . . . Grant?" Lincoln woke slowly, reluctant to rejoin reality. "Urgent, what?"

"The general has received some intelligence and requests your presence at his headquarters," the officer reported in his most military manner. "He seemed very upset."

"Then he won't mind my state of disarray," Lincoln observed, pulling himself off the bed and moving toward the entrance of his tent in a single movement. "Let us go in all haste, Colonel."

The first light of the false dawn had appeared, bright only to eyes that had grown accustomed to the night. Inside the tent that constituted the corps' headquarters it was still too dark to make out faces without a light. To Major Holland, there was something strange and painful visible in General Lincoln's eyes, even in the dim glow of the single lantern hanging over the map table. The big man was stooped over the table, studying his map, and occasionally glancing silently around at the assembled regimental commanders. He had put on a fresh uniform, but had not taken the time to shave. The stubble softened the hard edges of the general's face, making him appear almost fatherly. That, combined with the visible sorrow emanating from Lincoln's expression, gave the entire staff meeting an air of pathos before it had even begun.

"Gentlemen," Lincoln began when the last regimental commander had arrived. "Your men performed admirably yesterday. We held the Rebs and went to bed with every expectation of doing so again today."

Lincoln's gaze locked with that of Phillip Holland and the general tried to smile. Remembering his embarrassing hesitation of the day before, the young major looked away and stared self-consciously at the worn tarpaulin that covered the floor.

"Unfortunately," Lincoln continued in equally solemn tones, his magnificent voice conveying so much more than just words, "the situation has changed drastically.

"Last week Jackson's Iron Brigade managed to slip away from the siege of Washington. A few hours ago we received word that the entire corps has boarded steamships at Parkersburg. We can expect them to arrive the day after tomorrow."

There was a murmur of surprise and concern. The soldiers of the famed Iron Brigade were among the South's best troops. Their presence would change the entire fabric of the battle. Worse yet, Jackson was known for his wily ability to place his corps where they could discomfort the enemy the most. There was no telling on which flank the Rebs might appear.

"All of the other Union forces have been in battle two days longer than we have. They are both too tired and too depleted to act decisively. I have been ordered by General Grant to take what action I can to bring this battle to a timely conclusion." The statement silenced every voice. After a moment of confusion, Phillip Holland realized that the corps was located in the center of the Union position. There was only one way to approach the Confederate lines: straight at them. Lincoln's orders confirmed his conclusion.

"We are going to try to break their center. Grant has ordered diversionary attacks on both flanks at eight. We will move toward the Rebels at eight-thirty. I want every man, every cook and horse-holder, armed and charging with us. We mean to break their line and drive them back today. If we fail, the Union may well fall with us."

Again, Lincoln paused as he glanced at each of his officers in turn. No one spoke. The general's eyes were brighter now, alive with thought and planning.

"I will be leading the charge personally." Lincoln waved off the protests that followed with an abrupt gesture. "Your orders are being written now and will be delivered within the hour. Prepare your men."

As Major Holland left the tent he noticed that the glow of excitement had left the gaunt man's eyes, leaving only the dark sorrow he had noticed earlier.

It took Zach Bolton a few minutes to remember where he was. He ached, and his face was still coated with the grime thrown back from his musket. The blanket he had slept under was too short and his feet were very cold. Without thinking, he stood and stomped to return circulation to his tingling toes. A growl from Henderson about getting his fool head blown off brought the private fully awake, and he crouched down inside the trench.

They had spent half the night digging in the soft Indiana soil, using shovels, plates, even bayonets to build up the earthworks. Zach noticed that his hands were still covered with mud and his shoulders stiff from the unaccustomed effort of digging. Then he realized his legs ached from the four days of hard marching, and he decided that he simply hurt all over. Still, looking at the mound of earth they had heaped in front of where he sat, the young man from Chicago knew he would be much safer when the Rebs attacked again. Zach continued to be amazed at the courage the Rebs had shown, charging three times yesterday against the punishing fire of the 33rd. It had seemed both glorious and suicidal even as he had sat and fired ball after ball into them.

It was during a cold breakfast of crackers and cornbread that Zach realized he had been in a battle. More importantly, he had not run, and he had done his share. He was a veteran, fully equal to the men whom he had held in some awe the day before. This meant less to him than he expected. There was no excitement to it. He wasn't any different. As the private chewed on a cracker and sipped tepid water from his canteen, he realized that what seemed more important was to stay alive.

The order was passed down the line less than an hour later: "Get your bayonets ready." Almost at the same time, the rumble of distant cannon spoke of hard fighting to both the left and the right.

At fist Zach was confused, and he crawled up to look across the level field that separated them from the Confederate position less than a mile away. Were they about to be charged again? He couldn't see anything in front of the 33rd Illinois but the gray and blue piles of the dead.

Unsure what to do, Zach stayed at the top of the earthworks, looking out for first sign of the Reb attack.

"Don't be so anxious, boy." The voice sounded familiar.

Turning, Zach realized Major Holland was standing behind him. The sight of the new recruit scrambling to his feet to salute and then crouching back under cover in one quick action won a nervous grin from the battalion commander.

"We'll be out there soon enough," the officer said, and continued down the ranks. It was then that Zach realized they would be charging soon. They would be the ones to endure the same unbelievable punishment as the Rebs had received. He could feel himself go pale, and he slumped deeper into the trench.

"Don't let the Major scare ya," Henderson offered, misunderstanding Zach's concern. "He won't remember nothin' after we're done chargin'."

"I hope so," Zach quickly agreed, lest he be considered a coward.

Though still unsure of himself on horseback, Major Phillip Holland tried to ride straight in his saddle while he approached General Geary. He counted the riders and figured he was the last of the battalion commanders to report in. That made him even more painfully aware that he had never really led his men in a charge before, and that the men he was approaching all knew it.

"All the men ready and awaiting the order, sir!" Holland announced, saluting as best he could while still moving the last few paces toward Geary.

"Very good, Major," was the general's rather brisk reply once Holland had come to a halt a few feet before him. There was a moment of hesitation, almost as if Geary didn't want to move. Then the general audibly sighed and said, "You are welcome to accompany me while I ride to General Lincoln and receive the order to charge."

Having reported last, Holland found himself riding beside Geary at the front of the column of officers. This made him feel even more self-conscious as he recalled his earlier meeting with the man they were approaching.

The ride to where Lincoln and two other divisional commanders waited was accomplished in complete silence. All three looked very military in their dress uniforms and mounted on large, black chargers. Most men wore their best uniform for a charge. It guaranteed that if you died, you would be buried in it. To Holland's surprise, Lincoln actually greeted him with a slight smile as they approached. It was the kind of smile that is passed between two men who share a secret, though the smile hid nothing of the visible pain in the tall man's eyes.

"My division is ready, sir," Geary reported, once they had all come to a halt. "My commanders and I are ready to fight and die for you, the Union, and Illinois," he finished, removing his hat. Several of the other officers followed suit.

Lincoln seemed touched by the gesture. He had taken a good deal of criticism after not arriving at Centralia. It was some seconds before he could speak. Even then he kept his eyes averted and his normally resonant voice was soft and difficult to hear over the distant sounds of battle.

"I have received a message from General Grant confirming our orders," he acknowledged. "At the sound of two cannon firing, you are to lead your men against the Confederate positions opposite."

"Then can I return and begin this bloody business?" Geary asked. This time Lincoln didn't answer at all; he just stared at the ground and nodded slightly.

Geary took this as confirmation, saluted and spun his horse, followed by his commanders. A few moments later Lincoln, accompanied only by his two aides, spurred his own horse forward.

Somewhere nearby on his left, Private Zachary Bolton of the 33rd Illinois heard two cannon fire. Almost immediately the cry came for the men to form ranks in front of the earthworks. Just as quickly the cotton guns began to fire, blasting gaps in the three lines they were attempting to form.

"Forward, guide center, march!" General Geary ordered from somewhere not too far away. Zach scrambled to climb over the earthworks they had labored so hard upon the night before, and nearly fell when a cannonball passed close just as he crested the top.

The private had a glimpse of a horse's legs as a gloved hand steadied him. Looking up, he saw that it was Major Holland. He failed to note that the young officer appeared almost as frightened as he did.

The first few yards brought them out of the Confederate barrage. After that the shot and ball still hit, but in a much more random way. Officers and sergeants screamed for the men to dress their lines, even as the cotton guns tore those lines apart. Zach moved forward, moving at a fast march toward the Rebs without thinking. It was what he was supposed to do, and he was doing it.

They were nearly halfway there when a ball, probably from an old Napoleon gun, tore through the air just a few feet to Zach's left. It made a chugging sound, similar to but louder than any train he had heard in Chicago. The force of the air from the near-miss threw the young private to the ground. His ears were ringing as he stumbled to his feet and turned to help Henderson up. Zach actually had hold of his former friend's arm when he saw that the ball had taken off the man's head and part of his shoulder. Revolted, Zach Bolton dropped the arm and stumbled away, praying he could keep from being ill.

A swat from the flat side of a sergeant's sword drove the still-dazed private back toward the Rebel position. The bombardment had gotten worse and men fell in every direction. The sergeant disappeared, maybe encouraging others, maybe getting killed. Zach didn't know and hardly noticed.

The ground changed and Zach realized that they were at the foot of the ridge where the Confederates had dug in. He had caught up with what remained of the 33rd.

Suddenly they were within musket range, and the air filled with hundreds of angry wasps. When a ball hit a man, Zach heard a sound like a fist smacking into a hand. Most of the wounded didn't fall right away, but stumbled a few steps before they realized they were dead. Suddenly the man ahead of Zach turned and ran. Almost without thinking, Zach followed. It seemed right to get back and away from that deadly swarm of ball and bullets.

"At them or they'll slaughter us!" Major Holland bellowed as he passed Zach and swung his sword at one of the first men to retreat. The man stumbled, swore and then continued to run from the battle. The Major was mounted and quicker. He swung his sword again, this time using the edge, not the flat of the blade. The soldier fell, his head half cut from his shoulders. The shock of the sight jolted Zach. He and the men near him stopped and stared at the sight of a man killed by their own officer.

"Back to the line! Back!" Holland shrieked, trying to threaten a hundred men with his horse and a single blade.

Zach looked around. The artillery had stopped firing, for fear of hitting their own side or to reload with cannister rounds, he couldn't tell which. Around him the men of the 33rd straggled and stood in confusion. Behind them those who had remained in the battle had formed a ragged line and were trading uneven volleys with the Rebs, who were protected by a stone fence.

Without knowing why—perhaps it was the silence after the roar of the gun—Zach began to sing. He thought it was softly, to reassure himself, but half-deaf from the explosions and near-misses, it rang out loudly. He sang what first came to mind, a hymn, their marching song, "The Battle Hymn of the Republic." Holland fell then, the victim of a well-aimed rifle bullet. It no longer mattered.

The melodious, almost reverent song was incongruous amid the carnage and horror of the battle. Even so, the men near Zach joined in, with an energy born of fear and adrenaline. Within a few bars the entire mass of milling men were singing and had begun to rejoin the ranks. As they approached, even though they were parched and choked by the dust and powder smoke, the rest of the battalion and then most of the division took up the song. Some men sang different verses, and many croaked, unable to do more, but all sang. The rout stopped and, to a man, the Illinois divisions formed smartly under the withering fire and met the Rebs volley for volley.

The song faded as the Union ranks concentrated on firing at the better-protected Confederates. To Zach's right he heard a cheer. He turned and saw it was Lincoln riding along the line, ignoring the enemy fire. Even as the tall general approached, Zach was unable to hear what he was yelling, but the meaning was clear. It was even clearer when General Lincoln turned his horse to face the enemy and gestured for them to charge.

The yell the 33rd let out would have done any Rebel unit proud. They followed Lincoln up the slope and over the fence. More from shock than fear, the Southern line recoiled.

Zach found himself facing a grizzled man in gray. The fellow had dropped his musket, but drew a wicked-looking knife, and rushed at the private. Not sure whether his musket was loaded, Zach fired. He felt the heavy weapon tug against his grip, and a dark spot appeared on the Reb's belly. He fell at Zach's feet and lay unmoving.

For what seemed a long time the young man from Chicago stared at the man he had killed. Then he felt a tug at his arm, no pain, just a tug as if someone had pulled his sleeve to attract his attention. Turning, he was surprised to see no one was there. The melee had moved on over the slope. There was the sound of a splatter of rocks against the ground, and Zach looked around. He stood alone amidst the carnage near the wall. Most of the fighting was now on the other side of the ridge. In the distance he could see a battery of cotton guns being hurriedly limbered. The splatter must have been cannister, hundreds of musket balls in a bag so that they could be fired like a giant shotgun blast. He was surprised they had bothered to fire at such a lonely target as himself, and even more surprised that he had survived the attack.

When he raised his hand to wipe the grime from his eyes, Zach realized that it was covered with blood. At about that time his shoulder began to throb with pain. He had not survived unscathed.

Still unsure as to what to do, Private Bolton began moving slowly toward where what remained of the 33rd had disappeared over the hill. The Captain who stopped him was unfamiliar, but wore the patches of the 21st Illinois.

"You're wounded. We've done our job here," he assured the private who had stumbled toward him. "Get back before you bleed to death." The captain gave Zach a gentle shove back toward their original position.

Still unsure, the private took the path of least resistance, which was down the slope. Less than halfway to the bottom, he tripped and fell onto something soft and dark. Realizing that he lay against a dead horse, Zach pulled himself to his feet and looked around it. Still straddling the dead black charger was the body of General Lincoln.

It didn't seem right that Lincoln should lie there, all twisted and trapped. Using his good arm, the soldier managed to pull the body out from under the horse. As he propped the dead general up against his saddle, Zach could count three holes in the man's chest.

Not quite understanding the gesture, but feeling it was the right thing to do, Zachary Bolton of the 33rd Illinois rose and stepped back from Lincoln's body, saluting as smartly as he knew how. As he did, he noticed the surprisingly peaceful expression in the great man's eyes.

1872

The very first woman to campaign for the presidency was Victoria Claflin Woodhull, who, in 1872, ran on a platform of free love, women's suffrage, short skirts, legalized prostitution, and the right of women to orgasm. She was arrested and jailed on obscenity charges the day before the election when the magazine she published printed details of the Beecher-Tilton scandal, and she lost, of course, to Ulysses S. Grant.

Laura Resnick, the daughter of your editor and an award-winning author of ten novels in the romance field under the pen-name of Laura Leone, has chosen to write her first science fiction story (she has since written and sold five more) about the reign of President Woodhull and the effect it might have had upon the world at large—and on one particular Englishwoman who is less than amused.

We Are Not Amused

by Laura Resnick

The following letters have been excerpted from *Correspondence Between the Victorias: An Insight Into the Decline of Victorianism, 1872–1880* by Dr. Wiantha Woodhull. The author is a descendant of President Victoria Woodhull

(1872–1876) and Attorney General Zula Maud Woodhull (1904–1908). The book will be published in its entirety this spring by Femme Fatale Press, cover price $16.95.

SANDRINGHAM, 10th December 1872:

Her Majesty Victoria, Queen of Great Britain and Ireland, Empress of India, wishes to convey her sincere felicitations to the President Elect of the United States of America, Mrs. Victoria Woodhull. The Queen was *very strongly*, though not unpleasantly, surprised to learn from Mr. Gladstone that Mrs. Woodhull has succeeded to the highest elected office of her charming country.

The Queen applauds Mrs. Woodhull's commendable and publicly expressed gratitude to Mr. Cornelius Vanderbilt, who aided and abetted her bold campaign for the presidency. The Queen *knows little* of Mrs. Woodhull's background, and wonders if the Woodhull and Vanderbilt families have been intimate for *many years*.

The Queen has learned that Mrs. Woodhull did not rely solely upon Mr. Vanderbilt for financial support for her campaign, but also engaged in active enterprise in partnership with her sister, Miss Tennessee Claflin, first as New York stockbrokers and later as the publishers of *Woodhull and Claflin's Weekly*. The Queen admires such industrious behaviour and has *very often* encouraged it in her subjects! The Queen has been informed that a particular issue of *Woodhull and Claflin's Weekly* printed two days before the presidential election sold for forty dollars per copy. The Queen is most impressed that Americans are so eager to read, and she would very much like to know more about the contents of the *Weekly*.

Nevertheless, the Queen is well aware that it requires more than *mere money* to emerge victorious in a political campaign, having observed many such campaigns within her realm. Mrs. Woodhull may be surprised to learn that the Queen knows that, as early as 1870, Mrs. Woodhull enjoyed the support of Congressman Benjamin F. Butler of Massachusetts, who arranged for her to address the House Judiciary Committee.

It was certainly at this pivotal moment, when Mrs. Woodhull urged Congress to legalize women's suffrage under the Fourteenth Amendment (a speech for which, the Queen understands, the National Woman Suffrage Association delayed the start of their convention in Washington, D.C.), that Mrs. Woodhull's political career became of such interest to the British Prime Minister. The Queen commends Mrs. Woodhull on her successful efforts, since it is surely the woman's vote which has helped to place her so securely in office! The Queen is also sure that Mrs. Woodhull will agree that the Queen's own female subjects currently have all the rights and privileges they need and are in *no need* of suffrage like their distant sisters across the sea.

Although former President Grant cost Her Majesty's Government $15.5 million in the settlement of the *Alabama* incident (and Mrs. Woodhull may be assured that no one had informed the Queen that the British weren't supposed to sell ships to the Confederates during the American Civil War, much less that there was evidently a precise difference between Confederate rebels and Cuban belligerents, or Cuban rebels and Confederate belligerents), he was evidently nevertheless a rather popular president within his own country (leading the Queen to believe that the American people still harbor some resentment from 1812).

It has been implied within Her Majesty's Government that President Grant may well have won re-election, had not Mr. Greeley and Mr. Sumner been successful in their advocacy of an amendment to limit the president to one term. Perhaps Black Friday and the Santo Domingo affair contributed to the success of this amendment. Nevertheless, there can be no doubt that this surprising development, combined with the Republicans' *misguided judgement* in naming an actor as their next presidential candidate, contributed to Mrs. Woodhull's felicitous success. The Queen, known for her sense of humour, acknowledges the irony: Mr. Greeley succeeded in eliminating President Grant from the race, but he himself, as the Democratic candidate, suffered an overwhelming defeat at the hands of his female opponent, candidate of the Equal Rights Party!

The Queen has learned that a duck was somehow responsible for Mr. Greeley's defeat. Her Majesty is at a loss to understand how an ordinary farm animal could be instrumental in deciding the outcome of a presidential race, but she recognizes that Americans have lived in isolation for some centuries and may have unique values.

The Queen also wishes to take this opportunity to convey her felicitations to Mr. Frederick Douglass, the abolitionist and former slave who now stands beside Mrs. Woodhull as her Vice President.

The Queen concludes by advising Mrs. Woodhull to seek the advice and guidance of Mr. Woodhull, remembering as she does how greatly she valued and misses the strength and wisdom of her departed husband, Prince Albert.

BUCKINGHAM PALACE, 28th April, 1873:

The Queen has to thank President Woodhull sincerely for her letter of 15th February, and she is pleased to learn that the President felt her inauguration was a successful occasion!

The Queen further thanks President Woodhull for explaining how a duck caused her Democratic opponent to lose the election. The Queen expresses hope that all ducks have been *removed* from *his presence*, as well as all children and all persons of character.

The Queen finds it most enlightening that President Woodhull's sister Miss Tennessee Claflin initiated their association with the esteemed Vanderbilt family by administering a healing massage to Mr. Cornelius Vanderbilt. However, though she *seldom interferes* in the affairs of foreign nations, the Queen feels bound to suggest that Miss Claflin may not be the best possible choice for the post of Surgeon General, since her medical practices led to her being indicted for manslaughter in Illinois in 1864.

Thanks must also be extended to President Woodhull for the time she took in explaining her *Weekly*'s exposure of the Beecher-Tilton incident, though the Queen finds it quite difficult to believe such claims about a clergyman. Apparently the American people also found it difficult. The Queen is pleased to learn that President Woodhull and Miss Claflin have nonetheless been acquitted of obscenity charges.

On the issue of Mr. Woodhull, the Queen is somewhat bewildered, despite the President's explanation. If the Queen understands correctly, President Woodhull is the wife of Colonel James Harvey Blood, *not* the wife of Dr. Canning Woodhull. However, the President's former husband, the aforementioned Dr. Woodhull, now lives in the White House with the President and her husband.

Under the circumstances, the Queen agrees with President Woodhull that it might be wiser to seek advice from *neither man* for the time being.

The Queen is charmed to learn that President Woodhull is the proud mother of two children. From the President's description, the Queen concludes that Zula Maud is a child of remarkable resilience of character. The Queen expresses her sympathy that the President's son, Byron, has been diagnosed as a mental defective. Having recently read *Childe Harold's Pilgrimage*, the Queen can only conclude that this is often true of men named Byron.

Mr. Gladstone has informed the Queen of President Woodhull's Cabinet appointments. Evidently, Susan B. Anthony will make a vigorous Secretary of the Treasury, as she is now gamely grappling with the financial problems resulting from the American Civil War and Reconstruction; British subjects have already heard of a new currency called the "Susie Buck." Initiative should always be applauded!

The Queen also commends the President's wise decision to rejuvenate her nation's dealings with the American Indian tribes. They are still living far closer to civilisation than they really need to be, and perhaps the President's newly appointed Commissioner of Indian Affairs, Talks Much Woman, can convince them of this, being one of their own kind.

However, Her Majesty's Government is concerned that the posts of Secretary of War and Secretary of the Navy are to be abolished altogether and replaced by the Secretary of Love and the Secretary of Reproductive Freedom. Mr. Gladstone and the Queen would both appreciate a more thorough explanation than offered in the President's previous letter.

The Queen cannot also help wondering if Elizabeth Cady Stanton, though movingly described by the President as a lifelong crusader against immorality, is appropriately qualified for the post of Attorney General.

Finally, the Queen expresses her admiration for President Woodhull's unwavering commitment to Pantarchy, but would like to know what it is.

BALMORAL, 5th August 1873:

The Queen thanks President Woodhull for her letter of 4th June, though she found the contents of said letter quite disturbing.

The Queen was aware that President Woodhull had once assumed leadership of Section Twelve of Marx's International Workingmen's Association, but thought it would be in poor taste to remind the President of her youthful indiscretions. Nor did the Queen wish to presume about President Woodhull's character. After all, Mr. Disraeli may be a Liberal, but he is nevertheless a most agreeable person, as the Queen keeps pointing out to Mr. Gladstone.

However, Pantarchy, a supposedly perfect state wherein

children and property are managed in common by the members of society, sounds exactly like something those horrid Communists would propose. The Queen wishes to remind President Woodhull that *free love* and the break-down of the family are in direct opposition to the values held by the Queen and, therefore, universally held by her subjects.

The Queen is further dismayed to learn that the President's administration is encouraging the legalisation of prostitution. While the Queen cannot prevent the President from this folly, she *can certainly resist* the President's efforts to convince her to become a champion of legalised prostitution. Although the President's appeal to protect the lives and health of fallen women is most eloquent, the Queen assures her that no such problem exists in Great Britain (except possibly among the Irish who, after all, cannot help themselves). The Queen protests the figures quoted in President Woodhull's letter which indicate that Her Majesty's subjects enter brothels more frequently than they enter churches. While this is very possibly true of France, the figures are erroneous when applied to Her Majesty's realm!

The Queen recalls that the President's administration is instituting dietary reform, and she suggests that diet may well be at the very root of the problem. Some hearty roast beef, not to mention tea and clotted cream, might well minimize some of the President's more eccentric impulses!

The Queen understands from the President's letter that the Secretary of Reproductive Freedom will supervise research and legislation regarding abortion and birth control. Though the Queen cannot condone this, she does see how this could be considered necessary if everyone in America is going to start practicing free love, since primogeniture could become *extremely confusing*.

Evidently, the Queen misunderstood the President's purpose in appointing Talks Much Woman as Commissioner of Indian Affairs, as well as her goals in dealing with the American Indian tribes. Would it be too presumptuous of the Queen to enquire just *how much more* of the United States the President intends to give back to native tribes?

Finally, the Queen regrets to inform President Woodhull that her new American ambassador to the Court of St. James was arrested upon arrival. She was wearing a *short skirt*. A skirt which, the Queen is unhappily obliged to inform the President, exposed a considerable portion of her *limbs*. Mr. Gladstone was in a state of considerable excitement, the poor man.

WINDSOR CASTLE, 23rd October 1875:

Despite the Queen's firm resolve to have no further correspondence with President Woodhull after the remarks in her Christmas greeting of 1873, she now finds it necessary to appeal to the President to cease this relentless barrage of change which has *so afflicted* British society since the President's election.

The Prince of Wales has recently abandoned his wife, the Princess Alexandra, having explained to the Queen that he is now practicing free love in the American manner, finding it a charming and thoroughly civilised custom. The Princess objected until the American ambassador explained that free love is also *her* right, and she has since become the constant companion of Lord Tennyson (whose works are now sadly lacking in the fine moral tone for which he was once known).

The Queen's dearly beloved daughters, Princess Beatrice and Princess Louise, now habitually wear the *short skirts* first popularised by the President's select representatives in this country. Thousands upon thousands of young women have followed suit, and many of them have established rebellious musical groups which play Spanish and African instruments.

The Duke of York's eldest son has left home to go live with some of the American Indian tribes now settling in the eastern United States. Young men in Trafalgar Square

are wearing their hair in the style of Mohawk Indians and protesting the Government's involvement in India. They also protest the situation in South Africa, melodically insisting that they shall "overcome" someday, which puzzles the Queen.

Mr. Gladstone's office at 10 Downing Street is daily besieged by women demanding the right to vote, the right to apply for men's jobs and earn men's wages, and the right to receive paid maternity leave from their places of employment. Factories in Britain have come to a standstill as workers strike and demand safe working conditions.

Furthermore, traffic in London has been totally disrupted by a group calling itself the British Union of the Sisters of Mercy and Comfort. The prostitutes of London, having heeded President Woodhull's international call to unionisation, now daily parade around Piccadilly Circus in most indecent attire, refusing to leave the public limelight until the Government recognises and protects their places of employment. No doubt suffering from shock, Parliament has been unusually slow in taking any action whatsoever to stop these women from disturbing the peace.

The Queen has lived in seclusion at Windsor Castle for the past six months, waiting for the situation to improve. Mr. Gladstone has finally admitted that he thinks matters may continue on this downhill course for quite some time, though Great Britain, he assures his supporters, will never see a female Prime Minister!

To add to the Queen's woes, her once dear friend the Empress Augusta came to Windsor Castle for a visit this week. In a devastating blow to the civilised world, not only was the Empress wearing a *short skirt*, she also insisted that she adheres to President Woodhull's theory that every woman is entitled to . . . to . . . orgasm! After a most embarrassing discussion, the Empress made a number of comments about the late Prince Albert that the Queen really could not tolerate.

As abasing and humiliating as it is to admit these problems to President Woodhull, the Queen writes this letter in the hope that the President will see fit to eliminate her newly proposed medical, legal, and environmental reforms. Surely the President can see that they would be the downfall of civilisation!

The Queen holds President Woodhull entirely responsible for the chaos currently overwhelming Great Britain and now seeping into Europe, the alienation of her sons, the disgrace of her daughters, and the loss of a dear old friend.

In short, President Woodhull, we are not amused.

1876

Samuel Tilden actually won the 1876 election, but had it stolen by the supporters of Rutherford B. Hayes, who managed to engineer Hayes's election by a single electoral vote. (There were 20 contested electoral votes. Tilden legitimately owned a minimum of 8, and possibly as many as 13 of them—but all 20 went to Hayes, who officially won by an electoral total of 185 to 184.)

Tappan King, former editor of *Twilight Zone* magazine and co-author of *Down Town*, looks back from a vantage point some 16 years after the election and explores just what might have happened to Tilden had the daughter of Samuel Morse actually accepted the marriage proposal put to her by this 62-year-old lifelong bachelor.

Patriot's Dream

by Tappan King

Drums? Was it the sound of drums he heard, drawing nearer? Pray God it was not, for drums meant war, and there had been too much of war already.

He was running through a great city of white, polished stone. The walls rose up like canyons, high above his head. Snow piled high on every street corner, and the icy wind whistled through the streets, numbing him with its bitter chill. Above the distant spires he saw a flash of red in the sky, felt the pavement shudder beneath his feet.

Before him was a great building of marble, some monument to commerce or culture, flanked by a pair of recumbent lions, their eyes slitted and cold. Its doors and windows were boarded shut. As he looked up he stopped, halted by the sight of his own name inscribed in stone above the door.

He heard a shout. On the steps, he could see a group of figures huddled behind a rude barricade, warming their hands over a blazing dustbin. As he rushed past, one of the figures swung a rifle in his direction.

He froze, heart hammering wildly, peering into the dancing shadows, to make out the figure who held the gun. In a flash of fire, their eyes met. It was a woman's face, gaunt with hunger, haunted with bitterness and despair, stained with old tears. At first, she looked to be of middle age, but as she raised her face to him, he could see that she was still young.

There was a sharp crack behind him. The drums grew louder. He could hear the sound of marching feet. Wordlessly, he pleaded for his life. The woman lowered her gun for a moment, jerked the barrel in the direction he'd been going. He nodded his thanks, began running again, through the streets of that God-forsaken city.

Ever nearer came that harsh pounding, as loud as cannon fire, as insistent as a steam engine. It throbbed inside his breast, pounded his head. The wind wailed, carrying with it the shouts of men, the wails of women, the soft cries of children. . . .

"Father? Are you awake?"

"What?"

He'd been dreaming again. The room was dark, the gaslights dimmed. Outside, lightning flashed, thunder cracked, the wind moaned. Rain clattered against the windowpane. The pounding began again, his daughter's firm, insistent knock.

"Are you all right, Papa?"

"Yes, dear. Just—just a bad dream." Samuel Jones Tilden's voice cracked as he spoke, his hands trembling as he pulled himself up to a sitting position on the lounge. The exertion left him weak and trembling.

Why had they come back now, those dark and haunted dreams? He closed his eyes for a moment to shut out the bloody tide, opened them again when the fit passed.

The door opened, golden light spilling in from the hallway. A figure in white stepped in carefully, carrying a tray. For a moment, he didn't recognize her. "Windy?" In the fine dress she wore, his daughter looked remarkably like her mother.

"Shall I turn the light up, Father?"

"Yes—yes, go ahead," he whispered, too hoarse to speak up. He pulled his spectacles on, fumbling awkwardly with the ear wires, blinking at the bright gaslight. "What time is it, Windy, dear?"

"Ten o'clock, Papa."

Tilden started. "Ten! Damnation! Why didn't you— I have an interview this morning. . . ."

"It's all right, Papa. The reporter from the *Times* sent word that he would be delayed. The streets are beastly this morning with all this rain. And Mother thought you could use the rest." She set the tray down on the sideboard. "I've brought you tea—and your tonic, Father."

He made a feeble noise of disgust. "Cure is worse than the condition," he croaked.

"You mustn't talk like that, Papa. You need to keep up your strength." Windy draped a towel about her father's neck, then poured him a cup of tea, sweetening it with a spoonful of sugar. He took the teacup in trembling hands, sipped deeply. The hot liquid warmed the chill about his heart.

"Mrs. Reilly made scones and jam for tea, Father. I borrowed some from the kitchen, when she wasn't looking." Windy's eyes flashed with a touch of mischief. "If you take your medicine, I'll let you have some. I know you're not supposed to have sweets, but today is a special day, after all."

"A special day. . . ?" he whispered, suddenly unsure of her meaning. The confusion must have registered on his face, for Windy's brow furrowed, and she chided him.

"The convention, Father. Mr. Schurz will be sending a carriage 'round this afternoon. He said to make sure you wore a topcoat. The weather is frightful."

"The convention?" It took him a moment to remember. Ah, yes. They'd asked him to give the nominating speech for the vice presidential candidate at the party's convention this evening. Foolish business, really. They seemed to feel his presence was important to the occasion, though for the life of him he could not see why. Cleveland seemed sure of re-election.

The spectre of Thomas Watson in the White House was apparently terrifying the party regulars. Schurz was afraid that some of them were considering bolting to Blaine and the Republicans, in the belief that they had a better chance of beating Watson and the Democrats. He'd prevailed upon Tilden to say a few words to keep them in line. Perhaps Schurz thought the mere sight of an old fossil like himself would be enough to frighten the younger delegates into compliance.

At the thought, he laughed, a sharp bark that turned to a cough, spat into the spittoon by his chair, saw blood amid the phlegm.

Windy blanched, pulled a bottle from her apron, poured a spoonful of foul-smelling liquid into it. Before he could protest, she'd popped it into his mouth. Having no choice, he swallowed, shuddered, coughed again, washing it down with another swallow of tea.

"Ghastly," he muttered, breaking a scone with trembling hands. The scent of the biscuits was heady. Windy watched him with rapt attention. "Would you care to join me, my dear?" he asked with a dry chuckle.

"Oh, yes, Papa! Thank you. I wasn't going to ask. Mama says it spoils the appetite—and the figure."

"What your mother doesn't know can't hurt her, child. Come, sit down."

Beaming, Windy pulled a chair up across from him, and proceeded to ladle a heaping spoonful of strawberry conserve onto a steaming scone, stuffing it whole into her mouth, and brushing the crumbs away roughly with her lace-trimmed sleeve.

Tilden felt a twinge of bittersweet tenderness. For a moment, she was once again the little ragamuffin he was used to having underfoot, not the stylish young woman of fourteen who was growing up so swiftly.

Fourteen years? Could it be? The years had tumbled by like falling leaves. . . .

They ate together in companionable silence for a time. Tilden found himself lingering over his tea, filled with some inexplicable reluctance to finish this meal. "You'd best be dressing, Father," Windy said at last. "It's nearly half past."

Tilden nodded, reaching over for the bellpull. A moment later, he heard Jerome's footsteps on the stairs.

"Good morning, sir," Jerome said with a slight bow. "You're looking well this morning."

Tilden snorted. "You're cutting quite a figure yourself this morning, Jerome." Jerome was dressed in full livery. With his white gloves and mane of silver hair, Jerome looked more like some African potentate than a manservant.

"Mrs. Tilden seemed to think it proper, sir, seeing as how we're receiving visitors this morning, and I will be accompanying you to the convention in the afternoon."

"Doubtless she's right, Jerome. She usually is in such matters."

"Shall I help you dress, sir?"

Tilden sighed. The question was another fraud. His frail frame was almost useless to him now. It had been many months since he'd been able to dress himself unassisted.

"Yes, thank you, Jerome. Run along now, Windy, dear. Tell your mother I'll be down as soon as I'm dressed."

"Yes, Papa." With a kiss on the cheek that smelled of jam and lavender water, Windy was off down the stairs at a most unladylike gallop.

"All right, Jerome. Let's get on with it."

"As you say, sir."

With skill born of long experience, Jerome lifted him from his chair and undressed him swiftly, shaving him and combing his hair, and cleaning his withered body with a sponge soaked in pine soap. Tilden fought feelings of anger and helplessness as Jerome placed a fresh breechcloth beneath his underclothes as a guard against incontinence.

When at last his toilet was complete, Jerome opened the wardrobe door with a flourish. "The missus bought this for you, sir. Thought you'd want to shine a bit this evening."

"Did she, now?"

Within was a stylish new suit of soft gray wool, and a new-made shirt of fine damascened linen. Tilden eased himself into the trousers and shirt, though he needed assistance with the nacre shirt-studs and bright burgundy cravat Leila'd picked out for the outfit. He was relieved when Jerome allowed him to keep his slippers and favorite silk smoking jacket. At the moment the thought of that tight frock coat and collar were more than he could bear.

He cast a sour eye at his reflection in the looking glass, and was pleased to discover he did not look the decrepit crone he felt. He found himself looking forward to the occasion, though the prospect of a public appearance was daunting. The simple action of dressing had left him feeling drained and weak. Jerome sat patiently while he rested on the lounge, sipping tepid tea, waiting for his heart to still, then handed him his cane, and took him firmly under the arm, lifting him to his feet, guiding him carefully down the stairs to the parlor.

* * *

"Good morning, Tildy, dear!"

Leila was setting out the tea service as he entered. She was attired in a dress he'd never seen before, a gown of plum-colored silk trimmed with dyed feathers that complemented the rich auburn of her hair. It must have cost her a pretty penny on the Lady's Mile. How fortunate he was to have married a woman with a fortune of her own!

"Good morning, Leila. You're looking particularly fine this morning." She was even more handsome now at forty-two than the day he'd first met her nearly twenty years ago.

"Why thank you, Tildy," she said with a bright smile. "You look quite the dandy yourself this morning."

"You are a brazen liar, Leila, but I will forgive you. Thank you, Jerome," he said, relinquishing his servant's arm. "I believe I can manage, now." The tea and biscuits—and the dreadful tonic—had revived him somewhat, and he made his way slowly to his favorite chair next to the fire.

Leila fussed over him, settling him in the chair, and covering his legs with a lap robe. "Are you sure you're quite fit enough for this interview, Tildy?"

Tilden coughed. "I believe so, my dear. All I will have to do is talk, and that ability is one of the few I've not yet lost entirely."

"Oh, Tildy. . . !" At that moment the doorbell rang.

"That will be our visitor," said Leila, rising in a flourish of silk. "I'll go fetch him." As she kissed him gently on the brow, he wondered for the hundredth time what angel had smiled on him to provide such an old codger as himself with such a splendid wife as she. Doubtless a clerical error.

He leaned back. The soothing warmth of the fire made him drowsy. His eyes drifted shut, and the shadows of dark dreams began to gather. . . .

The drums were closer now. He ran with a dozen others down a narrow alley, breath rasping in the cold. The alley turned a sharp corner; ahead lay a high brick wall. The woman beside him sobbed, clawed desperately at the stone. Shots came from behind. Bending low, he boosted her up and over. A sharp pain ripped through his side. . . .

"Mr. Tilden?"

Tilden looked up, startled, for a moment unsure of where he was. There was a tightness in his chest, and his hands felt cold and numb.

"Mr. Tilden, sir?"

Before him stood a slim young colored man, who seemed barely out of his teens. He was attired in a well-cut suit of black worsted, and he carried a large notebook under his arm. Tilden blinked and stared, unable to find words to greet him.

"Samuel, dear, this is William Du Bois—the reporter from *The New York Times*," said Leila. She raised her eyebrows to signal her own surprise.

"A pleasure to meet you, Mr. Du Bois," said Tilden, extending his hand. The colored man took it in a firm grasp. "Forgive me if I don't get up. These frail old bones aren't what they used to be."

"Please sit down, Mr. Du Bois," said Leila. "Would you care for some tea?"

"Why yes, thank you, Mrs. Tilden." The colored man settled himself in the chair across from Tilden.

"If you will excuse me, Mr. Du Bois?"

"Certainly, Mrs. Tilden." With a swirl of color, Leila swept out of the parlor, leaving the scent of rosewater behind.

"I must apologize for my lapse earlier, Mr. Du Bois," said Tilden. "I had been dreaming by the fire, as old men do, and you caught me by surprise. I hadn't expected that the *Times* would be sending over—"

"A black man, sir?" said Du Bois, with a slight smile.

Tilden coughed. "I—I was going to say, someone quite so young as you, Mr. Du Bois."

"I am twenty-five, sir," said Du Bois. "I have recently completed requirements for my master's degree in history and political science at Harvard, and I am at work on my doctorate. I secured this position at the *Times* because I believe history should be studied where it is lived, as well as in the classroom."

"A commendable ambition, Mr. Du Bois," said Tilden.

"I must say, sir, I've been looking forward to this for quite some time. When I learned that you would be in New York City for the convention, I kept after my editor until he gave me the assignment." He was extremely well-spoken for a Negro, with an intense and enthusiastic manner. "I've done a great deal of reading about you, Mr. Tilden. Your life has always fascinated me. You are, after all, one of the most important surviving witnesses to a crucial chapter in our nation's history."

The colored man's words made Tilden feel suddenly ancient. "I'm flattered that you consider an old relic such as myself a worthwhile subject for your study, Mr. Du Bois," Tilden said with a dry chuckle. Despite his well-developed suspicion of the press, Tilden found himself warming to the young man.

A moment later, Leila returned with tea and scones.

"Would you care to join us, Mrs. Tilden?" asked Du Bois. Tilden nodded.

"Why yes, thank you, Mr. Du Bois." Setting down the tray, she settled herself in a nearby chair, gathering her skirts behind her, and began pouring tea. "Sugar, Mr. Du Bois?"

"Yes, thank you, Mrs. Tilden," said Du Bois.

"Now then," said Tilden, "where would you like to begin.

"With a question for your charming wife, sir. I'd be interested to know how you came to meet, and marry, Mr. Tilden. You were quite a young woman at the time, twenty-four, I believe. And Mr. Tilden had been a bachelor for over six decades. What first attracted you to him?"

Tilden pushed his glasses up on his nose, peering intently at Du Bois. This young man was sharper than he seemed. He would bear watching. Still, he had no doubt that Leila would be more than a match for him.

Leila set her tea down carefully. "I was attracted to his intellect at first, Mr. Du Bois. Also his kindness and his generosity, his good humor and quick wit." She lowered her eyes. "He was also a very handsome man, Mr. Du Bois. He quite captured my heart."

"There my Leila is embroidering the truth. I was rather a stick, actually. But as to your question, I'd in fact known Leila for several years before we wed. As you may know, I'd been retained by her family to settle her father's estate. That was a tangled skein if there ever was one. . . ."

"Her father, sir?"

"Samuel Morse."

"The inventor who perfected the telegraph? I understand he left quite a fortune behind."

"A good thing, too," Tilden cackled. "Otherwise they would have said she was after my money!"

"Samuel!" Leila blushed, took a sip of tea.

Du Bois smiled, swiftly jotting his words down in his notebook without looking at them. "Do you recall how you made the decision to forsake your bachelor ways, Mr. Tilden?"

"Indeed I do, Mr. Du Bois. It was shortly after the election of 1876," Tilden began, warming to the story. "We were having a modest victory celebration next door at my old place at Number 14 Gramercy Park. Leila had come with her cousins. It was a most merry evening, with many toasts and libations."

"This was before the Temperance Acts, of course, Mr. Du Bois," Leila interjected.

"Quite so," Tilden continued. "At any rate, some wag was going on about how, as president, I should have a wife to assist me in social matters. I was prompted to choose which of the young ladies present I would consider as a bride. I had always been extremely fond of Leila, and asked her if she would enjoy the life of a First

Lady. To my surprise, she took my remarks altogether seriously."

"What did you say, Mrs. Tilden?"

"I'm afraid I was a bit of a wet blanket, Mr. Du Bois," she answered after a moment's thought. "I said that he was trifling with my affections, and a proper proposal shouldn't be made in jest."

"I was a bit taken aback," said Tilden. "I apologized, and let the matter drop. That might have been the end of it if the *Tribune* hadn't printed an account of the matter. I suspected some of my friends at the paper of a misguided attempt to make me seem more youthful than I was."

"How did you react to the story, Mrs. Tilden?"

"I was mortified, Mr. Du Bois. It is one thing to speak such trifles in private, quite another to explain them to family and friends. When Mr. Tilden sent me an invitation to his yearly Christmas party, I very nearly refused. When I did arrive, we got into a terrible row."

"What sort of row?"

"Well, Mr. Tilden began again, teasing me about marriage in front of everyone, promising me a White House wedding," Leila answered. "I'm afraid I wasn't very civil. I told him that the way he was handling things he might never get into the White House at all."

"What an extraordinary statement, Mrs. Tilden!" said Du Bois, sitting forward in his chair. "Whatever brought you to that conclusion?"

"Though most people have forgotten the whole affair, Mr. Du Bois, there was considerable controversy over irregularities in the voting during the 1876 election," Leila answered. "Although the Democratic Party had won a clear majority of both the popular and electoral votes, the Republicans had contrived a plan to contest the election returns and to force the issue into the Senate, where they held a majority. Mr. Tilden had been counseled by his advisors to stay above the fray and wait them out. I questioned the wisdom of that position."

"Indeed she did, Mr. Du Bois! In mighty intemperate language, I'll have you know!"

"Samuel!"

"But I am only speaking the truth, my dear! Why, I'll venture to say that if Leila had kept her temper that night, I might never have been president. Instead, she said to me: 'Mr. Tilden, you should be ashamed of yourself!' just as brazen as a boy! 'Few men are ever given the opportunity you have been given,' she told me, 'to alter the course of history itself by your actions. And yet you stick your head in your shell like an old turtle, while others are stealing this election out from under you! I am only a woman, sir,' she said, 'but were I a man like you, I would not throw away that opportunity—as you have so many others!' And then she stormed out into the night, slamming the door behind her."

"I was very vexed," Leila said quietly.

"No more than I," Tilden replied. "I was fit to be tied! I can tell you, I didn't cotton to a young girl telling me my own business—particularly in front of kith and kin. It put me in a black mood, and the party didn't last long after that."

"Not a very auspicious beginning, sir, if you'll pardon my saying so," said Du Bois.

"On the contrary, Mr. Du Bois. As it turned out, it was just the thing. That pretty speech gave me much to think about. I value truth above all things, and I had just been given a great walloping dose of it to swallow. I retired with my mind in a turmoil, and suffered through a most unsettled night. By the next morning, Christmas Day, I had to admit Leila was right, though it wounded my vanity to do so." He paused for a moment, staring off into the distance.

"You see, Mr. Du Bois," Tilden continued quietly, "I realized that I was letting the prize I had toiled all my life to gain slip away without a fight. And, as I sat there musing, it also occurred to me that the prize itself was worth nothing if I had no one to share it with. It was then that I resolved to make this remarkable woman my wife.

"As luck would have it, Leila had left her shawl in my parlor. The proper thing would have been to have a servant take it 'round, with perhaps a nosegay and a brief note. Instead, I marched bareheaded out into the street and returned it to her myself. Soon I was down on my knee to her, proposing in earnest. I was pleasantly surprised that my rusty old bones could still manage that, even at sixty-two!"

"And did you accept his proposal then, Mrs. Tilden?"

"Not at first, but over time he wore down my defenses. He used a most cunning stratagem. He described to me the great aspirations he held for this nation, and then told me he could not accomplish them without me. What woman could resist such an appeal?"

Tilden could remember clearly the moment she'd said "yes." She'd been dressed in a gown of cream-colored silk, her cheeks flushed, lips red as cherries, her hair unpinned and gleaming in the fire's glow. He'd grown flinty and cold over the years, withdrawing more and more from the world of flesh and blood into the realm of facts and figures. When they'd kissed to seal the bargain, he felt the warm breath of Indian Summer thawing his stony heart. They'd announced their engagement on New Year's Eve, to the delight of his family, who loved Leila dearly.

"I understand, Mr. Tilden, that your decision to marry subjected both of you to rough usage from your political rivals."

"Quite so, Mr. Du Bois. The results of the election were still in dispute, and my enemies attempted to discredit me by portraying me as a lecherous old rake. For example, shortly after our engagement was announced, a cruel broadside, entitled 'The Cradle Robber of Gramercy Park,' began circulating, which featured a drawing of me dressed in a nurse's gown pushing Leila about in a perambulator! I was, of course, used to such calumnies, but it wounded Leila deeply."

Leila smiled. "I was very young, Mr. Du Bois, and unprepared for the rough-and-tumble world of politics. The attacks affected me deeply, not so much for my own sake, but for Samuel's. It seemed so unfair that so good a man should be the object of such vile abuse."

Tilden had never found the source of the slanders, though he suspected it lay close to home. Several of his oldest political cronies had bitterly resented his marriage. His secretary and lifelong friend, John Bigelow, had been the most strongly opposed. He'd stressed Tilden's frail health, and the disparity in their ages. He'd intimated that Leila was a fortune hunter, which seemed comical in light of the fact that it was Tilden's own offices that made her independent of his own considerable fortune. And, betraying more than a little jealousy, he claimed she would be a 'disruptive influence' on his career.

There, at least, Bigelow had been right. She'd certainly turned his orderly little world topsy-turvy. She'd persuaded him to dismiss his personal physician, Dr. Simmons, whom she called a charlatan and quacksalver who was schooling him in hypochondria. She undertook to restore his health herself, getting him out of his office and off to weekends at Newport as often as she could. That hadn't set well with his advisors.

"You mentioned earlier, Mrs. Tilden," Du Bois continued, "that you feared Mr. Tilden would be deprived of the presidency by the actions of the Congress. Mr. Henry Adams, in an article in the *North American Review*, suggests that you attempted to influence the outcome by personally pleading your husband's case before Justice Bradley, who held the deciding vote on the Electoral Commission appointed to resolve the dispute."

Leila colored deeply. "Since Mr. Tilden was constrained by his position from acting, I felt it was my place as his wife-to-be to petition Judge Bradley on his behalf. I appealed to him to avert a divisive conflict that could harm the nation. In the end, Mr. Bradley chose to honor the will of the American people, and cast his vote for Mr. Tilden."

Tilden laughed to himself. Again Leila was telling only half the truth. It hadn't been only rhetoric that had swayed Judge Bradley. The Tilden faction had eight votes to Hayes's seven until Justice Davis, a sympathetic Republican, had been suddenly called into the Senate. They'd replaced him with Joseph Bradley, a career Republican who'd apparently been paid well to keep his vote in the Hayes column. Leila decided to fight fire with fire.

She had visited Bradley's home on the evening of March first, the night before the final vote, and used every wile at her disposal to change his mind. "I began with logic, and ended with tears," she'd told him later that evening. "No man can resist tears. His lady had a harder heart. To her, I offered money. The issue is decided, Tildy. You will have the presidency, and I, my White House wedding."

"Mr. Tilden?"

He'd drifted off again. "I'm sorry, Mr. Du Bois. Would you be so kind as to repeat the question?"

"Certainly. Several of your biographers have noted a marked change in your political philosophy after you became president. There are those, as you know, who credit the change to your wife's influence—"

"That's not true!" Leila protested. "My husband has always been a champion of reform, Mr. Du Bois. It was his moral vision, and his alone, that brought this nation through the dark times of the past decade!"

"I didn't mean to imply . . ." Du Bois began.

"If I played a part, it was only in doing what any fit wife should—providing the moral support he needed to continue his fight in the face of virulent opposition." She rose abruptly to her feet, and Du Bois followed.

"I sincerely hope I haven't said anything to offend you, Mrs. Tilden."

"No, Mr. Du Bois. You are merely repeating what others have said. Now, if you will excuse me, I need to see to the preparations for this evening." She lifted the tea tray, and carried it swiftly out of the parlor, closing the door firmly behind her.

"I seem to have struck a nerve, Mr. Tilden," said Du Bois. "My apologies."

"I shouldn't worry about it, Mr. Du Bois. My wife, as you have observed, is a very passionate woman where my reputation is concerned. She is sensitive to criticism that she might be overstepping her role, even today. I remember, during the fuss over the Cypher Telegrams, that Mr. Nast prepared a caricature of Leila leading a donkey about by the nose, a donkey that bore a strong resemblance to me! It bore the caption 'Without me, this old ass couldn't make up its mind!' She was livid, I can tell you. She wrote a most immoderate letter to the *Times*, and would have sent it had I not talked her out of it. Eventually, when her temper had cooled, she responded by inviting Mr. Nast for tea. They have been fast friends ever since. Please, go on."

"All right, sir. You mentioned the Cypher Telegrams. How did you feel when the Republicans produced evidence that your own staff had attempted to steal votes in the 1876 election?"

Tilden's eyes narrowed. "At first, I saw it merely as a brazen attempt on the part of the Republicans to reverse the results of the election. But when I saw the telegrams with my own eyes, and learned that members of my own staff—men I had trusted—had encouraged 'bulldozing' in the southern states, I was deeply shocked."

"But surely it was common knowledge—"

"Nothing excuses fraud," Tilden said sharply. "You campaign hard, Mr. Du Bois. You exploit every legitimate advantage and point out your opponent's weaknesses in the sharpest terms. You muster your canvassers and ward heelers like an army. But you do not buy votes, nor intimidate voters, nor bribe officials. That is beyond the pale.

"What galled me most about the whole affair was that

the Republicans were guilty of far worse connivance and chicanery than the Democrats. And yet Mr. William Orton, who was then president of Western Union, had turned over copies of telegrams which implicated Democrats to Mr. Hewitt, but deliberately withheld those that would demonstrate malfeasance on the part of the Republicans."

"Yet such telegrams did, at last, come to light, did they not, Mr. Tilden?"

"Yes, they did," said Tilden. He regarded Du Bois closely, wondering how much of the truth he knew. "Fortunately, an executive of the American Telegraph Company saw the travesty taking place, and released a group of telegrams which implicated the Republicans."

It was Leila who had procured the telegrams. As a "telegrapher's daughter," she knew just where to look. But she had exacted a high and bitter price. She insisted that everyone involved in the affair be dismissed from his staff: Wooley and Marble, Havemeyer and Weed—all the members of his inner circle. It was bitter medicine for him, but Leila was adamant. "You must cut them loose, Tildy. The press must have its meat."

It was hardest to let go of his nephew, Will Pelton, whom he'd always treated as a son. Leila made it clear that he was no longer welcome in their home. He'd made sure that Pelton got a commission in the foreign service, and he prospered there, after a bit of seasoning. They met infrequently after that, and only when Leila was out of town.

In the aftermath, she'd scoured his personal affairs for any trace of scandal, feeling his narrow victory made him vulnerable to further attack. The house-cleaning had cost him dearly. She made him pay over $150,000 in back taxes, and settle his part in the Terre Haute & Alton Railroad dispute for $100,000, telling him the investment in his reputation was cheap at twice the price. Her intuition had proved right. . . .

"Perhaps we should turn to a more pleasant subject, sir."

"By all means."

"Tell me a bit about your life in Washington. According to the newspapers, the White House became quite a center for art and culture during your administration."

"Ah. There I do credit Leila for most of the work. We were married in June of 1877, in the Rose Garden, amid much hoopla in the press. Shortly afterward, Leila's Sunday afternoon teas became quite the thing. She had a habit of inviting the most curious combinations of people—politicians, painters, scientists, musicians. Yet somehow it all seemed to work.

"Once, she managed to snare the humorist, Mark Twain, who'd been a Hayes supporter in the election. And you know what he said? 'If I had known there were such creatures among the Democrats, Mrs. Tilden, I would have bolted years before.' I remember one afternoon, I came down late for tea to discover the house was filled with suffragists! As it turned out, Leila had been a school chum of Alice Stone Blackwell, daughter of Henry Brown Blackwell and Lucy Stone, the feminist."

"So it was your wife who introduced you to woman suffrage?"

"Well, I'd always supported the notion in the abstract, Mr. Du Bois. But I certainly got an earful about it that afternoon!" Once that doctrine had entered Leila's head, there was no talking her out of it. She would argue in her passionate way that if each uneducated Negro man deserved one vote, then an educated white woman deserved two. She was also shrewd enough to realize that the party that did give women the vote would instantly gain thousands of new voters.

"I understand the birth of your daughter caught both of you a bit by surprise."

"I should say so! I had so long ago given up any hope of children, that it caught me completely off my guard.

When Leila told me the news, I was speechless at first, then overwhelmed with delight."

He'd made clear to her that she was not to expect much of him in the way of conjugal duties. She'd laughed, and told him she hadn't married him for his ardor, but for his brain. And yet, on those quiet evenings beside the fire, their gentle affections had often given way to more passionate embraces. Only a few months later, Leila announced that she was with child. With that rough wit of hers, Leila described the blessed event with such epithets as "God's little prank," and "our windfall." When their daughter was born the following summer, they'd nicknamed her "Windy," in reference to the jest. Everyone assumed it was just a pet name for Gwendoline.

Looking down at that small, fragile creature, his whole perspective had changed. Through her, the stream of life flowed forward into the future. Here, incarnate, was the reason he must strive to create a better world.

Tilden looked up, saw Du Bois waiting patiently. He leaned forward, addressing the reporter in a low voice. "If you don't mind my turning the tables for a moment, Mr. Du Bois, I have a question for you."

"Yes, sir?"

"In listening to your questions, I get the impression you have a point you are trying to get at. Perhaps it would be best if you would simply state it outright."

Du Bois frowned. "I'm not sure how to put this without sounding critical of you, sir."

"Go ahead, Mr. Du Bois. A politician develops a very thick skin over the years."

"Well, sir, I must say you present a bit of a puzzle to me. Before you became president, you were closely identified with the wealthy and the powerful." Du Bois reached into his breast pocket, and pulled out a well-worn notebook and a pair of gold-framed eyeglasses. He peered at his notes for a moment, then looked up. "You represented Jim Fisk, the railroad baron. You owned a large amount of railroad stock yourself, and your sharp business practices earned you the title 'The Great Forecloser.' "

"I'm not sure I take your point, Mr. Du Bois," Tilden answered.

"My only point is this: Prior to 1876, you seemed lukewarm to reform—labor relations, the rights of women, the plight of the destitute. And, if you'll pardon me, sir, you did not have a reputation as a great friend of the black man. And yet, despite all of this, you became the architect of some of the most profound changes in this republic since the Bill of Rights. I have always wondered what caused you to change."

"Ah!" Tilden replied. "That explains your close questioning of my wife. You are looking for the skeleton key—the alchemy that turned the Great Forecloser into the Great Reformer."

"Yes, sir," said Du Bois sheepishly. "I suppose I am."

"Well, I will tell you the secret," he whispered. "I had a dream!"

"A dream, sir?" said Du Bois.

"A dream, young man. In my first inaugural address I spoke of a great vision for our nation: 'a vision of a rich and abundant nation filled with shining cities and prosperous towns, a land where every citizen enjoys equally the blessings of liberty.' Surely you must recall it. They quote the damned thing *ad nauseam* in all of the official biographies, the ones the little schoolchildren read."

"I recall the quote, sir," Du Bois replied.

"Well, that vision was not a metaphor. It was an actual dream that first came to me on Christmas Day, 1876!"

"The day you proposed to Mrs. Tilden," said Du Bois.

"Precisely!" Tilden replied. "I had the dream right after that great galumphing quarrel with Leila. In the dream, I saw clearly the road that lay ahead for the nation, and understood the part I must play in making that dream a reality. I am not a particularly religious man, Mr. Du Bois, but I have always believed that vision was given to me by the Almighty to remind me of the work I had to do here on Earth."

It was a lie. But it was a lie with a purpose; a lie that held a strange kind of truth. It was a lie Tilden had told to only a handful of people. Leila was the first, and he suspected that the lie, more than any other single thing, had won her heart. Now he was telling it again to this skeptical young colored man, who seemed clearly moved by the story.

The truth could not be spoken. How could he ever explain that it was no noble dream he had seen that holiest of nights, but a hellish nightmare? A nightmare of a dark and bloody road that twisted far ahead into the mists. Of skies blackened and fields blighted, rivers and oceans fouled and lifeless. Of a world divided into warring camps, ravaged by fear, want, and unending strife. Of men slaughtered by the millions, women bound in chains, wretched children begging on the streets.

Whatever perverse deity had delivered him that vision had also cursed him with the knowledge that it was within his power to turn from that road—but only if he threw his body upon the wheel of history. Over the years, he had come to understand the enormity of that curse. Only when he devoted his every waking hour to the pursuit of the light did the darkness for a time subside.

For the past few years, the dreams had been infrequent, and he had come to hope that the burden had been lifted from him. But in the past few months, they had returned, more terrible than before. Once again, that black road stretched out before him. . . .

"Samuel?" Tilden shuddered; the visions fled. Leila was bending over him, her face wreathed in concern. "Are you all right, dear?" she asked.

"Yes, dear," he answered, though his body felt weak and cold. "My apologies, Mr. Du Bois. I'm afraid this has tired me more than I realized. Perhaps we could continue the interview after lunch?"

Du Bois rose, pulled a large gold watch from his pocket. "Certainly, sir. It is now nearly noon. Shall I call again at, say, one-thirty?"

"That would be fine," Tilden said weakly, despite Leila's obvious discomfort.

"I'll show you out, Mr. Du Bois," Leila said. She kissed Tilden on the brow, whispering "I'll be back in just a moment, Tildy, dear."

Tilden leaned toward the fire, staring into its depths, hoping the bright memories the reporter's questions had recalled would banish the long, dark shadows that threatened to engulf him. When Leila returned, she seemed pained.

"Why did you consent to continue this interview, Tildy? The *Times* has never looked on us favorably, and that young man is relentless in his questioning—"

"It's all right, Leila, dear. It's for the best."

"But look at you, Tildy! You are trembling and pale. You should be resting, not subjecting yourself to an inquisition. You must conserve your strength for your appearance at the convention this evening."

"Sit down, dear," Tilden whispered. "Let me explain." Leila pulled her chair close, resting her hand on his arm. "You know that I have always had one love above all others, and that is truth. That young man is history, come to judge me. I must make a good accounting of myself while there is still time. Would you rather I left it to the undertakers?"

"You mustn't talk like that, Tildy!" said Leila angrily, blinking back tears. She pulled the lap robe up about his neck. "Try to rest, Tildy, dear. I'll wake you when it's time for lunch."

"I will, Leila. I have work yet to do . . ."

Tilden woke somewhat refreshed, but the remainder of the interview was exhausting. Though Du Bois was unfailingly patient and polite, he seemed determine to cross-examine him on every important moment of his career.

He seemed especially interested in the "War of Redemption," those dark years when the Democratic victory had unleashed a wave of lawlessness and vengeance throughout the South, pitting the black race against the white in a virtual second civil war.

In the first crisis of his career, Tilden had nationalized the militia, and sent them into the South to keep order. It was one of the most brutal episodes since the war. It had taken months to quell the riots. By the time they were over, black families by the thousands were leaving the South and emigrating to Kansas, Oklahoma, and Louisiana.

Du Bois was also fascinated with the events that had led to the formation of the Liberal Party in 1880. He seemed to understand well enough why the Democrats, anxious to hold the "Solid South," would have repudiated Tilden and nominated Sam Randall. But it seemed strange to him that the Republicans, the party of Lincoln, would have turned to Jacob Cox after his remarks about the "hereditary deficiencies" of black men. But Tilden pointed out that both parties were dominated by men who feared a racial war.

"All the malcontents came to me, Mr. Du Bois," Tilden explained. "Free Soilers, 'soft money' types, labor reformers, teetotalers, Negro leaders, even woman suffragists, who saw in our new party their best chance to gain the vote." It was they who had forged the planks in the Liberal Party's platform: "Four T's for Tilden," as the slogan went: Temperance, Trust-Busting, Tax Reform and Total Suffrage.

Tilden had chosen as his vice presidential candidate General Winfield Scott Hancock, who had served him so well during those bloody months of 1878. They had "risen between two stools," winning the election by a slim plurality while the two other parties tore each other to pieces. When Hancock had won in 1884 with Cleveland as his running mate, he'd repaid Tilden by appointing him Chief Justice of the Supreme Court.

Though he'd been exhilarated by the power of the presidency, Tilden had always been a lawyer at heart. It was there, aided by the justices he'd appointed while president—O'Conor, Root, Douglass, and Davis—that he'd begun the great work of extending the rights and liberties granted to all citizens by the Constitution. During those happy, if hectic, years, he had slept well. . . .

"I would like to thank you again, Mr. Tilden, for this opportunity. You've made a great many things clearer to me," Du Bois was saying. "I'll make sure the *Times* sends you a proof copy before the story goes to press." Tilden was barely aware of his remarks, lost in contemplation of the improbably strange turns his life had taken.

After Du Bois left, Leila fed Tilden more tea and tonic, and helped him dress for his star turn at the convention. Windy was aflutter with excitement after her mother had given her permission to attend.

The rain was sluicing down as they stepped out on the curb to await the carriage. All traffic was snarled by the foul weather, and Tilden was soaked to the skin by the time they were safely inside. The rich food he'd consumed was contriving to give him dyspepsia, and he had developed a hacking cough he could not shake.

Once at the armory, he was bustled inside, where Jerome and Leila fussed over him in an antechamber, trying to repair the damage to his facade. They took their seats in a roped-off section filled with uncomfortable folding chairs, and Leila had to give him a bit of her laudanum to still his cough. It left him a bit vague, but filled with good feeling.

Windy had struck up a friendship with a young girl about four years her junior, the niece of the young congressman from New York who had been chosen to introduce him. She'd amused them all by declaring her ambition was to become president herself one day.

Leila was introducing him to a slim, scholarly-looking woman, a Miss Bates, who seemed overwhelmed to be in his presence. Though he could barely hear her over the din, she seemed to be speaking of a poem she had written on a visit to Pikes Peak that was to be performed to music after he spoke.

"When I heard you would be speaking at this convention, I sent a copy of it to Mrs. Tilden. It may be immodest of me, sir, but I like to think it captures the spirit of your great dream."

"My dream?" he asked.

"That great vision you spoke of in your inaugural address, Mr. President. I do hope you like it, sir."

Before he could reply, an aide was whispering with Leila, motioning frantically toward the dais.

"It's time, Tildy," she was saying to him. "You will be speaking as soon as Mr. Roosevelt finishes. It's a long walk up there, and we'd best get started. Do you have your speech?"

Tilden coughed, patted his pocket, and levered himself up into Jerome's waiting arms. His hands would not stop trembling, and his legs felt as if they were swaddled in lead. Leila kissed him on the cheek, her eyes glistening. "Make it a rouser, Tildy!" she whispered in his ear.

". . . and so, it is my distinct honor and privilege to present to you a man who, more than any other individual, bears the glory for this gathering tonight." Roosevelt's voice carried far out into the hall, its hearty tone commanding silence. The podium seemed impossibly far away, and Tilden wondered for a moment if he had the strength to reach it. And they'd placed all manner of obstacles in his path that barked his shins and impeded his progress.

"Gentlemen—and ladies—fellow delegates, I give you the dean of this great party, the Great Reformer, *Samuel Jones Tilden!*"

The applause hit him like a wall of noise, causing him to falter. As he labored up the last few steps, he heard a rising chant, accompanied by noisemakers and explosions: *Tilden! Tilden! Tilden!* All of the delegates had risen to their feet in ovation. The noise grew louder as Roosevelt took his arm and led him to the podium. He gripped it tight, swaying, waiting long minutes for the tumult to subside. When at last it grew quiet, he began to speak, but his dry throat caused a racking cough that made his chest burn. When Roosevelt handed him water, his eyes glistened with gratitude. At last, he found his voice.

"You can all sit down now," he said, wishing he could do the same. A warm wave of laughter swept over the audience. "I have very little to say, so I will be brief.

"You are gathered this evening in a solemn, and I might even say sacred endeavor: to choose the leaders you feel will best serve our nation in the years to come." As he spoke, a warmth began to spread throughout his body, and he suddenly felt youthful and strong. "Each of you has in your hands a mighty power, one which your forebears gave their life's blood to preserve: the power to determine the nature of the world in which your children, and their children, and countless generations after, will live." The power inside of him filled his lungs, making his voice ring to the farthest rafter.

"Sixteen years ago I spoke of a dream, a dream of a nation where greed and want and hatred and fear are forgotten wraiths of the distant past. With the help of the Almighty, I have devoted my life to the battle for that dream—a battle that will soon be over for me." There was a murmur of negation from the crowd, but Tilden continued. "It has been my privilege, and my burden, to be its custodian these many years. But now it is time to pass it on. Tonight, I entrust that dream into your hands—and the hands of those you have chosen to lead you."

The hall resounded with thunderous applause. The warmth in his limbs began to ebb, and his heart beat wildly in his breast. Summoning his strength, he lifted one palsied hand, and the delegates fell silent again. With a hoarse whisper that carried out to the farthest rafters, he spoke again.

"And so, it is my singular honor and duty to place in

nomination for the vice presidential candidacy of the Liberal Party the Honorable Susan Brownwell Anthony, of Massachusetts!"

The thundering applause began again. A slim, white-haired figure dressed in somber gray rose slowly and made her way to the podium. As she shook his hand, he felt a wave of dizziness, and the roaring filled his head so that he could not hear. He stumbled from the stage into Jerome's arms, helpless to move as his servant carried him back to his seat. Leila cradled his head to her breast, mopping his brow with her kerchief.

Faintly, he could hear Susan Anthony's voice addressing the convention, but he could not make out the words. Her voice was echoing faintly in his ears. Tilden smiled, feeling the warm glow spread through him again, washing away every trace of pain.

Far away, music began to play, a sweet and haunting melody. As he listened, the drums were stilled and the shadows departed, and a bright and glorious road stretched out before him. At its end stood a woman in white, looking like an angel, her hands clasped to her breast, her bright, birdlike voice singing a song of hope and promise:

O, beautiful! For patriots' dream
That sees beyond the years.
Thine alabaster cities gleam
Undimmed by human tears . . .

America! America!
May God thy gold refine
Till all success is righteousness
And every gain divine . . .

1880

In 1876, Samuel J. Tilden was literally robbed of the presidency in a back-room deal, after winning the popular vote and seeming to win a majority of the electoral votes. Four years later James A. Garfield won the presidency, but was shot and killed before he could have any lasting effect on policy or history.

Tilden did not run again in 1880. But what if he had, and what if he had defeated Garfield just as dishonestly as he himself had been defeated four years earlier?

Michael P. Kube-McDowell, author of such best-selling novels as *Alternities* and *The Quiet Pools*, poses the question, and then offers an intriguing answer.

I Shall Have a Flight to Glory

by Michael P. Kube-McDowell

On the avenue outside Booth's New York Theater, the post-curtain bustle was more pronounced than usual. Black hansom cabs and carriages jockeyed for places at the curbside, where top-hatted men and women in fine evening dress waited, their coat collars upturned against the chill November air.

Despite the cold, it was a happy crowd, still enthused by the performance they had just witnessed, and by their privileged status. In all of America, only these few thousands could claim to have been present for the American debut of *Adrienne Lecouvreur* and its star, the legendary Sarah Bernhardt.

"General Garfield! General Garfield!"

The voice was shrill for a man's, and cut through the clamor of laughter and conversation. Only a few steps beyond the lobby doors, General James Abram Garfield paused and let the dispersing audience flow around him as he peered questioningly in the direction of his accoster. Taller by a head than most of those around him, Garfield quickly spotted an eager-faced man pushing his way through the crowd on the walk.

"This way, General," said the man at Garfield's elbow. "I see our carriage."

"A moment, Will," Garfield said.

William Evarts frowned, but signaled the chauffeur to wait. Then he moved protectively close to Garfield, scrutinizing the approaching man as he did.

The stranger wore a flat-brimmed black hat, much like an Ohio Amishman's, and his beard billowed out around his chin like a black ruffled collar. Though he wore no greatcoat, his cheeks were reddened, as though he had been standing in the cold for some time. His waistcoat was stained with a streak of brown gravy, or perhaps a dribble of tobacco.

"General Garfield!" the man repeated as he closed to within an arm's length. "What a pleasure! I heard that you were in the city, and I had to come see you. You honor us with your presence, General. Or, should I say, Mr. President?"

"It will be some days still before we know whether I've earned that honor, sir," Garfield said, tugging on his gloves.

"I have every confidence, every confidence," the little man said animatedly. "I gave a splendid speech here on your account a month ago, you know. I warrant there wasn't a Tilden supporter left in the hall by the time I was finished. You can count on New York, I'm certain of it. Did you see the show?"

"I did, on Mr. Arthur's urging," said Garfield.

"Splendid! Myself, I gave up my ticket so that Senator Conkling's sister might attend. I expect to see a later show, of course. May I ask what you thought of Sarah Bernhardt?"

"Miss Bernhardt is as fine an actress as her notices declare," said Garfield, correcting the stranger's pronunciation by example. "Though as a Christian man, I confess I'm somewhat troubled by the morality of the tale to which she lends her talents."

"I'm a Christian man, too," the man said hurriedly. "A theologian, in fact. And I must agree I do find a touch of idolatry in the acting profession, to say nothing of libertinage. But no more than on the stage of politics, I daresay. And I should not want to be so Christian as to prevent me from enjoying a woman like that, wouldn't you agree?"

Garfield cocked an eyebrow quizzically. "A theologian, you say? I took you for a newsman, sir. You have the manners of one."

"No, no," the man said, in horror. "I thought I had already made it clear. I am Guiteau, Charles Guiteau. You must remember—I posted you a copy of my speech. I'm a Stalwart, a Grant man. But a Republican first and last, as I know you are. And I have every confidence your presidency will reunite our party. It's our natural right to lead this country. Only our own fractiousness could hand the White House to Tilden and the damned Democrats."

"Yes—no doubt. If you will excuse me, Mr. Guiteau, my host is waiting."

Garfield tipped his hat and turned away, but Guiteau pursued him, interposing himself between the general and the carriage. "I wonder if I might have the chance to speak with you sometime in regard to the Paris consulate."

"It is far too early to speak of such things, Mr. Guiteau," said Garfield. "If you will excuse me."

"Move along now, there's a good man," said Evarts in a stern voice.

"Am I too confident of victory?" Guiteau asked. "I think not, but—perhaps if I came to Washington once the electors have voted?"

Garfield shrugged. "Should the vote favor me, I will be obliged to interview candidates for a great number of posts. Though I hardly look forward to it."

"Good. Very good. Thank you, General. I'll see you in Washington, then, a few weeks from now." Guiteau bowed and backed away, leaving the path to the carriage clear.

"Fool," muttered Evarts, watching Guiteau leave.

Garfield caught a handhold and swung himself up onto the step of the cabriolet. "Is that meant for me, Will? Was I too short with him?"

"Too patient, General," said the secretary of state, following Garfield into the carriage. "I know every Stalwart of consequence, and this Guiteau is not among them. Did you see his clothes? He looked more a street beggar than a friend of Conkling's circle. For that matter, if this Guiteau were what he claimed, he would have known *me*. I take him for a hanger-on, and a pretender. We won't see him tomorrow, you can be sure. Pay him no mind."

The Stalwarts had seen to it that Garfield had a comfortable suite with a generous bar, a solicitous hotel staff, and a sunrise view of Central Park. But the amenities had not succeeded in softening his resolve or blunting his wariness.

"General, let me offer one last time— I would be happy to conduct this meeting for you," Evarts said, coming up behind Garfield as he stood at one of the tall, narrow windows.

"That won't be necessary, Will."

"I strongly advise it—"

"Why?"

"To make it that much more difficult for them to trap you into a commitment. I have a great deal of experience in these things. And I do represent the party's interest."

Garfield shook his head. "Just so. You're the party's lawyer, Will, not mine. I'll speak for myself. I don't expect the meeting will last long enough for me to grow hoarse."

The Stalwart legation arrived just after nine, and numbered three: Roscoe Conkling, his fellow senator Thomas Platt, and the vice-presidential candidate, Chester Alan Arthur. Both of the other men deferred to Conkling from the start—Arthur in particular, who joined Platt on a long settee and said little.

"Did you enjoy the play?" Conkling wanted to know.

"Very much indeed," Evarts said. "Ms. Bernhardt's voice is quite extraordinary."

"Good. Good," said Conkling. "I thought it would do us all well to escape from Washington for a while, from the post-election fuss and the press. Ms. Bernhardt offered as good a pretext as could be asked for. Who would say that the queen of the Comédie Française isn't worth a train ride to New York?"

"Let's get on with it," said Garfield.

"Of course," said Conkling. He retrieved a small bundle of paper bound with a ribbon from his inside coat pocket and passed it across to Evarts.

"What's this?" Garfield asked, reaching out and claiming the bundle.

"A list of our patronage appointments," said Senator Conkling.

Garfield tugged the ribbon loose, unfolded the sheaf, and scanned the first page. "Postmaster of New York, of Albany, of Rochester, etcetera— Collector of customs for the port of New York—" He thumbed the first page back and went on to the next. "The vacancy on the court of appeals for the Second District— You seem not to have overlooked much." Garfield riffled the last few pages cursorily and then tucked the bundle against his leg.

"It was a difficult fight against Tilden, especially here," said Conkling. "We worked hard for you. We deserve to share in the spoils."

"That's to be expected," said Evarts. "And we're prepared to be reasonable."

"I'm not," said Conkling. "If it isn't clear, New York belongs to us again. No more of the kind of interference Hayes tried to push down our throats. If it's a federal job and it touches this state, the name comes from me. Nothing else is acceptable. Understand?"

"Your meaning is unmistakable," said Garfield, his expression portrait-placid.

"Good. There are two more appointments I want to talk about, which aren't on that list—which are the real purpose for this meeting."

"And those are—" asked Garfield.

"Senator Platt," Conkling said with a nod, "has expressed an interest in becoming attorney general. And Alonzo Cornell is willing to accept the post of secretary of state."

"New York belongs to you—but the White House belongs to the President," said Evarts. "You can't make demands at the cabinet level. But we'll be glad to consider all eligible candidates—"

"No," said Garfield.

Evarts looked quizzically at him.

"President Hayes was right. Patronage is a shabby, back-scratching, palm-greasing business that serves politicians better than the public," said Garfield calmly. "I'm going to build on Hayes's work, not undo it. Your payoff for your part in the campaign is right there." He pointed at Arthur. "Your boy's going to be vice president."

Conkling's expression had turned cold. "A lot of people did you a lot of favors—"

"They did *you* favors, Senator. I never asked for anything but an honest vote. Pay them off yourself." Garfield picked up the appointment list from beside him, ripped it in half and in half again, and let the pieces fall in a scatter to the carpet. "I'll appoint who I want. And I want people who can do their jobs without bowing to Roscoe Conkling first."

Stunned, Evarts mouthed an oath. "Mother of Jesus, James—"

His mouth twisted into a snarl, Thomas Platt leaped up and took two threatening steps toward Garfield. "Do you think it's too late for us to hurt you? The vote that matters is still five weeks away. We taught Tilden that lesson last time. We can teach you the same damned way."

Garfield came to his feet. "Do what you will. I'm still not going to give you so much as one damned dirt-town postmaster. I don't like you, and I don't intend to *be* like you."

"Politics is not about liking," Conkling said slowly, collecting his satchel from beside his chair. "Politics is about needing. And you don't know yet how much you need me."

The bill for the suite and services arrived an hour later. It was padded by at least half, but Garfield paid it cheerfully from his own pocket.

"I'll pack the gin for the train home, Will," he said. "We can drink it in good conscience now."

The Georgetown house in which all five of Lucretia and James Garfield's surviving children had been born could not be called a mansion by Washington standards; in his days as a Reconstruction congressman, Garfield had not dipped too deeply into Credit Mobilier's barrel of Union Pacific gifts and favors.

But by the standards of Cuyahoga County, Ohio, the house was mansion enough—a well-groomed lawn for bowls and youthful games, stable space for six horses, rooms for Garfield's mother and for a small clutch of servants, and a narrow cobblestone drive that pierced a wall of maturing trees and curled past a large and imposing front door.

Ordinarily, the racket of iron-shod carriage wheels and horses' hooves against the cobbles announced the approach of visitors to the general's Negro houseman long before the doorbell's musical call. But that January afternoon, the vigorous ringing of the bell and the insistent pounding on the door which accompanied it both erupted without preamble.

"I must see General Garfield," the man on the portico blurted as the door was opened. His bearded face was pinched by distress. "Something's gone terribly wrong!"

The houseman, a former Union infantryman, could not be rushed into panic. He took a moment to take measure of the caller: the legs of his trousers were soaked through nearly to the knees, as though he had traversed blocks of street slush, and he smelled more than faintly of manure. Then he looked past the caller to the empty driveway, and concluded that he was dealing with a beggar.

"General Garfield is not available," he said curtly. "And the household is not hiring at this time."

"No!" said the caller, jumping forward before the door closed again. "Tell him Charles Guiteau is here. He knows me—we went to the theater together in New York, November last, to see Sarah Bernhardt. He'll remember. Tell him I have news from the New York caucus. Tilden has stolen the election!"

In Garfield's study, three men huddled around a well-rubbed dark oak desk and scrutinized the drawings scattered across its broad surface.

"You see, General, the flaw in the steam engine is the great amount of energy needed to boil the water," John Gamgee was saying. "But if we *replace* the water with an element which boils at a lower temperature, the engine will require less fuel."

"And you propose ammonia?" asked Garfield.

"Yes. Which boils at zero degrees centigrade. So as long as the outside temperature is above freezing, my zero-motor will need no fuel at all."

Garfield looked sideways to the third man. "And this seems reasonable to you, Mr. Isherwood?"

The Navy engineer pointed to the drawing before him. "The ammonia is condensed back to a liquid here, just as the water would be—except on leaving the condenser, it should instantly begin to boil anew. It's more than reasonable. It's a most exciting prospect—a tremendously clever creation."

Gamgee said, "General, consider this—a warship powered by the zeromotor could circle the world fueled by nothing but the heat of the water in the sea beneath it."

"You daresay," Garfield said, shaking his head. "Remarkable."

"There'd be no need any longer for the Navy to keep coaling stations all over the world," said Isherwood.

"You could pour that money into building more ships, instead of blowing it out the stacks of steamers," said Gamgee. "The American Navy would be second to none—master of the seas."

Garfield straightened. "An attractive prospect, to be sure. Very well, Mr. Isherwood—if you're convinced that the principle is sound, it seems that an investment in Mr. Gamgee's invention would be in order."

"If you want my opinion, it should be a priority once you take office, sir."

"That's not far from my own opinion. Mr. Gamgee, what do you estimate as the cost of building a working model?"

Before Gamgee could answer, there was a knock on the study door.

"Yes?" called Garfield.

The door opened under the houseman's hand. "Excuse me, General, but a Mr. Guiteau is calling, claiming to have news on the election—"

Just then, Guiteau appeared in the hallway behind the houseman, squeezed past him and sprang to the center of the study, leaving a trail of dirty wet footprints on the floor.

"I'm sorry, sir—" began the houseman.

"General Garfield," Guiteau said breathlessly, "I came as soon as I could. The electors for New York are frauds—every one of them a Tilden man. Thousands of Republican votes were destroyed or given to Weaver and the Greenbacks to cover the crime. When the President of the Senate opens the certificates tomorrow, you're going to lose by eighteen votes."

All three men stared at the unlikely messenger. "Where did you hear this?" Garfield demanded. Behind him, Gamgee began hurriedly to gather his papers together.

"We Stalwarts, we know Mr. Tilden, know him very well. He's not the saintly reformer he poses as, no, not by half. There were rumors the day Tilden announced he would run again. There were handbills the day he was nominated. 'Right the Wrong,' they said. 'This Time, Tilden.' "

"Excuse me, General," said Gamgee, his drawings rolled under one arm and clutched protectively in both hands. "I must be going." Circling wide around Guiteau, Gamgee slipped out the door as though escaping from a mistake.

Looking nearly as uncomfortable, Isherwood hastened to follow on Gamgee's heels, saying, "We'll take this up again another time," though it was not clear to whom he spoke.

His gaze fixed on Guiteau, Garfield did not seem to notice either man's departure. "Did you build this conspiracy from a rumor and a handbill?"

"Oh. no," Guiteau said, shaking his head. "I kept my ears open. I have contacts. I listened for what was said, and not said. A mouse can enter many rooms, after all. I heard how you refused Senator Conkling's demands. I heard how Conkling said 'Let Garfield hang.' And then later I heard about half-burned ballots, lost ballots, the recounts that turned against you."

The doorbell sounded, and Garfield waved a hand at his houseman, still frozen in the doorway of the study. "And why did you take this burden on yourself?"

"Sometimes God allows me to see what must be done."

Garfield frowned and shook his head. "You're a madman, Guiteau."

"No, General. A loyal Republican. Though some would say that there's no difference."

Squinting, Garfield threaded his fingers through his beard. "But Arthur is on the ticket. I can't believe that he would sacrifice his own man, throw New York and the White House to the Democrats, simply to spite me—to prove I needed him. Arthur hasn't much pride, but that insult would rouse even him—"

"No, no—you don't understand," Guiteau said. "The ballots from New York carry the names of both favorite sons—Tilden for president, and Arthur for vice president. You and Hancock were snubbed entirely."

As Garfield gaped, heavy footsteps sounded in the corridor, and two men swept into the room with the presumptuous familiarity of friends and regular visitors. The first through the door was Evarts; the second was James G. Blaine, the Plumed Knight, leader of the Half-Breeds, and Garfield's choice to succeed Evarts as secretary of state. As though disconcerted by their presence, Guiteau surrendered the center of the room, backing away toward a side window.

"Something's up, General," said Evarts. "The Pennsylvania vote has finally arrived, and if paid gossip can be trusted, every Republican elector has thrown himself behind Tilden. There's talk that electors from other states may have done the same, in ones and twos. The counts we made on the popular returns are no good. I don't know where we stand."

"What have you heard about New York?"

"New York? New York is reporting half a million Greenback votes, for God's sake. But Weaver took no electors." Then Evarts took note of Guiteau and stopped, staring. "What is *he* doing here?"

"Giving me better counsel than you, it appears. Mr. Guiteau tells me New York has gone for Tilden."

"What? Impossible. I've heard nothing of this."

"You have now. What do you say now of where we stand?"

"Without New York, you can't win. But this is absurd. Why believe this man?"

"Have you forgotten Pratt's threat?" Garfield glanced sidewise at Guiteau. "Mr. Guiteau, where are you staying?"

Guiteau flushed, embarrassed. "Unfortunately, my resources are strained at the moment, being as I left New York on short notice. I've taken up the hospitality of Mrs. Green's boarding house, on 3rd Street, north of the station."

"Very well." Garfield looked to his houseman, who had trailed the new arrivals into the room. "Send someone to collect Mr. Guiteau's belongings. He'll be staying here for the interim. And close the door after you. We have business to discuss."

Fat flakes of new snow were blowing through the darkness as the carriage bearing James Blaine creaked to a stop in the drive. With Blaine's arrival, the gathering in the study had swollen to six men, but like the others who preceded him, Blaine brought only further gloomy news.

"Neither Senator Conkling nor Mr. Arthur can be found anywhere," Blaine announced.

"Chester doesn't want to be found, I daresay," said a sour-faced man in an army uniform. "I doubt he's proud enough of this business to defend it."

"Find one and you'd find the other, I wager," said Evarts. "Holed up somewhere drunk and laughing. I'd throttle the two of them if they were here this moment."

"Did you try the brothels?" asked another man sarcastically. "That's where whores can usually be found."

"I was able to see Chief Justice Waite, though I couldn't persuade him to join us here," Blaine continued. "He believes the Court will decline to intervene. They won't want to be in the position of crowning the king—"

"So much for the loyalty of one Ohioan to another," said Joseph Keifer, himself an Ohioan.

"—and the heads of the New York and Pennsylvania delegations refused to see me."

"Predictable," said Evarts. "They were the last to show, and they'll be the first to leave. They'll do their dirty little deed and scamper."

"Well," said Garfield, "at least we can see the shape of it now."

"This is New York's revenge for '76." Blaine said bitterly.

" 'He who lives by the sword,' " said Garfield.

"I should have known that a fix was in when Tilden changed his mind and agreed to run again," Blaine went on.

"How loudly can we cry foul?" Garfield asked. "Four years ago, it was *our* fix that made Rutherford Hayes president. You were the architect of it, Will, and everyone here blessed it. *We* sent Tilden home as the loser, when everyone here knows he won." Garfield snorted. "The compromise of '77, we grandly called it. But all we compromised was our honor. How can we be surprised if the electors are sympathetic to Mr. Tilden—if they think he was robbed? The fact is, he was."

"Even so—we wouldn't be having this conversation if you hadn't broken with Conkling, if the Stalwarts hadn't turned their backs on us in New York," said Evarts.

"That's unfair, sir, and I demand you retract it," said Guiteau, rising from the chair where he'd been quietly sitting. "We are proud to be Republicans. New York was stolen by Democratic thuggery."

Evarts scowled at Guiteau, then turned his back on him. "General, I wish you would send this man packing—"

"Will, you don't see what's happened," said Garfield. "We were outflanked, plain and simple. Last time around, the Southern states let themselves be bought, so we could seat a minority president. But they didn't stay bought. They got what they wanted from Hayes—the federal troops recalled from the South. Now, with that behind them, they're showing their true colors. Scratch a Confederate, and you'll find a Democrat underneath."

"Well—how do we fight this?" Keifer asked. "I'm afraid I must tell you, we can't win this time if it comes to a vote of the House. Not since the mid-term, with Sam Randall as speaker. No one hates an Ohioan like a Pennsylvanian, unless it's a Michigan man."

"We can delay the vote," Blaine said. "I'll have the Maine delegation declare an elector ineligible, withdraw our vote."

"Is that allowed?"

"There are no rules for this, Joseph, or at least none Machiavelli didn't know," said Evarts. "If you get away with it, it's allowed."

"I still think the Supreme Court is our best answer," said Stanley Matthews. "Even if the Chief Justice ties his own hands, Noah Swayne will give us a hearing—and an injunction to stop the certification. I'm sure of it. We could give them a fight to make the Vanderbilt probate scrap look like a church tea party."

"What good will delay serve?" asked Garfield.

Evarts said, "We can challenge the Pennsylvania and New York votes, submit our own elector list, our own vote, just as in '77—we have two months to work with—"

Garfield began shaking his head. "William, I don't want that."

Wordless, Evarts stared. "You're talking nonsense."

"I went to the convention to make James Sherman president, not to become a candidate myself," Garfield said, softly chiding. "My God, what is there in that place that a man should ever want to get into it?"

"You're tired, James, and letting your weariness speak for you."

"I *am* tired, Will, that much is true. But I'm not so tired that I can't tell that this is our own young chicken, come home to roost. Or realize that we'll have to eat it, feathers and all."

"General Garfield!" It was Guiteau, his voice full of righteous indignation and his face full of horror. "I don't like the sound of this at all! You can't be thinking of *accepting* this abomination."

"What choice have we?"

"My preference is *this* abomination be plucked, butchered and served well-done," Evarts said, looking directly at Guiteau before joining Blaine in chuckling over his own joke.

Guiteau ignored them. "General, this back-stabbing war is as grave a threat to the existence of the Union as the war you served in so nobly. Only a truce will save us. The Compromise of '81 must be forged between you and Samuel J. Tilden—the generals of the two armies of the Potomac. Otherwise, we'll lay waste to this great nation as surely as if the cannons were still roaring."

"Oh, please," Evarts said in disgust, coming to his feet and turning his back, moving to the window.

But Garfield was silent for a meaningfully long time. Cocking his head, he pressed the fingers of one hand to his lips as he considered. "Thank you, Charles," he said finally, pulling himself slowly to his feet. "I had missed what there was in this uncivil war to be justly angry about." He looked harshly in Evarts's direction. "I stood for it once, holding my nose. But here we are in the same muck again. How many more times will we play this game? The vote belongs to the people. When will we give it back to them?"

He was answered only by uncomfortable silence.

"You see, your answer is the same as mine. Never," Garfield said, more softly. "So it must end now, before it goes any further. I will go and see Mr. Tilden—tonight, if possible. William, will you arrange it?"

"No," said Evarts curtly, and stalked out of the room.

"I will," said James Blaine, standing. "Though I have little hope for the venture. But I can't stand in the way of trying."

* * *

Later that night, Garfield's study was dark save for a single desk lamp, its wick turned low, and deserted save for Garfield himself, standing at a window watching the swirling flakes of snow. The houseman entered quietly and came up close behind him.

"Yes, Thomas," said Garfield.

"Mr. Blaine sent a message," said the houseman. "Mr. Tilden will see you in the morning, at the Capitol."

Garfield turned, disappointment clouding his face. "I'll not sleep well tonight, then. Has Mrs. Garfield turned in?"

"She has. And your mother as well."

Nodding, Garfield said, "Take a drink with me, Thomas?"

"Thank you, sir."

Garfield poured two glasses, surrendered one, and drained the other. "A sorry business, eh?"

"There's muck in every field."

"It seems to me that two reasonable men ought to be able to work out a reasonable solution."

"Ought to," said the houseman. "But seems to me like when there's gold in the room, it can be nigh impossible to find two reasonable men. Polite rules and manners, seems like those are for rich men, who can afford them."

Refilling his glass, Garfield grunted. "If he'd been a soldier, I'd know how to talk to him. But a New York railroad lawyer—we don't eat at the same table." He shook his head. "I'm itching to go roust him out of bed and wring this out."

"Maybe it's best you can't," said Thomas, "lest you get carried off on one of your enthusiasms."

Showing a maudlin smile, Garfield refilled his houseman's glass. "No danger of that, Thomas. My enthusiasm for this business vanished weeks ago. Duty is all that's left."

They met the next morning in the deserted Senate cloakroom, only an hour before the certification count. Although the House chamber where the joint session would be held lay at the far end of the opposite wing, Garfield could nevertheless sense its proximity. It was a magnet, a focus for the gathering moment.

He knew then why Tilden had put off their encounter until the morning, knew that the issue was lost. A slender hour and a walk of a few hundred paces were all that separated Tilden from the presidency, and that fact stood between the two men and absorbed Garfield's words like a sponge. It armored and enlarged Tilden, bringing out a gloating arrogance of which Garfield had previously only heard rumors.

"Governor Tilden, I should think that you would be the last man who would want to take this office on fraud."

Arms crossed, Tilden showed a half-smile which was nearly a smirk. "Tell me, what gift do you have which tells you not only the outcome of an event which has not yet happened, but the moral temper of it as well?"

"You've made a name standing against corruption—"

"Perhaps that's why so many have rallied to me when they saw corruption strike me down four years ago."

"—and for reform. You've battled the Tweed Ring, dishonest judges, the Canal Ring, and beaten them all."

"And now I've beaten the Republican chicanery machine as well, your Steal-warts and Half-wits." Tilden's laugh was not a pretty sound.

"But only by the very means you profess to despise."

Tilden bristled. "I've done nothing dishonest—not the first thing. If you have proof to the contrary, produce it—or withdraw your words."

"You know what was done on your behalf."

"No," said Tilden. "Tell me. What are the charges? What are the names? Or is innuendo as far as you go?"

"If you truly don't know, it can only be by turning a blind eye—"

Tilden jabbed a finger in the direction of the House chamber. "Very soon, a man will open a series of envelopes, and another will sum a column of numbers, and four hundred others will witness to the fact that Samuel

Jones Tilden of New York is president-elect of the United States at last. And in two months, this city and this country will begin to learn what it means to give an honest man the power to make changes at the top."

"You don't need to wait that long," said Garfield, taking a step toward his adversary. "You can start right now."

For just a moment, the glint of triumph disappeared from Tilden's eyes. "What do you mean? What can be done now?"

"In these last two decades we've endured a bloody civil war, a president struck down by bullets, a national election tainted by fraud, and now another stands to be taken in fraud as revenge. We're too young a nation to suffer a battering like this without harm."

"None of that can be undone."

"We can go to the House floor together and renounce the system that brought us to this pass," said Garfield. "We can repudiate the vote of the electors, and demand Congress do the same—that they call for an honest accounting of the popular vote and certify the winner of that tabulation—"

Tilden snorted derisively. "There's *never* been an honest accounting of the popular vote, and never will be."

"—and we can insist on amending the Constitution to abolish the electoral college—"

"They will never do it," Tilden said, vigorously shaking his head.

"They *must* do it. It's become a cynical corruption of the political process."

"They do not care. They are equally corrupt."

"Then we must make them care," said Garfield. "In 1876, the people elected Samuel Tilden president. In 1877, the electoral college elected Rutherford Hayes. Whose coat hung in the White House closet these last four years?"

"The wrong man's," Tilden said, bitterness coating the words.

"Then let's make certain by what we do today that such a wrong never happens again."

Holding himself aloof, Tilden locked his gaze on Garfield. "There is no injustice in a Tilden victory today," he said deliberately. "No matter what the circumstances. A wrong will be righted—"

"A wrong will be compounded, you mean."

"You fool," Tilden said, shaking his head. His voice dripped contempt. "The electors have *never* been obliged to follow the electorate. It's tradition, nothing more. They make no promises. They *exist* to ensure against the foolishness of the public mind. You want to trust the rabble to know its own interest? I trust Conkling more. I can deal with a thief or a scoundrel. But the ignorant, the weak-minded, are too unpredictable—imagine if women were given suffrage! No—there's no injustice looming. Just the opposite. I can do more with this opportunity than anyone. I will not share it, I will not surrender it, and I will not apologize."

"You're poisoning the well we all drink from."

"No," said Tilden. "The taste has been bitter for some time."

Garfield drew back. "You're not the man I believed you to be—not the same man you were four years ago. Not the same man at all."

"Quite right," said Tilden stiffly. "I am much more—enlightened. You may thank Rutherford Hayes and his friends for that."

The corridor outside the cloakroom had been quiet and nearly deserted when Garfield and Tilden kept their appointment, but had swiftly grown busy as the coronation hour approached. Now the bustle had migrated in the direction of the House chamber, and the corridor was quiet once again, with only an occasional hastening page or tardy senator visible along its length. The one unchanging landmark was a slightly built, bearded man wearing a round-brimmed black hat and ill-fitting coat.

Guiteau attended absently to the changing activity as he hovered nervously outside the cloakroom door, wandering a few dozen paces from it, then always returning within arm's reach, as though it were a touchstone, or he hoped to hear the conversation underway beyond it. He was near the apogee of his orbit, staring down a bust of William Rufus King, when the lock turned and the cloakroom door opened.

Tilden was the first to emerge. Taking no notice of Guiteau, he turned toward the House, his long, unhurried strides carrying him down the empty corridor. Then Garfield appeared, answering Guiteau's questioning look with a shake of the head and a look of resignation.

"No?" Guiteau asked, disbelievingly.

"He would not bend," said Garfield.

A mask of outrage settling over his face, Guiteau fumbled in the pocket of his overcoat and brought forth a white-handled bulldog pistol. Lips taut and twitching, body trembling, he raised his arm and shakily pointed the gun in the direction of Tilden's retreating back.

But in the moment of uncertainty, before he could squeeze the trigger, Garfield sprang at him, seized his hand, and snatched the gun away.

"You don't understand," Guiteau said, his voice childlike. "We have to do it now, before the votes are opened. Then you'll be president."

"Shut up," Garfield said, looking both ways down the corridor for witnesses. Finding none, he buried the pistol in his own pocket, seized Guiteau roughly by the elbow, and hustled him down the hallway and outside into the bitter air and January sunshine.

"You shouldn't have stopped me," Guiteau said, starting to turn.

"I should have *shot* you," Garfield said, shoving the other man toward the steps and the Capitol plaza below. "Goddamn you for a fool. What did you think you were doing?"

"I was going to make you president."

Garfield spat at Guiteau's heels. "Idiot. You were going to make Winnie Hancock president. If you could have killed the governor with that toy in the first place. If you could even have hit him. What am I going to do with you?"

"I want to be consul-general to Paris."

Stopping short, Garfield shook his head disbelievingly. "It would serve the French right. Keep going."

Wounded pride stifled any reply.

At the foot of the facade, Guiteau suddenly turned to Garfield and broke his silence. "I want to thank you for stopping my impulsiveness, and preventing my mistake."

"That's progress."

"Because I'm the wrong person to do it," Guiteau quickly added. "But it still needs to be done."

"Let's be finished with this nonsense once and for all," Garfield said tersely. "The last chance we had was the truce we came here to get, and could not."

"Not the last chance," insisted Guiteau. "A physician amputates a limb he's unable to heal."

"How would killing Tilden change anything?"

"Because the trial will be a national sensation—if *you* pull the trigger," Guiteau said. "The extraordinary trial of James Abram Garfield, assassin, will fill the front page of every newspaper for weeks on end. Why did he do it, they'll whisper. And we'll tell them. We'll expose Tilden as a traitor, and show you to be a great patriot. Our defense will be offered to a jury of millions. Every tongue will wag, and they'll speak for our cause, whether they side with us or not—saying 'something must change—this must not be allowed to happen again.'

"And in the end, they will do what must be done." His fervor fading, Guiteau smiled weakly. "I am afraid that were I his assassin, they would just hang me and be done with it."

"We *would* be hanged, in the end, and that's all that's certain."

"I do fear hanging," Guiteau said, nervously rubbing his throat. "It's a cruel business. But life is a fleeting dream, and it matters little when one goes."

"It may matter rather more to Mr. Tilden than to you."

"I presume that the president is a Christian, and he'll be happier in Paradise than here. And it will be no worse for Mrs. Tilden to part with her husband in this way than by natural death."

"Is *this* your grand theology? Self-serving convenience? No. I'll have none of it." Garfield brushed past Guiteau and began walking resolutely toward where carriages of every description waited in ranks for the conclusion of the Congress's business.

Guiteau hurried after and drew up alongside. "How many did you lay in their graves at Shiloh and Chickamauga?"

"We were fighting to save the Republic."

"Yes. And so we are again. The President's death is a sad necessity—but it will save the Republic. Unless you've reconsidered your appraisal of the danger?"

Garfield stopped and stared at the ground ahead of him. "In truth, I am more convinced now than before I spoke with him," he said slowly.

"Then I leave it to you to judge what a patriot, knowing what you know and believing as you believe, would do."

Garfield turned his back and raised his eyes to the trees, still refusing to look at Guiteau. "You assume that I *am* a patriot."

"You assumed I was a madman."

"Was I wrong?"

"No. Am *I* wrong?"

Garfield turned and met Guiteau's gaze. "No," he said at last, slipping a hand in his pocket and finding a grip on the pistol. "You were not wrong." He hesitated. "A sad necessity, you said."

"Yes."

"And this *will* bring the change that must come."

"We'll plan it with every care—so there can be no mistake about who or why—"

"No," said Garfield. "It's to be done now, in front of the world."

"Yes," Guiteau whispered. "Yes. God will be with you."

"Yours may be. I have doubts about mine," said Garfield. He squeezed his eyes shut for a long moment. "Ask Him to see that your cartridges are dry and well-packed. I will attend to the rest myself."

"I shall come with you."

"No," said Garfield. "Take the carriage home and tell Thomas—tell Thomas that it was a duty, not an enthusiasm."

Then he turned and started back up the Capitol facade, climbing the broad stone stairs steadily and resolutely, the bone-handled pistol growing hot in his hand.

1888

The second woman to run for president was Belva Ann Lockwood, who was among the many also-rans in 1888, in an election dominated by Benjamin Harrison.

Janet Kagan, author of *Hellspark, Mirabile,* and many popular short stories, has chosen to show you a scene from President Lockwood's run for re-election in 1892 against Grover Cleveland—and to demonstrate that not all triumphs come after the votes are counted.

Love Our Lockwood

by Janet Kagan

You have heard too many lies about the second of November. Now you shall hear the truth. I was there from the beginning and I shall tell you what I saw.

The morning was gray and chill, as it so often is in Washington. My stump ached with the cold, as my daughter Essie hastened to build a fire. As fortune had it, the storefront chosen for this year's polling was rich enough to possess a Franklin stove. The fire at last made, Essie moved our table and lockbox close.

Mr. Harry Worthington chose the left side, huddling as close to the stove as he dared. I believe his arm stub ached as badly as my leg. The warmth soothed us equally.

We had an amiable argument over the time, for Mr. Worthington had set his watch to railroad time and I had set mine to District of Columbia time. In the end, we agreed; he would accept ballots cast to railroad time and I to suntime.

As we had both arrived early, we had little to do but wait. We spent our time in reminiscence: we spoke of friends lost in the War of Secession. We could have spoken for a month and not named them all. The day seemed grayer, as if dawn would never arrive.

Essie kept watch at the window through which ballots would be passed, for she did not want to draw it open to the chill until such time as this was necessary. As this was the first time she had assisted us, she was naturally in a state of high excitement. When she exclaimed from the window, "Oh, Father! It's a parade!" even Mr. Worthington laughed.

We had seen electioneering before, he and I. The average man will do the most peculiar of things to call attention to his chosen candidate. I have often joked that Mr. Barnum learned his trade from the politicals. I now repeated the joke to Mr. Worthington, who found it quite amusing.

Essie turned from the window. "No, Father, you don't understand. It *is* a parade. They are all coming down the street together, coming *here*!"

She flung open the window and a gust of cold air struck us. I pulled my lap robe more tightly about my stump. Mr. Worthington snugged into his shawl. Essie, risking her health still more, leaned out the window for a long look.

When she drew back in, she had a smile such as to warm even a veteran's heart. "Mrs. Lockwood has come to vote, and all of her friends have accompanied her."

At that, I knew why Essie had volunteered to assist us this morning. Essie is reading law. Some years ago, when Mrs. Lockwood began her practice, it was she who adjudicated my pension. From that day forward, I heard little from Essie but words that she had learned from Mrs. Lockwood. However much I might worry that the legal profession might damage my daughter's prospects, I was forced to agree to permit it when she argued that Mrs. Lockwood alone could not try all the pension cases.

Mr. Worthington was astonished. "Mrs. Lockwood is a woman," he said.

"She is the President," said Essie. She turned back to the window. "Oh, Father! You must see! Come, I'll help you!"

As I am hard put to deny the child anything, I allowed her to help me to the window. What I saw was indeed a parade, one of which even Mr. Barnum would have been proud.

First came the Mother Hubbard Clubs. They would do for the clowns had not their purpose been so good-hearted and serious. The men, young and old, had pulled huge shapeless Mother Hubbard dresses over their street garb and each had replaced his hat with a beaked cap. They carried brooms and the words of their song drifted through the early morning air.

"My soul is tired of politics," they sang, "Its vicious ways, its knavish tricks. I will not vote for any man, But whoop it up for Belva Ann!" With that, they gave a collective whoop and brandished their brooms high. "Clean sweep!" they chanted. "Clean sweep!"

"Ducks," said Mr. Worthington, who had left the fire to stand beside me. "They waddle like so many giant ducks." I could not deny it, for the beaked caps made them seem so. But their striped and flowered dresses brightened the street.

Mr. Worthington sent our young soldier to halt them the proper distance from the polling booth. This was proper, even though Essie thought it was a shame.

"We will do the same for Mr. Harrison's supporters, my dear. You will be glad of it later. When two parties strike up chants in opposition, you would think the world was coming to an end. We keep them back that we might hear each other speak."

Now, to the amazement of both Mr. Worthington and myself, came an entire regiment of veterans, all known to us. Two of those who had survived the War without injury carried Mr. Thomas, who had lost both his legs to a cannonball. Mr. Worthington and I readied ourselves to receive ballots but, to our further amazement, the regiment, on Captain Haricut's order, wheeled and formed an honor guard along the street. The guard led directly to our window.

Next came a contingent of Red Indians, led by Sitting Bull. They, too, did not come to the window to cast their ballots. Like the veterans, they lined the street on either side. Then a contingent of Negroes did the very same.

Essie smiled and pointed to their leader, a tall distinguished gentleman. "That is Samuel Lowry," she said. "He is an ex-slave. It was Mrs. Lockwood who introduced him to legal practice before the Supreme Court."

The crowds broke into a sudden wild cheer. The veterans all raised their swords in salute. And through the lines of this most peculiar of honor guards came the strangest sight my eyes have ever seen.

At the head of the line was Mrs. Lockwood in her tricycle. I had seen her often enough, pedaling about the town. Unlike many, I do not find it scandalous, for she took great care to prepare a dashboard that her skirts do not fly up and shame her. It strikes some odd that a president should not use a carriage, but I admired her economy. Since the tax, I prefer a president to some economy.

Today, however, she did not pedal at her usual brisk pace. She moved no faster than a man might walk and she smiled and waved now and then to those who lined her way. Then we saw why she had set such a pace. For, behind her, all in Sunday best, walked hundreds of women. Their arms were linked, they were all smiling, their ribbons and laces aflutter. They were of all ages and, strange to say, they were of all races as well: white,

Negro, Red Indian, even a few Chinee. Odd to say, I did not find the sight either shocking or scandalous. It seemed as if fitting—as no two women wore the same dress, no two wore the same skin. The sun chose that moment to appear, however wanly, and all of the colors blazed.

Even Mr. Harrison's supporters, who had now arrived in some number, paused and stood respectfully back, as the President braked to a stop a few yards from where we stood.

Mr. Love, her vice president, offered his arm and assisted her from her vehicle. Captain Haricut led his men in a second salute. Yet another cheer came from the crowd. Even a number of the men in support of Mr. Harrison joined in, giving their duly elected President proper respect.

Mr. Love escorted Mrs. Lockwood across the street. They walked briskly toward us. Mrs. Lockwood looked no different than she had when she tried my case before the Court. She is a grandmother. Her hair is gray but her high forehead lends her a handsomeness that many younger women lack. Perhaps it is her force of character that so ornaments her bearing.

I could not help but glance at Essie. She seemed to be holding her breath, but her eyes were bright and sparkling. She smiled at Mrs. Lockwood, who smiled in return. Essie, too, had that handsomeness of character.

A hand came through the window to proffer me a ballot. I reached to take it and was shaken when Mr. Worthington grasped me sharply by the wrist. "She is a *woman*," Mr. Worthington said. "I will take *your* ballot, Mr. Love."

Mr. Love is a very quiet man. He made no fuss, nor did he raise his voice. He merely took two steps back and indicated the women. "Ladies first," said he.

Mr. Worthington snorted. He drew himself up and stared at Mrs. Lockwood, as if by force of glance he might will Mrs. Lockwood away. He should have known better. She met his eyes easily and once again offered her ballot.

"You are a woman," said Mr. Worthington, yet again.

"To that I plead guilty," said Mrs. Lockwood.

Rubbing his stub for the pain, Mr. Worthington leaned through the window and addressed the crowd. "Any man who wishes to cast his ballot may do so now," he said. "Captain Haricut? Will you vote, sir?"

"Ladies first," said Captain Haricut—and all along the street took up the cry. "Ladies first!" they shouted. "Ladies first!"

The Harrison supporters pressed forward in an attempt to reach the window, but the women massed together and would not be moved. There was a brief skirmish toward the edge of the crowd, and I feared a riot.

I feared not for myself but for Essie and for the brightly dressed women. Captain Haricut gave an abrupt order, however, and the men formed protectively. It was only then that I realized that many of the women in the crowd were wives or widows of veterans. Even old Mrs. Terrint was among them. Her sons had been in our regiment. All five had died.

Mrs. Lockwood had turned away from me, toward Captain Haricut. "Captain," she called, and hers was the voice of command, "there will be no fighting. We are here peaceably. We shall vote peaceably." The captain acknowledged with a flash of his sword.

Mrs. Lockwood returned her gaze, this time to me. "We shall vote peaceably," she repeated. "But we *shall* vote."

"Father," said Essie, "she is the President. Will you not accept a ballot from the President?"

I turned to Mr. Worthington. "Will you call out the army to disperse these women?" I asked him. "She is their Commander in Chief."

The notion embarrassed Mr. Worthington. So I pursued it. "If the notion embarrasses you, will it not embarrass the entire country?"

He thought it over for a long time, time enough for me to hear my words whispered back to the very furthest reaches of the waiting crowd. "The *President*," he said, at last, "should be permitted to vote." He held out his hand.

Women craned to watch. Two of the soldiers on horseback leaned forward just as eagerly.

Mrs. Lockwood laid her ballot in Mr. Worthington's hand. Mr. Worthington put the ballot in the lockbox. One of the soldiers on horseback cried out, "Mrs. Lockwood has cast her ballot!" and a great cheer went up.

Mr. Worthington held out his hand for Mr. Love's ballot. I believe Mr. Worthington thought that to be the end of it. But Mrs. Lockwood had moved only to the side of the window, not away from it. I did not need to see her eyes to know her determination; I saw that very determination reflected in the eyes of my Essie.

Mr. Love once more crooked his arm. This time he received for escort the Honorable Mrs. Lavinia Dundore, Justice of the Supreme Court. Like Mrs. Lockwood before her, she held out her folded bit of paper. I took it from her hand.

Mr. Worthington hissed at me, but I did not hesitate to place the ballot into the lockbox. The same soldier on horseback cried out, "Mrs. Dundore has cast her ballot!"

As before, a cheer rose from the crowd. "Would you embarrass our country by denying the vote to a Supreme Court justice?" I said to Mr. Worthington.

"That is enough, then," said Mr. Worthington. "There are no more women who are presidents nor are there more women who are Supreme Court justices. Now the men will vote."

But still the men could not approach the window, for the way was obstructed by that multitude of women in their brightly colored garb.

Over their heads, I could see that Captain Haricut was now engaged in conversation with a member of the local police force. The import of this was not lost on Mrs. Lockwood. One of the Cleveland supporters had called for enforcement. Mrs. Lockwood made a gesture and the ladies parted politely to permit the gentleman through.

I believe he was much surprised to discover both Mrs. Lockwood and Mrs. Dundore the leaders of this insurrection. He saluted sharply, but his face was full of bewilderment. "I have been asked to uphold the law," he began.

"Just so," said Mrs. Lockwood. "As Mrs. Dundore and I have sworn to uphold the Constitution."

"The ladies must leave off obstructing the polling place and return to their homes."

"The ladies must vote. I have sworn to uphold the Constitution and I shall do so."

"Mrs. Lockwood . . ."

"The Constitution permits all citizens to vote."

Mr. Worthington could not contain himself. "A citizen in the Constitution is referred to as 'he.' "

Mrs. Lockwood was pleased. "That is my contention, Mr. Worthington. Now—what does the Constitution say of the President of the United States?"

Essie gave a cry of delight. Clapping her hands together, she said, "The President is likewise referred to as 'he'!"

"Yet I am the President, Mr. Worthington. Therefore, 'he' may refer to a woman. Or do you contend some wizardry has made me male?" Mrs. Lockwood smiled again.

The young policeman had been listening carefully to this exchange, although his eyes were clearly fixed on Essie. Seldom have I seen a young man so taken so quickly. When he spoke, it was not to Mrs. Lockwood, but rather to Essie. "Miss?" he said. "What is your name?"

"Miss Essie Twineham."

"Would you be a citizen?"

The young will ask the young in matters of opinion.

Essie did not inquire of me nor did she inquire of Mrs. Lockwood. It was, I believe, her own soul she consulted.

Having consulted, she drew herself up more proudly than I had ever seen her stand before. She gave the young man a radiant smile and said, "I *am* a citizen, sir. The Constitution grants me the right to vote."

I could not deny her pride, nor could I detract from it in any fashion. To the policeman, I said, "Young man, my leg pains me greatly. I would be most obliged if you would step aside, thus permitting the ladies and gentlemen to vote and be on their separate ways." I stretched out my hand to a young black woman in gingham. "Your ballot, please, miss or mistress."

I had seen the turning on of an electric light, yet I had never seen a light the equal of that which lit the young woman's face as she placed her ballot in my palm. When she had seen me place the ballot in the lockbox, she gave a great shout of joy and threw her arms about Mrs. Lockwood.

With a great sigh, Mr. Worthington accepted the next ballot, that of an old Chinee lady. As if a floodgate had opened, the ballots crackled through the window. The Mother Hubbard Brigade once again struck up their song, as the Cleveland supporters strove to outsing and outchant them.

The young policeman stood by, stiffly erect, but every now and then he gave a shy glance in Essie's direction. "I shall stay," he told her, "to keep order."

Essie nodded, smiling. "And to uphold the law," she said.

More wonders were yet to come, for the word had run through the streets of Washington as fast as electricity through a wire.

The next time I stretched out my hand to receive a ballot, I saw yet another face I recognized. "Mrs. Cleveland," I said politely, "and a good day to you."

Mr. Worthington was utterly aghast. I believed he expected Mrs. Lockwood to protest Mrs. Cleveland's ballot. I could see Essie and her young man almost did. But Mrs. Lockwood seemed, if anything, all the prouder with her accomplishment.

Perhaps even Mrs. Cleveland expected some objection from Mrs. Lockwood, for she turned to her and said, "I did not vote for you, Mrs. Lockwood."

"You voted," said Mrs. Lockwood. "I count myself triumphant in that."

Some strengthening understanding passed between the

two in that moment. Then Mrs. Cleveland embraced Mrs. Lockwood. Together the two of them watched as yet more women came to cast their ballots.

"I had hoped," Mrs. Lockwood began, "to see Mrs. Harrison as well."

Mrs. Cleveland shook her head. "I did not expect so much. She is as frightened a woman as her husband is a man. You could not convince them of the safety of the electric lights in their own home."

"I had hoped . . ."

"Mrs. Lockwood," said Mrs. Cleveland with a smile, "you had hoped that all women had your courage and your strength of purpose. They do not, nor do all men." She was silent for a moment. "You have given me strength, though, and for that I thank you."

At last, all had voted. The last two ballots into the lockbox were none other than the young policeman's and Essie's. Essie stirred up the fire as Mr. Worthington and I eased our limbs at last.

When the men came for the lockbox, I had a thought that disturbed me. "Go home, Essie, and take your rest. I shall accompany the gentlemen to watch the counting of the votes."

"But, father, your leg . . ."

I kissed her on the cheek. "I will not mind my leg," I told her. "Mr. Worthington will see you home."

I gathered my crutches and followed the men with the lockbox. Mr. Worthington would see Essie home safely; I would see her vote home safely. I intended that each and every ballot we had collected the day long was duly and properly counted.

Mr. Cleveland was duly elected president that day. But I believe that Mrs. Lockwood won, and so did my Essie.

(For Lee Burwasser and Val Ontell,
Librarians Extraordinaires.)

1896

Three times William Jennings Bryan ran for the presidency, and three times he lost. He came closest in his first campaign, in 1896.

Martha Soukup, author of many superb short stories, offers you the unique perspective of Mary Baird Bryan, who, like so many spouses in similar positions, is torn between her desire for tranquillity in her declining years and her husband's greatness.

Plowshare

by Martha Soukup

From the journal of Mary Baird Bryan, May, 1915:

I have spent the better part of the week turning poor Fairview from a home into a monument. It is a strange thing to think of the halls where our children, Ruth and William and Grace, once ran, as a path for tour guides and visitors curious about Lincoln's favorite son to tread, reading somberly from little pamphlets and pointing things out to each other.

A President's home must sooner or later become a museum, but it makes me feel fossilized to think about it happening so soon. It is only the fossilization of my joints that makes us move permanently to Florida this year. In this unseasonably cold, rainy spring weather those selfish joints argue with my heart about where home should be. Will is right that we should leave, but I shall miss dear Fairview.

Will says he is ready to move on, and I know he believes it, as we have never lied to each other, but there is an atmosphere of melancholy about him.

If any descendant of ours reads this, he or she may doubt my judgment. The President has so many great victories behind him, after all. The youngest presidential nominee to carry the standard of the Democracy; the youngest man elected to the White House, by the largest popular vote (though heart-stoppingly near Major McKinley's!); he pushed free silver through against the best efforts of Wall Street, if at less than the planned 16-to-1 rate (the rising supply of gold was helping to ease money pressures at the same time); he began the railroad reforms; he successfully prosecuted the war against Spanish imperialism in Cuba, and saw those islands, Puerto Rico and Hawaii, established as constitutional nations.

I can remember when a younger and less understanding wife begged him not to take so much on himself, and to sometimes let an unpopular issue go by. A man so much in the public eye can suffer cruel taunts and attacks when he refuses to compromise to the expedient; sometimes I could hardly think that it was worth the issue, even when Will sat in the White House and made decisions that affected the nation. In time he made me understand that he could never be happy if he smothered his beliefs to live simply with past accomplishments. "Politics is compromise," Will says, "and if I am to begin with a compromised stand already, what good will I accomplish? Let me take a more radical stand, so that when the compromise is reached there will still be good left in it." And so after his term of office, after he refused the renomination (a president should serve one term, he said, except in time of national crisis, as during the Civil War), an "elder statesman" in the vigor of his prime, he continued to press for reforms: so that now women have the vote, and shortly, with the help of the women's vote, we can also expect a national Prohibition.

To this day he continues his summer Chautauqua lecture circuits, speaking to appreciative audiences on Christian faith and the politics of the people, and though there have always been critics and political enemies, he may count as many true friends and admirers as any other man I know in public life.

So why, you putative great-grandchildren must ask, does his wife say Mr. Bryan seems thoughtful and subdued, with all those victories, and more, behind him?

Perhaps it is just that: these moral battles, which gave him the strength to speak twelve hours in a day on the campaign trails, are behind him. I trust to God that there will be work ahead, but what? And when?

Deciding what to take to Florida, and what to leave here for the museum, is a difficult task. A few choices are obvious. The painting of Thomas Jefferson, my "Holländische Dame," the small sandalwood bust of Will presented to him by the President of Hawaii, will all come with us, and of course the whole library of books, including the copy of *Resurrection* presented and autographed to my husband by the great Count Tolstoy himself.

Quickly, though, one is brought face to face with the thousands of gifts brought to Will by the enthusiastic delegations that trampled our garden during the '96 campaign, and later presented to him during the White House years and after. I have never had the heart to discard them. There are too many to ascribe sentimental value to them all (there must be three hundred canes alone!), but some I shall want to keep.

But by now, Will will already have on his black alpaca coat, and I must put on my new lace dress for the small reception Will's brother, the mayor, is having for us today.

Mary Baird Bryan listened attentively to her husband's speech on women's suffrage, smiling and nodding slightly each time he caught her eye. It was not the first time she had heard him advance "the mother argument," which had helped bring the Twenty-third Amendment to passage, but it remained one of her favorites of his oratory, and he was in good voice.

"The child is the treasure of the mother," William Jennings Bryan declaimed in his warm baritone, nearly as compelling as the youthful chime whose Cross of Gold speech swept him to the nomination of the Democracy, and then to the White House, but tired, she thought. "She expends on it her nervous force and energy; she endows it with the wealth of her love." He made a protective gesture, as of a mother stroking her child's brow. "Oh, when mothers' dreams come true, what a different world this will be!"

Murmurs of agreement from the audience. It was, after all, a sympathetic group, of Nebraskan Democrats and longtime Bryan friends and supporters, with a smattering of visiting dignitaries. And it was a speech about the past—although the recent past, with the Woman Suffrage amendment just ratified in 1913.

Bryan brought the speech to conclusion by discussing the effect of the women's vote on the fight for Prohibition, and speculating on how their suffrage in Europe would surely bring to an arbitrated end the carnage taking place in their great war. There was enthusiastic applause from the assemblage.

"My dear Mr. President!" said the ambassador from Hawaii, bounding up and shaking hands vigorously. "A fine speech, very inspiring."

"Thank you, Ambassador," said Bryan with a modest smile. Mary signaled him with her eyes and he adjusted his string tie, which had gone crooked. "You are looking well, sir. But where is your lovely wife?"

"Back in our hotel room, I'm sorry to say, not feeling her best," said Ambassador Kauiliho. "Nothing too serious; the rigors of the trip. She says she'll be better when we're settled in Washington. She sends her best to Mrs. Bryan."

"Please thank her for me, and give her my best wishes for her health. It is a long trip. Fortunately, Mr. Bryan and I have always adapted well to travel. I hate to think what we would have missed otherwise!"

"I'm just glad this last part can be taken by rail." The ambassador smiled ruefully. "I make a poor representative of an island nation, I'm afraid. If we had had to make the trip all the way around Cape Horn, I think I would be green for a month after."

"They are bound to finish the Nicaraguan canal someday," Mary said.

"Someday, I'm sure," the ambassador agreed, "but in the meantime, give me a sleeping car and I shall snore my way across this enormous continent, recovering from the rolling of the ocean. Even without the rigors of sea travel, the train trip would be worth it just to hear your excellent speech, Mr. President."

"You're far too kind," said Bryan. "I fear I just rehearse the obvious. In my religious speeches, now, I hope to do a little good."

"I'm sure you do," said the ambassador. "As most of the citizens of Hawaii know you did well for us, when Congress was ready to annex Hawaii."

"That would have aped the imperialism we fought against in Cuba," Bryan said. "You say, *most* of the citizens?"

The ambassador looked a little uncomfortable. "Some

few worry about Japan," he said. "With what happened in the Philippines, you know. They think it would be safer to be part of the United States, with war fever all around."

"I'm sure you can count on the United States to aid your defense, if necessary," said Bryan. "Though it's a Republican administration, so of course I can't really speak for them!" They chuckled, and the ambassador moved aside for the next well-wisher. Mary, having seen the trace of a frown twitch her husband's wide mouth at the mention of war, took his arm and squeezed it, and he smiled down at her.

"You did do well, you know," she said quietly to him.

"With God's help," he answered. "Ah, Charlie, there you are."

"Mr. President," his brother said, with a formal bow.

"Mr. Mayor." Bryan returned the bow. "How good of you to put aside differences for the sake of the party!"

Charlie grinned and clasped his hand. "A mayor just about has to let a former president into his home, even if that president did tease him mercilessly some—oh—forty years ago." Mary smiled.

"I'm certain I just gave you instruction for your betterment."

"It makes a good theory. You could do a speech on it. Anyway, it's the most interest there's been in town since Theodore Roosevelt passed through last month, you and your hero's sendoff."

"I wish Mr. Roosevelt would stick to domestic issues," said Bryan, shaking his head. "He isn't too bad on those, for a Republican."

"I've even heard him agree with you once or twice," Mary said.

"The situation in Europe, though, calls for mediation, not the addition of American arms, which Mr. Roosevelt fails to understand. He has the ear of the administration, as well as the attention of the reading public, and may do real damage."

Mary sighed. "I think he has an overly romantic view of battle, since his regiment didn't have the chance to join in the Spanish-American War. You've read his novel, *The Big Stick*, haven't you, Charlie? About the war hero who becomes president?"

"It was an interesting frame for his political arguments," said Charlie, "but I think less successful than his more straightforward essays and memoirs. And as you say, terribly romanticized. Do you think that if he had seen the actual battlefield he would take a less rosy view of war?"

"I am certain of it," said Mary.

"Well, he has achieved more success writing about battlefields than most men do fighting on them," said Charlie. "People were talking about him for the White House next term."

"I wouldn't say his chances were good," said Bryan, warming to a debate about the next campaign.

Before he could take another breath, an effusive woman came up to thank Bryan for his "brilliant!" lecture on the Prince of Peace the past Sunday, and the talk turned away from politics.

Mary sat reading aloud in the late afternoon sun as her husband chopped away at a tree behind Fairview. She didn't feel it incumbent on her to point out that the administrators of the museum could remove the tree if they thought it was in the way, or that the new home in Florida would doubtless have many trees to chop. Or that the poor tree had never bothered him before. He needed some physical work to make him feel useful. She would have asked him to help her sort out mementos, but that did not seem a wise choice. Will was not sleeping well. She knew it was the business of packing up his old life.

Better, almost, she thought, that he had had to run twice, or three times, before achieving office. Even back in college, debating, he had always shone on the negative side. He came most to life when he had ills to fight against, but now he was adrift between battles. It was selfish of her to wish the battles had lasted longer—though still won, of course!—but if a woman could not be selfish for her husband, then for whom?

God gives no burdens that cannot be borne, she reminded herself.

She stopped reading and looked across the lawn. "My goodness, look who's here."

Bryan looked up, face creasing into a grin, put down his ax and went to hug their daughter Ruth and the two grandchildren. "You didn't tell us you were coming," he scolded.

"I had a chance for some speaking engagements," Ruth said, "and I thought while I was traveling I'd see if you and Mamma needed some help with the packing."

"Come inside and have some lemonade. Would you like some lemonade, Ruth?" Mary asked the younger Ruth, a tall girl of ten, who hugged her grandmother in answer.

"I'll finish chopping this up," Bryan said. "You'll help, won't you, John?" he asked the nine-year-old, as the women of the family started for the house.

"Pappa is looking well," Ruth said, slicing lemons.

"I expect he is, now that's he's seen you. Tell me about your lectures."

Ruth explained she was on a limited tour speaking for the Women's Peace Party, an anti-war organization founded by Jane Addams, Bryan's college debating colleague and a mentor of Ruth's from when she worked at Hull House as a young woman. "You should think about speaking, too, Mamma," she said. "You'd be good at it." She handed the lemons to her daughter, who started squeezing them out with some energy.

"Now, you know you get all that talent from your father's side," Mary said. "Do you think there is a danger we'll enter the war?"

"People talk about it," said Ruth. "There are people who want to enter the war on either side. If a big enough reason could be found by one side or the other, I think it very likely the public could be convinced."

"One hears terrible things from both sides," Mary said. "I can hardly bear to read the papers, ever since the Kaiser ordered his Zeppelin airships to drop bombs on Antwerp last year. On innocent people, sleeping in their beds. War is even worse a sin than it used to be. And yet, we've met the German ambassador, Count Bernstorff, and he was a very pleasant and civilized man. I'm sure his country and her enemies can be reasoned with, if we are firm and intelligent. Now, where is your father?" She raised the kitchen curtain and laughed. "It looks like he and John are at work on another tree. We'll be waiting for them a while."

After they finished their lemonade and had set the rest aside for the tree-choppers, Mary allowed Ruth to talk her into being helped with the packing. The younger Ruth she sent to the library, telling her to pick out which books she might like for herself. That would probably take her the rest of the day, since she would want to read them all to find out.

"Good heavens, Mamma, you still have this stuffed eagle?"

"I never knew what to do with it!" Mary said, laughing. "The four live ones, at least, we could send to zoos. This poor bedraggled bird won't come to Florida with us, I think. The museum administrators can either figure out where to hang it, or I suppose the University Museum might want it."

Ruth was going through some old papers. "They'll want this for the Bryan Museum," she said, holding up the McKinley telegram. Mary knew it by heart: *I have been informed that the election is to be yours. I beg you to receive my congratulations and best wishes.* And Will's return: *I have received your courteous message. The American people know you have served them well in the past and, as God wills, shall do so again.* "I have always thought Major Mc-Kinley was an honorable man, congratulating Pappa the way he did. That was so unusual, and civil." Under the telegram Ruth found a leaflet illustrating Bryan in fool's motley, waving a sword labeled WILD-EYED FINANCE over an unhappy worker's neck, shielded only with a silver coin. *A Mighty Risky Experiment*, read the caption. "I'm not so sure about that Mr. Hanna of his, though."

"Don't speak ill of the dead, Ruth."

"I won't, if you insist. But at least it put a stop to these dreadful leaflets for a while when the Republicans lost him."

"We plan to take all the papers with us, for now," Mary said. "There will be time enough later for the museum to have them. Your father and I have papers in us yet!"

Ruth put the telegram and leaflets back into their box. "Oh, look at this old plowshare!" she said. "Why wasn't it sold with the farm?"

"That's not an ordinary plowshare," Mary said. "It was presented to your father after the Spanish-American War, by a Philippine citizen who was grateful we did not do what so many in Congress called for, and make them a territory. It was made of swords, you see, melted down and recast."

"Very literal," Ruth remarked.

The doorbell chimed. Mary put down the cane made of macerated newspaper editorials (it was such a strange item, she would have to take it with them), stood, dusted her hands on her apron, and went to see who it was.

It was Charlie Bryan. "The Germans," he said. "They've sunk a British ship. With Americans aboard. The *Lusitania*."

"Oh dear," Ruth said. "I must telegram Chicago. This will change my speaking tour."

Back of the house, the tall Bryan and his grandson were silhouetted in the setting sun, working at the tree stumps with their axes. Mary handed Charlie the lemonade and went back to tell them.

From the journal of Mary Baird Bryan, May, 1915:

It seems half of Lincoln would volunteer to fight the Germans today, with the news of the *Lusitania*. The papers drum it up, and quote a great deal from a recent speech of Mr. Roosevelt's, particularly liking his "big stick" talk. There are editorial cartoons showing American boys in uniform crushing the Kaiser with clubs, which seems a brutal enthusiasm for a newspaper to arouse.

It is like 1898 all over again, when the bloodthirsty in the country looked for a new war to win. A less brave man than my husband could not have led the people back to their natural love of peace. But it seems that thirst for victory on the battlefield was only suppressed for a while. The papers are full of ill talk about "the ill-advised 'anti-imperialism' first promoted by the Bryan administration," even suggesting that the war in Europe might not have happened if the United States had taken a stronger position in the world after 1898—by use of warship and cannon, of course. The opposing voices are drowned in drum-beating.

I do not know what the Republican administration will do. It seems only the pro-German Secretary of State is staying the President's hand, and there are calls for his resignation. Some are suggesting the ever-present Mr. Roosevelt as his replacement. I do not want to see a Big Stick in the White House now, when it so important we stay neutral and continue to support an arbitrated peace.

Ruth and the children have returned to Chicago, and Will is not sleeping at all. When I told him of the *Lusitania*, he said, "I wonder if that ship carried munitions of war? I must investigate to see if England has been using our citizens to protect its cargo!" Word is not so swift from our friends in Washington. There has been no warning from the administration not to sail on British ships that might secretly carry contraband known to the Germans, but that does not prove anything, Will says.

There have been meetings of Will's discussion group, Fortnightly, and that of us women, Sorosis. Even some of those good Democrats, even one or two of the bright-minded women of Sorosis, wave war banners, though unhappily. Americans are dead, and it is hard to look past that tragedy. Will was disheartened not to convince all of them to wait for more news, whether our citizens were used by the British as a shield for munitions. He has spoken both to the newspapers and briefly in public, and has taken some abuse for it, though there have been telegrams of support for his call for America to be peacemaker, not warmaker.

I think we will put off the move to Florida a little while. I am not putting any more Chautauqua engagements on his calendar until we see how things go.

The only silver lining to this uncertainty is that it gives me more time to pack.

Mary shut and locked the door to the suite that had been her parents', satisfied that everything within was finally in order to leave. Walking slowly, because her knees pained her, she went to the back porch. Her husband sat there beside the Philippine plowshare, running his hand thoughtfully down its blade. She sat beside him and took his other hand.

"That gift shows how the Philippines loved you for their independence," she said.

"They may not love me now," Bryan said. "Japan took them after all."

"That does not mean you did the wrong thing," Mary said firmly. "You could not read the future. If the Philippines had had a little more time to consolidate their government, it might not have happened."

"The newspapers practice reading the future. They say

if the United States does not stand against the Kaiser, there will be no stopping the war. The country is full of Big-Stickers. Do I know more than they do?"

"God does."

"I know He does, and I know He knows what must be done, but He has not told me," Bryan said. "This White House is indecisive, but that will probably not last. After next year I expect the nation to be led by someone else. Possibly Roosevelt. He is in his glory. He is campaigning already, I think."

"Who does the Democracy have who will stand against war?"

"Not many who care to speak up now," sighed her husband. "Not many to stand against the Big Stick."

"If there is a solution, God will show it," Mary said. She took her husband's second hand and they sat together, heads bowed, praying.

From the journal of Mary Baird Bryan, June, 1915:

Will has his energy back. There may be hard months ahead, but his eye is bright and his voice strong. Telegrams are pouring in; it is a trial to keep them in some sort of order as we prepare to take the train to Florida, especially as Will tends to stuff the ones he means to answer next in his Gladstone bag, using his foot, if necessary!

The Philippine plowshare, melted down, has made more than a hundred little miniature plowshare paperweights, all of which Will handed out to supporters within a day or two. I have located a supply of old swords and Civil War bayonets, and placed an order with the foundry to cast them into more paperweights. Will's plowshares are beginning to cause nearly as much talk as Mr. Roosevelt's "big stick." Some of it is ridicule, of course, but even the ridicule gets people to thinking, Will says.

It does not look like Florida will be retirement. I never thought it would, when Will knew what he wanted to do, but I did not expect this redoubled speaking schedule. Only a younger Bryan could outspeak the schedule he has set for himself. He will be on the road while I settle our goods in Florida. The Chautauqua season is about to start.

Many Chautauquas are trying, their organizers wire us, to book Mr. Roosevelt, and have the pair debate in their tents. While I do not believe Mr. Roosevelt has ever spoken at a Chautauqua lecture meeting, there is much interest among the public. It would be interesting to hear. Ruth and young William are speaking, too, and have written asking for their share of paperweights to distribute.

Will tells the papers he is not running for President again, and I know he would be content to encourage another plowshare Democrat to take the office. I would be content not to have to organize another Oval Office! But I remember how last time the office sought the man before the man sought the office.

The papers call Will a wild-eyed radical, but they have called him that before. Whatever happens now, we leave in God's hands. It may be hard, but He has armed his servant with a plowshare. Can that be a heavier burden than the cross of gold?

1912

Theodore Roosevelt was almost too many men to fit in a single body: writer, naturalist, outdoorsman, politician, explorer, president. He left the presidency in 1908, but, dissatisfied with the way his hand-picked successor, William Howard Taft, was running the country, ran again in 1912 as the candidate of the Bull Moose Party. He was shot in the chest during the campaign, and by the time he had recovered, victory had slipped away from him.

But what if the bullet had missed him? I thought I would examine what Roosevelt's second presidency might have accomplished, and where the visionary man from Sagamore Hill might have failed.

The Bull Moose at Bay

by Mike Resnick

I don't care what may be his politics, I don't care what may be his religion, I don't care what may be his color. I don't care who he is. So long as he is honest, he shall be served by me.

—Theodore Roosevelt
Speech at Cooper Union Hall,
New York, N.Y., October 15, 1886

Personally I feel that it is exactly as much a "right" of women as of men to vote. I always favored woman's suffrage, but only tepidly, until my association with women like Jane Addams and Frances Kellor changed me into a zealous instead of a lukewarm adherent to the cause.

—Theodore Roosevelt
Autobiography (1913)

The date was October 27, 1916.

It was a birthday party, but it resembled a wake.

The President had invited only his family and a few close friends to his retreat at Sagamore Hill on this, his fifty-eighth birthday. He walked from room to room in the huge old mansion, greeting them, trying to joke with them, but unable to keep a dark scowl from periodically crossing his face. Even Alice, his oldest daughter, who had distracted her share of cabinet meetings and press conferences, seemed unable to distract him tonight.

"Well?" demanded the President at last.

"Well, what, Theodore?" asked his wife.

"Why is everyone tiptoeing around me?" he demanded. "I'm not dead yet. There are worse things than taking an enforced vacation." He paused. "Maybe I'll go back to Africa again, or explore that river the Brazilian government has been asking me to map for them."

"What are you talking about, Mr. President?" said Elihu Root. "You're going to spend the next four years in the White House."

"This isn't a political rally, Elihu," answered Roosevelt. "It's a quiet party, and you're among friends." He sighed deeply. "You've seen the papers, you've heard what the pundits say: I'll be lucky to win six states."

"I believe in you, Mr. President," insisted Root.

"You're my Secretary of War," said Roosevelt, managing one of his famous grins. "You're *supposed* to believe in me." The grin vanished, to be replaced by a frown. "I wish I could say the same of the Republican Party."

"They're still angry at you for running and winning as a Bull Moose four years ago," said Edith, standing in front of her husband and stroking his hair lovingly. "Some of them probably wish that fanatic who tried to shoot you in Milwaukee had been a better shot. But when they're faced with a choice between you and Mr. Wilson, they'll do what's right."

Roosevelt shook his head. "If I can't win the Congress to my cause, how can I expect to win the people?" He strode restlessly across the parlor. "The choice isn't between me and Mr. Wilson; if it was that simple, I'd have no fear of the outcome. It's a choice between their principles and their prejudices, and given the splendid example of the Congress"—he spat out the word—"it would appear that their prejudices are going to win, hands down."

"I just can't believe it," said Gifford Pinchot.

"Gifford, you're a good man and a loyal man," said Roosevelt, "and I thank you for the sentiment." He paused. "But you're my Director of National Parks, and trees don't vote. What do you know about it?"

"I know that you came into office as the most popular American since Abraham Lincoln—probably since Jefferson, in fact—and that you managed to win the war with Germany in less than a year. We've become a true world power, the economy's never been stronger, and there aren't any more trusts left to bust. How in God's name can they vote you out of office? I simply refuse to believe the polls."

"Believe them, Gifford," said Roosevelt. "You've got less than three months to find employment elsewhere."

"I've spoken to Hughes, and he thinks you're going to win," persisted Pinchot.

"Charlie Hughes is my running mate. It's in his best interest to believe we're going to win." Roosevelt paused. "That's one thing I'm especially sorry about. Charlie is a good man, and he would have made an excellent president in 1920. A lot better than that fat fool from Ohio," he added, grimacing at the thought of William Howard Taft, who had succeeded him the first time he had left office.

"Speaking of Charlie," said Root, surveying the room, "I don't see him here tonight."

"This is a birthday party, for my friends and my family," answered Roosevelt. "I'm sick of politicians."

"*I'm* a politician, Theodore," said Root.

"And if that's all you were, you wouldn't be here," answered the President.

"What about *him*?" asked Root, nodding toward a tall, well-dressed young man who seemed uncomfortable in his surroundings, and viewed the world through an elegant *pince-nez*.

Roosevelt sighed. "He's family."

"He's also a Democrat."

"At least he's still speaking to me," said Roosevelt. "That's more than I can say for a lot of Republicans."

"He's too busy looking down his nose to speak to anyone," commented Pinchot.

"He's young," answered Roosevelt. "He'll learn. And he's got a good wife to teach him."

A tall, grizzled man clad in buckskins entered the room. Everyone stared at him for a moment, then went back to their drinks and conversations, and he walked across the parlor to where the President was standing.

" 'Evening, Teddy," said Frank McCoy.

"Good evening, Frank," said Roosevelt. "I'm glad you could come."

"Brought some of the stuff you asked me to hunt up," said McCoy.

"Oh?"

McCoy nodded, and pulled a wrinkled folder out of his rumpled jacket. "Two hundred thousand acres adjoining the Yellowstone, a couple of lakes, nice little river flowing through it, even got some buf and grizzly left, and yours for the asking."

"You don't say?" replied Roosevelt, his eyes alight with interest.

"And I found another one, out by Medora in the Dakota badlands, right near where you used to own a ranch."

"Medora," repeated Roosevelt, a wistful smile crossing his face. "It's been a long time since I've thought of Medora." He paused. "Stick around when the party is over, Frank. I'd like to go over these brochures with you."

"I won't hear of it!" snapped Pinchot. "You're going to be the President of the United States for four more years!"

"So who says the President can't own a ranch out near the Yellowstone?" asked McCoy.

"You should be out campaigning for him, not finding retirement homes," continued Pinchot angrily.

"Gifford, I've always been a realist," said Roosevelt. "I'm going to lose. It's time to start planning the next phase of my life."

"I won't hear of it!" said Pinchot.

"I admire your loyalty, but I question your grasp of politics," said Roosevelt gently. "The people will speak one week from today, and neither you nor I are going to like what they have to say—but we're going to have to abide by it, and I'm going to have to find something to do with myself."

"But you're *right*!" said Pinchot. "Can't they see it?"

"Evidently not," answered Roosevelt.

"If it wasn't for that bastard Morgan . . ." began Root.

"It isn't J. P. Morgan's fault," said Roosevelt. "He's opposed me for years, and I've always beaten him. No, you can lay the blame for this at the doorstep of the Republican Party. They're still bitter that I ran as a Bull Moose and beat Bill Taft—but they're slitting their own throats to have their revenge on me, and I can't seem to make them understand it." He sighed again. "Or maybe it's my own fault."

"You're not backing off what you've been fighting for, are you, Teddy?" asked McCoy, arching a bushy eyebrow.

"No, of course not," answered Roosevelt. "But obviously I didn't get my message across to the people who count—to the voters."

"How could you?" asked Root, taking a drink from a liveried servant as he passed through the room with a large tray. "The Republicans own three-quarters of the newspapers, and the rest think that God speaks directly to Woodrow Wilson."

"I should have realized that it was in their best interest to oppose me and gone out on the stump and spoken to the people directly. I've done it often enough before." The President shook his head. "What I can't understand is why the Democrats didn't grab this issue and wave it like a flag once the Republicans wouldn't have anything to do with it."

Root snorted contemptuously. "Because they're Democrats."

"And maybe they were afraid if they took *it*, they'd have to take *you*, too," added McCoy with an amused grin.

"It could turn their party around," said Roosevelt seriously. He looked across the room at the tall, well-dressed young man who was carefully inserting a cigarette into its holder. "Look at my cousin," he said, lowering his voice. "An effete blue-blooded snob, who dabbles in politics the way some men dabble in stamps and coins. Yet if he came down on the right side of this single issue, he could be in the White House fifteen or twenty years from now."

"God forbid!" laughed Pinchot in mock horror.

"Mark my words," said Roosevelt. "This is an issue that isn't going to go away. You and I may wind up in history's ashcan, but not what we fought for. It's as inevitable as the stars in their courses, and I can't seem to make a single Republican senator or congressman see it!"

An almost animal growl of anger came forth from the President's lips, and Edith immediately approached him, bringing him a soft drink, straightening his tie, smoothing his hair.

"You must try to control yourself, my dear," she said soothingly.

"What for?" demanded Roosevelt. "I thought I was supposed to be among friends tonight, not politicians. If a man can't express disgust for the Congress to his friends, then who *can* he express it to?"

"Please, Theodore," said Edith. "You don't want to make a scene."

"Why not?" he said irritably. "A president has the right to make a scene if he wants to."

Edith shrugged. "He's all yours, gentlemen," she said to Root, McCoy and Pinchot. "I can't do a thing with him when he's like this."

She walked off to supervise the butler and servants.

"What is everyone staring at?" demanded Roosevelt, for all talk had stopped when Edith had approached him. "Isn't a beaten candidate allowed his tantrums?"

"You're not beaten yet, Father," said Alice.

Roosevelt shook his head impatiently. "Of course I am," he said, addressing the room at large. "But that's not the issue. *I'm* not important. I've put in eleven years at this job. It's time I moved on to other things: I've still got books to write and distant lands to see. The important thing is what's going to happen to the country." The President's voice rose in anger. "You can't simply disenfranchise sixty percent of it and expect things to run as they've always run."

"My cousin, the Samaritan," muttered the tall man with the *pince-nez* and the cigarette holder, and a number of people around him chuckled in amusement.

"Laugh all you want!" thundered Roosevelt. "That's what the Congress did, too. You want to vote me out of office? Go ahead, that's your right—*if* you happen to be a male of the Caucasian race." He glared at them. "Doesn't it bother you that more than half the people in this room *can't* vote me out of office no matter how much they disagree with me?"

"It bothers *me*, Cousin Theodore," said a plain-looking woman, who had been standing unobtrusively in a corner, reading some of the framed letters from other heads of state that were displayed on the wall.

"Well, it ought to bother *all* of you," said Roosevelt. "How can we build a country based on the principle that all men are created equal, and then refuse to give women the vote? We freed the slaves more than half a century ago—and we've erected so many barriers that more Negroes voted *before* the Civil War than vote now!" He paused. "How can I be President of all the people when six out of every ten of them can't vote for me or against me?"

"I believe we've heard this song before," said one of the guests, a one-time hunting companion from the Rockies.

"Well, *I* don't believe you've heard a word of it!" snapped Roosevelt. "What makes someone an American, anyway?"

"I don't think I understand you," said the hunter.

"You heard me—what makes you an American?"

"I . . . ah . . ."

"You were born here and you're breathing!" said Roosevelt. "Does anyone know of any other qualification?" He glared pugnaciously around the room. "All right, now. What do you think makes you better than any other American?"

"I consider that an insulting question, Mr. President."

"You'd consider it a lot more insulting if you were a woman, or a Negro, or an immigrant who received his citizenship papers but can't pass a literacy test at the polls—a test that nine out of ten college graduates couldn't pass!"

Roosevelt paused for breath. "Don't any of you understand? We're not living in a Utopia here. We haven't reached a plateau of excellence from which we will never budge. America is a living, growing experiment in democracy, and sooner or later, whether you like it or not, women *are* going to get the vote, and Negroes are *not* going to be harassed at the polls, and immigrants are going to be *welcomed* into a political party."

"If it's inevitable, why are you so worked up about it?" asked a distant relative. "Why did you let it cost you the presidency?"

"He hasn't lost anything!" snarled a younger man. "Those are fighting words! Step outside and—"

"He's right," interrupted Roosevelt. "It did cost me the election."

"But Mr. President—"

"That's a fact," continued Roosevelt. "And facts can be many things, pleasant and unpleasant, but the one thing they always are is true."

"Then I repeat—why did you let it cost you the presidency?"

"Because I believe in the principles of the Republican Party," answered Roosevelt.

"The Republicans voted almost ten-to-one against your proposals, and it took you six ballots to win the nomination once you decided to merge your Bull Moose party with them," continued the man. "What makes you think this has anything to do with the Republican Party?"

"Please!" said Edith, coming back into the parlor. "We didn't invite you here to fight. This is supposed to be a birthday party."

"It's all right, Edith," said Roosevelt. "It's a fair question; it deserves an answer." He turned to his questioner. "I believe in the Republican Party," he said, "and I tell you that the party will rise or fall on this single issue. It's as simple as that."

"How can you say such a thing?" demanded the man incredulously.

"How can you not see it?" retorted Roosevelt. "How can *they* not see it, those fools in the Congress? It's only a matter of a few years, a decade at most, before women get the vote, before we stop harassing our minorities at the polls. Can't anyone else see that the party that fights most vigorously for their rights will count them among their numbers? Can't anyone else understand that an influx of voters greater than the number that already exists will totally change the balance of political power in this country?" He paused, and his chin jutted out pugnaciously. "No matter what you think, I haven't been waging this war for myself—though I pity the man who has to tell my Alice that she can't vote for her father on Election Day. I'm waging it because it's the right thing to do, whether I win or lose—and because if the Republicans don't realize what the future holds, then sooner or later the Democrats will, and we will permanently become the nation's minority party."

"Calm yourself, Theodore," said Root, laying a hand on his shoulder. "We can't have the President dying of a stroke a week before the election."

Roosevelt jumped at the touch of Root's hand, then blinked his eyes rapidly, as if suddenly realizing his surroundings. "I'm sorry, Elihu," he said. "The election is all but over, and here I am, still campaigning."

"It's an issue worth campaigning for," said the plain-looking woman.

"The problem is that nobody who agrees with me is allowed to vote for me," said Roosevelt with a wry smile.

"That's not so, Theodore," said Pinchot. "I agree with you."

"And I," added Root.

"Me, too, Teddy," said McCoy. "You know that."

"That's probably why none of you holds elected office," remarked the President with dry irony.

The party continued for another three hours, as still more relatives and old friends stopped by to pay their respects, and to see Roosevelt one last time while he was still the President of the United States. Politicians and Rough Riders, New York dandies and Indian chiefs, men of letters and men of action, black men and white, women of all political stripes, mingled and rubbed shoulders in the Sagamore Hill mansion, for the President had made many friends in his fifty-eight years. Even F. C. Selous had taken time off from a safari to cross the Atlantic and celebrate his most famous client's birthday. Roosevelt, for his part, was soon so busy greeting guests that there were no more outbursts.

At ten o'clock Edith had the servants bring out a case of champagne, which everyone except the President imbibed. Then came the cake, and a chorus of "For He's a Jolly Good Fellow," and then, one by one, the guests began departing.

By midnight only a handful of people remained: Root, McCoy, Selous, two grizzled old Rough Riders, and the plain-looking woman.

"I see your husband's left without you again," noted Roosevelt.

"He had business to conduct," replied the woman. "Politicians are just the opposite of flowers: they don't bloom until the sun goes down."

Roosevelt chuckled. "You always did have a fine wit."

"Thank you."

"I'll never know what perverse whim caused you to marry a Democrat," he continued, "but I suppose he's no worse than most and probably better than some. Grow him out and I imagine he'll turn out all right."

"I plan to, Cousin Theodore." She paused. "By the way, I fully agree with what you said before. The party that reaches out to the disenfranchised will dominate the next half-century of American politics."

"I'm glad *someone* was listening," said Roosevelt.

"Listening and taking notes." She smiled. "Well, mental notes, anyway."

"How about your husband?" said Roosevelt. "I've never asked before—but what's *his* position on enfranchisement?"

"The same as yours."

"Really?" said Roosevelt, suddenly interested. "I didn't know that."

"He doesn't know it, either," answered the plain-looking woman, "but he will when I get through speaking to him."

Roosevelt grinned. "You're a remarkable woman, Cousin Eleanor."

She smiled back at him. "Why, thank you, Cousin Theodore."

"Play your cards right and you may be the second First Lady named Roosevelt."

"I plan to," she assured him.

1920

Everyone knows that Franklin Delano Roosevelt was elected to the presidency in 1932, and proceeded to win an unprecedented four terms. But how many of you know that Roosevelt was the defeated vice presidential candidate in 1920?

Jack Nimersheim, author of numerous nonfiction books and articles, knows—and in this, his first science fiction story, he postulates a victorious 1920 Democratic ticket and a secret meeting with a very ambitious German politician.

A Fireside Chat

by Jack Nimersheim

A chill permeated the room. Its only source of heat was a single fireplace set against the north wall. Within this brick proscenium flames danced wildly, performing daring pirouettes and *grands jetés* above the makeshift stage of a cast-iron grate. But the warmth generated by the four logs orchestrating that fiery ballet withered long before it reached a small alcove on the opposite side of the room. There, a tall man sat in a straight-backed chair, staring out the window, his hands folded delicately across his lap. A thin shawl was draped with equal delicacy across the man's broad, powerful shoulders, shoulders slumped only slightly forward. The long days of arduous travel leading up to this cool September night had fatigued him much more than they should have, much more than they would have just a few years earlier.

Sitting there alone, fireplace ballerinas casting Sleeping Beauty shadows on the walls around him, the man gazed out across the Rhone River at the city's old quarter. What was the rhythm of life, he mused, over there? Was a kindly old lamplighter making his rounds, gently brushing back the evening shadows with the warm kiss of flame to wick? Were men and women passing through the open porticoes of cafés and coffee houses, pausing as they came and went, exchanging warm greetings with friends and neighbors they had known and trusted all their lives? Did horses still canter down the narrow, winding cobblestone streets?

This imaginary journey beyond the opposite bank recalled the distant shores of his own youth—a Hudson Valley childhood nurtured in the elegance and affluence afforded by old money. There were other images as well. The memories of long-ago autumn evenings spent running beside the cool, clear waters of the Hudson. And of the endless hours he'd sit quietly on that river's edge, looking below its slowly rolling surface, confidently plumbing the depths of a young man's hopes, his dreams, his aspirations.

Both he and the world had changed since then.

Over here, north of the Rhone, in that city within a city the natives called St. Gervais but the rest of the world referred to as "new Geneva," businessmen and bureaucrats, deal makers and diplomats, plied their trades. Over here, the evening shadows were shoved aside by the harsh glare of electric lights. Over here, the streets were all straight and wide and evenly spaced, their intersections surveyed to a perfect 90 degrees. Over here, the nearest thing to a neighborhood was a daily crowding together of strangers in the newly built stores, hotels, embassies, and office buildings that clawed their way up from the wide roads. Roads, not streets. Roads cast in solid, unyielding concrete. Roads lined with sidewalks filled with people walking—no, running; no: *scurrying*—to keep their next appointment. The buildings threatened to choke the sky. The strangers worked together every day and did not even know each other's names. And they rarely if ever said hello.

Pulling off his glasses, he closed his eyes and gently massaged the bridge of his nose, rubbing it slowly, up and down, between thumb and forefinger. Would the new world reflected in St. Gervais be able to reclaim the virtues of old Geneva, he wondered? And could it do so in time to survive the challenges that lay ahead?

Leaning forward and reaching down to his legs, the tall man with the powerful shoulders and tired eyes twisted a pair of metal rings, one encircling each knee, until they locked into place with a reassuring *clang*. Pushing himself unsteadily to his feet, he grabbed the two metal crutches leaning against the chair and slowly made his way to the window, three steps that seemed to take an eternity. Pausing briefly, he closed the red velvet drapes, drawing an opaque veil across his memories and the darker thoughts that accompanied them.

It was better this way, he thought: detached, isolated, separated from the serenity of autumn evenings that lay an ocean to the west and a lifetime in the past. Here and now, on this particular September night, he could not afford to let his attentions wander. Rather, he needed to concentrate completely on the difficult and distasteful task that lay ahead.

Such opulence! Crystal chandeliers; solid oak desks, tables and wainscoting; deep, plush leather chairs; equally deep and luxurious carpeting. And gold . . . gold everywhere! Even the bell used to summon the idiots who reigned over this gilded palace was gold. (Or, more correctly, gold-plated—a perfect metaphor for a thin veneer of prosperity.) Nor could he help but note the colors adorning the walls and woodwork. Pastel green with a garish coral trim! No professional painter possessing a liter of common sense would place these hues within ten meters of one another!

It did not surprise the little man with the stern countenance, passing judgment as he passed quickly through the hotel lobby, that his American counterpart had arranged to meet in such conspicuous surroundings. After all, the Atlantic Ocean had effectively insulated that country from the full horror of the recently ended World War, a misnomer if ever there was one. For while this land, *his* land, still bore the ugly scars etched into its hillsides by four years of bitter conflict, a large part of the world, including the so-called United States, had emerged from that conflict virtually unblemished. Consequently, Americans visiting Europe expected to encounter the quaint beauty and old-world ambience historically associated with life on "the Continent." Lamentably, there was no shortage of individuals and institutions (most of them Jews or under Jewish control, no doubt) willing to cater to these fantasies.

He bitterly remembered how the rebuilding began almost on the day the killing stopped. But this renaissance was not directed toward to a renewal of European resolve and spirit, as would have been the case in a logical world. Rather, it represented a vain attempt to gloss over the physical damage inflicted upon the so-called "cultural" centers of Europe—in truth, the breeding grounds of commerce and capitalism. All the recent reconstruction amounted to nothing more than an economic face-lift, cosmetic surgery on a continental scale, designed primarily to keep a steady stream of foreign currency pouring into numbered accounts and national treasuries. But was this not to be expected? Did it not reflect the Jewish credo? Was wealth not the ultimate god of the Hebrew heathens into whose pool of resources this blood money eventually flowed?

A quick slap of his palm on the gold-plated bell sitting atop a solid oak desk produced a sharp, solitary, resonant *ding.* The concierge, a dark-haired man with a prominent nose and probing eyes, turned and smiled.

"Yes, sir. How may I help you?"

Another *verdammt* Jew, the small man thought. Probably thinks accommodating me will line his pockets with an extra mark or two. How sweetly they all smile when the scent of money is in the air.

"Please inform President Roosevelt that Reichschancellor Hitler has arrived," was all he said.

Though numerous lower-level meetings had preceded this one, each leader, for his own reasons, had wanted to face his counterpart with no bureaucratic underlings around.

"And how was your trip, Herr Roosevelt? Not too tiring, I trust. Long sea voyages are never enjoyable, and the journey from America to Europe has been known to tax even the strongest of men."

"To the contrary, Chancellor, I found it to be quite pleasant—invigorating, actually." Roosevelt felt no obligation to reveal the extent of his fatigue, especially in light of the subtle implication in Hitler's remark that he was somehow less capable of withstanding the rigors of travel than another man might be. "The accommodations available on today's modern steamships have all but eliminated the discomfort previously associated with a transatlantic crossing."

To a proverbial fly on the wall, this exchange would have seemed like nothing more than two men sitting before a fire, indulging in small talk—the kind of polite but inconsequential discourse people pull out of a closet marked "Courtesy" whenever they have little of real import to discuss. As Roosevelt's minor deception implied, however, the conversation was mere camouflage. Beneath the surface, beyond the words, each man was probing the other. A thrust here to uncover whatever weaknesses he might possess, a parry there to discover his strengths.

"That being the case, maybe I should plan to visit your country someday, eh?"

"It's a beautiful land, Chancellor, one I'm sure you would enjoy."

"Oh, I'm certain I would. Yes, I'm *quite* certain I would." Hitler nodded, raising one eyebrow as he did so. His eyes narrowed almost imperceptibly before he continued. "Speaking of America, I understand that you were raised in a part of that country referred to as the Hudson Valley. Is that correct?"

"Yes, it is. My family lived in Hyde Park, a small city located in the southern portion of the state we call New York."

"Hyde Park. New York. Those names also are of English origin, are they not?"

"Why, yes. I suppose they are. That's not surprising, though, given the close ties that have traditionally existed between America and its British allies."

For a moment, Roosevelt had the impression that the German chancellor was debating whether he should pursue this topic further, perhaps to make discreet inquiries as to the current status of American/English relationships. Instead, Hitler directed the conversation back to the topic of childhood.

"Tell me, Herr Roosevelt, were you happy as a child?"

Several seconds separated query and response. Images of the sun-baked Hudson Valley countryside replaced the dark and shadowy room in which they sat. For a brief moment, Roosevelt was once again young and strong and madly racing alongside the Hudson, challenging currents he knew could never be captured. Not that this had ever discouraged him. Back then, the chase itself was all that mattered.

"If you had posed that question at the time, Chancellor, I'm quite certain I could not have given you an answer," Roosevelt replied, stepping back into the present. "To a child, after all, childhood is neither happy nor unhappy. It simply exists. He feels no compulsion to pass judgment upon it at the time. Only later, after that child has passed into adulthood and possesses the experience required to put the patterns of his life into perspective, can he make such an evaluation. Today, upon reflection, I would have to admit that, yes, I had a very happy childhood."

Within the fireplace, the flames flared momentarily as the bottom log, weakened by heat, collapsed beneath the weight of those above it. Sparks danced up, down, back, out, hurling themselves against chamber and screen before floating gently down to join the growing pile of spent embers and ash gathering on the hearth. The German leader, watching this fiery display, sighed and leaned back slightly in his chair. It was the first time Roosevelt had sensed weariness in his guest.

"Would that all adults could feel that way about their lives," was all Hitler said.

Charles Warner had been right, Roosevelt mused: politics does indeed make strange bedfellows. An American aristocrat and an Austrian peasant. How strange for the two of us to be sitting here discussing our youth, now that each steers the course of his respective nation. Almost as strange, he reflected, as the chain of events that had brought him to this place, at this time.

Only the most dedicated Democrats gave James Cox a snowball's chance in hell of winning the 1920 presidential election. After all, the political wisdom of the time maintained, it had taken Cox an almost unprecedented forty-four ballots to secure his own party's nomination, hardly a mandate designed to instill confidence in the American electorate. Roosevelt agreed to share the ticket primarily for the exposure campaigning at the national level, even in a losing effort, would provide—exposure he believed ultimately could be used to advance his own political ambitions.

Roosevelt's personal vision of the future collided with reality two months into the campaign. That's when Cox's opponent, fellow Ohioan Warren G. Harding, died suddenly of a stroke. Most Americans accepted the official report that Harding had succumbed to the rigors of an overly ambitious campaign. As was always the case in such circumstances, however, other voices hinted at other, more mysterious, possibilities. Probable causes not withstanding, the effects of Harding's death were no mystery. With the Republican ticket in disarray, Cox and Roosevelt emerged triumphant in the November election.

Five weeks later, the victory celebration ended as unexpectedly as it had begun. That's when Cox himself fell victim to a madman's perception of how *true* Americans made their political opinions known. *"Join the legion of the dead, not the League of Nations!"* the crazed assailant had screamed—a reference to one of the more emotional issues in the recently-ended campaign—just before he plunged a dagger into the President-elect's chest and proceeded to carve the heart out of democracy.

So it came to pass that, on Thursday, January 20, 1921, Franklin Delano Roosevelt became the twenty-ninth man to assume his nation's highest elected office. No one appreciated more than the new President the irony of his situation, given the *lack* of choice the American public had exercised in elevating him to that august position. It was not the most auspicious of beginnings for an administration faced with the unenviable task of reuniting a country so recently and deeply divided by political turmoil, personal tragedy, and the polarizing effects of a war that, although its military outcome had been decided almost three years ago, carried with it political ramifications that were only now starting to reveal themselves.

Always the pragmatist, Roosevelt realized he had to parlay the cards destiny had dealt him into a winning hand. He succeeded brilliantly. The new President quickly converted an American tendency to canonize its fallen leaders into widespread support for the League of Nations, one of his former running mate's favorite causes. Under increasing pressure from its constituents, Congress reversed its previous stance and voted to support U.S. participation in that international organization, thus ending the isolationism that, in the opinion of some, had delegated America to the role of a second-rate world power for too many decades.

For a while, the new and surprisingly popular President played his hand brilliantly, drawing kings and aces seemingly from nowhere to trump any political or personal opposition he faced. Unknown to Roosevelt, however, Fate had shuffled an extra wild card to the bottom of the deck, one it turned over in the summer of his first year in office.

"Does it cause you much pain?"

Roosevelt was rubbing the upper thigh of his left leg. Reacting to the warning signs of an approaching muscle spasm had become so intuitive that he did not even realize he was doing this.

"The polio itself? No, not anymore. After three years, any discomfort associated with its initial onslaught is thankfully behind me." His honesty surprised him. "Every so often, however, I have to remind those muscles that do still function just who rules the Roosevelt roost."

Hitler smiled, in spite of himself. His advisors had informed him of the American President's penchant for self-deprecating humor.

"Were you aware that it was a German physician, Dr. Wickman, who first confirmed the infectious nature of your illness?"

"A German, eh? No, I must admit I was not. Well, now that the legendary Aryan intellect has determined the cause, do you think you could convince a couple of your countrymen to drop whatever projects they're currently working on and begin searching for a cure?"

"I can state categorically, Herr Roosevelt, that *all* scientific research taking place within my country is directed toward the betterment of mankind," Hitler asserted—perhaps a little too categorically.

Whatever weariness Roosevelt had detected earlier in his guest vanished as quickly as it had surfaced. Whatever affinity had passed momentarily between the two men dissipated, or was being consciously repressed, in response to Roosevelt's innocent remark. (Why should the German leader be so defensive on this topic, Roosevelt wondered? He made a mental note to have the appropriate departments investigate the current activities of Germany's scientific community upon his return to Washington. Somehow, he sensed this knowledge would prove invaluable in the years ahead.) Hitler's next pronouncement, though delivered with nowhere near the fervor of his previous response, was no less resolute.

"Did you know, Herr Roosevelt, that you and I are very much alike?"

The quiet confidence with which Hitler posed this question surprised the American President. According to all the information he'd been given—and the amount of this information, gathered in preparation for their current meeting, was prodigious, indeed—he and Hitler did not at all resemble one another. They were, if anything, polar opposites. Order and chaos. Light and dark. Day and night. Hot and cold. Kind and cruel. Any contradictory image one could conjure up, he had once been told, could be applied to these two leaders. And yet, the German Chancellor had expressed his opinion with such conviction that Roosevelt felt compelled to explore the rationale behind it.

"What do you mean, Chancellor?"

Hitler leaned slightly forward and stared directly at his American host. The reflection of the fire off the little man's dark eyes only added to the intensity of his gaze.

"I have spent several months studying you. Don't look so surprised, Herr Roosevelt. My staff briefed me extensively on your personal background, just as I'm certain your own advisors provided you with no small amount of information about me, prior to our meeting. You would have been foolish to come to Geneva lacking such knowledge, as would I. Let us openly concede, therefore, that neither of us is a fool."

This time it was Roosevelt who nodded. For in spite of all the negative attributes enumerated in all the various reports he'd received on Hitler, no one dared to characterize the German chancellor as a fool. A fanatic? Definitely. A racist? Yes. Possibly even a madman. But a fool? Never. For beyond his fanaticism, beneath his racist rhetoric, below whatever madness might motivate Hitler, there existed a cool and calculating opportunist—one who had expertly exploited the social upheaval and political unrest that permeated postwar Germany to his own advantage. Hitler may have been many things, some of them deplorable, but he was no fool.

"In the course of reviewing your life, I discovered some very interesting facts about you. I was previously unaware, for example, that several members of an anarchist organization in your country once attempted to assassinate you. That was in 1919, if I remember correctly, while you were still an assistant secretary to the Navy."

"You are only partially correct, Chancellor." Roosevelt said, recalling the incident. "For while it's true that my home suffered extensive damage in the bombings to which you refer, no clear determination was ever made as to whether I or Mitchell Palmer, the attorney general at the time, was the intended victim."

"A glorified lawyer? Hah! The men who planted those bombs would not waste their time on such an inconsequential bureaucrat. An overly intrusive legal system, after all, only increases the social chaos anarchists embrace as their political goal. But a military leader responsible for several major reforms in American naval policy? That type of man, a man dedicated to order and efficiency, would certainly warrant the attention of such zealots. Make no mistake about it, Herr Roosevelt, you were the true target of that night's violence."

The logic was hardly irrefutable. Still, Roosevelt once again nodded in agreement. At this late date, Hitler's hypothesis could neither be proved nor disproved. The point seemed too minor to warrant any other response.

"Were you aware that similarly misguided individuals in my country have made similar attempts on my life? They, too, were anarchists. They, too, had ties to Russia, as did the people responsible for the attempt on your life. It seems as though we both have, how shall I put it, attracted the attention of that country's new Bolshevik regime. And the Great Bear, it further appears, would feel much more comfortable, were he not forced to share his forest with visionaries such as you and I."

"You do me a great honor, Chancellor. But I don't see myself as a visionary. I'm merely a man who was chosen by his fellow countrymen to reflect *their* vision of what America represents."

"Oh, come, now, Herr Roosevelt. Your modesty may be endearing, but in this instance it is misguided. All great leaders—and I include the two of us in this category, another trait we share with one another—are visionaries. Admitting this openly allows us to cast off the unnecessary encumbrances associated with maintaining a facade of false humility, and advance our visions quickly and efficiently."

Was Hitler a "visionary" and a "great leader"? Questions of this nature had been posed many times by many experts and analysts, both in and out of government. Given the ambiguous and subjective nature of those attributes, however, no one seemed willing to commit themselves to a definitive answer. Everyone did agree, however, that the Aryan leader was efficient. His meteoric rise to the top of the German power structure bore witness to this fact.

Since becoming President, Roosevelt had been kept constantly apprised of Hitler's political ascendancy. During this same period, he'd also attempted to identify and understand the man's personal demons. Hitler's own writings, most notably *Mein Kampf*, revealed much about this ambitious little man who believed that the same hands that once held a painter's palette now held forth the promise of Aryan ascendancy:

"The nationalization of the broad masses can never be achieved by half-measures, by weakly emphasizing a so-called objective standpoint, but only by a ruthless and fanatically one-sided orientation toward the goal to be achieved.

"Existence compels the Jew to lie, and to lie perpetually, just as it compels the inhabitants of the northern countries to wear warm clothing.

"The aim of a German foreign policy today must be the preparation for the reconquest of freedom for tomorrow."

Roosevelt vividly recalled these and a dozen other chilling passages from Hitler's crude but forceful autobiography, which the chancellor had dictated over a five-month period following the successful 1922 Burgerbrau Putsch. And they were merely words he'd read in a book. The people paid to know such things had informed him that Hitler's skills as an orator were, if anything, even more compelling. "Hypnotic," was an adjective that appeared in briefing after briefing, as did "coercive," "commanding," "aggressive," and "persuasive."

"It's clear," one of the earliest intelligence reports to cross Roosevelt's desk had posited, *"that a fusion of Hitler's blistering philosophies, his penchant for inflammatory rhetoric, and the political instability currently spreading like wildfire throughout Europe only serves to exacerbate an already explosive situation."*

"It's equally clear," the President had quipped to his staff upon reading this passage, "that some of our own advisors possess a flair for the dramatic rivaling that of our potential rival."

Since he'd first made that comment, however, the situation in Europe had deteriorated to a point that no longer lent itself to facile wit. And perhaps the greatest irony of all was the degree to which the rise and fall of Roosevelt's own personal and political fortunes had contributed to his German counterpart's climb to power.

It was he, after all, who had coaxed America out from behind a curtain of isolationism and into the limelight of world affairs. Then, just as America was growing comfortable with its new role in the center stage of global politics, a microscopic virus bearing an impressive name struck down her leading man.

Poliomyelitis. Roosevelt had never heard that word before the chief resident at the George Washington University Medical School identified it as the cause of the fever, sore throat, headaches, and vomiting that had plagued him for several days prior to Eleanor's insisting he see the White House physician. ("It's only the flu," he'd insisted just as strongly at the time. In the democracy that governed the Roosevelt family, however, his wife won all tie votes, without his even being permitted the courtesy of a recount.) That initial checkup turned out to be but the first step in an endless parade of examinations, diagnostic tests, and medical evaluations that culminated in his being admitted to George Washington one grim afternoon in the summer of 1921. That same afternoon an equally grim-faced physician added *poliomyelitis* to his vocabulary, after which he proceeded to outline a treatment regimen only a sadist would have prepared . . . and only a masochist could adhere to.

During Roosevelt's recovery, the posture within the House, the Senate, and a dozen other power centers in Washington was pretty much that of business as usual. America, after all, had almost 150 years of political inertia to keep it rolling—if not always with the precision of a well-oiled machine, at least like one on which only a few bearings were beginning to wear. Consequently, the ebb and flow of domestic politics were only slightly disrupted by the fact that the United States was now being directed by a commander in chief *in absentia*.

Across the Atlantic, however, a radically different situation arose. Since America's entry into the League of Nations, that organization had become overly reliant on its most prosperous and stable charter member. While the United States was necessarily preoccupied with the task of keeping its own ship on course, therefore, the League—and, by extension, all of Europe—suddenly found itself set adrift in a sea of political turmoil. For a while, the League seemed incapable of finalizing its own lunch menu, much less resolving the major issues facing a continent still recovering from the trauma of the recently ended World War.

One man sensed opportunity in the obstacles facing the League. And not being the type to let opportunity pass him by, Adolf Hitler, the newly elected President of the Nationalist Socialist German Workers Party, stepped in to commandeer the helm of a floundering continent.

Realizing that a defeated nation was a nation ripe for manipulation, Hitler wisely chose Germany as the initial target for his political and ideological assault. He and his Nazi party attacked that country's postwar leaders with constant accusations of cowardice for their refusal to repeal the Treaty of Versailles. Hitler further condemned the German government for what he perceived as collusion with "Jews, subhumans, and other bloated bourgeois capitalists"—a collaboration whose ultimate purpose, he proclaimed to anyone who would listen, was to keep the German economy so weakened that it could not support a much-needed Aryan rearmament. Hitler's strategy over this period culminated with the Munich uprising of 1922, in which he planned and executed the now-infamous Burgerbrau, or "beer house," Putsch, effectively taking control of the German state of Bavaria.

By the time Roosevelt emerged from Warm Springs in the summer of 1923 to once again become America's active—albeit, semi-paralyzed—chief executive, a disgruntled German citizenry had heeded Nazism's siren call of hatred and bigotry and replaced former President Friedrich Elbert with a new leader: Adolf Hitler. Hitler's first official act was to dissolve the Weimar Republic. His second was to create and then claim the title of First Chancellor of the Third Reich of a United Germany.

* * *

"I'll let history decide whether or not I am a great leader, Chancellor. It seems to me that making such an assumption about one's own stature could cause a man to confuse his personal visions with a much greater destiny—one over which, in the end, he exerts little influence."

"If you truly believe that, Herr Roosevelt, then it's possible I have misjudged you. Maybe you do have a streak of foolishness running through you, after all. Destiny is not a predetermined set of conditions one must blindly accept. Rather, it is the blank slate on which we write our own future history, one in which it is the duty of visionaries like us to ensure that our visions ultimately triumph."

The condescension in Hitler's voice did not bother him. If anything, he welcomed it. The time for pretense had ended. If his struggle with polio had taught Roosevelt anything, it was that with few exceptions, obstacles could best be overcome, problems most effectively solved, only through direct confrontation. Had he cautiously and patiently waited for the tiny virus that had invaded his body to run its course, the President had no doubt but that he would still be lying flat on his back in Warm Springs or, even worse, imprisoned within an iron lung until that mechanical monstrosity artificially drew his last breath.

"That sounds as if you perceive your destiny—and, by extension, the destiny of your nation—to be in conflict with the rest of the world. Correct me if I'm wrong, Chancellor, but I was under the impression that Germany signed a peace treaty several years ago stating its intent to avoid such conflicts."

"Wrapping a piece of paper around the problems of the past does not magically transform them into a gift for the future, Herr Roosevelt. Europe and, more specifically, Germany have a long way to go before they can truly enjoy the peace and unification supposedly consummated by the Treaty of Versailles."

"I am aware of that, Chancellor. As you yourself previously pointed out—and despite the more recent caveat you attached to that observation—neither of us is a fool. Like it or not, however, we are both in the position of governing nations the rest of the world turns to whenever it finds itself in need of strong leadership, as is the case now. My reason for requesting that you and I meet like this was to see if we could come to some sort of an arrangement, one that would allow us to set aside whatever personal and political differences exist between us, and provide that leadership in a responsible manner."

"An 'arrangement,' Herr Roosevelt? It's been my experience that people generally pull out that word whenever they need a polite euphemism for compromise. Are you suggesting, therefore, that my country compromise its goals in deference to your vision of how the world should function?"

"Not necessarily, Chancellor. What I am proposing is that Germany and the United States work together to maintain what can best be described as a precarious peace. What I'm suggesting is that we become allies in a coordinated effort to eliminate the disorder and discord which currently permeates Europe, threatening to plunge that continent—and, therefore, our respective nations—into another world war, one beside which the recently ended conflagration would most assuredly pale by comparison."

"Germany and the United States, allies? I must admit that the idea intrigues me, Herr Roosevelt. There is, however, still the small matter of what is best for Germany. I'm sure you understand that, as Chancellor of the Third Reich, my first obligation is to my own nation. Furthermore, I have always believed that leading the German nation into a glorious future was, if you'll forgive me a moment of arrogance, my personal destiny."

"I don't really see that as a problem, Herr Hitler," Roosevelt replied sardonically. "After all, according to your own philosophy, whatever destiny you have will ultimately be determined by your own hand. Surely, anyone who perceives his fate as clearly as you profess to won't be deterred by my proposed 'arrangement,' the sole purpose of which is to guarantee that the world does not obliterate itself before your destiny can be fulfilled."

"Hah! I like you, Herr Roosevelt! And I retract my previous observation. You are no fool. Rather, you are a shrewd man. First, you half-heartedly entice me with the bland carrot of something as altruistic as world peace, then you firmly prod me with the irresistible stick of my own ambitions. I see now why your countrymen recently re-elected you to office by an overwhelming majority." Hitler paused thoughtfully. "Very well, Mr. President, we shall forge your proposed alliance: Germany and America, working together to solve the world's problems. I only hope the world appreciates our efforts."

The flames had dwindled. The fire now provided only a small measure of light and warmth to the man sitting quietly before it. The long hours he and Hitler had spent laying down the broad brush strokes of their newly formed alliance had pushed him far beyond his previous exhaustion. Now, however, the deed was done. For better or worse, Roosevelt realized, he had just entered into a political marriage with the devil himself. All that remained was for the negotiators and nameless bureaucrats responsible for such things to fill in the details that would consummate the union.

"I only hope the world appreciates our efforts." These words, spoken by Hitler earlier that evening, echoed in Roosevelt's mind. That the world would *remember*, he had no doubt; a democracy and a dictatorship climbing into bed with one another, even in a marriage of necessity, was not the kind of coupling the world could soon forget. That the world had been irrevocably altered by the events of this night—of this Roosevelt was equally certain. But would the world *appreciate* the changes he had wrought? This question Roosevelt could not answer. Only some

future history, written in some future time, would determine that.

Locking his leg braces into place, the President rose from the chair and slowly crossed the room. Standing in the alcove before the window, he reached out to once more pull back the red velvet drapes. Halfway there, his hand stopped. Suddenly, Roosevelt could no longer bring himself to look upon that small corner of a less complicated world just beyond the river's opposite shore.

Behind the tall man with the powerful shoulders and tired eyes, the embers continued to cool.

1924

Robert La Follette, the great liberal senator from Wisconsin, ran for president as the candidate of the Progressive party in 1924, and actually won some electoral votes.

Kristine Kathryn Rusch, senior editor of Pulphouse Publishing, editor of *The Magazine of Fantasy and Science Fiction*, and winner of the 1990 Campbell Award for Best New Writer of the Year, examines the La Follette presidency from a dark, unusual angle.

Fighting Bob

by Kristine Kathryn Rusch

I still believed that the Club was La Follette's personal kingdom, even though the King, Robert M. La Follette, had been dead for nearly six years. I had to remind myself that it was 1931 as Joe and I drove up the winding path that led to La Follette's domain.

When I was a child, I loved the Club. Secluded in a nest of trees at the edge of Lake Superior, the building itself looked more like a large home than the meeting place for the powerful men of the state. At night, the floor-to-ceiling windows in the drawing room cast light on the black waters, sparking the imagination of young boys. I used to play with La Follette's son, Philip, on that rocky beach. We'd scout the rough waters for pirates and pretend that we were going to conquer the world, while our fathers sat inside and discussed foreign policy, Theodore Roosevelt, the progressive tradition and economic theory. The Club seemed purer then and the world more exciting. Philip and I had not spoken to each other—and I hadn't been to the rock beach—since the night Fighting Bob La Follette died.

Joe shifted uncomfortably beside me. His round face was flushed, his eyes too bright. I opened a window, even though the roadster's leather-scented interior wasn't hot. I probably should have briefed him more, but we hadn't had time. Just two short weeks ago, he came into my office, wearing a borrowed suit and a derby ten years out of style, and asked me to help him finance a 1932 senatorial bid. He knew that I was one of the few wealthy men in Wisconsin who would sponsor a run against La Follette's oldest son, Bob, Jr. I told Joe I would use my connections to fight the toughest political battle the state had seen in thirty years.

I kept a grip on the wheel. Even though the Club kept the road well graveled, the roadster hated the final two winding miles. Joe probably thought we were going to the edge of nowhere; most people did. The Club was hidden, from both the forest and the lake, and the staff received a good salary to make sure that it stayed hidden.

Finally we rounded the corner into the driveway. Dozens of cars were already parked in neat rows. Joe gaped at the tree-covered, manicured lawn. The door to the colonial-style red brick building stood open and the butler—once our gentleman's gentleman—waited on the top stoop, greeting new arrivals.

I pulled up beside the valet. Joe swallowed hard, then took a deep breath and stepped out. His feet crunched against the gravel. "Good evening, sir," the valet said to me as he opened my door.

I got out, handed the valet my keys and a large tip. "Good evening, Winston."

As he drove my roadster to my favorite parking spot, another car inched up the driveway and stopped. Fola La Follette peered at me over the dash, her small gloved hands clutching the wheel. Belle, her mother, sat at Fola's side; only the white strands mixed in her dark hair gave any evidence to Belle's advancing age.

Another valet helped Belle out of the car. She looked old-fashioned despite her fashionable skirt that fell to mid-calf. She came over to me, hand extended, and I got a very faint whiff of her lavender perfume. "Russell," she said, "if your father knew what you were doing, he would question the wisdom of letting you inherit."

I took her hand and bent over it perfunctorily. As I stood, I smiled. "My father always allowed me an open mind."

But she had already turned her attention to Joe. "You must be Mr. Stanislawski," she said.

Joe's posture was stiff, but his expression was friendly. A lock of black hair had fallen across his forehead. "Yes, Ma'am."

"I believe I met your family in '24," Belle said. "They were trying to stop that railroad strike in Milwaukee."

"Yes, Ma'am."

"They thought it so odd for a woman to come and negotiate, even if she were the wife of the President-elect."

"Yes, Ma'am."

I stiffened. Belle smiled. Fola moved closer to the conversation. Joe ignored her.

"You wouldn't have trouble with a woman in that kind of situation, would you, Mr. Stanislawski?" Belle asked, her tone the same as it had been for all the other questions.

"Not at all, Ma'am," Joe said. "I believe in the same rights your husband believed in. I believe in equality under the law."

Fola snorted. "Until you're elected."

Belle pursed her lips. "Fola. Allow the young man his ideals. Sometimes I think that's more than my son has."

"Bobby is following Daddy's plan."

"Precisely. He needs a plan of his own." Belle touched Joe's hand lightly. "Best of luck to you, young man. They'll probably be vicious inside."

Belle took Fola's arm and together they walked up the brick sidewalk. Belle's skirt swayed slightly, and she leaned a little too hard on her daughter. From the back, La Follette's widow looked like an old woman.

Joe took a deep breath. "She's good."

She was old, but she hadn't lost any of her power. "Sixty years at her husband's side," I said. "They always claimed she was his strength."

"And she probably did half his thinking for him too."

"If you're going to malign Fighting Bob La Follette, I'm going to put you back in the car and take you out of here. You can't take this state's only president and shred him among the people who financed his election."

Joe looked at me, his eyes wide. "I didn't mean that as an insult. The lady is smart. Two intelligent people are always better than one. It makes me wish I had a woman like that beside me."

"You have me," I said. "And for now, that's enough."

Joe nodded once. I ignored him and took my customary glance around the estate. The evening was warm, but not too warm, and the lake smelled like a fresh rain. The pine trees swayed slightly in the breeze. The summer night made me feel like walking in the woods. Alone. No hunting, no social events. Just me, the trees and the lake. I could stand on the rock beach and chase those imaginary pirates in my mind instead of the real ones I'd been fighting for nearly six years.

"We ready to go in?" Joe asked. That shock of black hair curled around his forehead, making him look about twenty years old. I didn't know much about the man. Perhaps I didn't know enough to sponsor him into this club.

"You meant what you said to Belle?" The question slipped out before I had a chance to stop it.

Joe smiled and shrugged. "I'm as much of a politician as her husband was."

I nodded and started up the walk. The walk had been made with the remaining brick from the building itself, and the pieces were unevenly laid. Some of the members had fought to replace the brick, but I believed in leaving traditions as they were.

Beside me, Joe seemed steadier than he had before, as if reminding himself that he was a politician had given him strength. When we reached the door, Joe handed the butler one of his cards, and the butler placed it in the bowl that kept all the cards from guests for the past few years.

The narrow hallway was dark, the newly installed electric lighting doing little to dispel the gloom caused by the paneled walls, thick red carpet and low ceiling. The smell of tobacco permeated the air. Conversation filtered in from the main room. We rounded the corner, and I stopped, as I always did, in awe of the wall of floor-to-ceiling windows overlooking the lake. About fifty people filled the room, holding drinks and standing in small groups. None of them seemed to notice our presence except Ira Knudsen, who nodded at me. Ira's wife, Ruby, and I had grown up together. When La Follette and his Progressives supported the suffragettes in bill after bill, Ruby took advantage of her new rights and became one of the shrewdest business people in the state. She and her husband had joined the Club together.

I led Joe to the bar tucked in the corner near the windows. I ordered a brandy and braced myself to defend Joe's beer order. But he shook his head. He didn't want anything, preferring, I supposed, to keep his mind clear.

A hand clapped me on the shoulder. "So this is the young man who is going to wrest the power away from the La Follettes."

I didn't have to look to know who the booming voice belonged to. "Joe," I said. "This is Timothy Van Hise, president of the University of Wisconsin system."

Van Hise's hand swallowed Joe's. Joe looked like a rag doll next to the larger man. "So why should I vote for you when the La Follettes know Washington and have made this state the great place that it is?"

The conversation in the room hissed to a stop. Van Hise's words echoed in the silence. Joe glanced at me, once, and I didn't move. We had discussed this. I had explained that he needed these people. He needed their support, their encouragement and their money to defeat Bob, Jr. Joe's I'm-a-working-man-just-like-you tactics wouldn't work in this room.

"Because, sir, I'm young, I'm fresh and I have my own ideas." Joe's voice sounded a bit shaky.

"We all have our own ideas, young man. But most of us stay out of politics. And most of us know better than to challenge an experienced politician who has established himself within one of the most powerful bodies in the world."

I took a sip of my brandy to cover a sudden attack of nerves. Van Hise had been chosen spokesman. Joe's trial had begun. Joe glanced at me again, and I knew then that he wasn't going to follow my advice.

"Forgive me, sir," Joe said, "but the Senate gained its power in the Stalemate of 1925, a stalemate caused by the Senate's disagreements with President La Follette himself. That his son has gained a measure of respect in that body is, perhaps, a tribute to the La Follette charisma and nothing more. Wisconsin is not represented on the more powerful committees and in the past five years, we have voted along with the business dollars that President La Follette died fighting."

Someone gasped. Fola, standing off near the double oak doors, clutched her purse as it were a naughty child. Belle sat in an overstuffed chair, legs crossed and eyes closed. Bob, Jr., half hidden by the back of his mother's chair, watched the events with a slight smirk on his leonine face. No one discussed the Stalemate of '25—La Follette's major defeat—in these rooms. No one dared mention how

La Follette was the only president who had allowed the legislative branch to deadlock the executive. And in the past six years, no one had mentioned La Follette's death either.

"If we're not careful," Joe said, "this drought of the past two years could become an agricultural depression which will lead to a major, national economic downturn."

"And you can solve these problems?"

"One man can't solve them, but I can work at solving them better than a man who carries the La Follette name, but not the La Follette spirit."

I turned away then, and walked toward the window. I set down my brandy glass, afraid that it would shatter between my clenched fingers. My father had lost most of his fortune when La Follette circumvented the Congress and tightened the reins on domestic money speculation. La Follette claimed he had avoided a major economic collapse, but if he had looked among his old friends in his home state, he would have seen examples of the economic turmoil he had caused all over the nation. The 1920s had been a bust decade, and that had been the fault of Fighting Bob La Follette.

I had been a young man then, half-believing in La Follette's ideals. I still spoke to Philip, and we discussed politics, as our fathers had. My father became more and more convinced that Robert M. La Follette had let his political power go to his head. My father tried to stop La Follette, first with words and friendly persuasion. But when the Progressives turned their back on Wilson's postwar foreign policy, my father used the last of his fortune to finance the fight that eventually denuded the executive branch of much of its power and caused (or so said the press) Robert Marion La Follette to die of a heart attack a month later. By that time, my father had become a bitter man, financially ruined and despised in the state of his birth.

I had to restructure the bank, the only business remaining in the family. And while my father spent his last years refighting a fight he thought he had lost, I rebuilt his fortune, penny by penny, cautiously planning for the time when I could finish the job of defeating the La Follettes.

"What do you know of the La Follette spirit?" Fola asked. For a moment, I thought she was talking to me. Then I remembered where I was. The window reflected the entire scene against the darkness of the lake. Fola had moved in front of her family, as if she were protecting them. Belle and Bob watched her. Philip had arrived. A poorly tied ascot and his uncombed hair made him look young and wild—like he had been these last few years. Philip was a La Follette without a direction. He had never been able to step out of his father's shadow, and somewhere along the way, he had stopped trying. He lounged in the corner, seemingly as uninvolved as his mother.

"I am a working man," Joe said. His voice had a ring to it and a power, and I knew that the expression on his face, even though I couldn't see it, would be intense and driven. "I grew up reading *La Follette's Magazine*, believing the dream that everyone—male or female—had a chance in this country—"

I started. My father had burned copies of *La Follette's Magazine*, claiming that it was no more than a progressive propaganda rag and no politician, especially no president, should run his own publication. I agreed, even though *La Follette's Magazine* had once been required reading in my youth.

"—I watched your father fight the great trusts and battle for the poor people, the underprivileged." Joe's voice warbled a little, giving that touch of heartfelt emotion that always drew a crowd to a politician. "My father died in a railroad accident that wouldn't have happened if the Stalemate of '25 hadn't prevented your father's Railroad Regulation Act from passing—"

"So you say you support my father?" Fola asked.

Philip pulled a tobacco pouch out of his pocket and rolled a cigarette. "So it would seem, darling sister, though

Lord knows why Russell would put up the money for this campaign."

Ira Knudsen stood up. Ruby placed a hand on his arm, as if to restrain him. "The Railroad Regulation Act would have constricted the hand of business, would have forced it to make costly changes that would have forced the closure of several rail lines."

"We just discussed how your family did not support the La Follette position during the rail strike of '24," Belle said.

Joe whirled on her. "My family needed work and money. The rail strike lost them their jobs. My father had just been rehired when the train derailed because of faulty connectors—"

"That would not have been fixed even if the Railroad Regulation Act had passed." I set my drink down. "The Act would have squeezed the money out of the railroads and closed down lines. Thousands of people would have lost jobs and the economic turmoil that marked the 1920s would have increased."

The room was silent. The entire group watched as Joe and I faced off. We were supposed to be supporting each other, not fighting in public.

"I have a personal stake in the issue," Joe said. The words came out like an apology.

"The best politicians always have a personal stake in what they do." Belle reached out a hand toward Joe. He glanced at it. Such a small gesture, so symbolic, but if he took that hand, he would line up against me and everything I believed in.

"What stake did Fighting Bob have in giving jobs to women?" Knudsen asked. Ruby reached for him again, but he shook her off. "He was a white man. He should have been supporting the white man."

"It seems to me that you benefited from those laws, Ira," Belle said. She rested her hand, palm up, on the arm of the chair. Joe hadn't moved. "I seem to remember from the last stockholders' meeting that Ruby is the one who supports your membership here now."

Joe took a deep breath and clasped his hands behind his back. I stared at those hands, now hidden from Belle's reach, and realized what he was doing. He was doing what I had told him to do. He was winning the support of the La Follette backers here, and trying not to alienate his true supporters—men like me. My blunder, arguing with him in public, had actually helped him gain that La Follette support.

"I think we're discussing the wrong issues," Joe said, his voice honey-smooth. "We're standing here, drinking legal whiskey and talking, men and women, because La Follette supporters managed to get some of his bills through after his untimely death. I think each of us, deep down, is proud to be from Fighting Bob's state. I think the problem, as I stated to you out front, Mrs. La Follette, is that no one—including your son—is upholding the La Follette traditions any longer."

"And you think you have to defeat my brother to do that." Philip's cigarette was nearly gone. He still hadn't looked in Joe's direction.

"I don't think that inheriting the La Follette name means that you all have inherited the political wisdom and savvy necessary to fight for what you believe in."

"And what do you believe in?" Van Hise asked. "Russell has sponsored you. He's not a La Follette man."

"But he was once, weren't you, Russell?" Philip stubbed his cigarette in the cut-glass ashtray.

Everyone gazed at me. I felt a flush rise on my neck. I wasn't used to public action. I hated being in the limelight. I had opened my mouth when something pounded against the window.

I turned. The glass in front of me shook and shimmered. A woman stumbled across the patio. She used the window to brace herself as she propelled herself toward the light. Her hands left bloody prints as she moved.

Van Hise stepped past Joe and pushed open the patio

doors. The woman came inside. Her clothes hung in shreds around her body and she didn't even try to cover herself up. Her eyes were wide and glazed. Blood from cuts all over her black skin dripped on the red carpet below her.

"Please," she said, "they're going to kill him."

"Who?" Van Hise asked. We all hovered around her, afraid to get too close.

"My husband." She pointed toward the direction she came. "Please . . ."

Ira Knudsen glanced at me from across the circle. I could see the disapproval on his face. My heart was pounding so hard I thought it would come through my throat.

"Don't stand there." Belle was on her feet. "Someone call a doctor and help this child." No one moved. She snapped her fingers at the butler. "See to it that she gets cleaned up and covered up."

The butler pulled off his jacket, pushed his way past us, and wrapped it around the woman. She collapsed against him. A few of the men, Joe and Van Hise among them, were already outside. I went with them, followed by the La Follettes. Through the window, I saw Ira pick up his glass and settle into a chair as if nothing had happened at all.

The air was cool this close to the lake. Blood spattered the grass. The woman had left a trail going into the trees. We didn't need to follow it. The snaps of a whip crackled the air, followed by the whinny of a horse and men's laughter.

I walked toward the edge of the trail, careful not to step in the blood and stain my shoes. My stomach had gone queasy. This was not the kind of test I had planned for Joe. In fact, after his showing inside, he didn't need to do anything else. He was probably strong enough to gain the support of the La Follette backers. If he made a mistake out here, in the forest with the men who truly hated everything La Follette stood for, we would lose everything we had just gained.

Philip kept pace with me. I ignored him, and stayed with the group. We rounded the corner into a small clearing. Five men wearing the white robes of the Klan watched as a sixth whipped the already shredded back of a black man tied to a pine tree. The man leaned facedown against the tree, seemingly unconscious; only the way he was tied kept him from falling to the ground altogether. Several horses waited at the edge of the clearing.

"Enough of this!" Van Hise shouted.

Joe slipped into the trees. I moved to follow him, but couldn't see where he had gone. I hoped he probably went back to the club to get extra help—and to stay uninvolved. He had come out, seen the damage. That was enough. A fight with the Klan this early in his career would only hurt him. I had to hold myself as rigidly as I could to keep myself from shouting like Van Hise was.

The Klansmen turned. Their robes were spattered with blood. The tallest man stepped forward. "Senator," he said. I started when I heard his voice, then felt my flush of anger grow. Fritz. He ignored me and directed his remarks to Bob, Jr. "Did you come to help us tame the nigger?"

Bob stood straighter. "You're breaking the law," he said in his best stentorian voice.

"Nigger lover." The fat man in the middle, Richard, walked toward us. "We wouldn't have to take care of this ourselves if you and your father hadn't—"

A gunshot made us all turn. The horses screamed and bolted, leaving Joe standing across the clearing, unprotected except for the derringer in his hand. Fritz grabbed Bob and placed a gun against his head. My mouth went dry. The death of Bob, Jr.—here, now—would ruin everything. There would be investigations, publicity, and recriminations.

"We're all gentlemen here," said Fritz. He looked at me.

"In fact, many of us have the same goals. Let us leave and there'll be no further violence."

"Let him go, Fritz," Joe said. "You're not solving anything."

Belle came up beside me, the only signs of worry on her face a slight pursing of her lips. She grabbed my arm. Then I knew that she recognized the voice, too. Fritz was my attorney. He had met with Joe last week as had, probably, most of the other white-sheeted men in this clearing.

"If you have a grievance about the way things are being run, then you go to Bob or you come to me," Joe said. He stepped into the clearing, the derringer leveled on Fritz. "Let him go. Or this will get very unpleasant."

No one moved. I swallowed. The evening hadn't gone at all like I had planned. Everything was out of control. I thought I had orchestrated this evening carefully, and no one had listened to me. No one followed the plan we had set.

And the last thing we needed was for my candidate to shoot one of the most prominent attorneys in the state while a United States Senator was held hostage.

"Let him go," I said. Fritz's blue eyes looked alien under that white hood. They had never looked alien before. "I mean it, Fritz. I want you to let him go. Now."

Belle's grip on my arm tightened. I didn't have to look at her to know that she understood my calm, disgusted tone, understood more than I wanted her to.

Fritz dropped his hold on Bob. Bob stumbled forward. We stood at a stalemate for a moment, facing each other like La Follette and Congress in 1925. Only Joe and I seemed to be standing with the wrong side. Then Van Hise hurried over to the man tied to the tree. The Klansmen turned and walked away, moving with as much dignity as pallbearers at a famous man's funeral. No one else moved until the trees had swallowed the white robes.

"You're letting them go," Bob said, his voice rising in pitch.

"Of course." Belle stepped behind him and put her arms around him. "Are you all right?"

Bob nodded, wiping the sweat from his forehead.

Van Hise finished untying the black man. He fell forward in a cloud of blood. Not dead, but injured enough to serve as a warning.

Fola stood in the center of the clearing, her legs and shoes spattered with mud. "You knew them," she said to Joe.

He slipped his derringer back into his pocket. "I'm sure we all did."

"And yet you didn't do anything."

"There are other ways to take care of them," Joe said.

"Yes." Fola drew herself to her full height, looking like a younger version of Belle. "You can do nothing and let them continue."

"Or we can bring political and economic pressure to bear," Belle said. She wasn't looking at her daughter. She was looking at me. "These are lawyers, doctors and bankers we're dealing with, not working-class men. We can stop them in other ways, can't we, Russell?"

I didn't say a word. A flush rose hot against my chest. They weren't supposed to be out tonight. Fritz had no power to call a meeting, not even if the wrong sorts of people showed up in the area and needed to become examples. Tonight was supposed to have been a quiet night, a night for aboveboard political action. Instead, my chances—and Joe's chances—for defeating the La Follettes on their home turf had been ruined.

Fritz knew that power came through many avenues, not just political ones. But he didn't have the sophistication to know when to use politics and when to rely on violence. My instructions not to hold a meeting tonight should have been more explicit, but I was unable to be too explicit the week before, during the meeting with Fritz and Joe.

"Joe." Belle had let go of her son, and once again extended her hand to my candidate. "My husband used to say that there are two kinds of people in this state: thugs and honest men. And he was always afraid that the thugs would take over the government once again, giving us witch-hunts and terror that we haven't seen here since aught-two. If I asked you for the names of those men, would you give them to me?"

Joe looked at me, his wide gray eyes filled with an emotion I didn't recognize. Or perhaps it was one I didn't want to recognize. He took her hand. "Yes, Ma'am. I will."

"Then perhaps you, Bob, Jr., and I need to discuss strategy. It might be better to have two good men in office, even if one of them has to be in the House, than none at all, wouldn't you agree?"

"Well, Ma'am, we need to talk about a definition of good."

"Indeed we do."

I walked away. The ground squished beneath my feet. I was protected. They could do nothing to me, tie nothing to me. I had lived a quiet life and only taken one overt political action—Joe's sponsorship. And, as far as I was concerned, it had failed.

A hand touched my shoulder. I whirled, half-ready for a fight. Philip stood behind me. A leaf had fallen into his wild shock of hair. "Didn't mean to scare you, Russell," he said. "I want to walk with you."

We had walked together once before, the night his father died. We had walked on the rock beach and instead of comforting each other, we had screamed at each other about rights and principles. I yelled that his father had ruined the economy by trying to give an equal share of the pie to everyone, and Philip had said that building a world in which equality and freedom existed in business as well as politics was a slow, but worthy task. Now, years later, he had done nothing, having lost his drive and focus somewhere, and I had become a quiet, bitter man like my own father, acting out my frustrations in secret, after dark.

"We have nothing to say to each other," I said.

Philip bit his lower lip. I could feel the remnants of the old friendship, almost as if we could shed our years and return to that beach, where we had once fought a common—if imaginary—enemy.

"What changed, Russell?" he asked softly.

"We grew up, Philip." I said.

Philip's gaze was intense. Until that moment, I had never seen a resemblance to his father. But it was there, around his eyes. "I know that, Russell. You don't. You never have."

His words hit like a blow. The blood on the grass had dried. White sheets and violence—a child's game gone awry? I shook my head. We suffered from something more insidious than that.

I looked at him. He didn't see it, and I hadn't until then, either. "We lost, Philip," I said. "We pushed against your father and lost."

"We made our own choices."

A flush rose in my cheeks. All these years, he had watched me and not judged me. His father would have said that only cowards hid behind white sheets and the cloak of darkness. Robert La Follette, Sr. would have written me off as a thug and a ne'er-do-well. Philip hadn't written me off at all.

"What do you want from me?" I asked.

Philip smiled, a slow ancient grin that I had forgotten he possessed. "Walk with me, Russell. I promise. I won't try to change you."

He started through the blood-covered grass, heading toward the rock beach. After a moment, I followed, head down. I had avoided that lake shore all those years, I thought, to avoid Philip and the ghost of his father. I had really been avoiding the self I had left there so long ago.

I wondered if that self was still there.

I half-hoped he was.

Philip wasn't changing me. He was just bringing me home.

1932

1932 marked the first of Franklin Delano Roosevelt's four presidential victories, and the beginning of the New Deal. Roosevelt took over during the depths of the worst economic depression in America's history—so you would think that a story in which Roosevelt didn't defeat the incumbent President, Herbert Hoover, would of course concern itself with Hoover's handling of the Depression.

Well, think again—because Lawrence Watt-Evans, Hugo-winning and best-selling author of *Nightside City* and *The Blood of a Dragon,* jumps ahead to the early 1950s and takes a sharp look at the most important single change in American (and world) society had FDR *not* been elected.

Truth, Justice, and the American Way

by Lawrence Watt-Evans

"Damn!" said the Secretary of State.

His aide looked up, startled by the outburst. "What's the matter?" he asked.

"It's this man Rosenman," the Secretary said, flinging down the telegram. "The Japanese say they won't recognize him as our ambassador."

The aide blinked at him in astonishment. "Can they *do* that?"

"Well, why the hell not?" his superior said, swiveling his chair about so he could glare out the window more easily. The cherry trees were in full bloom on the Mall, but he couldn't see them from this particular window, which added to his frustration. "What are we going to do about it, go to war again? We did that already, nineteen years ago, and it doesn't seem to have done us much good, does it?"

"Maybe we should have done it more thoroughly the first time," the aide suggested. "I mean, if they keep making trouble like this, we may wind up fighting them again eventually."

"Oh, we might someday," the Secretary agreed, "But not today. And not over this Jew, Rosenman. No one's crazy enough to go to war over the Jews."

"Why should the Japanese even care?" the aide asked. "I mean, Japan isn't a Christian nation."

"Oh, they've been listening to the damn Germans again," the Secretary growled. "Or the British, going on about Zionism as a threat to world peace. World peace, ha! It's a threat to their damn Empire, that's what it's a threat to. They just want to make sure there's nobody in Palestine who knows how to point a gun."

He lapsed into moody silence. The aide picked up the telegram; it was signed by Undersecretary Sumner Welles, and dated April 4th, 1953.

"Damn!" the Secretary said again, under his breath.

"It's all Stimson's fault," the Secretary told the President. "If he hadn't gone so easy on the Japanese back in '37 they wouldn't dare do this. They took it as a sign of weakness."

The President sighed. "I suppose you think he should have gone ahead with the invasion of the home islands, and dragged the war out another year or two, and lost another million men? Fine shape we'd be in now if he'd done that. Look, you know as well as I do that Henry Stimson only started the war in '34 to get the country out of the Depression, since Hoover's programs weren't doing the job. He wasn't looking to stamp the Japanese into the ground."

The Secretary leaned back in his chair. "And I suppose that it didn't matter that the Japs were killing our people in China, and walked out of the peace conference and repudiated the naval treaties?"

"Not much," the President replied. "If they really were."

"Oh, they were, sir—no doubt about it."

"Well, I don't think anybody here at home really cared—or at least they wouldn't have if Stimson hadn't stirred them up. Old Bert Hoover didn't think any of that was enough to start a war, did he?"

"No, sir, but Herbert Hoover was a Quaker pacifist. He wouldn't have started a war until the Japs were bombing Hawaii. If then."

"Then I guess it's a good thing that Stimson and Congress hated him enough by then to declare war anyway, isn't it?"

The Secretary shifted uneasily in his chair. "I don't think Stimson hated Hoover. He was just trying to distract everyone."

"Or get himself elected president in '36," the President suggested sourly.

"How could he know Egg Curtis was going to drop dead a month before the primaries started and leave Hoover without a veep?"

The President almost sneered. "You think anyone would have voted for Curtis?" he asked. "You may know foreign affairs, but you don't know shit about getting elected—and I do, Mr. Secretary, I do. I may not know what's happening in every third-rate country in the Balkans or wherever the hell you've been sending people, but I know the American people. Roosevelt would have won easily against Curtis. Hell, Hoover only beat Roosevelt by two electoral votes in '32 as it was, even with Al

Smith's third party messing up the Democrats, and Stimson didn't exactly get a landslide in '36."

"Nobody wants to change parties in the middle of a war, though," the Secretary ventured.

"Ha!" the President replied.

The Secretary thought he saw a long lecture on domestic politics approaching, and he spoke quickly to head it off. "We're getting off the subject, sir," he said. "About this man Rosenman. The Japanese won't take him as our ambassador. So do we just apologize to him and tell him to go home?"

"No, damn it, we don't. He's earned a post somewhere—the man's brilliant, and he's been a good party man for years. He worked on all three of Roosevelt's campaigns, as well as both of mine, and damn it, we owe him a post." The President sat back in his chair, thinking. Then he leaned forward and said, "Look, you find him a place. It's your baby—do it."

"Yes, sir," the Secretary said, unhappily.

His wife gave a puzzled little frown. "I don't understand," she said. "What's the problem?"

"The problem is," the Secretary said, "that there's nowhere to send him."

"Oh, that's silly. There must be. Where are there vacancies?"

"Nowhere," the Secretary said, slumping into the chair by the radio. "We'll have to recall someone if we want to make Rosenman a full ambassador. Or more likely we'll just send him along as plenipotentiary somewhere, and let him make up the job to suit himself. I don't want to recall anyone, though."

"Well, then, just make him a what-do-you-call-it."

"Okay, fine, maybe that'll do—but where do we send him?"

"I don't know," his wife said, throwing up her hands. "You're the Secretary of State."

The Secretary grimaced. "Well," he said, "I don't know, either. That's the problem."

"Well," his wife suggested, "his people came from Germany, didn't they? Can't you send him to Germany?"

"Oh, God, no! Of course not!"

His wife glared. "Why not?" she demanded. "They shot that idiot Hitler back in '38, and those generals are still running things."

"Yes, of course they did—but the Nazis are still the biggest single party, and the generals don't want any trouble with them. Besides, the Nuremberg Laws are still on the books. I wouldn't dare send a Jew to Germany under *any* circumstances—not even for a day, let alone a regular posting."

His wife considered. "Pardon a stupid question," she said, "but if the Nazis are still the biggest party in Germany, then what on Earth did the Germans shoot Hitler for?"

"For invading Czecho-Slovakia," the Secretary explained. "Nobody in Germany except that one lunatic wanted a war—once Chamberlain and Daladier stood up to Hitler's threats the generals knew the Czechs and the French and the British would beat the pants off 'em, even assuming the Soviets didn't get into it. I think France and Britain were almost looking for an excuse to fight—we'd made 'em look bad by whipping Japan and getting China back on its feet while they all just stood on the sidelines watching, and they'd probably have loved a chance to whip Germany." He paused. "But we might have had a second World War if they hadn't. Even so, the Nazis are still popular—while they were in power they got the economy going, pulled off the Anschlüss with Austria, all the rest of it. The generals don't want any trouble with them. The Nazi leader's Hermann Göring now—a lot brighter than Hitler ever was, even if he's not half the orator."

"And they still don't like Jews?"

"Anti-Semitism is basic to their whole philosophy."

"And the Czechs and the French didn't do anything about it in '38?"

"No. Why should they?" asked the Secretary. "Roosevelt tried to make something of that in the 1940 campaign, actually—said it was our duty to fight the spread of Fascism, or some such thing—but nobody paid much attention. Didn't help him any at the polls, either. We'd had our war with Japan, and that was enough; nobody was about to go to war over the Jews!"

His wife thought for a moment, her fingers busy with her crocheting, then asked, "I suppose the other Fascist countries are all out, too?"

The Secretary hesitated.

"Well," he said, "I don't think any of the rest are as bad as Germany, but in general, yeah. Which eliminates Italy and Spain and Hungary and Romania and Portugal in Europe, and Argentina, Paraguay, and Brazil in South America."

She nodded. "And I guess I know why you don't want to send him to Russia or Poland or Lithuania or Latvia."

"It's not so much that he'd be in trouble himself, really," said the Secretary, "but we don't want him making a fuss, protesting the pogroms. Wouldn't do any good, and it would just stir up a lot of ill feeling."

"If the Communists had stayed in power in Russia maybe things would be better—weren't a lot of them Jewish?"

"I don't really know," the Secretary admitted. "Hitler used to talk a lot about the Jewish-Communist conspiracy, but I don't know if there was anything in it. Doesn't seem like anybody knows much of anything about what Communism was really about, not since they kicked Stalin out. No one but the Russians ever tried it—though there were rumors that Roosevelt was a Communist. Maybe we'd have found out if he'd gotten elected."

"Maybe that's why he was so anti-Fascist, if there really *was* some connection between Communists and Jews, and he was a Communist."

"Maybe—but he sure wasn't Jewish."

His wife nodded, and asked, "What about Estonia, or somewhere in Scandinavia? Nobody seems to mind Jews much there."

"They might do," her husband admitted. "But the idea is to *reward* Rosenman, not freeze his ass off."

"Scandinavia's supposed to be very pleasant . . ." she began.

"I don't think so," he said, cutting her off. "But maybe, if we can't find anything else."

"What about England, then? They even speak the same language."

"Well, sort of, they do," the Secretary admitted, "but they've got the whole anti-Zionist thing. They're obsessive about Jewish plots against their empire in the Near East."

"But Rosenman's not a Zionist, is he?"

The Secretary shrugged. "Not that I know of," he said, "but I don't think it matters. He's definitely a Jew."

"Maybe France?"

The Secretary sighed. "I don't know," he said. "It might be all right. But they're still talking about the Dreyfus affair, after all this time." He hesitated. "I wonder if we really need to send him overseas at all, though? Maybe we can find him something in another department." He sighed. "At least it would be out of *my* hands, then!"

"Sir," he asked, "Couldn't you find him something here in the States? It'd be a lot easier."

The President swiveled his chair around to stare at the Secretary.

"Come on," he said at last, his voice cold. "You know better than that!"

"I didn't mean here in the White House, sir!" the Secretary said hurriedly. "I was thinking of a job with Interior, maybe, out west somewhere . . ."

"Don't be ridiculous," the President snapped. "A Jew out west?"

"I guess not," the Secretary admitted.

"If there were some way to keep him in New York, I suppose that would be workable," the President said. "But I don't have anything for him to do there. And for that matter, I'm not sure I want him where he's got so many of his own kind around to stir up."

"No, sir," the Secretary agreed, "I suppose not."

"And I sure don't want him here in Washington, where he might take it into his mind to come around every so often."

"Would it really be . . ."

"It would be a bad precedent, is what it would be," the President interrupted. "Rosenman's all right; I've talked to him now and then—but I don't want any of his people getting the idea they belong here."

"Yes, sir."

For a moment, both men were silent. Then the President spoke. "You can't find him anything?"

"Not very easily, sir."

"Well, neither can I," the President said. "Why do you think I waited this long before trying to post him to Japan? You need to pay more attention to domestic affairs, instead of spending all your time worrying about Europe and Asia. I did try to find him something stateside." He sighed. "I do have one possibility, but I don't like it. We could post him to the Philippines, on the governor's staff."

"That sounds fine, sir," the Secretary said, puzzled. "What's wrong with it?"

"Oh, nothing really—it's just that the governor there's a good man, and I hate to do this to him. But I guess the rest of the world's got plenty of Jews without taking any of ours."

"Sure," the Secretary said. "And with all this fuss down South the last year or two, you can tell the governor to look on the bright side—at least we aren't sending him a nigger."

1936

Roosevelt won an overwhelming victory in 1936, winning 46 states to Alf Landon's 2. However, it is entirely possible that Roosevelt's toughest electoral challenge would have come from within his own Democratic party, had not Huey "The Kingfish" Long been assassinated the year before.

Barry Malzberg, John Campbell Memorial Award winner and author of such underground classics as *Galaxies, Herovit's World,* and *The Gamesman,* had already submitted his 1960 story to this anthology—but during lunch with me he began musing about what might have happened had the Kingfish lived to vie with Roosevelt for the Democratic nomination, and before long I was telling him to stop musing and go write the story.

So he did.

Kingfish

by Barry N. Malzberg

Every man a king, every king a saint, each and every one of us on our own piece of holy ground. That's what he said. That's what he said to the little guy in Berlin. I was there at the picture-taking after the private conferences, I could hear what Huey said to him over the sounds of the reporters, the hammer of the flashbulbs. Just look this way, boss. You and me and cousin Henry, Aunt Anna and Moses down the lane, there's a glory for each of us and it can be yours too. The little guy kind of jumped and twitched when Huey squeezed him on the shoulder. The interpreter was yammering away in that German of his, but somehow I think the little guy got the message already. He knew more English than he let on. He knew a lot more stuff than he let on about everything.

What do you say there, Adolf? Huey said, and gave an enormous wink. I could have dropped my teeth on the floor. You think we can get this rolling, just the two of us? Hey John, Huey said, motioning to me, don't stand there like a stupe on the sidelines, join the photo session. This here is my vice president, Huey said to the little guy.

The little guy said something in Huey's ear, up close. That's right, Huey said. That, too. He's everybody's vice president. He is the second in command, isn't that right? He gave me a Louisiana-sized wave, clasped my hand. Holding his hand that way, backing into the Führer, I had the little guy boxed against Huey. We had him in perfect position, trapped. We could have stood and tossed him over the Reichstag. But we didn't, standing there frozen in the eye of the world, the press roaring, the sounds drifting around us and in that small abyss Huey squeezed my hand for attention and gave one perfect, focused wink. *Got him*, the wink said. *Got him, didn't I tell you?*

Got you too.

This was the meeting in the Bayou in November of 1935, the famous secret meeting. Never mind where. Huey's boys got to me and said be in Amarillo at midnight and leave the rest to us. We'll get you past the border and leave the delegation at home. It was easy to get away, I was back home for Christmas then. The President wouldn't even have known I had blown town. It had gotten harder and harder to get Roosevelt's attention; it wasn't even worth trying anymore. Now and then I had fantasies of sneaking behind his wheelchair during the

State of the Union and pulling the podium away, showing his shrunken parts to the world. But I never would have done that. Damn near would never have done anything if Huey hadn't gotten in touch. Came into the parish humping my way in a big black car, it could have been Capone's chauffeur up there in front, the guys with me in the back Capone's party boys. But I wasn't scared. Who shoots the vice president? Easier to park him under a rug and let him die. I'm going to go for it, Huey said to me. This isn't to bullshit you, I'm coming straight out. I'm running for president.

That's no surprise, I said. It wasn't. The word had been out for years, this Senator wasn't running around Washington for the graft, filibustering for the sake of opening his yap. *Every man a king.* He wanted to be president, all right. If not Roosevelt, then why not him? But Roosevelt seemed to have the banged-out vote pretty well sewed up. I told Huey that. You can't run as the man of the people against this guy, I said, he knows the people too well. He's a sitting president. You'll just have to wait your turn.

I'm not waiting my turn, Huey said. Up close he was intense, even more so than on the radio. There was something in his eyes, something in the set of his body that made you not want to explore his depths. All of this was in a room one-on-one, he wanted no one in there with us. After I got shot at, Huey said, grabbing his arm, I got this insight. There's no sense waiting. You wait, you're just as likely to die. Two inches either way on the gun hand and the guy wouldn't have gotten me in the shoulder, he would have had me in the heart. I would have died there on the Capitol floor.

I know all about it, I said. I read the papers too.

You read a hell of a lot more than the papers, Huey said. You don't pull that dumb cowboy shit on me, John Nance Garner, you're the Vice President of the United States and no goddamned fool. I was calculating, let him have the two terms and run in 1940. But when I saw the blood spouting out of my arm, heard the screaming, saw that cocksucker lying dead on the floor instead of me, I said what the fuck is this? This is all bullshit. I'm making plans, biding my time, while the man on the plow is dying and I could have been dead. I'm going for it now.

That's your prerogative, I said. You've got a tough one ahead of you. But I can wish you well. I got no quarrel with you.

Maybe you should, Huey said. You Texans, you think we're all a bunch of savages and Cajun voodoo lovers here. Or grave robbers. But if you can take it, I can. I want you to run with me, he said. That's the only way. You run with me, we can split him away.

Run with you? I said. You're crazy. Bolt the party, give up the office?

Who said to give up? Huey said. You're Vice President. You're a constitutionally elected official, you're in as solid as him. He can't impeach you and it's only eleven months until the election anyway. Instead of running as a Democrat you run with me as an Independent. I don't want to go in the party anyway.

Never heard of anything like it, I said. I have to tell you, I was astounded. Ever since that thirty-hour stem-winder in the Senate when Huey had worked with apple-jack and a tin can strapped to his leg to stop the government cold while he argued the budget and the Book of Genesis and a hundred other things, I had known he was a man to reckon with, no one to underplay, but this was something entirely new. This went outside my experience. Shit, I said, you're crazy.

So I'm crazy, Huey said. You think I'm out of place here? It's all crazy. We got ourselves a country in collapse, we got ourselves a situation that won't quit. Got thirty million men wandering the roads of America, ready to kill for a slice of bread, got thirty million women who would hump for the price of an apple or some clothes for the baby. Think it's going to turn around? Think again.

We're in critical times, boy. It's all falling apart on us. It's time for someone to take over who cares for the people.

Frank cares for the people, I said. In his way.

His way, Huey said. He gave me that smile, opened his mouth, showed me all the lovely white and open spaces. Just two guys on the Bayou talking sense, he said. Got all the doors closed. Want some whiskey? I got me a bottle of the finest here. He busted Prohibition, I'll give your guy that.

I don't care, I said. I never turned down any whiskey. Huey took a bottle from inside his coat, opened it, passed it to me. Here, he said. Got compunction? Want a glass?

Never heard of that, I said. I took a swig deep down—not bad stuff—and handed it over. You serious? I said. You really mean it?

Sure I mean it, he said. If you come over, I figure we got this election. It all falls into place. You've made a considered judgment, that's it. You're going with the real man of the people. Franklin will have a fit but what can he do? Maybe he can get Lehman to run with him. Two New York kikes, Huey said, and took a swig and giggled. Not that I got anything against kikes, he said. Kikes and shines and Micks and Polacks, hunkies and Cajuns and Injuns and all the rest of them, they're all the soul of the country. But I want this to be a done deal, I don't want to fool around. I want your commitment *now*, and then we'll go on from there.

And then what? I said. How do I go back to Washington and face the man?

You don't have to face him. You can stay on the ranch. You're constitutionally elected, remember? There's nothing he can do to you. We'll wait a couple of months, then we'll hold a joint press conference and announce.

Not Democrat, I said. You want to go third party.

Right, Huey said. He looked at the bottle, shrugged, took another sip. We could probably beat him in the party if we went out for it but we'd bust it wide open and then he'd probably go third party on *me* and split the thing.

No, we'll do it ourselves. The money is there. Don't worry about the money.

Just have my ass there, I said, that's what you're telling me?

That's what I'm telling you, he said. Listen, you don't like this guy anyway. That's no secret. And I'll tell you something, all right? He held the bottle out to me. I shook my head. (They have me down for a drunk but it is all part of their misunderstanding. No one goes as far as John Nance Garner has by being a simple drunk. Of course there are other factors.) Here it is, Huey said. I want to be a one-term president, that's all. I'll step aside in '40. You can have it then.

You got it all figured out, I said. What a generous offer.

I'm serious, he said. If I can't make this thing work in one term, I can't do anything in two. Besides, I don't want to be president all my life. I want to lie down here in the sun, run the dogs, know me another woman or two. But I got a few plans. In '40 I can put you over the top.

I didn't believe a word of it. Up to this point I had pretty well taken what Huey had said as he had presented it, but this part was not to be believed. It didn't bother me, of course. Long view or short, you cultivate the situation more or less as it is found and don't push for explanations. I'll think about it, I said. It's going to be ugly stuff. The Republicans want to be heard from.

Republicans! Huey said. Who they got? Hoover again? Charles Evans Hughes? Maybe Styles Bridges? I say the word *Hoover* three times a day until November, I don't have to say anything else. So much for the Republicans. Franklin will be tough but with his vice president jumping ship and every man a king, I think I got a chance. You think I have a chance, Big John?

Yes, I said, I think so. I want to think on this some.

Don't think on it too long, he said. You're getting first offer and best offer but you aren't the only one, you understand. There are a lot of people outside the parishes who see things the way I do, who would be happy to come along. The next person I ask is Rayburn. You think he'll turn it down?

I don't know, I said.

Well I do, Huey said. He turned it down. Conditional. He said I should ask you first, courtesy of the line of succession and all that. But if you don't want it, he said, I should ask him again. That good enough for you?

I'll have another sip of that whiskey, I said. I do declare that ain't bad whiskey, considering.

Yeah, Huey said. You know, I looked down at that blood on the floor of the Capitol and I said, it could have been *my* blood and no one would ever have known what I could have been. There are moments that change you, Big John. Maybe you've had a few.

I think I've had one just now, I said. I took the whiskey bottle from him and palmed it. It felt like a grenade in my hand. I ran the palm over it, up and down, down and up, then drank deep. I'm tired of this job, I said finally, this is a shitty job. Maybe you can give me something to do besides hold a gavel and wait around for you to drop dead.

We'll have plenty for you to do, Huey said. We're gonna be a goddamned *team*, Big John. And in 1940, things work out the way I hope they will, you can have the whole goddamned thing. We'll probably be in a war by then anyway, ain't doing you no favors.

Landon was a clown. Huey was right, the Republicans had nothing, there was no way that they could campaign, nothing that they could say. That was the summer of the dust bowls, the failed crops, the riots in the Capitol. Roosevelt wanted me to step down when he got the word, and then he threatened to impeach me, and then he said he'd send me out to inspect the goddamned Navy in California for six months if I didn't shut up and get in line, but I just laughed at him. There was absolutely nothing that he could do. He was licked and he knew it. He had a sitting vice president who had shifted to an Independent ticket headed by a better man and there was no provision in the Constitution or in the articles of state that could touch me. He couldn't even say too loud that I was a piece of shit because, after all, he had picked me the first time around and I had enough friends in the party to embarrass him on the renomination. Anyway, the Governor of New Jersey ended up as the fool's candidate for vice president and Huey and I took to the road.

We stirred the pots in Metairie and prayed with the ministers in Dallas; we lit fires on a reservation in Albuquerque and then we went to a meeting with Father Divine in Brooklyn. The Father Divine stunt was a ripper, it looked for a couple of days that it would cost us everything, that we would blow the election on that, but then the East came roaring in with the editorials and Rayburn was able to hold Texas and the rest of the South in line just as I knew he would. Father Coughlin went crazy and the Klan had some mighty doings in Florida and outside Atlanta, but Father Divine stood up in Times Square and on 125th Street and then Independence Square and said, these are good men, these are men who understand, I take the curse of racism and hatred from these men because having come from the fires of Satan, the hardest place in the country, they know the truth that will set us free. The Governor of the State of New York—Franklin's state—met Huey in Grand Central Station and shook his hand. Out in the Midwest, crawling from stop to stop, we saw crowds like I had never seen in a hundred years in politics, and in California the farmers and the soldiers and the old soldiers came in a long line to Huey and shook his hand and wept. We know you got something for us, they said. We think you understand. Grandmas wiped his face with their handkerchiefs and now and then, seeing a hungry baby, Huey cried. Landon was flabbergasted, he gave it up in early October and went back to Kansas and just about sat on the front porch. Roosevelt fought and fought—no legs but enough courage, I had never denied that—but it all slipped away from him. As Vice President

I slipped off to Washington now and then to preside over the Senate, get my face in the papers and pound the gavel and cloakroom a little.

We got 341 electoral votes. We got New York and Pennsylvania. We got California. We lost Ohio and Illinois and we almost lost Texas too, and we sure as hell lost Georgia and Florida, but we didn't lose too much else and in the early morning Wednesday when it was at last over, Huey turned to me and handed me a bottle, that same bottle I swear, and said, We did it, John. *You* did it and I swear I'll never forget. I want to do good, John, he said. You got to believe that, I've only wanted all my life for the working man to have a break—and the working man in this country, he's been screwed right out of his inheritance and his heart. We're going to set this country aright, John, you hear that? For the first time we're going to do it *his* way. I owe it all to you, John. Rayburn snuck in when it was all over, of course he couldn't do anything officially then or later, but he made his position clear. Huey went out the next day and had the press conference.

It was the goddamnedest thing I had ever seen. I had been Vice President of the United States and now I was going to be Vice President again and it was *still* the goddamnedest thing that I had ever seen. I guess I knew at the time that nothing could ever touch it again like that but I didn't care. There are only a few moments in life, as Huey himself said, and if you are lucky you know when they are there and you use them and you try to run with them all to—and maybe, if you are very smart and lucky—past the grave.

But it started to go badly, early on. By the time of the Olympics, even before the election, we knew that Adolf was no temporary phenomenon, that he was the real thing and that it was a bad situation. The worst. Adolf did things with crowds that even Huey couldn't do. We could see that in the clips. And the news drifting out was worse and worse.

We're in trouble, Huey said. This was in spring of '37, only the third time I had gotten in to see him since he had been triumphantly inaugurated. It hadn't taken long for him to turn me back into a vice president. This guy is murder, he said. I don't worry about Mussolini so much, he's an Eye-talian and he goes whichever way the wind goes, but Adolf is a killer. He's a killer boy, do you hear that? He is taking us to war.

So what can we do? I said. I fell into the role easily enough, feeding Huey lines, taking his whiskey—he always had a bottle now—and trying not to think about the times past. What the hell, it wasn't worth a pitcher of warm spit anyway, I had known that before. So I had just switched wives, that was all. It was the same bunch of crap and John Nance Garner knew it. Besides, the only real populist is a dead man, I was smart enough to know that. What are we going to do, take Adolf out?

He's killing Jews and Gypsies, Huey said, and ugly-looking types and enemies and a lot of good Germans too. He's killing everything that takes his fancy and he's dead serious about this. He is one out-of-control loon and he is putting us on a war footing, do you understand that?

I understand a lot of things.

I can't go nowhere, I can't do the kind of things that got to be done with one eye on that guy. We're going to go over there and try to reason with him. We're going to set up a run to Berlin.

I think not, I said. I think I'll preside over the Senate.

You too, Huey said. We'll take a slow boat, bring along some good whiskey and maybe a few friends. We'll have a nice cruise and we will try to reason with this gent. Maybe he can be persuaded to try reason. If not, we'll still get some good pictures out of it and they'll see that the President was willing to go a ways trying for peace.

I think this is a big mistake, I said. I think we ought to hunker down and wait this out.

Wait what out? Think he's going to stop? His country is leaking Jews. Soon as he's killed everyone he can there he's going to turn outward, want to go other places. This guy likes killing, you understand? We wait him out, he'll be in California.

What can I say? I said. I had another swallow of whiskey. I was always swallowing whiskey in those days. It's your play, I said. You always wanted it your way, Kingfish, so I'm not going to stop you. You want me to go over on an ocean liner with you, I'll go, I just hope it's not the *Titanic*. What the hell, I said, why don't we go all the way? Smuggle a thirty-eight caliber into a state meeting and shoot the fucker in the throat. You think that would solve the problem?

Huey gave me a long odd look. You think I haven't considered that? he said. I am ahead of all you Democrats. But it is not a wise plan. Not at this time.

You think he's a faster draw?

I think that we're at the Reichstag when we try it, that isn't too smart, Huey said. That's all I think. But it is something to be tabled for future reference.

I should have said something then. But vice presidents are not paid to say things other than *in accordance with the Constitution I cast the tiebreaking vote in favor of this resolution*. Or, *I support our great President*. Or *it ain't worth a pitcher of warm spit*. Trust a vice president to know protocol.

After Berlin, Huey put the invitation right out. Come to Washington and we'll try to settle this thing. But Adolf had other plans, other stuff on his mind about then, and so for that matter did the Kingfish, things were getting cudgeled about in the provinces and Franklin, no quitter, was rallying the Democrats and talking about a people's coalition in 1940. The basic question, Franklin was saying, had to do with what Huey had *done* since the Inauguration and aside from going to Berlin to have his picture taken and making some good speeches against the Wall Street capitalists, Huey hadn't done much at all. These were powerful points and gave the Kingfish pause, or at least kept him preoccupied. So there were some lively times here and about when the food riots started to occur on a regular basis. Business was reviving a little and Hollywood was telling us that things were great but down on the Great White Way or the places where the Commies dwelt, there was a different cast to the situation. And the Commies were getting stronger; anyone, even the Vice President, could see how much real appeal they were finding in the cities.

But by that time it just didn't matter that much. There comes a time when your destiny confronts you and if you don't accept it, you don't begin to work in accord with that destiny, well then you're just a fool. I wasn't going to be president in 1940. I wasn't even going to be vice president by the end of that year; I had been sucked in and served my little purposes and now I was going to be frozen out. The Kingfish had gobbled me up, just a medium-sized fish in the tank. I would be dumped and Huey would run again, maybe win, maybe lose to Franklin this time, but that was going to be the end of it. And by 1940, it was going to be a changed situation anyway. I just didn't give a damn; I wanted to get back on the ranch, I wanted to see the old times out with as much dignity and as little whiskey as I could manage and the hell with the rest of it. So my accommodation was to simply hang on and go on my way. Huey was going to stay out of local statehouses and he had some pretty good protection. Even Capone or Legs Diamond would have had a hell of a time nailing the Kingfish by that time. No fortunate accidents were going to catapult me to any place that I hadn't already been.

But then, just when it seemed settled, it wasn't settled. After Munich, after he gobbled up the rest of Czechoslovakia, Adolf had Göring pass the word direct to Harry Hopkins. He wanted to take up Huey's invitation. He wanted to come over, explore a few things, do a little business.

Peace in our time, Huey said. He's looking for that now, right? Why should the son of a bitch take us up on this now? He's cleaning out the country, he's ready for war. What the hell does he have in mind?

Why are you asking me? I said. I haven't been in here twice in nine months, Huey, I got nothing to tell you.

Don't sulk, Big John, Huey said. I got you in mind all the time, it's just that I've been preoccupied. This is a big country, you know, and there are lots of problems. Maybe we'll get that redistribution working, maybe all of this stuff will come out in the long run, but it isn't going to be nearly as fast as I thought when I was a young man. Got to cultivate patience, that's all.

I have lots of patience, I said, I had it a long time ago. You were the one who was going to turn things around, make it all different by 1940, remember? I didn't say that it was going to happen.

Huey said, you're taking this too hard, John. You're taking it personally. Sit back and help me through this. I want you to meet the guy when he comes off the boat in New York, I want you to escort him around. The Statue of Liberty, maybe Liberty Square in Philadelphia on a day trip. Then you can bring him here and I'll meet him at the White House and we'll talk over things. But I need your support here, I don't want to go trotting out for him, it doesn't suit my purposes.

I'm not a messenger boy, I said. I'm the Vice President. You got to take the office seriously even if you got no use for me.

Ah, nonsense, John, the Kingfish said. You've said yourself what you think of this job and you were right, all the time. I got a crazy plan, John. I think we're going to save the world twenty years of agony and maybe a few million lives. I think we're going to arrange to plug this guy, if not at the dock then maybe when he's walking down Pennsylvania Avenue. We'll have an accident arranged for him.

That's crazy, I said. Our own lives won't be worth shit.

A head of state killed in our protection? They'll go to war the next day.

Göring and Himmler? Goebbels? You think these guys want war? They just want what we have, John, they just want their part of it, that's all. They won't do a goddamned thing. They'll be relieved, they think this guy is crazy too. Every synagogue in the country will have the lights on all night the day he dies. Even Chamberlain will thank us. We'll be treated like heroes. I think the world will fall down and give us everything we want, we get the deed done. That's what I think and your own part is clear. You're going to help me, John, and that's the end of it.

And then what? I said. It's a crazy plan, Huey. And even if it works, can we deal with the consequences?

Well sure, Huey said. I've been dealing with consequences all my life. I *love* consequences, they're all we got. We don't know what *causes*, we only know what *happens*, you understand? I love these talks, I want you to know that. Just the two of us in a room with a bottle, beautiful, I don't know what I would have done if we hadn't had that. Have a drink, John, it's too late.

Too late for what?

Too late not to have a drink, the Kingfish said. So set them up.

So what was there to say? The rest seems very fast in memory although of course it was agonizingly slow in the development, waiting all through it in a suspended anguish, waiting for that heavy thud that would ejaculate us into the latter part of the century. Meeting the prancing, dancing little dictator and his company right off the boat, doing the ceremonial thing, then whirling them through Jimmy Walker's glittering, poisonous city. The Staten Island Ferry, Radio City Music Hall. Two Rockettes flanked Hitler, put their arms around him at my direction, mimed kissing his cheekbones. He glowed, seemed to expand. There was supposed to be a mistress but there was no woman in the party, no woman close to him. Just

Himmler, Göring and the impossibly fat Streicher who always seemed to be confiding something to the Führer. We had a private dinner at the Waldorf, talked through the interpreters of cattle and of conditions in Austria during the World War and of the shadows in Europe. Grover Whalen poured wine. I mentioned the Sudetenland, just to have it on record, but the interpreter frowned and I could see that there was no translation. Later, the dictator wanted to see Harlem at midnight. We drove there quickly in covered cars, then back to the Waldorf. At the corner where Father Divine had embraced the Kingfish, women looked at us indolently, poking knees through their skirts. The Führer rumbled in the car but said nothing. We wheeled down Fifth Avenue until the lights glowed softly again, then back into the underground garage. I felt something like a blow at the back of my neck and the thought *Like the Statehouse.* These were the conditions. If it was going to happen, the place would be here. It would be now.

Seated next to the dictator I leaned over to whisper—what? What would he have understood? I had no German. Nor did I know what I would have said. Dead Jews, Gypsies, burning bodies in their graves, the awful aspects of war. I thought of this and leaned back. There was nothing to say. We stopped, the door came open. I got out first and then the guard in the jump seat and then Streicher from the front, panting in sweat, and then Hitler. Hitler came last of all, straightened, looked at me with those strange, focused eyes, that face like a claw. *Raus*, he said in a high voice, *raus*—

His head exploded. One eye seemed to expectorate, fall to the stones of the garage, then fragments of him were cast upward. In the heavy embrace of someone I could not see, I stumbled back. The grasp was enormous, absolutely enfolding, it felt like swaddling, like death, like ascension. The dictator was floating. The dictator, in pieces, was floating in the air.

Now we can begin the business of living, I thought I

heard Huey say, his voice enormous in my head. Except of course, that there was no Huey there, only that stricken embrace, and then the broken screams in the garage, the sound of gabbled German, hysteria—

Hitler sifted over me in the sudden darkness.

Under the silt of Hitler, I fell.

The Kingfish sent shocked condolences and offered to accompany the body back to Berlin. But the party and their coffin were already on their way before the announcement at the press conference and then in the dawn, the first reports came of the attacks upon the Embassy. The declaration of war followed by noon.

Chamberlain was furious with us.

But the Kingfish was at the top of his mood, the happiest I had ever seen him.

I always wanted to be a war president, he said. I guess that this was what I was aiming for from the start. We're going to save them, John, he said excitedly, we're going to get them out, we're going to stop the machine. We're going to save them all, Huey said. We're going to save *them all.*

Salvation from the parish.

1944

Thomas E. Dewey ran for the presidency in 1944 and 1948, and lost both times. One result of his 1944 loss was that Harry S Truman got to make one of the most difficult decisions in political history: whether or not to drop the atomic bomb.

Barbara Delaplace, in her first professional sale *(she has since made six more)*, presents Dewey with that same choice—and then with an even *more* difficult one.

No Other Choice

by Barbara Delaplace

"Don't you see, Mr. President? You have no other choice." The general's face was weary as he looked at the man at the head of the table. This had been talked out so many times.

"I see your point of view, certainly, General. And I know you've persuaded the Secretary of War around to your way of thinking as well, in the last couple of days."

The two voices protested.

"Sir, I haven't tried to influence—"

"He has not persuaded me—"

President Dewey held his hands up. "Peace, gentlemen. It wasn't meant as a criticism. General, you're a professional warrior, and I expect you to present me with what you feel is the most appropriate military action in this situation. You're simply doing your job, and doing it well."

The general nodded in acknowledgment. "But this is not only a military situation, and I'm sure you understand that." He turned to face the other man. "There is more at stake here."

The Secretary of War looked at the unremarkable man in the seat of power, resentment in his eyes. "He hasn't 'persuaded' me to anything, sir—I came to my own conclusions. As things stand now, I see no other alternative but to drop it on either Hiroshima or Nagasaki. It's the only way to convince the Japs that we mean business."

John Bricker, the Vice President, spoke. "Sir, you must realize the immense power of The Bomb." His voice somehow added capital letters when he spoke of it. "We simply can't drop it on a city of innocent bystanders with no warning."

The general sighed inwardly as he listened to the professorial voice. *These ivory tower types . . .*

"Of course, John," the President replied, "nor will we. We will warn the Japanese in unmistakable terms about its destructive power."

"Then you agree, sir?" the soldier asked hopefully.

"About a demonstration? Certainly. The Japanese government must indeed be convinced. But I don't agree that we should use it on what is essentially a civilian target." The Secretary of War frowned and seemed about to speak. "No, Mark, I'm firm on that. I've read the reports, and so have you. I simply can't allow such a horrifying weapon loose on *any* group of human beings."

"But, sir—"

"Mark, surely you've thought about what you've read?"

"Of course."

" 'Of course,' just like that, eh?" The President smiled grimly. "Then you must have a stronger stomach than I do, or a more limited imagination. I'm not talking about the destruction of property itself—I'm talking about the destruction of *people*. Condemning thousands to an oblivion so rapid they won't even realize it. Damning tens of thousands more to a lingering and painful death as they suffer dreadful burns and infections."

"The Japs—"

"Are our fellow beings, Mark, not slant-eyed monsters, despite the behavior of some of their leaders and the descriptions of our propagandists. Do you realize the heat from the blast can *melt eyeballs*? You have a four-year-old daughter; how would you feel if that happened to her?" The Secretary's face whitened. "Thinking about it a little more carefully, I see. That's good."

The scientist, up to now an observer, cleared his throat. "Sir, don't forget our reports mentioned there may be other effects, long-term ones. You must understand, the atomic bomb is not simply a more powerful sort of high explosive. It's an entirely new weapon, using nuclear forces we have little experience with. We have no idea what such massive amounts of radiation may do to human beings exposed to it."

"Robert, I appreciate the cautions of your team. But right now I'm not concerned with what *might* be. I've got enough problems with what *will* be."

There was a pause. Then the general spoke, choosing his words carefully. "You say you agree to a demonstration, sir."

"Quite right, General."

"But you don't wish to drop the bomb on either of the two proposed target cities. What sort of target *do* you have in mind?"

"An uninhabited island. After all, the point is to show the destructive power we now have at hand, and an island will serve just as well as a city for the purpose. We will invite Japanese observers, of course, and they can carry a report back to their government. And you and your team, Robert, will have that big test blast you're so eager for. Bikini Atoll, wasn't it?" The scientist nodded. "Tim, can we arrange for a few discreet visitors?"

The Secretary of State nodded in his turn. "It will take a few days to get the diplomatic wheels rolling, sir."

The President smiled. "I expect it will take a few days to get all the wheels involved rolling."

The general looked doubtful. "Forgive me for sounding cold-blooded about this, sir, but I'm not sure the destruction of some atoll will be as effective as the bombing of a city in compelling a Japanese surrender. Tojo and his people . . ."

"I know, General, but whatever else they are, they're not crazy. I don't believe they could see such a demonstration and not rethink their position. It seems to me we have nothing to lose and a surrender to gain. And now, gentlemen, if we could get down to the details . . ."

The face of the silver-haired man in uniform remained worried as he turned to take papers from his briefcase. *Tojo's bunch* are *fanatics. I wonder if you truly realize that, Mr. President? Or how easily the behavior of fanatics crosses the line to recklessness?*

Thomas Dewey awoke from a restless sleep, the dream still running through his head. *Wind of fire,* the faceless voices had cried, *wind of fire.* He stared into the dark and the voices faded, giving way to the quiet breathing of his wife beside him. But the restlessness didn't fade, and he slid out of bed, reaching for his robe. The spring night was cool through the open bedroom window, making him shiver and fumble for his slippers as well. Robe wrapped around him, slippers in place, he reached for the doorknob, then paused. Why disturb that poor Secret Service fellow too? He turned and padded over to the window and gazed out at the night.

Why did I ever go into politics? he asked himself. *I'm getting too old for this.* He smiled wryly—how many times had he silently said those words over the years? Too bad he couldn't rekindle the exhilaration he'd felt on Election Day, a few months ago—he could use the energy. *Damn it, Roosevelt. I expected to inherit a war; I didn't expect to inherit a doomsday weapon. Why did you ever agree to develop such a hellish thing? Three terms . . . maybe that's too long, and one loses touch, surrounded by all those experts. . . .* He sighed. *I wish that body of yours hadn't given out when it did.* Well, perhaps the Japanese would be convinced by the demonstration.

He prayed to God they would be convinced.

"So, Tim, how are the arrangements coming?"

"The Japanese have agreed to send three observers, sir. They'll be arriving at the end of the week. Secretary Higashi added a note saying that nothing would weaken their resolve."

The Secretary of War pounced on that. "You see, sir? The Japs just aren't going to fold up and quit over a test explosion."

Dewey looked at him sharply. "Are you trying to say 'I told you so' before the fact, Mark? That hardly becomes you." The Secretary had the grace to look slightly abashed. "They've agreed to come; we can't ask more than that at this stage. General, I know you've arranged for our guests' transport to the observation vessel."

"Yes sir. We'll be using the carrier *Antietam*, along with two battleships and five cruisers. We'll make use of this opportunity to impress them with a little show of Navy strength. Our intelligence reports the Japanese fleet is in poor shape."

"Good thinking." The President smiled. "I'll take any advantage you can give me. Robert, I assume everything is ready to go with your team?"

The scientist nodded. "We're all in place. Running checks on the monitoring equipment and so on. We'll be set for next week."

"Thank you. Thank you all, gentlemen, for a fine job. Let's hope your efforts will have the desired effect on the Japanese observers. And now, lest we forget"—a wry smile—"we've got a war on. General, if you could brief me on the situation in . . ."

* * *

Again he awoke with words from a dream running through his mind: *Forgotten shadows. Now where the hell did that come from?* he wondered irritably. A glance at the luminous dial of his watch told him it was well before dawn. Maybe he could fall back to sleep if he didn't think about . . . no, too late. Today was the day of the test blast. With a sigh, he sat up.

"All right?" his wife mumbled sleepily as he adjusted the pillow behind him.

"Fine, dear. Go back to sleep," he said softly.

He stared into the blackness, his mind's eye picturing a fiery mushroom-shaped cloud rising over a warm blue ocean. *Please, God, let this convince them. Let this bring the war to an end before more have to die.*

The mushroom cloud rose higher and higher.

> . . . obvious the Japanese observers were badly shaken by the damage caused by the test blast, Mr. Matsushita in particular. It was pointed out that this was a small demonstration weapon, and that larger bombs were in place and ready to be delivered to any desired target in the Pacific theater of war. They declared they would convey that message with the utmost clarity . . .

Dewey looked up from the report. "It sounds like the test made quite an impression on our guests."

"They weren't the only ones."

"I noticed you looked a little shaken yourself when you came back, Tim."

"Yes." The short reply caused the President to glance sharply at the Secretary of State.

"Want to discuss it?"

"Not particularly. I . . ." Dewey waited as his colleague collected his thoughts. "Sir, up to a few days ago, I thought of the atomic bomb as just another bomb. More powerful, yes, but nothing more. But now . . ." His voice faded away.

Finally the President spoke. "Well, Tim, to state the obvious, we can only sit and wait."

"Yes, sir." He gave Dewey a crooked smile. "We might cross our fingers, too."

"That we might."

"They refuse to surrender."

Dewey's face turned an ashen gray. "I see I owe you an apology. They didn't fold up and quit."

The Secretary of War looked unhappy. "I'm not particularly thrilled about being right, sir."

"And you, too, General. Your assessment was correct."

"I wish it hadn't been. This places us in a very difficult position regarding our next move, sir."

The President nodded. "Very difficult indeed."

The officer paused, collecting his thoughts, and then spoke. "The situation has developed to the point where we have no other military option. There's no point in having a weapon if we're not prepared to use it. And that was what the demonstration was about."

"Hiroshima or Nagasaki?" said the Vice President bitterly. "Who gets to toss the coin? Who gets to play God, General?"

The President interrupted before the general had a chance to reply. "It's not quite that simple now, John."

"You regard deciding the fate of helpless women and children 'simple'?"

Dewey's jaw tightened, but his voice remained composed. "I find it appalling to have to make a choice at all, John, but the problem now is not whether to bomb Hiroshima or Nagasaki. As the General pointed out, we've already run our demonstration, and it didn't convince the enemy. Now we're faced with deciding whether to bomb Tokyo itself."

The Vice President went pale. "You can't be serious, sir!"

I should never have let them talk me into taking John for

my running mate. He's the wrong man for wartime. "I assure you, I'm fully aware of how serious it is."

"Sir, I don't think you have much of a choice," said the Secretary of War. "If we bomb Tokyo, Japan will *have* to surrender. If instead we invade the home islands, we'll lose—at a conservative estimate—a million men." He paused. "Men we now know that we don't have to lose. *American* men."

"That was why Roosevelt okayed the development of the bomb," said the general. "He felt it would bring a quick surrender, and save American lives."

'But if we drop the bomb on Tokyo, Robert's team estimates the civilian death toll will be far higher than that," noted Dewey.

"Possibly eight million, sir," said the scientist. "And again, I remind you there may well be more casualties. We simply don't know what high levels of hard radiation will do. The city itself might be uninhabitable for years to come."

The faces around the table looked at the scientist with varying degrees of disbelief.

"You don't know that," said the Secretary of War. It wasn't a question.

"No, we don't know for sure. But our studies suggest . . ."

"Uninhabitable for years? Eight million dead?" The Secretary scoffed. "This is something out of a fairy tale!"

"I'm not in the habit of making things up, Mr. Secretary," the scientist replied angrily. "If you want to argue—"

"Enough." Dewey's voice cut across the table. "Thank you for your information, Robert. We must, of course, deal with what we know to be facts." *Eight million deaths? Could it* really *run that high?* "And the facts are these: either we invade the home islands, or we must drop the bomb on Tokyo. Either choice will cause an enormous loss of life. We have to ponder this very carefully."

"I'm afraid you won't be able to ponder it too long, sir," said the Secretary of State. "There've been intelligence reports that the Japanese are planning a new offensive near New Zealand. The Kiwis suffered badly the last time. If we're to stop this one, we must act soon."

The President frowned and was silent for a moment. "All right, gentlemen. Your advice, please?"

"Mr. President, my best advice to you is to bomb Tokyo."

"Thank you, General. Mark?"

"I agree with him, sir."

"John?"

"We simply can't use this monstrous weapon. It's morally wrong and I feel we must—"

"Thank you, John. I'll bear your thoughts in mind. Tim?"

"Sir, I . . . before I watched the test blast, I wouldn't have hesitated to say 'Bomb Tokyo.' But I saw that mushroom cloud rising into the sky . . ." The Secretary of State paused, then looked up at Dewey with haunted eyes. "Sir, it will cost American lives, but I can't in good conscience agree to dropping an atomic bomb on Tokyo." A long silence followed the Secretary's words.

Then the President spoke again. "Gentlemen, thank you for your thoughts. I'll consider your words carefully, and let you know my decision as soon as possible."

Funny. I always thought the expression about having the weight of the world on your shoulders was just a figure of speech. Dewey's face was deeply troubled as he stared at the rain-speckled windowpane. The June shower had washed the summer heat from the day, and the air was fragrant and cool.

What do I do? How do I weigh the lives of American soldiers against the lives of Japanese civilians? What scale do I use? How can I say "These human beings are more valuable than those human beings?" That's what Hitler did in those camps of his.

He thought of the young men—his fellow citizens—who would be fighting if he made the decision to invade. One of them might be the next Babe Ruth. Or the next Robert Oppenheimer. Or the next Carl Sandburg. Or the next Thomas A. Dewey.

Then he thought of the children with leaf-shaped brown eyes who would die in a blaze of hellish fire if he decided to bomb Tokyo. One of them might be the next Shakespeare. Or the next Bach.

He thought of the mothers and fathers, both blue-eyed and brown-eyed, who would mourn their children no matter what choice he made.

His clenched fist slammed down. *Damn you, Roosevelt! How could you leave me with a choice like this?* No one *should have to make a decision like this!*

He stood up and walked over to the window to look at the summer flowers outside, glowing in fresh-washed colors. He smiled grimly. *You might have had the grace to stay alive, you old bastard. Then at least I'd have someone I could discuss this with, someone who'd sat behind that big desk in the Oval Office.*

Someone who'd taken the oath to serve the American people. That's where his duty lay—to the people who had elected him. He owed it to them to spare as many of their soldiers as he could.

But those million American lives will cost . . . what did Robert say? Eight million Japanese lives. What a satanic equation! Where does *your duty lie, Tom Dewey? Are you an American first, or a human being first? Whom do you spare? How do you like playing God, eh?*

He stared out the window, but he no longer saw rain-washed grass. He saw broken and blackened buildings, broken and blackened people. And the sounds he heard were of weeping.

The dreams came again in the night. This time he dreamed of black rain falling on a ruined city.

"Gentlemen, I've made my decision." The sober faces around the table looked at him, noting the pale face and shadowed eyes of weariness. "I took an oath to serve my country. And I've decided the best way to do that is to minimize the loss of American lives on the battlefield, and bring this war to an end quickly. We will drop the bomb on Tokyo." He paused. "I feel that there is no other alternative."

"I think you've made the proper decision, Mr. President," said the general. "After all, what's the point in being the most powerful man in the world if you can't protect your own people?"

"What's the point, indeed?" said Dewey.

And the most powerful man in the world gazed wistfully out the window and wished, for the hundredth time that day, that he was somebody, *anybody* else.

1948

One of the closest elections in history came in 1948, when Ohio finally gave Harry S Truman a victory over Thomas E. Dewey at five o'clock in the morning. Perhaps the most famous political photo in history is the one that shows a smiling Truman holding up a copy of the *Chicago Tribune,* which had jumped the gun and printed DEWEY DEFEATS TRUMAN on its front page.

That's what Glen Cox had to work with when he sat down to write his first science fiction story. And this is what he came up with.

The More Things Change . . .

by Glen E. Cox

"Roper's poll—after the convention, mind you—has Truman with sixty-four percent of the vote. All he has to do, Tom, is keep quiet. Only Truman can defeat Truman."

Thomas Dewey looked across the table at his chief political advisor, Harold Stassen. "Is that your opinion, Harold? Are you joining Truman's campaign?"

"Now, Tom." Stassen shook his head. "Don't get riled up. I'm just putting it before you in cold, hard facts." Stassen leaned back in his chair, crossing his arms over his prodigious belly. "Truman isn't unbeatable. But, even with our best efforts, he must still stumble before he can take a fall. Our only chance is to make him stumble."

Dewey wiped the sweat off his brow with his handkerchief, then dabbed his short, black mustache. The silence in the conference room seemed to make a third to their discussion. Dewey, Stassen and the silence were the only ones left after a campaign planning session that had already lasted well into the morning hours. "What's your suggestion, Harold?" asked Dewey, covering a yawn with his hand.

"To make him stumble? Why, we have to stick our legs out, and by that I mean our necks. No Republican is going to have a chance at this election unless they take some chances. Given the present climate, I think our best bet is anti-Red."

Dewey sighed. "What's to prevent them from leveling the same charges against us? I'm about as much of a Communist as Truman is!" He shook his head. "I'm afraid that I cannot accuse the President of the United States of being a Communist even if he is a Democrat."

"Not the man, Tom—the party! Nixon has some shocking evidence that suggests the Reds have infiltrated high-level positions and that the Democrats in Washington know it. Why, Nixon showed me the results of a lie-detector test that he had this Chalmers man take—and the man they accuse is a high official in the State Department. *In the Department of State*, can you imagine!"

"I've seen Nixon's evidence," Dewey said. "And I sincerely doubt that you could get an indictment with it, much less prosecute."

"But that's just . . ." Stassen started to say, then stopped and drank from his nearly empty glass of water. "Look, Tom—you barely won the nomination. Sure, the party is going to be behind you because you're the candidate, but consider the message that's already been received by the American people: that the Republicans are not unanimous for their candidate. Plus, you were up last time and you came back a loser. . . . Now, wait Tom." Stassen held up his hand, stopping Dewey's angry retort. "I'm putting this bluntly because I don't think there's time to pussyfoot and I don't think you would want me to. Now, I'm behind you, Tom, I'm your man. I just want you to win. Just look what you did when you went after the Mob in New York! Why, what are Communists but the Mob written large on the world? I know you—if it was a gangster in the Department of State you'd be right there with a Gatling gun!"

Dewey laughed at that, his anger gone as quickly as it had come. "I just wish I had more evidence, Harold."

"Nixon, Taft and McCarthy are coming by tomorrow with a bill they've drafted to outlaw Communism in our government. Why don't you talk with them about it?"

"Tom, Tom!" Frank Jaekle, one of Dewey's senior campaign aides, called to him from down the hall. Dewey stopped and waited for him outside his hotel door. "Do you have a minute?" asked Jaekle. "I found that letter from Hugh Scott I was telling you about this morning."

"Sure, Frank. Let's just step back into my office." Dewey led Jaekle into his office, offering him a seat on the ottoman. Dewey closed the door, then sat on the edge of the mahogany desk. "Hugh's the Republican district chairman for D.C., right?"

"Right. He's the managing editor of *The Washington Post*. Listen to this: " 'Speaking to the ASNE . . .' " Jaekle started reading, then stopped and said, "That's the American Society of Newspaper Editors."

Dewey nodded.

" 'Speaking to the ASNE, Truman gave the dull, prepared radio address which I am sure you listened to. But once off the air, Truman continued speaking, obviously not from his notes, on national problems. Surprisingly, the audience loved it. I can only fear what might happen if Truman should start this sort of thing in front of the layman.' "

Jaekle finished, handing the letter to Dewey.

"This is what you meant by Truman taking it to the people in the meeting?" Dewey asked.

"Hugh's not a man to exaggerate. He goes on to say that Truman tells the ASNE that he plans to do an old-fashioned train campaign—you know, the ol' stop-at-every-stop-say-howdy campaign they did before radio."

"Well, I guess the news I got this morning was even better than I thought," Dewey said. "You and Hugh will be happy to know that Truman's got laryngitis and won't be doing any speaking at all for at least three weeks. If that's all, Frank, I've got a dinner appointment at seven."

". . . when the head of the Carnegie Endowment for International Peace—Peace! Communism is *certainly* for peace, as we've seen from their *peaceful* takeovers in Europe and Asia—when a high official in our Department of State such as Mr. Alger Hiss, a man trusted to look after the best interests of our country and world peace—when a man like this is found to be a no-good, lousy Communist spy, we must demand a review of our government. How could a man both be for Peace and be a Communist? Obviously he can't, and that's because it is his intention all along to work for the Russians . . . and where there's one, there's sure to be more! Mr. Truman has said our charges are a red herring—well, at least he got the *red* part correct. And he blames our fine Republican Congress for the ineffectiveness of his administration, or, in his words, " 'do-nothings.' Well, I blame his administration—him and his Democratic cronies—for doing nothing about these infiltrators in our government!"

Dewey stepped back from the rail of the caboose as the crowd cheered. But quickly he stepped forward again, holding his hand up for quiet, then continuing in a calmer tone. "Friends, it is sobering to think that the people you have elected—or might elect—are liars and traitors. The times are hard, and the enemy is smart. The Reds won't have to attack us if they destroy us from within. It is in your power, though, to demand loyalty and honesty. The goals of international Communism have no place in our system of government! You know of my record in New

York, where I led the battle against Mob rule. With your help I can lead this fight against Communism. Remember, D stands for Dewey and Democracy!"

This time Dewey stood back from the railing and waved at the crowd for a few moments. He yelled, "Thanks for coming!" before disappearing into the caboose in which he had spent the better part of the last month. Stassen met him inside with a smile.

"Wonderful speech," Stassen said. "Only a hundred forty-one more to go."

Rrrring! The telephone by the hotel bed rattled on the hook. Tom Dewey rolled away from his wife and managed to grab the receiver just as it started its second ring.

"Hello," he said, sleepily.

"Tom, Tom! Have you seen the morning paper?"

"Is that you, Harold?" asked Dewey. "What time is it?"

"It's six o'clock . . . oh, what's the time difference, it's five o'clock there. Get out of bed and see if the newspaper's outside your door. You are not going to believe me unless you see it yourself."

"Okay. Let me see. Be right back." Dewey sat up. He and Dorothy had just arrived in Chicago for a week of rest before the last week of the campaign. He put on his slippers, then grabbed his housecoat lying on the chair next to the bed as he made his way to the front door. The chill late-October morning and his disorientation with his new surroundings made the phone call seem like some dream or nightmare. He opened the door, grabbed the paper and started unrolling it as he returned to the bedroom. But he stopped when he saw the headline: MAN ARRESTED IN NEW YORK FOR GIVING BOMB PLANS TO RUSSIANS; ATOMIC SECRETS SOLD TO RUSSIANS IN 1945.

"Oh my God!" Dewey said, then ran back to the phone to immediately begin planning new campaign strategies with Stassen.

Unnoticed on the bottom of the page: ROPER'S LAST POLL PREDICTS TRUMAN WIN WITH 60 percent.

* * *

Streamers, confetti, horns: the celebration was well underway in the New York streets outside the Hotel Roosevelt. Inside, Western Telegraph pages ran through the hallways, delivering congratulatory messages. A young boy, obviously part of the campaign organization by the buttons covering his chest, arms and back, ran all the way through the Victory Suite, #1527, to the second floor balcony where the President-elect stood before reporters' microphones and cameras. The messenger boy handed the man of the hour a newspaper, an early morning edition of the *Chicago Daily Tribune*, and whispered to him, "Compliments of Mr. Stassen, sir."

Glancing at the headline, the 34th President of the United States grinned broadly, then turned to the press, raising the newspaper above his head, and read it aloud to his audience.

"'Truman Defeats Dewey!' To paraphrase Mr. Twain, 'The rumors of my defeat have been greatly exaggerated.'"

1952

Dwight David Eisenhower won the Presidency in 1952 and 1956, both times defeating Adlai E. Stevenson. During both campaigns, especially the earlier one, the literate and highly articulate Stevenson was branded as an "egghead" (an intellectual, which was not a good thing to be in the 1950s) and accused of being soft on Communism.

1952 was a time of Red-hunting and McCarthyism. What if Stevenson had actually won in 1952, and had to function in such an atmosphere of fear and hate?

Best-selling novelist and screenwriter David Gerrold, author of *When Harlie Was One* and *The Man Who Folded Himself*, offers this startling possibility.

The Impeachment of Adlai Stevenson

by David Gerrold

Washington, D.C., in August smells bad even when Congress *isn't* in session. The days are humid, the nights are just oppressive; the whole city swelters under a soggy blanket of dead air. When Congress is in session, it's even worse. Then the air is filled with lies and whispers. I wished I could line the whole pack of them up against a wall—

The Philco in my office was tuned to CBS. That nasty little creep, Walter Cronkite, was going to host a news special on "The Unraveling Presidency." I didn't want to watch it. I'd had my fill of bad news this summer, but I didn't have the courage to turn it off either. I felt like a relative of the guest of honor at a hanging.

As if things weren't bad enough, the air-conditioning still wasn't working. Even this late in the evening, it was so muggy in my office that finally, in desperation, I had shrugged out of my jacket and tie, and rolled up my shirt-sleeves. I was staring at the umpteenth draft of the speech, and I hated it. This was not a speech I wanted to write, and I was having a tough time of it. The President wanted to see a final draft by midnight. I didn't think I was going to make it; but a White House press conference had been called for ten o'clock tomorrow morning, so I'd be here until the speech was finished.

Some of the others on the White House staff hoped that Cronkite's broadcast would be a call for sanity—that maybe when the American people truly confronted the enormity of the moment, they would back away for a second thought. My own feeling was a lot less optimistic. I always assumed the worst.

Television had abruptly become our nemesis. It was an unleashed monster, even more powerful as an enemy than as a friend. Ed Murrow, for instance—there was a case; all he did was sit in his goddamned chair smoking his goddamned cigarettes, and talk to people. Yet, somehow, he still came across like God sitting in judgment on everything that passed before him. More than once this month, I'd prayed that he'd choke to death on one of those goddamned smokes. Over on NBC, those cretins Huntley and Brinkley weren't much better, dispassionately reading through the news as if the country weren't being hurt by the torrent of words. They were like a hundred thousand tiny knives, each one taking another slash at the authority of the President.

There was blood in the water and the sharks were gathering. *Hm.* Blood in the water? I wondered if I could use that image in the speech. I started to write it down on my notepad, then abruptly crossed it out. No, I wanted to avoid calling attention to the President's injuries. I didn't want to do anything that acknowledged his weakness. But how could you write a resignation speech without acknowledging why?

I felt frustrated.

This should have been one of the high points in my career—speech writer for the President of the United States. Instead, I was one of the last rats left on a sinking ship. The half-empty bottle of Coke on my desk was warm and flat. I pushed the cap back on the bottle and dropped it into the wastebasket by the side of my desk, where it resounded with a loud metal clunk. Those little green fluted bottles were probably the only thing in this world that would never change. I thought about going down the hall for another one, but I didn't even have the energy for that. The wet August night had drained it out of me. Besides, the broadcast was starting. I leaned back in my chair and watched; it creaked alarmingly, but it held.

Cronkite began with the 1952 election campaign. That had been a good time. The Republicans had marched out of the convention hall happily singing, "I like Ike," and Harry Truman had promptly remarked, "I like Mickey Mouse, but I ain't going to vote for *him* either." Two days later, Herblock published that famous political cartoon in the Post, showing Eisenhower with a pair of big black Mickey Mouse ears framing that sappy smile of his and suddenly the campaign had a theme. Was there anybody home behind that vacuous grin? That, plus the insinuation that Walt Disney had personally put a lot of money into the Republican campaign was the first crack in the Republican armor.

Nevertheless, according to Cronkite, Eisenhower could

have won the election. After all, it had been twenty years since there had been a Republican in the White House; many felt that the country was overdue for a change; and he was popular and well known. Unfortunately, he chose the wrong man for the office of vice president—that's what doomed the ticket.

John Nance Garner was right. The vice presidency wasn't worth a bucket of warm spit. The evidence of past elections suggested that even if the American voters had their doubts about the fellow on the bottom half of the ticket, that wouldn't stop them from voting for the guy on the top half, if he was their first choice. But in this case, Eisenhower's vice presidential nominee clearly cost the Republicans the election.

First, there was that business about Korea. Cronkite had most of it right. When Ike said, "I will go to Korea," he took a three-point jump in the polls. The American public automatically assumed that the general who had won World War II would bring a quick end to the growing mess in Asia. I remembered the agonized meetings we'd had about an appropriate response. It was obvious to us that candidate Stevenson could not say the same thing without inspiring laughter. What could an egghead do? But then, before we'd even had a chance to react, Ike's vice presidential candidate had added, "And if we have to use the atomic bomb and vaporize a few cities to bring those little yellow monkeys to their senses, then that's exactly what we'll do." That had been the first appalling mistake—and we had capitalized on it immediately. From that moment on, we treated the Republican vice presidential candidate's outrageous remarks as if they represented Eisenhower's opinions too, the party platform, and the political ideology of every Republican from William Howard Taft to Harold Stassen. We hoped enough people would be terrified by the specter of a war with Red China that they would be scared into voting Democratic. "The Republicans want to send your son overseas again!" That was my line. We talked about their greed and their desire to return to a wartime economy; but we knew who would really foot the bill. Wasn't inflation bad enough already? Gasoline was nearly a dime a gallon!

We hit him pretty hard on that issue; we milked it for nearly a month; but Ike was enormously popular and he was a good campaigner. Our best hope was for the vice presidential candidate to put his other foot in his mouth—and then shoot himself in it. We crossed our fingers and waited.

And sure enough, in the last week of September, the idiot was filmed at a private fund-raiser, waving around a sheaf of papers and claiming that the State Department was full of Communists, homosexuals, and Jews. He had the list right there in his hand, and what was the Democratically controlled government doing about it? Nothing. Somebody slipped Ed Murrow a copy of the film and the firestorm that followed was wonderful to watch. We didn't have to say a word. And in fact, we didn't. The Grand Old Party did our work for us.

Half the Republican Party was appalled and the other half kept trying to defend the candidate by explaining what he had really meant. It took Eisenhower over a week to disavow his vice presidential candidate's remarks, but that only made it worse. The VP candidate promptly snapped back that the country didn't need "another lace-pantied imitation Democrat, but a red-blooded Republican who isn't afraid to call a spade a spade." It would have been hysterical if it hadn't been so tragic; the Republican ticket was tearing itself in half. The vice presidential candidate was acting like he was the voice of the ticket. Eventually, they managed to muzzle him, but everybody knew he was muzzled, and the press was playing a great game with "Tail-Gunner Joe," trying to bait him into saying something else he shouldn't.

Before October was half over, Ike's well-orchestrated campaign had become a discordant cacophony. We weren't just running against Mickey Mouse. We were running against Mickey Mouse and Goofy. If ever there were a loose cannon in American politics, the Senator from Wisconsin was certainly it. Why Eisenhower ever chose Joe McCarthy for his vice president was a mystery that none of us on this side of the aisle were ever likely to understand.

Cronkite's broadcast was focusing almost completely on Eisenhower's campaign, and abruptly, I realized what he was doing. He was showing us that Stevenson hadn't won the election as much as Eisenhower had lost it. By implication, Stevenson shouldn't have been elected. Eisenhower should be president now, and, also by implication, he would have been a much better one. He barely even mentioned our October offensive. I had written what many people felt was the single best speech of the entire campaign:

"They've been calling me 'the egghead.' They've been saying that I'm too intelligent to be president. Can you imagine that? Too intelligent? Well, if stupidity is the qualifier, then by that standard Eisenhower's vice presidential nominee is the most qualified man for the office! And Eisenhower is the second most qualified man, because he chose him! What the Republicans are offering you is a witch-hunt at home and a land war in Asia. And frankly, I don't think it takes too much intelligence to recognize that either of those options would be a big mistake for the United States of America.

"But enough of the jokes. The Republicans have given us the best jokes of the campaign, and I'm not going to try to top them. I'm going to talk seriously about the future of this country. An election isn't a popularity contest. It isn't about who you like the most. What's at stake is too important to be decided so casually. An election has to be about two things: first, who's most qualified to run the country? And second, where is he going to take America?

"Let me tell you what the Fifties are going to be about if a Democrat is elected president: they're going to be about peace and prosperity. We're going to create jobs, we're going to build houses, we're going to build shiny new cars and great interstate highways to drive them on. We're going to build radios and television sets so that Americans can be

informed and entertained. We're going to build hospitals to take care of our sick and schools to educate our children. And most of all, we're going to build a strong economy, an economy based on freedom and prosperity for all. We're going to demonstrate to the entire world how democracy really works.

"This is a nation of courageous men and women who have demonstrated over and over again that Americans are not afraid of hard work. We have worked our way out of a terrible depression, we have fought and won the most terrible war in the nation's history, and we stand second to no one in our commitment to the rebuilding of war-torn Europe and Asia. Our children are going to know a world of shining cities, a world that is clean and safe and bright. Our children are going to know a world that is free from war and sickness and hunger. Our children—"

It was the "Our Children" speech, and that became the theme of the campaign for the last three weeks. It crystallized the entire election, and Eisenhower slid disastrously in the polls. We put up posters with pictures of Joe McCarthy, and the caption read, "What is this man going to do to your children?" With Eisenhower, we were a little more respectful. We went back to the earlier theme, "General Eisenhower wants to send your children to Korea." It was enough.

We had dictated the theme of the campaign, we had defined the choices. The Republican campaign never found itself and by the time the first Tuesday of November rolled around, fifty-three percent of the American people voted for the Democratic candidate, forty-five percent voted for the Republican. Not a landslide, but not an embarrassment either. The people chose fairly.

During the commercial I went to pee. I passed one of the Negro custodians in the hall; he nodded to me sadly. "You watchin' the broadcast? Mr. Cronkite sure ain't being nice to the boss."

I shook my head. "I don't trust Walter Cronkite. I wouldn't buy a used car from him."

"Wouldn't buy a used car from him!" The old Negro cackled at the joke. "Hee hee hee. That's a good one, all right."

I continued on down the hall; with a little luck, by morning that remark would be all over Washington, D.C. It wouldn't help the boss any, but it sure would make me feel better.

When I got back to my office, there was a note on my desk. *The President would like to see you after the broadcast.* I crumpled it up and tossed it into the wastebasket after the Coke. He was going to ask me how the speech was going. And I was going to have to tell him that I couldn't write it. "Sir, you're a statesman," I wanted to say. "A statesman doesn't make speeches like this."

But I knew what he'd reply. "No, I'm not a statesman. I won't be a statesman until I leave office. Until then, I'm the man who has to make difficult decisions."

"But not this one, sir!"

"Yes, even this one."

We'd had the argument a dozen times. And each time, there were a few less voices saying that the President should resist the cries for his resignation.

Cronkite came back on the air then. Now, he began chronicling the unraveling presidency of Adlai Stevenson. He worked his way steadily through all six years of it. The endorsement of Oppenheimer, even though J. Edgar Hoover said he was a known Communist. The commutation of the death sentence of convicted atomic spies Julius and Ethel Rosenberg. The President's public opposition to the hearings of the House Committee on Un-American Activities. The Berlin Wall embarrassment. The Soviets' growing atomic stockpile. The continuing failures of the Vanguard missile system. The Northrop vs. Symington Flying Wing scandal. The attempt on Khrushchev's life at Disneyland. The Soviet demonstration of a 100-megaton nuclear weapon. The breakdown of relations with France because of the President's refusal to back them in Indochina. The public break with J. Edgar

Hoover, resulting in the firing of the Director of the FBI—and didn't *that* one set off the howls from the right. Simultaneous inflation *and* recession. The civil war in Cuba—and the *very* unpopular decision to send in troops to support the Batista government. And then—goddammit—*Sputnik*, the Russian satellite. It seemed that nothing that Adlai Stevenson did was the *right* thing to do.

The founder of the John Birch Society insisted publicly that the President was a Communist agent; that was the only logical explanation for the floundering of America—Stevenson was trying to bring the country to its knees so that the Soviets could triumph without firing a shot. "Khrushchev says that he will bury us—and Adlai Stevenson wants to give him the shovel." Stevenson's response: "No, I'm a capitalist. I'll sell him the shovel." But the joke fell flat. It's a bad sign when even the press corps doesn't laugh at the President's jokes. Even worse, the late-night TV talk-show hosts, Steve Allen and Jack Paar, were starting to make jokes that were hostile to the President. Those jokes would be repeated in a hundred thousand stores and offices the next day and the day after that.

And then, that grandstanding little son of a bitch—the congressman from Van Nuys—stood up in the House of Representatives and introduced a Bill of Impeachment. He charged the President with "non-feasance in office," whatever that was. Maybe he'd meant it as a joke to call attention to the rampant hostility on the Hill, or maybe he'd intended it as a way to get himself a little public attention, or maybe he'd meant it only as a political stunt, deliberately designed to embarrass the President—or maybe he just meant it.

Whatever the case, the press took it seriously. And because the press took it seriously, so did the American public. And within two weeks, a House Committee was drawing up Articles of Impeachment and holding hearings. The House Republicans were still angry about the slapping down they'd gotten over the Committee on Un-American Activities, so they were only too happy to go after the egghead—"You can't make an omelet without breaking eggheads."

But there was no support on the left side of the aisle either. The Democratic Party's unity was fractured so badly, there was talk it might break apart into two new parties. The South wanted out because Hubert Humphrey, that babbling little Porky Pig senator from Minnesota, had been trying to introduce a civil rights plank into the party platform every year since 1948. The closing of unnecessary military bases all over the country had further undermined the President's support in every town that had lost jobs as a result. The shutting down of all those unnecessary air-defense and missile-building projects hurt Southern California the worst. And Detroit was claiming that the administration's rigid insistence on auto-safety standards and smaller cars and gasoline efficiency had shut down half the assembly lines in America; so he couldn't depend on much support from Labor.

But an impeachment—at least that was something that Americans could agree on. Adlai Stevenson's campaign pledge had abruptly come home to haunt him: "We're going to demonstrate to the entire world how democracy really works."

The broadcast concluded with a recap of last Friday's uproar in the House of Representatives and the mean-spirited vote to impeach. The Senate was already organizing for the trial. From where I sat, they looked like a bunch of kangaroos laying railroad tracks to oblivion.

Cronkite hadn't told it all; he'd missed all the backstage squabbling and infighting, but he'd replayed most of the worst news—and in retrospect, the cumulative weight of it was crushing. Even I found myself thinking, "Maybe the President is right." Maybe it's impossible to continue under these conditions, and unfair to the American people to try.

Abruptly, I knew what I wanted to write. I rolled a fresh sheet of paper into the typewriter and quickly tapped out: *"The problems of America and of the Free World demand the full attention of our elected leaders. This country needs a full-time executive. It is unfair to the nation and to the office of the presidency to continue trying to operate in the current atmosphere of public dissatisfaction and distrust. Accordingly, this Friday, at twelve o'clock noon, I shall resign the office of the presidency."*

I wondered how long Vice President Kennedy would last in front of the jackals. Already he was a laughing-stock for marrying that silly blonde actress from Hollywood. (The *new* Monroe Doctrine: "Ooh, ooh, aaaahhhhh.")

Never mind that. I rolled another sheet of paper into the typewriter. *"The presidency of the United States is not a popularity contest. It is not a prize or a reward. It is not a laurel wreath to be given or taken away by the winds of hysteria. The presidency is only a job—sometimes it is a great responsibility, sometimes it is a terrible and crushing burden—but once the ceremony and ritual have been stripped away from the presidency, what is left is the responsibility for making difficult decisions, decisions that need to be made to protect the interests of America and the Free World. Sometimes those decisions are bitter medicine—but like bitter medicine, we take those steps because in the longer term, we know that we shall be healthier for it.*

"I have had to make many of those difficult decisions. They were the best decisions that I and my advisors could make at the time; they were based on the very best information that we could get. It is my firm conviction that most of those decisions were the correct ones, and I believe that history will vindicate those choices.

"When I was elected in 1952, and reelected again in 1956, I did not promise a pot of gold. The rewards I promised were those that would only come from hard work. Today, we are stuck in the middle of that course—and we are having a crisis of confidence. If we succumb to this crisis and abandon our larger goals, we will not simply be quitting a difficult task in favor of momentary comfort; we will be abandoning our leadership of the Free World.

"When I accepted this responsibility, I accepted the difficult as well as the great. I refuse to abandon the goals of America. I refuse to quit the job. I refuse to give up, halfway across the rushing river.

"If I do not resist this shameful course of action to the fullest of my ability, then I will be damaging the integrity and authority of this office for all of those who succeed me. My love of this nation and my responsibility to this office demand that I protect the constitutional balance of power.

"Accordingly, I am calling a special session of the Congress of the United States. I will present myself to a joint session to answer any and all charges that they wish to raise against this Administration. When all of the facts are spoken, it will be demonstrated that I am guilty of nothing more than being unpopular. Being unpopular isn't exactly an honor, but it is certainly not a crime—and it is definitely no cause for impeachment. More important, if the people of this nation allow themselves to be stampeded into turning their backs on the twin responsibilities of hard work and difficult decisions, the shame will not be mine, but America's.

"I remain confident in the wisdom and good faith of the American people, that this will not happen.

"Thank you. Good night."

I looked at the two speeches, side by side. Not quite my best—I would have preferred a few more jokes; but neither of these speeches lent themselves to the famous Stevenson wit. I put each one into a folder and headed up the hall to the Oval Office.

His secretary looked red-eyed, as if she had been crying, but she just nodded at me without actually meeting my eyes. The door was standing half-open. "Go on in," she said.

I knocked on the door and pushed in. "Mr. President?"

He was sitting at his desk, reading through a stack of leather-bound briefing books. He held up a finger, a familiar "wait-a-minute" gesture, while he finished reading. He nodded, initialed the book, scribbled something on it, closed it, and put it in the OUT basket. He looked old, much older than his years—and tired too. But that was given; nothing aged a man like the presidency. Almost automatically, President Stevenson reached for the next one, opened it, checked out the summary page, then closed it again and put it aside on his desk. At last, he looked up at me. "The work piles up. Even on the eve of impeachment." He sighed. "What have you got for me?"

I passed across the two folders.

"Two drafts?"

"Two different speeches, sir."

"I see." He massaged his nose between his thumb and forefinger, then readjusted his glasses and opened the first folder. He read it quickly. "Well, that's short and to the point."

"I don't think anything more than that needs to be said."

"You're probably right. Your judgment in these areas has always been on the mark. What's the other speech?"

"Read it."

He opened the second folder. I watched his features intently, looking for a clue to his reaction. He frowned, and at one point he shook his head, but I'd seen him do that even with speeches he approved of. At last, he finished, and closed the folder. He laid it on top of the first one. "A good speech, Drew," he said.

"But?"

"But nothing."

I sat down in the chair opposite him. "Mr. President—don't resign. It'll look like weakness."

"For what it's worth, Vice President Kennedy agrees with you. He's only forty-one, you know. I think he's a little afraid of the responsibility. But he'll handle it, I'm sure."

"There's nothing I can say, is there?"

"You said it all in the speech."

"You don't agree, do you?"

He shook his head.

"In one respect, you're absolutely right. If I resign, it

will weaken the office of the presidency for all who come after me. It *will* set a precedent."

"And you don't see that as a reason to fight?"

"No. If anything, it's a better reason to resign. The office of the presidency has become much too powerful. Roosevelt was the most powerful president the country has ever had. Think of what he could have become if he had been motivated like Hitler. Maybe it's time to rein in the presidency and make the office more responsible to the voice of the people. Maybe I can leave this country with a presidency that's less *dangerous*."

"You want to trust Congress with the future of the country?"

"The last I heard, that's how democracy is supposed to work. We trust our elected officials."

"Mr. President, resigning will destroy trust in the Democratic Party. You know what that will do to the election process—it'll give the Republicans a stampede."

"The Democratic Party is not America. And they'll recover. They always do. Maybe after they've lost a few presidential contests they'll lose some of their arrogance and rediscover some of their purpose. I hope so." He took off his glasses and rubbed his nose again. "I'm tired. I'm beaten and I want to go home. I did my best. I'm not ashamed of that. But I know when it's time to quit. It's time." He reached across the big desk to shake my hand. "Thank you. You've done good work for me. I've always appreciated your loyalty and your advice."

"Yes, sir." It was a dismissal. I accepted his thanks perfunctorily and headed for the door. I suppose I should have thanked him for the chance to work for him, but I was hurting too badly. I could see why so many people hated him. Maybe the Republicans had been right all along; Adlai Stevenson was too smart to be president. . . .

I headed down the hall, back to my office, and finally began doing what I should have done weeks ago. I started cleaning out my desk.

Adlai Stevenson had too much compassion and too

much integrity and he respected the so-called wisdom of the American people far too much to do any real good as president.

Okay, Mr. Stevenson. Go ahead. Resign. Forget the dream. Forget the promises. If you can't stand the heat, get out of the firestorm. Quitters are failures. A dumber man would have kept on fighting, until he outlasted his enemies.

I slammed the last empty desk drawer in angry disgust. "Next time, I'm going to work for a man who's too stupid to know when he's beaten!"

Hmm.

The senator from California hadn't declared yet, but he was certainly the front-runner for 1960, and many people were already looking to him to restore the nation's pride and confidence in itself. They said he had the kind of stern statesmanlike quality the country needed right now. I didn't particularly like the man, but he was a great poker player. He'd probably be one hell of a president. Best of all, he'd once remarked to me at a White House reception that he wished he had a speech writer who could write an "Our Children" speech. At the time, I hadn't given the comment any thought, but it was clearly a hint.

Okay, I wasn't exactly thrilled about working for a Republican, but what the hell? I could learn. And Richard Nixon was exactly what this country needed and deserved.

1960

The most exciting presidential race within the memory of most of our readers is undoubtedly 1960, where—thanks to charisma, television, or perhaps Chicago's Mayor Daley—John F. Kennedy edged Richard M. Nixon by less than 120,000 votes out of 69,000,000 votes cast.

Barry Malzberg, who has explored Kennedy's presidency in such brilliant novels as *The Destruction of the Temple* and *The Sodom and Gomorrah Business*, now examines the other side of the coin.

Heavy Metal

by Barry N. Malzberg

Let me tell you about Ohio. Ohio is where they did this to me, he said, extending his right hand, showing us the puffiness, the faint red streaks, the stabs of infection. Ohio, he said, fifty thousand, maybe sixty thousand handshakes, dangling my arm past that crowd all the way in from Erie to downtown. They almost tore my arm off in that state, I must have smiled my way through a whole generation of baby Republicans. Look at that, he said, the numbers streaking the screen, making it a big tote board. Thirty-two electoral votes the other way. What did Tricky do to get them? Don't answer that, he said, that fine head tilting upward, the hair flying, the teeth coming from the grayness of his face to dazzle, dazzle. This is not a night for answers, he said, it is a night for questions.

We're going to lose this election, he said. We're going to lose this fucking election, Dave. Oh no, Powers said, clasping his shoulder, winking and squeezing, oh no, Johnny boy, it's not over yet. Wait until Cincinnati comes in, he said, pointing at the figures over Cronkite's shoulder. Oh no, Jack said, *you* wait until Cincinnati comes in and buries us. I'm going to go out for a little walk down the compound.

Old Joe in the corner said, Stay awhile Jack. It's going to be a long night. There's a lot coming in; it's too early to go a-walking, a-walking. Jack stared at him. Take a flying, Dad, he said. No, that is not what he said, I have to retract that, but it is what he thought, I being in a position to tell this from my peculiar and special vantage point. I need to ponder some, Dad, is what he said. He heaved up from the couch. No, don't hold him, Joe said to the boys. He needs to be off to himself a bit, he does. We all need to be by ourselves sometime. A curious, weepy look passed across the old man's features, not characteristic under the circumstances. Such strength he had been, such ungiving optimism. But it was a long night, the edge was off, Ohio was going down and now it turned on the West and then on Daley.

Jack and I left the room quickly. No one noticed my departure. Though I am his most trusted confidant, the true partner in his endeavors, I have never been able to attract much attention or respect from the Circle. Powers explained it to me once, that wild Irish rose, the reasons for this, but I paid them little attention.

Why did we do this? Bobby said. This was after Johnson had said that he would take the nomination. No one thought he would. He would turn it down and we would go to Symington or somebody, no one had quite figured it out yet. But Johnson, shambling and stuttering in his own fatigue, had been pulled into a room by Rayburn and locked up there for a long time and when he came out he said that he would go. I can't believe this, Bobby said. He was frantic, his shirt was open to the waist and his eyes were streaming. This is what comes from staying up all night and not thinking things through. What are we going to do now? Where is Jack? Where is that brother of mine? This is no time for him to go to a room.

But it was such a time. Humping and pumping, showing his blonde campaign worker a New Frontier, locked to high attention on the double bed in room three-zero-three, the one kept in reserve for special use, listed to one D. Smith of Brockport, someone's idea of a pun, the next President of the United States had other things on his mind, heavier considerations of state. It is not necessary to be graphic. I *want* to be graphic; it would be a pleasure to describe every twist and shout, every bounce and jounce, but this is not really my function and it would be interpreted as an act of betrayal, benign as my purposes might be. It was a riotous and earthy fuck, at least from the point of view of the candidate, who had a tendency to overestimate his performance. Testimony from the blonde was not available. She was yet another in that long, interrupted skein of collisions from here to there and in all of the states of the union, another in that series of mysterious disappearances, sudden abscissa in daylight, strange lateness for appointments. No one except me could bring witness or documentation and I, of course, would never betray confidences or eyesight. Sufficient to say that the candidate had his discretion and his good points, he had a sense of control and an impatience for repetition, meaning that he spread far and wide and interchangeably.

We've got to talk to him, Bobby said. Maybe there's a way out of this. Where *is* he? As if I didn't know, Bobby said. He thinks I'm stupid, he thinks that none of us know what the hell is really going on. But he's got to stop this. This kind of thing can't go on; it's going to take everything away from us, we aren't talking Hyannis Port now or the Mayfair, this is Municipal Stadium and the Coliseum and prime time. They'll murder us, they'll leave us for dead. I've got to *get* him, Bobby said. There's got to be a way around this situation. He looked at me and for just a moment I thought our gaze would lock, that my true and secret knowledge would be confronted, but then, of course, his gaze passed through. How could he see me? He couldn't see me, of course. I was in the room with the blonde, the candidate having already left, the blonde slowly and weepily reassembling herself, fumbling for her lipstick, her face streaked in the soft and surprising daylight. Had it really happened? the blonde wondered. A lot of them get to wondering that. This was not the way I thought it would be, if it happened. They think that a lot too. Over the years I have heard a lot of these internal monologues, and it is a depressing thing to witness, I want to tell you, although, of course, they are entitled to no sympathy. I will not allow sentiment to get in the way of my perception: lots of them, almost all of them do it because they want to fuck a senator, maybe someday a president, not a man. The institution, the office, not the person. This is something I would impart to them if I had the patience.

No, he said to Bobby, there's nothing that we can do. This was a couple of hours later, holed up in the small suite, Sorenson and O'Donnell trying out the acceptance speech on each other in the next room. A deal's a deal and that's that.

I never thought he'd take it, Bobby said. Two hours of sleep, snatched in the candidate's absence, had made him sullen, meaner, had not relieved him at all. He crossed us up. It was that son of a bitch Rayburn. He was going to shove it back in our faces until Rayburn got him alone in that room.

Mr. Sam is a tough one, Jack said. You don't want to get alone in a room with him, not unless you have a chastity belt.

We're going to have trouble, Bobby said. It's going to

be trouble all the way. You think Lyndon Bird is going to shut up and get out of the way? Maybe he'll have another heart attack.

And maybe he won't, Jack said. Take the positive view. We need him. He locks up the South.

He'll be in Lynchburg, talking about nigras. *Nigras, nigras*, he'll be saying. You think that stuff is going to go over? He'll have the New York press on his tail then, they'll print that stuff and we'll get killed.

Jack swatted him on the shoulder. You got something against Lyndon Bird? he said. This was your idea, remember that. This was all your idea. I didn't push nothing on you.

I never thought he'd take it, Bobby said. It was a conciliatory gesture. *Con-cil-ee-a-tory*, get it? Who would think the tall fucker would go for it?

Heart attack, Jack said. He had that whopper four years ago, maybe it's time to slow down. Can't be making deals in the Senate forever. That's what Mr. Sam told him, probably, time to semi-retire, Lyndon. And if the kid's back really goes out or he gets a bullet hole in his forehead, who is to say what the advantages of state might be? Jack giggled. Maybe Mr. Sam measured a rifle or two for him.

Oh, shit on this, Bobby said. Enough of this. We're stuck with it, aren't we? We can't get out.

Call him insurance, Jack said. Who's going to try to scramble my brains with Lyndon Bird in the wings?

Some Southern patriot might want to get real close. They take their politics serious in the South.

Let me tell you something, brother, Jack said, we take our goddamned politics pretty seriously in the North too, you understand? We got reasons for Lyndon Bird on this ticket and we're going to follow through, you understand? He's going to give us Texas for sure and probably the South and we're going to need every vote he can bring in for-sure. They're not so crazy about the Pope down there, you may have noticed.

The Pope? Bobby said, you want to talk about the Pope,

do you? You'd do better keeping your hands off the blondes for a while, you want to talk issues like that, you hear me? Lyndon Bird isn't going to bring in the adultery vote and that's for sure.

Do I hear you, Bobby? Do I hear you saying what I think you're saying? Is that true?

You hear, Bobby said. You think I'm a fool, he said, you think we're all stupid here. But we can tell a hawk from a handsaw and it's bigger stakes now than we've ever had. I hear you very well. I hope you hear me.

There is more to this discussion, a lot more, but it was at that point that I withdrew. Family matters deserve a certain privacy. Furthermore, I have heard much of it before and there is very little new, it is simply, as Bobby has pointed out, a new venue.

Out on the beach at Hyannis, his hands in his pocket, walking under the cold stars, the hard wedge of sky, the implacable night all around us, Jack said, It's going to come down to Daley, isn't it? Daley's the whole ball game.

I don't know, I said, there's still the whole West. California could go either way. We can sneak by without Illinois, I think.

Forget California, Jack said. California is Tricky's state. They may know him best, but there's pride and tradition. I can't get arrested in that state. I don't understand them. I don't understand the women and I don't like the weather.

There's Texas, I said, we have Texas, we'll get the Southwest too.

No, Jack said, you're missing the point. It's going to come down to Daley. If Daley can hold the count back, then we'll get Illinois. It depends on the downstate totals and whether they can be pried loose before he's ready to let them go. Don't argue with me, I know the setup.

I'm not here to argue with you, I said. I'm here to help.

Yes, he said, all of you are here to help. Sorenson, O'Donnell, Powers, Schlesinger. Lyndon Bird, Bobby, you're all my friends. Symington, Stevenson, my comrades at arms. He stopped, kicked the sand, turned abruptly and headed south, stomping at pebbles, hands in his pocket. Eleven o'clock on election night and the wind socking at his ears like a fist. Everyone is looking out for me, right? But who has to carry this? Who has to carry this through? I'm the train, you're the passengers. I feel like a fucking horse, sometimes. I wish I were a riderless horse.

I said nothing, concentrating on keeping up with him. When he is in one of these moods, Black Irish, a mood he can dive into so breathtakingly as to stun, it is best to say nothing, to cultivate a kind of distance. Maybe Powers knows what to do at times like these but I do not.

Well, there are limits, he said. There are limits to all of us. I gave it all I could and maybe it's not good enough. Bobby is going to blame me, he's going to lay it at my door but that's bullshit, I did everything that I could. There are limits to all of us, he said.

I understand that, I said. How could I argue? No one is more conscious of that limitation than I. You gave it a great run, I said.

I'm not a riderless horse, he said. I'm a forty-three-year-old Irish with a bad back and wife trouble and other troubles you wouldn't know and I have it all to carry on my own. He stopped, bent, grabbed a pebble and from a crouch threw it into the sea, then grabbed his back and slowly came from the crouch. Fucking back, he said. Fucking *back*. It hurts. It hurts all the time. They told me that it would but I never believed them. I thought it would go away. You want to know the truth? he said. Nothing goes away. *Nothing*. You just carry it and you carry it forever.

Maybe we should go back, I said. They're sitting in there, making trouble for themselves, looking at those returns, and maybe they'll get a call in and say something stupid. Bobby's not there, I said, so no one's really in command.

Fuck them, Jack said. But he turned again and started walking slowly toward the houses. The hell with them. Maybe old Harry was right, he said. You know what Harry said before the convention, that I didn't have the experience, that I needed some seasoning.

Truman's an old guy, I said. He's seventy-six. I think he's senile.

Yeah, he said, well me too, maybe. He's gone back, the old guy, he really has. How do you think I liked that? Seasoning! You think old Ave would make a better president. Ave, you can't tell if he's asleep or awake except maybe by the size of his cock. It's smaller when he's awake. He spat in the sands. Not that I'd want to check, he said. Seasoning! Well, I've been seasoned now all right. I've been salted and peppered.

There's always next time, I said foolishly. It isn't the last election.

He swatted at the back of his neck as if a bee had hit him, then turned toward me. That's bullshit, he said. Tricky, once he's in, he'll amend the Constitution if he has to. He'll declare martial law. He'll put the troops in the streets. He's *never* going to give up. He paused at the fence, laid his hand on the gate. Well, maybe he'll give it up, he said. He's an old poker player, Tricky, I don't think he'd put his life on the line to stay. But there's no way, he said. It wouldn't work. They'll say it was because of the Catholic issue, not the age or experience, but the religious business. Al Smith queered things for more than thirty years and had to die before someone else got a chance. Thirty years from now I'll be seventy-three. Except I won't be seventy-three, he said. You can bank on it. That's for sure. He trudged through the gate, held it, walked back slowly. No, this is the end for me, one-shot and out. You see this? he said, extending his swollen right hand. That's Ohio, all right, they almost broke it in Ohio and now they're taking me down. So if it happened there it will happen everywhere.

You're just depressed, I said, it's all piling in on you.

You're tired. It's a long night. There are a lot of returns coming in. It's not over, not at all. You may not even need Daley.

Yeah, he said, pausing at the door, then pushing through. Right, I may not even need Daley. I didn't need Lyndon Bird either, did I? Everyone knew who I needed or not but we're in this goddamned count for good and I just blew Ohio and that's for sure.

Nothing's for sure.

All right, he said, you have a point there all right. The absolute certainty of uncertainty has always appealed. He almost smiled then but in the diminished and difficult light it was hard to tell. Not that my attention was fixated in that way, of course.

White followed us around, he sensed early the way that it might be going and he knew there was a book in it. Even if Jack lost it would still be a big book, a best-seller, an insider's look at the process. That was what White the old *Times*man called it anyway. You're the right candidate at the right time, he said to Jack, and this is the pivotal election of the American century. He said a lot of things like that, kissing it for all it was worth. Of course in the book he would come off as objective or, if we lost, full of admonition. I think we should get rid of this guy, Powers said, he means us no good, and O'Donnell pretty much felt the same way, but in relation to White only Bobby mattered and Bobby was adamant. He stays, he said, we give him what he wants, he'll give us what *we* need. What we needed of course was a *Time* endorsement or at least an even shot. We needed Luce to get off our ass. Everyone remembered what he had done to Adlai. We play ball with this guy, Luce will go along, Bobby said. We clam up on him or push him away and we'll get the full treatment in *Time* and that's the end of it. And another thing, Bobby said, for these four months, Jack, you've got to play it straight. There's too much press, too much attention. We can't take the risks.

Jack said, I don't know what you're talking about.

Bullshit, you don't know what I'm talking about. There are no secrets and there's no time for that crap now, Jack. For four months you act like Old Joe at a family weekend. Afterwards, we'll talk about it.

They wouldn't print anything, Jack said. They wouldn't touch this.

You don't know *what* they'll do, you get Luce mad enough. Which is why we're letting Teddy White through the door. You let him in, you make the kind of concessions I made here, you let old Lyndon Bird run loose out there in Galveston and New Orleans and talk about the *nigras* in our name, you're not going to screw us up at home. You hear that, Jack? You hear me?

I hear you, he said. I always heard you. You know what it's like? You know what it's like to be out here pushing, pushing? I hurt all the time, Bobby; my back can't take it, there are times I want to cave in.

Pussy won't change it. Doesn't change a goddamned thing. Besides, with back trouble, what are you humping away for? You want to be on a wood board on the floor, reading draft speeches, that's what you want.

You really want this, Jack said. You really want it bad, don't you, Bobby? Sometimes I think you want it worse than I do. And that means a whole hell of a lot.

We're in this to win. No point going into anything as bad as a national campaign and losing. I don't want to lose, Jack.

What if we do, Bobby? What if we lose?

There's something in you that wants to give up, isn't there Jack? I have it too, I know it's in you. But this is the kind of stuff you've got to keep down, it doesn't matter. You understand that, brother?

I understand everything, Bobby. Still, just for the hell of it. It's just the two of us in this room, nobody's listening, nobody's hanging around outside the door at four in the morning. Even Powers said his little prayers and gave it up two hours ago. *What if we lose?*

Well, Bobby said, if that's the case, I'll go to the Teamsters, I guess. Ask Hoffa for a job.

Do that, huh?

He knows I've got the skills, Bobby said. He can't be uncertain on that.

Just so you have a job. The Senate doesn't look so bad to me sometimes, you know?

It's too late, Bobby said. You know why it's too late?

Sometimes I think I don't know anything. It's a whole New Frontier out there, remember?

I'll tell you why it's too late. Because you'd have to go back there and serve with Lyndon Bird who will not only remember that he lost to you at the convention, will not only remember that he ran under you for the most useless job in the country, tits on a boar hog, but that because of you he *lost*. He'll blame you. And he'll make your life miserable.

Thanks a lot, Bobby. Why don't you tell that to White, give him a sidebar?

Jack, you'd better tell that to yourself. Because if we lose, we have no future. We're in his sights. And that's why you're going to calm down and hold onto yourself for three months.

There was more of it, a lot more. They would go on this way sometimes all night, would abandon any pretense of sleep and just have at it. They were brothers, they loved each other, that too. But at a certain point, it was all too much for me. I had other things on my mind and I did not have, as they would say, their commitment.

Tricky banged his knee getting out of a limousine in October and got it infected, Tricky's luck. We thought that that would do it, when he had to take to his wretched bed for almost a week and cancel all campaigning. That and the debates seemed to take him down, there was a point in mid-October when it was all crowds and shouting, thunder in the air and the clean, high purpose of victory. The motorcades, the crowded podium downtown, the pumping, prancing bands, the colors of the Fall, all of them seemed to mesh and carry us forward in one vast, surging pennant that swallowed and wrapped us in the history to be made. The Bishop's speech had worked or at least that was what Gallup was saying, and Lyndon Bird was putting out his all, doing what he was supposed to do and apparently keeping it from the Northern papers. In those days, Jack grew larger, redder, firmer, he seemed to shine with power and even the back relented a little, he was able to lean forward in the limousines, wave unsupported, make his way in and out of the banquet halls without stumbling. At the Smith banquet he laid them all out, even made Tricky smile his pained smile when Spellman came over and kissed him.

But Tricky was stubborn, he had a second-stringer's insistence and he got out of bed and came on. Eisenhower, a picture on the wall until then, began to make some noises, coming to understand for the first time perhaps that a man twenty-seven years younger, a junior officer and not a Republican, might come to change the guard and maybe revise a few ranks. We struggled on through the suddenly diminished arc of Fall, the darkness earlier, the flights bumpier, the motorcades ever more arduous and desperate. In New York there was a rally scheduled for five in the evening and a crowd of maybe 20,000, the largest crowd ever to gather for a candidate's rally, we were told, waited in the dusk and chill for three hours but Jack never came, the schedule had come hopelessly askew and he was still in Syracuse, shouting at a banquet of 500 young or younger Democrats until it was too late to get in there. It happened a lot in those gathering days, the sense of slow and careful unraveling and Bobby was helpless to deal with it, was not able to reach the top man here, the top contact there, we were told, picked up one disclaimer after the next. Tricky, undeterred by the Quemoy-Matsu shelling and the missile gap, plugged on and on, offering more Republican cloth coats. Daley finally caught up with us in Evanston, very late, after the campaign had gone to bed, after we had nearly canceled Chicago in the torrent of missed connections.

I want to know where your head is, he said, I want to know what the fuck you think you're fucking doing, that's all.

Jack stared at him. Listen, he said, I don't need—

Bobby put a hand on his elbow. That's just this guy's way, the hand pressure said. This is Dick Daley. Hear him out. Do nothing.

Yes you need, Daley said. You need all the help you can fucking get. You're screwing it up. The word is out.

I'm doing all right, Jack said. The polls—

Fuck on the polls, Daley said. He had come in with three silent men, large men, they stood with scarves over their shoulders and one of them rubbed Daley's back like a handler. You take the polls, you can read them in East Sheboygan picking up garbage. You're going to lose this, Daley said, you're on the way.

Now I don't think—

I don't care what you think. What you think is of no interest to me. You want to lose, that's okay, you got a safe seat in Massachusetts and you own half of fucking Hyannis and Boston, anyway. But you take me down in state, that's something else. You can hurt me, you hear that?

No one hurts you, Dick, Bobby said. You're beyond hurting.

Daley gave him a quick, sudden look, all jowls and curiosity. You think so? he said. Old Joe tell you to say that, you think that's the way to handle this? Well it isn't.

What do you want? Bobby said. Just tell me what it is.

Who talks? You talk? The brother is running for president, the wrong brother is making the deals. Who's the show here?

I'm the show, Jack said. He took his arm free from Bobby's grasp. What do you want? he said. You can't come in and shit all over me like this. You don't like me, okay, but I'm your party's nominee—

Ground Adlai, Daley said, that's the first thing you can do. Shut him the fuck up. We've had Adlai twice around the bend, it's enough Adlai. Every time he speaks he loses you five hundred votes. You already got every Jew on the West Side, there's nothing more he can do for you. Shut him up.

Adlai's not so easy to shut up, Bobby said.

You are an inexperienced man, Daley said. You are an inexperienced kid running a goddamned national campaign and you understand nothing. Adlai can be shut up. Anyone can be shut up. Haven't heard much from old Harry recently, have you? Been real quiet since the convention, hasn't he? But you got to get to Adlai. Tell him to shitcan it, you hear me?

We'll talk to him, Jack said. What's the other stuff?

You do more than talk to him, Daley said. You don't patronize me, young fellow, I wiped your daddy's ass many a time when he got it out of line. The other thing is I've got some stuff on Tricky you can use. He put a hand out, one of the handlers found an envelope, put it in the palm. Real good stuff, you take a look. You can feed it out.

Feed it out? Bobby said. He shook his head, laughed. To who? Who's going to print whatever you have there? The *Republication National Gazette*? We haven't got a publisher who would touch this.

You feed it out where you can, Daley said. You get it to the reporters and let it leak. Reporters know what to do, how to pass things along. They all hate Tricky, anyway.

Jack looked at the envelope. Do I have to open this? he said. Read it?

Not necessarily. Just pass it along.

Why don't you pass it along?

Because, you shit, Daley said, *I'm* not running for fucking President of the fucking United States, that's why. Because I'm just a wheelhorse, the big boss. You're the one with the credibility. Don't you understand campaigning?

We got pretty far without knowing anything, Bobby said. For a couple of rich kids we did pretty good, don't you think?

Daley shook his head. You fool, he said. You got through because I *let* you through, that's why. You don't get near the gates of the stockyards if I don't open them. And another thing, Jack.

What's that? Jack said. He handed the envelope to Bobby. Bobby opened the envelope and looked at the contents, shaking his head. What crap, Bobby said. Anybody could have known this.

Anybody could but nobody does, Daley said. Another thing, Jack. You quit the fucking around. I have my sources, I know what's going on.

Nothing's going on, Bobby said. We already talked about that.

Your information is wrong, Daley said. Your information is full of shit. You are only the brother, you don't know what the hell is going on. It's going on all the time.

Nothing's going on, I tell you, Bobby said.

Four-fifteen Tuesday, Daley said. At the Holiday Inn, room two-four-one. Seventeen minutes. She cried at the end. Cried at the beginning too, but not in the middle. You must be some guy, Mr. President, Mr. Senator. Got out of the room at four-thirty-two. You think I don't know? We know everything.

Bobby looked at Jack. Tuesday? he said.

Jack shrugged, stared at the wall. The henchmen, all three of them, laughed.

Shit, Bobby said. Shit, I thought we had a deal.

We had a deal, Jack said.

I can't control everything. I can't lead you around, Jack. I'm not Old Joe and you're not fourteen years old.

Okay, Jack said, okay, I hear you. I won't—

More and more, Daley said. You're going to do it more and more. You get elected, you'll think you can take on the world. You'll take on fucking Marilyn Monroe in Madison Square Garden, that's what you'll do.

Bobby said, This is too much, Jack. I don't want to handle this.

Okay, Jack said, okay, Dick. I'll stay clean.

Stay clean! You better get a nun's habit, you son of a bitch. You start screwing around in office, you think the whole country is Massachusetts, the press will cover up for you? You think Sam Rayburn is Joe Kennedy? You think Joe Martin is Dave Powers? They'll crucify you, you horny, tormented son of a bitch, and you'll take us *all* down. You cut it out, do you hear me? He turned, motioned to the henchmen, walked out of the room.

Jack ran after him, brushing Bobby's arm away. Dick! he said, and Daley, already in the hall, turned, looked at him. What is it? Daley said. I've said what I have to, there's nothing else to say. You got the word.

You don't walk out on me, Jack said. I'm running for goddamned president, you show some respect, you understand? I'm forty-three years old, you don't shit on me like this.

Anything else, kid? Daley said. His face was blotched. What else do you have to tell me?

No, Jack said.

Good.

I don't mean no, there's nothing else to tell you. I mean, no, I won't cut it out. I don't take orders from you. I live my own life, you hear me?

Jack, Bobby said, Jack, come back in the room.

I'm forty-three, Jack said, I don't have to listen to your shit. I listened to Old Joe's crap for years, that's enough of it. I hid him away and I'll hide you. I'm living *my* life, my way. You don't tell me what to do, you understand that?

Oh yes, Daley said, I understand. I understand good.

Go away, Jack said, get out of here. Go and play with the fishes. I don't give a fuck for you and your shit. He snatched the papers from Bobby's hands and threw them at Daley. Fuck your crap, he said. See? I can say fuck too.

I have a temper too. I got some ideas too. Get out of here, Jack said, go away.

I'll do that, Daley said. He bent, took the papers, put them into his coat pocket. His henchmen wiped invisible spots from his shoulders. He walked away.

Jack stood there, breathing hard, then his respiration slowly faded to normal. Shrugging off Bobby's touch, he walked back to the room. The hell with it, he said. I lose, I lose. I'll live longer, anyway.

Jack—

I mean it, Jack said, *I'll live longer*. How long would I last, listening to guys like Daley, taking orders from them?

Daley's the ball game, Bobby said. He's the ball game.

No, Jack said. He closed the door behind them, walked to the cabinet, took out a bottle and a pack of the cigarettes he never smoked in public. No way, he said, *I'm* the ball game. Win or lose.

We could have used that stuff on Tricky. It was solid stuff.

Fuck it, Jack said. Fuck the solid stuff. Maybe we go for dreams and air now.

Just like Adlai? Bobby said.

I don't care. Just like Adlai.

Powers said, We won't know any more until late morning. Go to bed, Jack. Lie down. It will still be there in the morning.

Illinois is coming in, Jack said. It will come in by dawn's early light. We'll hang around for it.

You never know, Bobby said. You never know. Consider the alternative.

I've considered the alternative, Jack said. All of them. You know what? What I told the son of a bitch that night is true, it's true, that's all. I'll live longer. So I'll give up the Senate seat. I'll write a book or something, one on my own this time. Maybe look for something else out there.

You think there's peace that way, Bobby said, peace for guys like us going that way? Losers? Losing?

Yeah, Jack said. He took a deep breath, blew it out, rubbed his back, showed his right hand to the room. When it comes down, he said, when the swelling goes away, I'll be able to jerk off again, anyway.

We all laughed at that. I laughed too. I had to, even knowing what I knew. He was a scrapper. He was, in or out of it, the toughest guy I knew, tougher than Old Joe could ever have measured. And never said a bad word to those other than what deserved it.

Let's have a drink, Jack said. Let's pray for Tricky.

We had a drink. Daley released the Chicago returns at 6:15 A.M. We lost Illinois by 240,000 votes and with it, the election.

1964

Lyndon Johnson won a landslide victory over Barry Goldwater in 1964. To many people, LBJ's victory and subsequent actions as president marked the *real* beginning of the 1960s (most of which took place, paradoxically, in the early 1970s).

Eileen Gunn, multiple Hugo nominee and author of many exceptional short stories, here offers up one of her typically off-the-wall fables, which is almost impossible to define or categorize, so we'll simply tell you that Goldwater won in 1964 and let Eileen take it from there.

Fellow Americans

by Eileen Gunn

". . . And now, the man you *loved to hate*, the man you *loved too late*, the man *everyone* loves to *second-guess*, America's own *Tricky Dick*!"

Applause, and the strains of "Let Me Call You Sweetheart." A tanned, well-groomed man in a blue blazer and gray slacks walks between the curtains.

He raises his hands above his head in the familiar double V-for-Victory salute to acknowledge the applause, then gestures for quiet.

"Thanks for the hand, folks." His voice is deep, quiet, and sincere. "You know, I needed that applause today."

A catch in his throat. "Right before the show, I was on my way down here to the studio . . ." He shakes his head slightly, as if contemplating the role that Chance plays in Life. "An elderly lady came up to me, and she introduced herself, and then she said, 'Oh, Dick, I'm so pleased to meet you, you know you were my all-time favorite presidential candidate . . .' " He lets the compliment hang there a second, as if savoring it. " ' . . . after Jack Kennedy, of course.' "

The audience laughs, appreciating the host who can tell a joke at his own expense. When the laughter has diminished, but before it stops completely, he continues.

"Speaking of politics, why is everybody picking on Dan Quayle these days?" He looks from face to face in the audience, as if for an answer. "He hasn't done anything." An artful pause. "And, as I know from my own turn at the job, he probably won't get to do anything in the future, either." More laughter, stronger.

He holds up a hand to stop them. "Seriously, folks, just the other day I was sharing a story with Dan—a story about two brothers." His voice is soft, as if confessing a family secret. "One ran away to sea and the other grew up to be elected vice president. . . ." He hunches his shoulders and looks down at the floor, shaking his head pensively. "Neither one of them was ever heard from again," he adds lugubriously. The audience howls with laughter and applauds enthusiastically.

The Governor of New York City looked out the small round window at the top of the ten-story Tower of Diminished Expectations and, through dirty glass, surveyed the 1990 New York World's Fair. He and Ethel had walked the 280 stairs to the top, and they were more than slightly out of breath.

Their hostess, a lovely young woman in a miniskirted uniform and a startlingly authentic retro-Sixties bubble haircut, pointed out the three festival areas they had just toured—the glass and steel pavilions of the Private Sector, the workaday plastic stucco of the Public Sector, and the tattered, colorful tents of the makeshift Alternative Fair.

The Private Sector, a promotional crankshaft for the wheels of industry, included the Minamata Pavilion, an entire building made from the byproducts of engineered bacteria raised on toxic waste; McRainforest, a model cattle ranch from the Amazon; and Weyerhaeuser's Walking Woods, a moving strip of biotope that rolled past onlookers as robot animals sang about the delightful variety of life in a clear-cut woodland.

In contrast, the Public Sector presented a cluster of low-budget homilies on the virtues of self-sufficiency and making-do-with-less—preparing people to live in a world of survivable nukes, reduced government services, lowered wages and raised taxes. Its highlights were a low-level nuclear waste dump, which was built right on the site and would be entombed there after the Fair closed, and a mammoth exhibit on Local Empowerment, made entirely by grade-school children out of papier-maché.

The Alternative Fair was an amorphous bunch of whole-earthers and punk-what-have-yous that had cadged land next to the Fair for their tent city and claimed to feed three thousand homeless people a day on the waste from the Fair's restaurants. Though the organizers maintained an aura of anonymity, the Governor suspected that more than one of his younger kids was involved. More power to them, he thought.

Behind him, the troop of wheezing reporters who had followed them up the stairs pushed into the room. The torrent of questions started.

"Governor Kennedy, do you have any comment on the proceedings against you?"

"Sir, will you be testifying in your defense?"

"No comment on that right now, folks," he said with a reflexive smile, and started back down the steps at a hearty pace.

When he got to the bottom, he paused for just a second. "You know," he said, for the benefit of the reporters braking to a stop behind him, "this tower reminds me of George Bush's budgeting procedure. You go around and around and around, and you end up just south of where you started."

Most of them laughed and some of them jotted it down. Flashbulbs popped. Leaving the tower, considerably ahead of Ethel, the guide, and the pack of reporters, he tried not to scan the crowd. There was no use worrying about it. He walked through the mass of people, waving, nodding to individuals, lightly touching people's shoulders.

There was a commotion to his right, and a slight, dark-haired man moved forward abruptly and shot him, point-blank, in the side.

"Just as well you're not hooked up to the lie detector yet, Dick," says Ed McMahon, shaking his head and chuckling, "or I'd make you confess who you stole those jokes from."

"Well, enough of this then, Ed, let's get me hooked up and get this show on the road!" He gives a lurching shrug and waves his forearms around stiffly. The audience loves it.

"Who are our guests today, Ed?" he asks as two young ladies in skimpy nurse outfits lead him to the dais between the two panels of contestants.

"Well, Dick, our guests today on the Republican side are . . . Zsa Zsa Gabor . . . and Arnold C. Hammurabi of Seattle, Washington. . . . And, on the Democratic side, Dick Van Dyke . . . and Ms. Suzanne Ackerly of Pittsfield, Massachusetts, back for her fifth week. Arnold, why don't you tell us a little about yourself?"

As Arnold talks, the nurses strap the lie detector to Tricky Dick.

Dick gives a brief, funny, and patently false weather report, allowing the participants to test their handsets. On the dais in front of each contestant, a colored panel shows how the contestant rates Tricky Dick's truthfulness. The panel changes through the spectrum from true blue for truth to choleric red for outright lies.

Home viewers can see an additional panel that shows how the lie detector rates Tricky Dick's truthfulness. It doesn't think much of the weather report, that much is clear.

The former president, retired now since 1973, stood in the doorway of his desert home and looked out across the city to watch the early morning sun strike the distant red and ocher arroyos.

Phoenix had been all rutted roads and ditches when he was a boy. In place of the dry-dirt farms that had taken water from the Salt and Verde rivers, there were now mammoth hydroponic farm-domes, controlled from glass towers, sucking in desalinated seawater from a pipeline and spewing forth tasteless vegetables. Suburban homes looked down from the mountains; each identical four-level home had its desal pool and its automated repair shop for the owner's helicopter and 2.6 cars.

Slowly and carefully, he drew in his mind a picture of the surrounding land as it would have been without the interference of the white man. He imagined the land stripped of the crust of human domination, cleaner even than it had been in his childhood. It looked good that way.

Glad I kept this old house, he thought. Happier here than in one of those damn futurama things. He walked slowly down the path to the hot tub, his cane making dull tapping sounds on the slate-blue flagstone. A good soak would ease the pain he felt in his knees, elbows, back, the artificial hips, all over, really. Where do these random stabs come from, he wondered. Now the left wrist, a really sharp one. Nothing the matter with the wrist—it'll still open jars—just a mean shot of pain right now. A reminder I'm still alive, I guess.

He tapped across the redwood deck to the tub, shed

his *yukata*, and, gripping the bars, lowered himself into the water. It was hot all right.

The pain was seeping away from his joints. He settled down further into the water and leaned his head back against the cedar rim of the tub. Quiet, this time of day, just the occasional clinking of dishes off at the kitchen end of the house as his housekeeper Lillian got the breakfast ready.

After breakfast, he had to meet with the crew from that PBS show, *Geraldo's Manifest Destinies*. Wasn't really sure why he'd agreed to do this—except Haldeman thought it would help with fund-raising for the museum. Always was uncomfortable with the primping you had to do for television. Now that running for office was happily behind him, all he needed was a blowdryer on the topknot and a little light makeup he could do himself.

Might even be fun to get someone out here—it had been kind of lonely since he finished his memoirs. He had no political agenda, just a little harmless PR puffery for the presidential museum to get those contributions rolling in. Guess he could spout off on just about any old subject he wanted, and let the chips fall where they may.

Birds were making a small racket at the feeder. Got to figure out how to keep those damn robins from eating all the seed before the doves and quail get to it. . . .

Lillian had left his *Washington Post* within reach, but he wasn't sure he wanted to know what was in it. Wouldn't be good news. AIDS, oil spills, violence. Bleeding heart editorials about the homeless.

Maybe I should just cancel the damn thing and stick to *Popular Mechanics*. Nah, he thought. Bite the bullet. Find out what they're saying back there.

He unfolded the paper. No major stories this morning.

NORIEGA TRIAL DELAYED. They'll never bring him to trial. Too many buried bodies.

RAD BABIES DENIED ENTRANCE FROM MIDEAST. Tough call. Damned if you do and damned if you don't.

FEDERAL JUDGE FINDS RAP LP OBSCENE. What's the world coming to? Who listens to this stuff?

Inside, the headlines were even less involving.

RFK TO RUN IN '92? Nah. Never gone for the big job, never will.

NEW SEASON FOR *TRICKY DICK*. Twenty years that thing's been on the air, about time he retired, wasn't it? Funny thing about Nixon—wouldn't have thought he'd make it on TV in any way, shape, or form. But some peculiar inability to concede defeat had led him to confront the medium and master it. Just as well he hadn't taken the same approach to politics. Never did trust the man.

He flipped quickly to the editorial pages, guaranteed to raise his blood pressure.

POLITICS AS USUAL? read the head on the lead editorial.

> Negative political advertising is nothing new. The present trend of sleazy innuendo started with the notorious 1964 campaign that drove Lyndon Johnson from office. But the current spate of smarmy sensationalism, everyone seems to agree, is the dirtiest yet, exceeding even the harsh 1988 campaign of—

Sonofabitch. All that stuff about Johnson was true, dammit. Sure, Ailes made the most of it, but there's no law against that—that's what a PR guy is for. Doggonit, the best thing about starting the day off with the *Post* was that it could only get better.

Members of the audience raise their hands to ask questions, chosen beforehand for their originality, sincerity, and capability of being answered with a lie.

The first few are too easy. "Do you agree with Andrew Jackson that there are no necessary evils in government?" "Do you think the U.S. should trust the Russians?" With questions that cut and dried, everybody can pretty much agree when Tricky Dick is lying and when he is telling the truth.

The best kind of questions for the show, all the regular watchers agree, are questions that result in an emotional reaction of some kind as well as a factual answer, or questions that bring forth an elaborate anecdote. This is where Tricky Dick is an artist with fact and fiction, heartfelt appeal and outright lie.

The living room had been radically rearranged by stylists from the Geraldo show, and now the two men, former president and respected PBS commentator, sat waiting in carefully angled armchairs positioned in front of a wall of books and kachina dolls. Geraldo's sculptured features were passive, his eyes blank. He got the signal to start, sprang vibrantly to life, and addressed the camera: "Rad babies! AIDS! Mutant rats! Is *this* the man responsible? We'll be back in just two minutes." The network cut to announcements, and Geraldo turned off again. A makeup girl appeared next to him, pushed a recalcitrant tuft of mustache into place, and misted it with a tiny can of hairspray.

Always hated this part of politics, thought the former president. Won't say I was born too late, but I'm damned sure I wasn't born a minute too soon—never be able to stand the rigmarole that politicians have to go through now.

The camera was back, and Geraldo revived again: "For better or worse, tactical nukes are now a way of life in troubled parts of the world. These baby bombs, first deployed by our guest today during the Vietnam War, are easy to use and tough to clean up after. What do you say, Barry, can we lay this mess at your doorstep?"

"Well, as I've said before, Geraldo, I wasn't the only one involved in deciding to use these weapons, but I accept responsibility for the decision, yes."

"I guess we know you stand behind your use of nukes in Vietnam, but don't you feel a little guilty about the millions of deaths that have resulted from the proliferation of these weapons?"

"As far as that goes, Geraldo, I think you have to look on these things as being the natural result of a free market econom—"

"Thanks, Barry. We'll be back with more, after these messages."

Why did I agree to do this, wondered the former president. Haldeman's got some explaining ahead of him.

A young man in the audience, hair a little long but neatly combed, raises his hand: "Sir, can you tell us, did you ever take LSD in the Sixties? If so, what was it like for you?"

The familiar hollow vowels: "I'm glad you asked me that question." Running a hand over the top of his head. "As a matter of fact, the truth is"—Tricky Dick's voice becomes dramatically husky—"yes, I have taken LSD." A subdued murmur of anticipation from the audience: what a great question!

"Of course, this was before it was declared illegal. I am not a— I've always believed in law and order.

"It began—it was some time back around 1965, after Pat and I had moved back to California. We had some, uh, show business friends, who had, who had experimented with LSD. Pat and I were going through a period of . . . of withdrawal from politics, and our friends thought it might help us, uh, make our peace with our destinies, if we took some of this LSD." He takes a deep breath. "Let me tell you what happened." The camera zooms in on his hands: he's wringing them nervously. "We arranged for this fellow to come to our house, to be our 'guide,' and he gave us two little white pills. This cost about three hundred dollars, which was a lot of money back then, as you might remember. Well, Pat and I just looked at each other. We were nervous, but we'd come this far, and we were determined to see it through.

"So we swallowed them, with the help of a little chocolate milk. Then we sat on the floor and listened to Leonard Bernstein records for a while. Pat took off her shoes, and I first loosened my tie, then took it off entirely."

As he relaxes into the story, Tricky Dick seems to confide in the audience. "Well I tell you, I didn't feel like my usual cocky, confident self there. I was full of restless energy. I fidgeted. I started to feel *very* uneasy. Then I realized that the problem was that I had no control over what was going to happen to me. I was accustomed to having control over even the smallest things in my life. And you know, my fath— My upbringing was such that I believed that a man had to be in control at all times.

"But as I struggled to remain calm, I realized that I did have a choice: I could relinquish control or continue to fight for it with the drug.

"I decided I would voluntarily give up control, and I made a gesture of giving, giving control over to the drug. At that moment a great peace descended on me, and I felt as though I had passed into another dimension. I cried freely, letting the tears run down my cheeks—and yet, I felt very happy, and I was smiling."

Eventually the reporters left the room and the Governor of New York City lit a cigarette and leaned back against the pillows. It was OK to light one, he told himself, as long as he just held it. He lifted it to his lips. As long as he didn't inhale, he amended. He didn't inhale. He couldn't, really, they had him strapped so tightly around the chest.

"Governor!" It was the day nurse. "What do you think you're doing?"

. . . She was right. "Damn," he said. "Wasn't thinking. Sorry." He handed her the cigarette.

Mollified, the nurse, an attractive blonde woman with gray streaks in her hair, smiled at him. "Your wife's on her way over, Governor."

" 'Bout time." He sure didn't feel great just now. They'd pushed it too close, letting the guy get off a shot. Could have shot him in the head, for Chrissake. He didn't want to blink out the way Jack had—too suddenly to put things in order, make proper goodbyes, say the things left unsaid. Though he wouldn't want to hang on for a decade like his father, either, tubes plugged into him at both ends, bringing stuff in at the top and taking it out at the bottom.

He wasn't ready to check out yet at all, thank you very much. At sixty-five, he still had the time and stamina to run for president. He could win, too, and he could do the job.

Funny, though, as a kid, he'd always been happiest in the supporting role. He could have done it for Jack, if things had worked out differently. And in '64, if that son-of-a-bitch Johnson had supported him for VP, he'd have taken it. They'd have beaten Goldwater, in spite of Ailes and his dirty tricks, dragging out the Jenkins thing and Johnson's past. . . .

"Hey, Ace, how you feelin'?" It was Ethel.

"I hurt like hell, is how I feel," he said. "What the fuck happened there?"

His wife turned to the nurse. "You can take a break now, if you'd like. I'll take care of him if he needs anything." The woman nodded and left them alone.

"I've just been hashing that over with your boys," said his wife. "After sticking to that guy like a second skin for three weeks, while he shadows you and buys the gun and writes like crazy in his diary, they lose him in the crowd at the last minute, just inside the gate."

"Jeez."

" 'Jeez' is right. This was a totally screwy idea. He could have killed you, vest or no vest."

"Well, he didn't. Don't borrow trouble. This is worth millions in press sympathy."

"What are you planning to do?" she asked sarcastically. "Announce you're running for president tomorrow, as you're released from the hospital?"

He answered seriously. "No, timing's all wrong. With the off-year elections coming up, the story would be old news real fast. But I'll be dropping some hints in the next few weeks, and by, say, January of next year, I should be ready to make a definite statement. . . ."

"You're out of your mind," she said. "Next time, they won't miss."

He turned on the television across from the bed. "It's time for *Tricky Dick.*"

"I know you don't hear a word I'm saying."

"We've already missed the opening monologue."

"I suppose you've got to do it, so go ahead, Bob," she said. "I don't have to like it. But next time you uncover a plot, have them pick the guy up right away, OK?"

The next president of the United States looked up at his wife and nodded his head. "I think I'll do that." He took her hand, and she curled up next to him on the bed to watch the show.

Tricky Dick's lips are pursed, his eyes slightly unfocused: he's transfixed by his own story.

". . . then I was the captain of a submarine, steering my vessel though seas populated by my enemies, watching them through the periscope, confident, knowing that not one of them knew where I was. Suddenly, I realized that I was the *submarine*, not the captain! For a moment, I wondered: who's the captain? who's the captain? and then I realized that I was *both* the captain *and* the submarine! And I was the sea as well, and the enemy ships! It was all a cosmic game, and we are all one, all the gameplayers and the game itself."

His voice deepens. "Well, I knew this was a really important insight, and I started to write it down, but just then I looked over and saw that Pat was weeping quietly under the grand piano. I realized that she was having a 'bad trip.'

"I piloted my sub over under the piano and extended my periscope, which was also my hand, toward her.

"She looked up at me, her eyes dimmed with tears, and as we looked at one another, I realized that she knew exactly what I was thinking, about the submarine and all, and that she'd been crying for each of us, the whole world, in our separate submarines, not knowing that we were really all part of the same game, all one, and I said to her, 'You know, don't you?' And she nodded, without speaking, because she didn't need to speak, she didn't need to say one word, she just needed to know, and she knew.

"Of course, afterward when we talked about it, I found out that she had been crying about all the music trapped in the piano, but on some level I think she really *did* know. You know?"

The Governor of New York City, propped up against the pillows of his hospital bed, laughed out loud. Stories like this were exactly the sort of thing that he tuned in to hear. The master, he thought, was not losing his touch.

The retired president hit the sound button on his controller and watched the people on the screen move their mouths ridiculously.

The son of a bitch looks *happy*, he thought, happy and healthy. Getting a little jowly, maybe, but I'll bet he still plays a couple of rounds of golf a week.

What does a guy like that think about? How could he turn his back on it all? Not so much on power—you don't get the power you think you'll have as president—but on the chance to change the course of history.

Could I have kissed it goodbye, he wondered, if things had worked out a little different? Stayed with the department store, maybe, or gone into some kind of commercial flying?

Nah, never.

He thought about these things a lot, now that Peggy was gone. Hadn't spent enough time with her and the kids, it was true. When he retired after his eight years, he had his flying, his ham radio, his photography. He'd figured that there'd be plenty of time, once he was too old to fly, to sit around with Peggy and watch *Tricky Dick* on the tube. How little we know. Peggy's probably happier where she is now, he thought wryly. She never cared much for TV, and she'd always hated politics.

In the evening, after dinner, the TV celebrity and former vice president wandered out onto his magnificent deck, and admired his spectacular view of the Pacific Ocean. The sun had set some time ago, and the sky, red at the horizon, shaded upward through a few dark wisps of cloud to clear yellow-green, to pale blue, and then to purple. Rather like the lie detector readout, he thought. The first stars were beginning to appear, and Jupiter was bright in the west.

Pat, martini glass in hand, came out from the living room and took his arm. "Dan and Marilyn must be wondering what's happening, Dick," she said. "You just up and walked out."

"I was just thinking," her husband replied, "what a great night it would be to just sit out here in the hot tub, under the stars. Tell them to get their drinks and come on out here."

"Dick, are you out of your mind? We barely know them. Besides, they're from the Midwest."

"Aw, let's get them out here. Let's give them a taste of the real California." He crossed the deck to the living room door. "You folks grab your drinks and come on out here," he called. "Don't you worry," he said to his wife in a low voice, "this'll be fun."

Dan and Marilyn came out onto the deck, smiling and politely curious.

"Beautiful night," said Dan. "What a view."

"Those flowers smell wonderful," said Marilyn.

"That's nicotiana, tobacco plant," said Pat. "It blooms at night, and it does have a heavenly scent."

"Have we shown you round the deck?" Dick asked, moving toward the steps that led down to the hot tub.

He remembered the first time he'd sat naked in a hot tub with other people, back in the Sixties. He'd felt very vulnerable, very awkward. Even now, he had to admit, it didn't feel completely natural. But there was something exhilarating in overcoming those feelings and, he had to be honest with himself, it was sort of fun to get new people to take off their clothes.

"On nights like this," he said, "we generally bring our drinks down here to the hot tub, just sit out here, smell the flowers, and get in touch with our feelings."

"Not so different from D.C.," murmured Marilyn. "Except we usually just fax any messages for our feelings."

Dick's twitchy smile flashed for just a second.

Of the four people in the hot tub, Dick thought, I'm the only one who's truly at ease. The thought didn't bother him.

The other man looked around nervously—not quite sure what to do with his eyes. His wife was cooler, a tough cookie with brains and backbone, but even she was holding herself a bit lower in the water than strictly necessary. And Pat, as usual, was embarrassed—more with his blatant power play than with casual nudity. She's come a long way from the prim housewife of the Fifties, he thought.

"So tell me about the Mars mission, Dan," he said. "That's your pet project, isn't it?"

Dan had the look of a golden retriever, and now Dick had tossed him a bone. He splashed a little and gave a self-assured smile.

"That's right, sir—uh, Dick. Fascinating planet, Mars." He searched for something to say.

Dick waited. He'd learned to let the other guy flail about in the game of conversational tennis.

"Could be a very important mission," Dan added helplessly. "We have seen pictures where there are canals, we believe, and water. If there is water, there is oxygen. If oxygen, that means we can breathe."

"Really, Dan?" said Pat, astonished.

Marilyn laughed gaily and winked at Pat. "Don't let him pull your leg," she said. There was a movement in the water, and Dick realized that it was Marilyn putting her foot on top of her husband's. Dan responded with a shake of the head and a big golden-retriever grin.

"Sorry, ma— Uh, Pat. Most of this stuff's classified."

Marilyn laughed again. "Danny likes to have his fun with the Mars stuff," she said. "Most of it's just a lot of technical jargon at this point—the usual logistical discussions—really pretty boring."

Dan nodded obediently.

"But you know, Dick," she said, "one of the things you might find interesting is this—they're implementing a biofeedback training program for the mission, to help the participants control their breathing rates and body functions in an emergency."

Dick looked at her. The archness in her voice—she was driving at something.

She continued. "I've heard you've had some training in this?"

He leaned back against the edge of the tub. "Well, way back in the Sixties, of course," he said. "Just about everybody I know did."

"So what's the story," she asked coolly. "Does it help you fool the lie detector?"

"Lie detector?" He was amused. "Lie detector?" he repeated. These political people. He was so glad he was out of Washington. "Marilyn," he said, "this is television. We don't *need* lie detectors." And again he flashed his famous crooked grin.

1968

To anyone who lived through it, there will never be anything remotely like the 1968 presidential campaign again: the murder of Robert F. Kennedy, the murder of Dr. Martin Luther King, Jr., Eugene McCarthy's "Children's Crusade," the spectacle of Lyndon Baines Johnson virtually a prisoner within the White House, and finally, climactically, the riots during the Democratic Convention in Chicago.

But what *really* happened at Chicago, beneath the smoke and tear gas? Pat Cadigan, Hugo- and Nebula-nominated author of *Mindplayers, Synners,* and a number of savagely brilliant short stories, offers one startling reconstruction.

Dispatches from the Revolution

by Pat Cadigan

Dylan was coming to Chicago.

The summer air, already electric with the violence of the war, the assassination attempts successful and unsuccessful, the anti-war riots, became super-charged with the rumor. Feeling was running high, any feeling about anything, real high, way up high, eight miles high and rising, brothers and sisters. And to top it all off, there was a madman in the White House.

Johnson, pull out like your father should have! The graffito of choice for anyone even semi-literate; spray paint sales must have been phenomenal that summer. The old bastard with a face like the dogs he lifted up by their ears would not give it up, step aside, and graciously bow to the inevitable. He wuz the Prezident, the gaw-damned Prezident, hear that, muh fellow Amurricans? *Dump Johnson, my ass, don't even* think *about it, boys, the one we ought to dump is that candy-assed Humphrey. Gaw-damned embarrassment is what* he is.

And the President's crazy, *that's what* he *is*, went the whispers all around Capitol Hill, radiating outward until they became shouts. *Madman in the White House—the crazy way with LBJ!* If you couldn't tell he was deranged by the way he was stepping up the bombing and the number of troops in Vietnam, his conviction that he could actually stand against Bobby Kennedy clinched it. Robert F. Kennedy, sainted brother to martyred Jack, canonized in his own lifetime by an assassination attempt. Made by the only man in America who was obviously crazier than LBJ, frothed-up Arab with a name like automatic-weapons-fire, Sir*han* Sir*han*, ka-boom, ka-boom. The Golden Kennedy had actually *assisted* in the crazed gunman's capture, shoulder to shoulder with security guards and the Secret Service as they all wrestled him to the floor. Pity about the busboy taking that bullet right in the eye, but the Kennedys had given him a positively lovely funeral with RFK himself doing the eulogy. And, needless to say, the family would never want for anything again in this life.

But Johnson the Madman was going to run! Without a doubt, he was a dangerous psychotic. Madman in the White House—damned straight you didn't need a Weatherman to know the way the wind blew.

Nonetheless, there *was* one—after all, hadn't Dylan said the answer was blowin' in the wind? And if he was coming to Chicago to support the brothers and sisters, that *proved* the wind was about to blow gale force. Storm coming, batten down the hatches, fasten your seatbelts, and grab yourself a helmet, or steal a hardhat from some redneck construction worker.

Veterans of the Civil Rights Movement already had their riot gear. Seven years after the first freedom ride stalled out in Birmingham, the feelings of humiliation and defeat at having to let the Justice Department scoop them up and spirit them away to New Orleans for their own protection had been renewed in the violent death of the man who had preached victory through nonviolence. He'd had a dream; the wake-up call had come as a gunshot. Dreaming was for when you were asleep. Now it was time to be wide-awake in America. . . .

Annie Phillips:

"There were plenty of us already wide-awake in America by that late date. I'd been to Chicago back in '66, two years to the month in Marquette Park. If I was never awake any other day in my life before April '68, I was awake that day. Surrounded by a thousand of the meanest white people in America waving those Confederate flags and those swastikas, screaming at us. And then they let fly with rocks and bricks and bottles, and I saw when Dr. King took one in the head. I'd thought he was gonna die that day and all the rest of us with him. Well, he didn't and we didn't, but it was a near thing. After, the buses were pulling away and they were chasing us and I looked back at those faces and I thought, 'There's no hope. There's really no hope.'

"When Daley got the court order against large groups marching in the city, I breathed a sigh of relief, I can tell you. I felt like that man had saved my life. And then Dr. King says okay, we'll march in Cicero, it's a suburb, the order doesn't cover Cicero. *Cicero*. I didn't want to do it, I knew they'd kill us, shoot us, burn us, tear us up with their bare hands and teeth. Some of us were ready to meet them head-on. I truly believe that Martin Luther

King would have died that day if Daley hadn't wised up in a hurry and said he'd go for the meeting at the Palmer House.

"Summit Agreement, yeah. Sell-Out Agreement, we called it, a lot of us. I think even Dr. King knew it. And so a whole bunch of us marched in Cicero anyway. I wasn't there, but I know what happened, just like everybody else. Two hundred dead, most of them black, property damage in the millions though I can't say I could ever find it in me to grieve for property damage over people damage. Even though I wasn't there, something of me died that day in Cicero and was reborn in anger. By '68, I had a good-sized bone to pick with good old Chi-town, old Daley-ville. I don't regret what I did. All I regret is that the bomb didn't get Daley. It had his name on it, I put it on there myself, on the side of the pipe. 'Richard Daley's ticket to hell, coach class.'

"Looking back on it, I think I might have had better luck as a sniper."

Excerpt from an interview
conducted covertly at Sybil Brand,
published in
The Whole Samizdat Catalog, 1972?
exact date unknown

Veterans of the Free Speech Movement at Berkeley also knew what they were up against. Reagan's tear-gas campaign against campus protestors drew praise from a surprising number of people who felt the Great Society was seriously threatened by the disorder promoted by campus dissidents. The suggestion that the excessive force used by the police caused problems rather than solving any was rejected by the Reagan administration and by its growing blue-collar following as well.

By the time Reagan assumed the governorship, he had already made up his mind to challenge Nixon in '68. But what he needed for a serious bid was the Southern vote, which was divided between Kennedy and Wallace. Cleverly, the ex-movie actor managed to suggest strong parallels between campus unrest and racial unrest, implying that both groups were seeking the violent overthrow and destruction of the government of the United States. Some of the more radical rhetoric that came out of both the student left and the civil rights movement, and the fact that the student anti-war movement aligned itself with the civil rights movement only seemed to validate Reagan's position.

That the Southern vote would be divided between two individuals as disparate as Robert F. Kennedy and George C. Wallace seems bizarre to us in the present. But both men appealed to the working class, who felt left out of the American dream. Despite the inevitable trouble that Wallace's appearances resulted in, his message did reach the audience for which it was intended—the common man who had little to show for years, sometimes decades, of hard work beyond a small piece of property and a paycheck taxed to the breaking point, and, as far as the common man could tell, to someone else's benefit. Wallace understood that the common man felt pushed around by the government and exploited this feeling. In a quieter era, he would have come off as a bigoted buffoon; but in a time when blacks and students were demonstrating, rioting, and spouting unthinkable statements against the government, the war, and the system in general, Wallace seemed to be one of the few, if not the only political leader who had the energy to meet this new threat to the American way of life and wrestle it into submission.

Some people began to wonder if McCarthy hadn't been right about Communist infiltration and subversion after all . . . and that wasn't Eugene McCarthy they were wondering about. By the time of the Chicago Democratic Convention, Eugene McCarthy had all but disappeared, his student supporters a liability rather than an asset. They undermined his credibility; worse, they could not vote for him, since the voting age at that time was a flat twenty-one for everyone. . . .

Carl Shipley:

"I hadn't been around Berkeley long when the Free Speech Movement started. Like, the university—Towle, Kerr, all of them were so out-to-lunch on what was happening with us. They thought they were dealing with Beaver Cleaver and his Little League team, I guess. And with us, it was, 'Guess what, Mr. Man, the neighborhood's changing, it ain't Beaver Cleaver anymore, it's Eldridge Cleaver and Wally just got a notice to report for his physical and maybe he doesn't want to go get his ass shot off in southeast Asia and maybe we've had enough of this middle-American conservative bullshit.' That's why they wanted to shut down Bancroft Strip. That was the first place I went to see when I got there and it was just like everybody said, all these different causes and stuff, the Young Republicans hanging in right along with the vegetarians and the feminists and people fund-raising for candidates and I don't know what-all.

"So we all said fuck this shit, you ain't closing *us* down, we're closing *you* down. And we did it, we closed the university down. We had the power and we kept it—and then in comes Ronald Reagan two years later in '66 and he says, Relax, Mr. and Mrs. America, the cavalry's here. I know you're worried about the Beave, but I've got the solution.

"He sure did. By spring 1968, a lot of campus radio stations all over California were off the air and the campus newspapers were a joke. No funding, see. And by then, everyone was too sick of the smell of tear gas to fight real hard. That was Reagan's whole thing—sit-ins and take-overs weren't covered by the right of free assembly, they were criminal acts. Unless you had to be in a building for a class, you were trespassing. I got about a mile of trespassing convictions on my rap sheet and so do a lot of other people. And Mr. and Mrs. America, they were real impressed the way Reagan came down on the troublemakers.

"Sure were a *lot* of troublemakers. Too many to keep track of. That's what happened to me, you know. Got lost in the court system. The next thing I knew, it was 1970, and nobody remembered my name, except the guards. And they could remember my number a lot easier. Still can.

"The thing is, I never burned my draft card. That was a frame-up. I wouldn't have burned it. I was ready to go to Canada, but I intended to keep my draft card. As a reminder, you know. And not even my parents believed me. By then, I'd been into so much radical shit, they figured everything the pigs said about me was true.

"But the fact is, everything I owned was in that building when it burned. So of course my draft card burned up with it! But I never set that fire. My court-appointed lawyer—this is me laughing bitterly—said if I told my 'crazy story' about seeing off-duty cops with gasoline cans running from the scene just before the explosion, the judge would tack an extra five years on my sentence for perjury. I should have believed him, because it was the only time anyone told me the truth."

Interview conducted at Attica,
published in
Orphans of the Great Society,
Fuck The System Press, 197?
(circulated illegally in photocopy)

Some say, even today, that Reagan wouldn't have taken such an extremist path if Wallace hadn't been such a strong contender. Nixon's mistake was in dismissing Wallace's strong showing, choosing to narrow his focus to the competition within his own party for the nomination. This made him look dinky, as if he didn't care as much about being president as he did about being the Republican candidate for president. That would show those damned reporters that they couldn't kick around Dick Nixon, uh-*huh*. Even if he lost, they'd have to take him seriously; if he actually won, they'd have to take him even more seriously. Which made him look not only dinky, but like a whiner—the kind of weak sister who, for example, might stand up in front of a television camera and rant about cocker spaniel puppies and good Republican cloth coats, instead of telling the American people that rioting, looting, and draft-card burning would no longer be tolerated. Even Ike's coattails weren't enough to repair Nixon's image, and Ike himself was comatose or nearly so in Walter Reed after a series of heart attacks.

The Republican National Convention was notable for three things: Rockefeller's last-minute declaration of candidacy, which further diluted Nixon's support, the luxuriousness of the accommodations and facilities, and its complete removal from the rioting that had broken out in Miami proper, where an allegedly minor racial incident escalated into a full-scale battle. The convention center was in Miami Beach, far from the madding Miami crowd, a self-contained playground for the rich. You couldn't smell the tear gas from Miami Beach, and the wind direction was such that you couldn't hear the sirens that screamed all night long . . .

"Carole Feeney" [this subject is still a fugitive]:

"I told everybody it was the goddam fatcat Republicans that we ought to go after, not the Democrats. But Johnson the Madman was running and everyone really thought that he was going to get the nomination. I said they were crazy, Kennedy had it in the bag. But Johnson really had them all running scared. I tried talking to some of the people in the Mobe. Half of them didn't want to go to either convention and the other half were trying to buy *guns* to take to Chicago! Off the pigs, they kept saying. Off the pigs. Jesus, I thought, the only pig that was going to get offed was Pigasus—the real pig that the Yippies were going to announce as the candidate from the Youth International Party. That was cute. I mean, really, it was. I said, let's go ahead and do that somewhere in California, film it and send the film to a TV station and let them run it on the news. Uh-uh, nothing doing. Lincoln Park or bust. Yeah, right—Lincoln Park *and* bust. Busted heads, busted bodies, busted and thrown in jail.

"So I wasn't going to go. Then I found out what Davis was doing. I couldn't believe it—Davis Trainor had been in on everything practically from the beginning. He was real good-looking and real popular, he had this real goofy sense of humor and he always seemed to come up with good ideas for guerrilla action. He actually did all the set-up work on the pirate radio station we ran out of Oakland and he worked out our escape routes. Not one of us got caught in the KCUF caper. We called it our Fuck-You caper, of course.

"Then I'm doing the laundry and I find it—his COINTELPRO I.D.—stuffed into that little bitty pocket in his jeans. You know, it's like a little secret pocket right above the regular pocket on the right. The one thing I always hated about the movement was that it was as sexist as the Establishment. If you were a woman, you always got stuck doing all the cooking and the cleaning up and the laundry and stuff. Unless you were a movement queen like Dohrn. Then you didn't have to do anything except make speeches and get laid if you wanted. Oh, they threw us a sop by letting us set up our own feminist actions and stuff, but we all knew it was a sop. We kept telling each other that after we changed things, it would be different and for now, we'd watch and listen and learn. Besides, everyone knew that the Establishment wouldn't take women as seriously as they would men. I wonder now how much any of us believed that—that it would really be different, that we could change things at all.

"Anyway, I went straight to the Mobe with my discovery, but it was too late—Davis discovered his pants were missing and he'd already split. I *really* didn't want to go to Chicago after that, but the alternative seemed to be either stay home and wait to get busted, or go to Chicago and get busted in action. I was still enough of an idealist that they talked me into Chicago. If I was going to get busted, I might as well be accomplishing something, and anyway, after the revolution, I'd be a National Heroine, and not a political prisoner.

"So, the revolution's come and gone and here I am. Still working for the movement—the feminist movement, that is. What little I *can* do, referring women with unwanted pregnancies to safe abortionists. Yes, there are some. Not all of us were poli-sci majors—some of us were pre-med, some of us went to nursing school. It costs a goddam fortune, but *I'm* not getting rich on it. It's for the risk, you know. You get the death penalty in this state for performing an illegal abortion. I could get life as an accessory, and there was a woman in Missouri who *did* get death for doing what I'm doing.

"Nobody in my family knows, of course. Especially not my husband. If *he* knew, he'd probably kill me himself. Odd as it sounds, I don't hate him . . . not when I think what good cover he is, and what the alternative would be if I didn't have such good cover. . . ."

Part of a transcript labeled "Carole Feeney"
obtained in a 1989 raid on a motel

said to be part of a network of
underground "safe houses" for tax protestors,
leftist terrorists,
and other subversives;
no other illegal literature recovered

The source of the DYLAN IS COMING! rumor never was pinpointed. Some say it sprang into being all on its own and stayed alive because so many people wanted it to be true. And for all anyone knows, perhaps it actually was true, for a little while anyway; perhaps Dylan simply changed his mind. The more cynical suggested that the rumor had been planted by infiltrators like the notorious Davis Trainor, whose face became so well known thanks to the Mobe's mock WANTED poster that he had to have extensive plastic surgery, a total of a dozen operations in all. The poster was done well enough that it passed as legitimate and was often allowed to hang undisturbed in post offices, libraries, and other public places, side by side with the FBI's posters of dissidents and activists. One poster was found in a Minneapolis library as late as 1975; the head librarian was taken into custody, questioned, and released. But it is no coincidence that the library was audited for objectionable material soon after that and has been subject to surprise spot-checks for the last fifteen years, in spite of the fact that it has always showed 100 percent compliance with government standards for reading matter. The price of a tyrant's victory is eternal vigilance.

This was once considered to be the price of liberty. Nothing buys what it used to.

Steve D'Alessandro:

"By Sunday, when Dylan didn't show, people were starting to get angry. I kept saying, well, hey, Allen Ginsberg showed. Allen Ginsberg! Man, he was like . . . *God* to me. He was doing his best, going around rapping with people, trying to get everybody calmed down and focused, you know. A whole bunch of us got in a circle around him and we were chanting *Om*, *Om*. I was getting a really good vibe and then some asshole throws a bottle at him and yells, *Oh, shut up, you fag!*

"I went crazy. Sure, I was in the closet then because the movement wasn't as enlightened as some of us wished it were. The FBI was doing this thing where it was going around trying to discredit a lot of people by accusing them of being queer, and everybody caught homophobia like it was measles. I ain't no fairy, no, sir, not me, I fucked a hundred chicks this week and my dick's draggin' on the ground so don't you call *me* no fag! It still stings, even when I compare it to how things are now. But then, I don't expect any kind of enlightened feeling in a society where I have to take fucking hormone treatments so I won't get a hard-on when I see another guy.

"Anyway, I found the scumbag that did it and I punched him out. I gave *him* a limp wrist. I gave him *two* of them. And I know I had a lot of support—I mean, a lot of straights admired Ginsberg, too, even if he was gay, just on the basis of *Howl*, but later, a bunch of Abbie's friends blamed me for creating the disturbance that gave the police the excuse they needed to wade in and start busting heads.

"Sometimes I'm afraid maybe they were right. But Annie Phillips told me it was just a coincidence. About me, I mean. She said they came in because they saw a black guy kissing a white girl. I guess nobody'll ever really know for sure, because the black guy died of his injuries and the white girl never came forward.

"I prefer to think that's what made Annie and her crowd go ahead with the bomb at the convention center. I don't like to think that Annie really wanted to blow anybody up. It was kind of weird how I knew Annie. Well, not weird, really. I probably owed Annie my life, or damn near, and so did a certain man of African-American descent. We were lucky it was her that walked in on us that day. She was enlightened, or at least tolerant, and we could trust her not to say anything. I didn't think she liked white people too much, but I'd heard she'd been with Martin Luther King a couple of years before on those marches and I couldn't blame her. Anyway, she couldn't give me away without giving away the brother, but to this day, I believe it really didn't matter to her—homosexuality, that is. Maybe because the Establishment hated us worse than they hated blacks.

"Anyway, I wasn't intending to be in the crowd that crashed the gate at the convention center on Wednesday. Nomination day. We'd been fighting in the streets since Monday and Daley's stormtroopers were beating the shit out of us. Late Tuesday night, the National Guard arrived. That's when we knew it was war.

"On Wednesday, we got hemmed in in Grant Park. People were pouring in by then, and nobody had expected that. It was like everyone was standing up to be counted because Dylan hadn't, or something. Anyway, there were maybe ten–twelve thousand of us at the band shell in the park, singing, listening to speeches, and then two kids went up a flagpole and lowered the flag to half-mast. The cops went crazy—they came in swinging wild and they didn't care who they hit or where they hit them. I was scared out of my mind. I saw those cops close up and they looked as mad as Johnson was supposed to be. On the spot, I became a believer like I'd never been before—Madman in the White House and Madman Daley and his Madman cops. It was all true, I thought while I curled up on the ground with my hands over my head and prayed some kill-crazy pig wouldn't decide to pound my ass to jelly.

"Somebody pulled me up and yelled that we were supposed to all go to in front of the Hilton. I ran like hell all the way to the railroad tracks along with everybody else and that was where the Guard caught us with the tear gas. Man, I thought I was going to die of tear-gas suffocation if I didn't get trampled by the people I was with. Everyone was running around like crazy. I don't know how we ever got out of there but somebody found a way onto Michigan Avenue and somehow we all followed. And the Guard followed after us. Somebody said later they weren't supposed to, but they did. And they weren't carrying popguns.

"Well, we ran smack into Ralph Abernathy and his Poor People's Campaign mule train and that was more confusion. Then the Guard waded in and a lot of Poor People went to the hospital that night (it was after seven by then). I'll never forget that, or the sight of all those TV cameras and the bright lights shining in our eyes. We were all staggering around when a fresh bus-load of riot cops arrived, and that's another sight I'll never forget—two dozen beefy bruisers in riot gear shooting out of that bus like they were being shot from cannons and landing on all of us with both feet and their billyclubs. I lost my front teeth and I was so freaked I didn't even feel it until the next day.

"I was freaked, but I was also furious. We were all furious. It was like, Johnson would send us to Vietnam to be killed or he'd let us be killed by Daley's madman cops on the Chicago streets, it didn't matter to him. I think a lot of us expected the convention to adjourn in protest at our treatment. At least that Bobby Kennedy would speak out in protest against the brutality. The name Kennedy *meant* human rights, after all. Nobody knew that Kennedy had been removed from the convention center under heavy guard because they were all convinced that someone would make another attempt on his life. I heard that later, before they clamped down on all the information. He was about to get the fucking *nomination* and he was on his way back to his hotel. They said Madman Johnson was more like Mad-Dog Johnson over that, but who the fuck knows?

"George McGovern was at the podium when we busted in. I hadn't really been intending to be in that group that busted in, but I got carried along and when I saw we were going to crash the amphitheater, I thought, what the fuck.

"I almost got crushed against the doors before they gave, and I barely missed falling on my face and getting run over by six thousand screaming demonstrators. And the first person I saw was Annie Phillips.

"I thought I was in a Fellini film. She was dressed in this godawful *maid's* uniform with a handkerchief around her head mashing down her Afro, but I knew it was her. We looked right into each other's eyes as I went by, still more carried along with the crowd than running on my own and she put both hands over her mouth in horror. That was the last time I saw her until she was on TV.

"I managed to get out of the way and stay to the back of the amphitheater itself. I just wanted to catch my breath and try to think how I was going to get out from all this shit without getting my head split open by a crazy Guardsman or a cop. I was still there when the bomb went off down front.

"The sound was so loud I thought my ears were bleeding. Automatically, I dropped to the floor and covered my head. There was a little debris, not much, where I was. When I finally dared to look, what I saw didn't make any sense. I still can't tell you exactly what I saw. I blocked it out. But sometimes, I think I dream it. I dream that I saw Johnson's head sitting on a Texas flagpole. I'm pretty sure that's just my imagination, because in the dream, he's got this vaguely surprised-annoyed expression on his saggy old face, like he's saying, *Whut the fuck is goin' on here?*

"Anyway, the next thing I knew, I was out on the street again, and somebody was crying about they were bombing us now, along with the Vietnamese. Which was about the time the Guard opened fire, thinking we were bombing them, I guess.

"I was lucky. I took a bullet in my thigh and it put me out of the action. Just a flesh wound, really. It bled pretty impressively for a while and then quit. By then, I was so out of my head that I can't even tell you where I staggered off to. The people who found me in their front yard the next morning took care of me and got me to a hospital. It was a five-hour wait in the emergency room. That was where I was when I heard about Kennedy."

Part of the data recovered
from a disk
taken in a raid on an illegal
software laboratory,
March, 1981

Jack Kennedy had died in the middle of a Dallas street, his head blown off in front of thousands of spectators and his horrified wife. Bobby Kennedy had narrowly missed meeting his end during a moment of triumph in a Los Angeles hotel. Ultimately, that seemed to have been only a brief reprieve before fate caught up with him. . . .

Jasmine Chang:

"Everyone heard the explosion but nobody knew whether it was something the demonstrators had done, or if the National Guard had rolled in a tank or if the world had come to an end. I ran down to the lobby with just about everyone else on the staff and a good many of the hotel guests, trying to see what was happening outside without having to out in it. Nobody wanted to go outside. That night, the manager on duty had told us that anyone who wanted could stay over if we didn't mind roughing it in the meeting rooms. I made myself a sleeping bag out of spare linens under a heavy table in one of the smaller rooms. The night before, the cops had cracked one of the dining room windows with a demonstrator's head. I wasn't about to risk my neck going out in that frenzy.

"Well, after the explosion, we heard the rifle-fire. Then the street in front of the hotel, already crowded, was *packed* all of a sudden. Wall-to-wall cops and demonstrators, and the cops were swinging at anything they could reach. They were *scything* their way through the crowd, you see—they were mowing people down to make paths so they could walk. It was one of the worst things I've ever seen. For a while it was *the* worst. I wish it could have stayed that way.

"The lobby was filling up, too, but nobody really noticed because we were all watching that sickening scene outside. The whole world was watching, they said. I saw a camera crew and all I could think was their equipment was going to get smashed to bits.

"I don't know when Kennedy came down to the lobby. I don't know why the Secret Service didn't stop him, I don't know what he thought he could do. He must have been watching from his window. Maybe he thought he could actually address the crowd—as if anyone could have heard him. Anyway, he was there in the lobby and none of us really noticed him.

"The demonstrator who forced his way into the revolving door—he was just a kid, he looked about fifteen years old to me. Scared out of his mind. The revolving door was supposed to be locked, but when I saw that kid's face, I was glad it wasn't.

"Then the cops tried to force their way in after him but they got stuck, there was a billy club jammed in the door or something. And the kid was babbling about how they'd blown up Kennedy at the convention. 'They threw a bomb and killed Kennedy! They blew him up with Johnson and McGovern!' he was yelling over and over. And Bobby Kennedy himself rushed over to the kid. I'm pretty sure that was the first any of us really noticed him, when it registered. I remember, I felt shocked and surprised and numb all at once, seeing Kennedy right there, right in the middle of a lobby. Like he was anybody. And nobody else moved, we all just stood there and stared like dummies.

"And Kennedy was trying to tell the kid who he was, that he wasn't dead and what bomb and all that. The kid got even more hysterical, and Kennedy was shaking him, trying to get something coherent out of him, we're all standing there watching and finally the cops manage to get through the revolving door.

"They must have thought the kid was attacking Kennedy. That's all I can figure. Even if that's not how they looked. The cops. They looked . . . *weird*. Like they didn't know what they were doing, or they did know but they'd forgotten why they were supposed to do it. I don't know. I don't *know*. But it was so weird, because they all looked exactly alike to me right at that moment, even though when I looked at them again after, they weren't anything alike, even in their uniforms. But they looked like identical dolls then, or puppets, because they moved all at once together. Like a kick-line of chorus girls, you know? Except that it wasn't their legs that came up but their arms.

"I know that when they raised their guns, they were looking at the kid, and I thought, 'No, wait!' I tried to move toward them, I was reaching out and they fired.

"It was like another bomb had gone off. For a moment, I thought another bomb had gone off, just a split second before they were going to fire. Then John Kennedy—I mean, Bobby, *Bobby* Kennedy—that's a Freudian slip, isn't it?—he did this clumsy whirl around and it looked like he was turning around in anger, like people do sometimes, you know? Like he was going, 'Dammit, I'm leaving!' And then he went down, and it was so awful because—well, this is going to sound really strange, I guess, but . . . well . . . when you see people get shot on a TV show, it's like choreographed or something, they do these kind of graceful falls. Kennedy was . . . they'd robbed him of his dignity. That's the only way I can think to put it. They shot him and humiliated him all at once, he looked clumsy and awkward and helpless.

"And I was outraged at that. I know it must sound weird, a man got shot, *killed*, and I'm talking about how he looked undignified. But that's like what taking someone's life is—taking their humanity, making them a *thing*. And I was outraged. I wanted to grab one of those cops' guns and make *them* into things. Not just because it was Bobby Kennedy, it could have been anyone on that floor at that moment, the kid, the manager, my supervisor—and I hated my supervisor's guts.

"Right then, I understood what the demonstrations were about, and I was against the war. Up until then, I'd been kind of for it—not really *for* it, more like, 'I hate war, but you're supposed to serve your country.' But right then, I understood how horrifying it must be to be told to make somebody into a thing, or be told you have to go out and risk being made into a thing. To kill, to be killed.

"All that went through my mind in a split second and then I started screaming. Then I heard this *noise* . . . under my screams, I heard this weird groan. It was Kennedy. They say he was dead by then and it must have been the air going out of his lungs past his vocal cords that made the sound. Awful. Just awful. I ran and pulled the fire alarm. It was the only thing I could think to do. And this other chambermaid, Lucy Anderson, she started pounding on the front windows and screaming, 'Stop! Stop! They killed Kennedy! They killed Kennedy!' Probably nobody could hear her, but even if anyone had, it wouldn't have mattered, because most of the people out there thought Kennedy was already dead in the explosion.

"It wasn't the Fire Department that used the hoses on those people. The cops commandeered the fire trucks and did that. And we were stuck in that hotel for another whole day and night. Even after they cleared the streets, they wouldn't let any of us go anywhere. Like house arrest.

"The questioning was awful. Nobody mistreated me or hit me or anything like that, it was just that they kept *at* me. I had to tell what I saw over and over and over and over until I thought they were either trying to drive me out of my mind so I wouldn't be able to testify against those cops, or trying to find some way to make it seem like I was really the one who'd done it.

"By the time they told me I could leave the hotel, I was mad at the world, I can tell you. Especially since that Secret Service agent or whoever he was told me I'd be a lot happier if I moved out of Chicago and started over somewhere else. He really screwed that one up, and it was lucky for me he did. I left, and I was far, far away when the shit really hit the fan. I started over, all right—I got a new name and a new identity. Everybody else who was in that lobby—Lucy Anderson, the manager, the other staff and guests—they all disappeared. The last anyone saw of them, the Secret Service was taking them away. The cops vanished, too, but I have a feeling they didn't vanish to quite the same thing as the others. And the kid killed himself. *They* said. Right, sure. I bet he couldn't survive the interrogation.

"Of course, all that was a long time ago. Hard to imagine now how things were then. I was only twenty, then. I was working days and taking college courses at night. I wanted to be a teacher. Now I'm in my early forties, and sometimes I think I dreamed it all. I dreamed that I lived in a country where people *voted* their leaders into office, where you just had to be old enough and not be a convicted felon and you could vote. Instead of having to take those psychological tests and wait for the investigators to give you a voting clearance. It *is* like a dream, isn't it? Imagining that there was a time in this country when you could be anything you wanted to be, a teacher, a doctor, a banker, a scientist. I was going to be a teacher. I was going to be a history teacher, but those are mostly white people. My family's been in this country forever, but because I'm Oriental, I've got conditional citizenship now . . . and I was *born* here! I suppose I shouldn't complain. If anyone found out I saw Kennedy get it, I'd probably be unconditionally dead. Because *everyone knows* that the rumor that Kennedy was shot by some cops with a bad aim in a hotel lobby is just another stupid rumor, like the second gunman in Dallas in 1963. *Everyone knows* Kennedy died in the explosion at the convention center. That's the official version of how he died and if it's the official version, government certified, that's the truth.

"Where I live, they have routine segregation, so I can't use any of the whites' facilities. I've thought about applying to move to one of the larger cities where there's elective segregation and nothing's officially 'white-only,' but I hear the waiting lists are years long. And somebody told me that everything is really just as segregated as here, they're just not as open and honest about it. So maybe I'd really be no better off . . .

"But I wish that I could have become a teacher—any kind of teacher—instead of a cook. I can't even become a chef, because that's another men-only field. I don't *want* to be a chef necessarily, because I really don't like to cook and I'm not very good at it. But it was all I could get. The list of available careers for non-whites gets smaller all the time.

"Sometimes, I think it actually wasn't meant to be this bad. Sometimes I think that nobody really wanted the military to take over the government for real, I think it was just panic about so many of the Democratic candidates dying along with the President in that blast and the rioting that wouldn't stop and all that. It did seem as if the country was completely falling apart and somebody had to do something fast and decisive. Well, sure, somebody should have. Somebody should have figured out who was the President, with Madman Johnson and Humpty Humphrey and all those Senators dead—there had to be *somebody* left, right? All of Congress wasn't there. I mean, if I'd known, if a lot of us had known how things were going to come out, I think we'd have just let Ronald Reagan be President for four years, run him against Wallace or something and kept free elections, instead of postponing the elections and then having them abolished.

"People panicked. That's what it all came down to, I think. They were panicking in the streets, they were panicking in the government, and they were panicking in their homes. Our own panic brought us down."

Undated typescript found in
a locker in the downtown
San Diego bus terminal,
April 9, 1993

Our own panic brought us down. For many who were eyewitnesses to certain events of 1968, this would seem to be a fitting coda, if coda is the word, for the ensuing twenty-five years . . .

Oh, hell, I don't know why I'm bothering to try to sum this up. How do you sum up a piece of history gone wrong? How do you sum up the fall of a country that believes it was saved from chaos and destruction? And who am I asking, anyway? I'm out of the country now, another wetback who finally made it across the border to freedom. There was a time when wetbacks went north to freedom, but I'm pretty sure nobody would remember that now. Mexico is sad and dusty and ancient, the people poor and suspicious of Anglos, though I'm so brown now that I can pass convincingly as long as I don't try to speak the language—my accent is still atrocious.

But the freedom here—nothing like what we used to have, but the constraints are far fewer. You don't need to apply for a travel permit in-country, you just *go* from place to place. Of course, it's not really that hard to get a travel permit in the U.S., they give them out routinely. But I'm of that generation that remembers when it was different, and it galls me that I would have to apply for one at all if I want to go from, say, Newark to, say, Cape May. I've deliberately chosen two cities I've never been to, just in case these papers fall into the wrong hands. God knows enough of my papers have been lost over the years. Sometimes I think it's a miracle I haven't been caught.

It's a hell of a life when you're risking prosecution and imprisonment just for trying to put together a true account of something that happened two and a half decades before.

Why I bothered—well, there are a lot of reasons. Because I've learned to love truth. And because I want to atone for what I did to "Carole Feeney" and the others. I'm still amazed that she didn't recognize me, but I guess twenty years is a long time after all.

I really thought I was doing the right thing at the time. I thought infiltrating the leftist groups was all right if it was just to make sure that nobody was stockpiling weapons or planning to blow up a building. Or assassinate another leader. I truly wish I could have arrested Annie Phillips and her group long before Chicago. Some of the people I talked to who were in the streets that night blame Annie for everything that's happened since, and I think that's why the authorities kept her alive instead of killing her—so the old radicals could hate her more than the government.

After I talked to Annie, I understood why she turned violent, even if I didn't condone it. If her voice could have been heard in 1964, maybe all these voices could be heard now, though they might not have so much to say. . . .

How melodramatic, "Davis." I can't help it. I was actually just like any of them in the year 1968—I thought my country was in trouble, and I was trying to do something about it. And—

And what the hell, we won the Vietnam war. Hooray for America. The Vietnamese are all but extinct, but we brought the boys back home. We sent them right back out to the Middle East, and then down to Nicaragua, and to the Phillipines, and to Europe, of course, where they don't protest our missile bases much anymore. That big old stick. We've gone one better than talking softly and carrying a big stick. Now we don't talk at all. . . .

In the weeks since I finally got out of the country, I've been having this recurring dream. I keep dreaming that things turned out differently, that there was even just one thing that didn't happen, or something else that did happen, and the country just . . . went on. And so I keep thinking about it. If Johnson hadn't run . . . if Kennedy hadn't been killed . . . if that bomb hadn't gone off . . . if it had only been half the number of demonstrators . . . if Dylan had showed up.

If Dylan had showed up . . . I wonder sometimes if that's it. God, the world should be so simple. Instead of simple and brutal and crude.

Even after putting together this risky account, I'm not sure that I really know much more than I did in the beginning. I was hoping that I might figure it all out, how, instead of winning the battle and losing the war, we won the war and lost everything we had. But it could have been different. I don't know why it's so important to me to believe that. Maybe because I don't want to believe that this was the way we were going no matter what. I don't want to believe that everything that was of any value is stuck back there in the Sixties.

Papers found in a hastily vacated room
in an Ecuadorian flophouse
by occupying American forces
during the third South American War
October 13, 1998

1972

The most emotional election of recent years occurred in 1972, when voters, after a decade of carnage in Vietnam, finally were given a clear-cut choice: they could vote for Peace With Honor (Richard M. Nixon), or they could vote for Peace With Alacrity (George McGovern). Nixon won the biggest electoral majority in history, some two years before he was forced to resign the presidency in disgrace.

But what if McGovern had won, and had begun the immediate withdrawal of troops that he promised? How would the Viet Cong have reacted?

Susan Shwartz, noted anthologist Nebula nominee, and author of *Heritage of Flight* and *The Grail of Hearts*, examines the consequences as they relate to a single family which, like so many others, is divided by the war.

Suppose They Gave a Peace . . .

by Susan Shwartz

Twenty-five years after the war, and my damned sixth sense about the phone still wakes me up at 3:00 A.M. Just as well. All Margaret needs is for me to snap awake, shout, and jump out of bed, grabbing for my pants and my .45. I don't have it anymore. She made me sell it as soon as the kids were old enough to poke into the big chest of drawers. I don't interfere when she makes decisions like that. The way things are going to the dogs, though, I'd feel a whole lot better about her safety if I had the gun.

So I stuck my feet into my slippers—the trench foot still itches—and snuck downstairs. If Margaret woke up, she'd think I was raiding the icebox and go back to sleep. I like being up and alone in my house, kind of guard duty. I don't do much. I straighten towels or put books back on the shelves—though with Steff gone, that's not a problem anymore. I don't like seeing the kids' rooms so bare.

Barry's models and football are all lined up, and Margaret dusts them. No problem telling the boys from the girls in our family. Barry's room is red and navy, and Steff's is all blue and purply, soft-like, with ruffles and a dressing table she designed herself. Now that she's at school, we don't trip on clothes all over the place. And I keep reminding myself we ought to yank out the Princess phone she got when she turned thirteen. Light on the dial's burned out, anyway.

I wish she hadn't taken down the crewelwork she did her freshman year. The flower baskets were a whole lot prettier than these "Suppose They Gave A War And Nobody Came" posters. But that's better than the picture of that bearded Che-guy. I put my foot down about that thing, I can tell you. Not in *my* house, I said.

I'm proud of our house: two-floor brick Tudor with white walls and gold carpet and a big ticking grandfather's clock in the hall. Classy taste, my wife has. Who'd have thought she'd look at someone like me?

Besides, dinner was pretty good. Some of that deli rye and that leftover steak . . .

As the light from the icebox slid across the wall phone, it went off, almost like it had been alerted. I grabbed it before it could ring twice.

"Yeah?" I snapped the way I used to in Germany, and

my gut froze. My son Barry's in Saigon. If anything goes wrong, they send a telegram. No. That was last war. Now they send a car. God forbid.

But Steff, my crazy daughter—every time the phone rings at night I'm scared. Maybe she's got herself arrested in one of her goddamn causes and I'm going to have to bail her out like I did in Chicago. Or it could be worse. Two years ago this month, some kids were in the wrong place at the wrong time up at Kent. Damn shame about them and the National Guard; it'll take us years to live it down. Hell of a thing to happen in Ohio.

I thought my kid was going to lose her mind about it. The schools shut down all over the place, all that tuition money pissed away, and God only knows what she got into.

Not just God. Margaret. Steff would call up, say "put Mom on," and Margaret would cry and turn into the phone so I couldn't hear what she was saying. I think she sent money on the sly-like, so I wouldn't make an issue of it. You don't send kids to college so they can get shot at. Steff would say you don't send anyone anywhere so they can get shot at. She's just a kid, you know. She doesn't really believe all that stuff. The kids shouldn't have been there. Anyone could tell you that.

"Hey, that you, Joey?" The voice on the other end was thick with booze. "It's Al. Remember me?"

"You son of a bitch, what're you doing calling this hour of night?" I started to bellow, then piped down. "You wanna wake up my whole damn family?"

"Thought you'd be up, Joey. Like we were . . . the time when . . ."

"Yeah . . . yeah . . ." Sure I remembered. Too well. So did Al, my old army buddy. It happens from time to time. One of us gets to remembering, gets the booze out—Scotch for me these days now that my practice is finally paying off—and then picks up the phone. Margaret calls it "going visiting" and "telephonitis" and only gets mad at the end of the month when the bills come in.

But Al wasn't from my outfit at the Battle of the Bulge. Weren't many of them left. Not many had been real close friends to start with: when you run away from home and lie about your age so you can go fight, you're sort of out of place, soldier or not.

Damn near broke my own dad's heart; he'd wanted me to follow him into school and law school and partnership. So I did that on GI bills when I got out. Got married, and then there was Korea. I went back in, and that's where I met Al.

"Remember? We'd run out of fuel for the tank and were burning grain alcohol ... rather drink torpedo juice, wouldn't you? And pushing that thing south to the 38th parallel, scared shitless the North Koreans'd get us if the engine fused ..."

"Yeah ..." How far was Korea from Saigon? My son the lance corporal had wangled himself a choice slot as Marine guard. I guess all Margaret's nagging about posture and manners had paid off. Almost the only time it had with the Bear. God, you know you'd shed blood so your kids don't turn out as big damn fools as you. I'd of sent Barry through school, any school. But he wanted the service. Not Army, either, but the Marines. Well, Parris Island did what I couldn't do, and now he was "yes sir"-ing a lot of fancypants like Ambassador Bunker over in Vietnam. At least he wasn't a chicken or a runaway ...

"You there, Joey?" I was staring at the receiver. "I asked you, how's your family?"

"M'wife's fine," I said. How long had it been since Al and I spoke—three years? Five? "So're the kids. Barry's in the Marines. My son the corporal. Stationed in Saigon. The Embassy, no less." I could feel my chest puffing out, even though I was tired and it was the middle of the night.

Car lights shone outside. I stiffened. What if ... The lights passed. All's quiet on the Western Front. Thank God.

Al and the beer hooted approvingly.

"And Steffie's in college. Some damn radical Quaker place. I wanted her to stay in Ohio, be a nurse or a teacher, something practical in case, God forbid, she ever has to work, but my wife wanted her near her own people."

"She getting plenty of crazy ideas at that school?"

"Steff's a good kid, Al. Looks like a real lady now."

What do you expect me to say? That after a year of looking and acting like the big-shot debs my wife admires in *The New York Times*, my Steffie's decided to hate everything her dad fought for? Sometimes I think she's majoring in revolution. It wasn't enough she got arrested in 1968 campaigning for McCarthy—clean up for Gene, they called it. Clean? I never saw a scruffier bunch of kids till I saw the ones she's taken up with now. Long hair, dirty—and the language? Worse than an army barracks.

She's got another campaign now. This McGovern. I don't see what they have against President Nixon or what they see in this McGovern character. Senator from South Dakota, and I tell you, he's enough to make Mount Rushmore cry. I swear to God, the way these friends of Steff's love unearthing and spreading nasty stories—this Ellsberg character Steff admires, you'd think he was a hero instead of some nutcase who spilled his guts in a shrink's office, so help me. Or this My Lai business: things like that happen in war. You just don't talk about them. Still, what do you expect of a bunch of kids? We made it too easy.

I keep hoping. She's such a good girl, such a pretty girl; one of these days, she'll come around and say "Daddy, I was wrong. I'm sorry."

Never mind that.

Al had got onto the subject of *jo-sans*. Cripes, I hadn't even thought of some of them for twenty years, being an old married man and all. What if Margaret had walked in? I'd of been dead. Sure, I laughed over old times, but I was relieved when he switched to "who's doing what" and "who's died," and then onto current events. We played armchair general, and I tell you, if the Pentagon would listen to us, we'd win this turkey and have the boys home so damned fast . . .

About the time we'd agreed that this Kissinger was a slippery so-and-so and that bombing Haiphong was one of the best things we could have done, only we should have done it a whole lot earlier . . . hell of a way to fight a war, tying General Westmoreland's hands, I heard footsteps on the stairs.

"Do you have any idea what time it is?" Margaret asked me.

I gestured *he called me!* at the phone, feeling like a kid with his hand in the cookie jar. My wife laughed. "Going visiting, is he? Well, let his wife give him aspirin for the hangover I bet he's going to have. You have to go to the office tomorrow and . . ." she paused for emphasis like I was six years old, "you need your sleep."

She disappeared back up the stairs, sure that I'd follow.

"That was the wife," I told Al, my old good buddy. "Gotta go. Hey, don't wait five years to call again. And if you're ever in town, come on over for dinner!"

God, I hope she hadn't heard that stuff about the *josans*. Or the dinner invitation. We'd eat cold shoulder and crow, that was for sure.

Fall of '72, we kept hearing stories. That Harvard guy, that Kissinger was meeting with Le Duc Tho in Paris, and he was encouraged, but then they backed down: back and forth, back and forth till you were ready to scream. "Peace is at hand," he says, and they say it in Hanoi, too. I mean, what's the good of it when the commies and your own leaders agree, and the army doesn't? No news out of Radio Hanoi can be any good. And the boys are still coming home in bags, dammit.

Meanwhile, as I hear from Margaret, Stephanie is doing well in her classes. The ones she attends in between campaigning for this McGovern. At first I thought he was just a nuisance candidate. You know, like Stassen runs each time? Then, when they unearthed that stuff about Eagleton, and they changed VP candidates, I thought he was dead in the water for sure. But Shriver's been a good choice: drawn in even more of the young, responsible folk and the people who respect what he did in the Peace Corps. But the real reason McGovern's moving way up in the polls is that more and more people get sick and tired of the war. We just don't believe we can win it, anymore. And that hurts.

I get letters from Barry, too. He's good at that. Writes each one of us. I think he's having a good time in Saigon. I hope he's careful. *You* know what I mean.

Barry says he's got a lot of respect for Ambassador Bunker. Says he was cool as any Marine during Tet, when the VC attacked the Embassy. Says the Ambassador's spoken to him a couple of times, asked him what he wants to do when he gets out of the service. Imagine: My boy, talking to a big shot like that.

And Margaret sent Stephanie a plane ticket home in time for the election. Sure, she could vote at school, but "my vote will make more of a difference in Ohio," she explained to me. She was getting a fancy accent.

"You gonna cancel out my vote, baby?" I asked her.

"I sure am, Dad. D'you mind?"

"Hey, kid, what am I working for if it isn't for you and your mom? Sure, come on home and give your fascist old dad a run for his money."

That got kind of a watery laugh from her. We both remembered the time she went to Washington for that big march in '69. I hit the ceiling and Margaret talked me down. "She didn't have to tell us, Joe," she reminded me.

No, she didn't. But she had. Just in case something happened, she admitted that Thanksgiving when she came home from school.

I didn't like the idea of my girl near tear gas and cops with nightsticks when I wasn't around, so I pulled a few strings and sent her Congressman Kirwan's card. *Mike,* the Congressman says I should call him when he comes to the lawyers' table at the Ohio Hotel. And I wrote down on it the home phone number of Miss Messer, his assistant. If anything goes wrong, I told her, she should call there. And I drew a peace sign and signed the letter, "Love and peace, your fascist father."

She says I drew it upside down. Well, what do you expect? Never drew one before.

Anyhow, she'll be home for Election Day, and Barry'll vote by absentee ballot. I'm proud that both my kids take voting seriously. Maybe that school of hers hasn't been a total waste: Steff still takes her responsibilities as a citizen very seriously.

Meanwhile, things—talking and fighting both—slowed down in Paris and Saigon. I remember after Kennedy won the election, Khrushchev wouldn't talk to President Eisenhower's people because Ike was a lame duck. As if he weren't one of the greatest generals we ever had. I tried to listen to some of the speeches by this McGovern Stephanie was wild for. Mostly, I thought he promised pie-in-the-sky. Our boys home by June, everyone working hard and off welfare—not that I'd mind, but I just didn't see how he was going to pull any of it off. I really wanted to ask Barry what he thought, but I didn't. Might be bad for morale.

Then things started to get worse. They stepped up the bombing. Tried to burn off the jungle, too. And the pictures . . . Dammit, I wish I could forget the one of that little girl running down the road with no clothes on, screaming in pain. Sometimes at night, it gets messed up in my mind with that thing from Kent, with the girl kneeling and crying over that boy's body. Damn things leap out at you from the newspaper or the news, but I can't just stick my head in the sand.

Maybe the kids . . . maybe this McGovern . . . I've *been* under attack, and I tell you, there comes a time when you just want it to *stop*. Never mind what it costs you. You've already paid enough. I think the whole country's reached that point, and so McGovern's moving way up in the polls.

* * *

Election Day started out really well. The day before, letters had come from Barry. One for me. One for his mother. And even one for Stephanie. I suppose she'd told him she was going to be home, and APO delivery to the Embassy in Saigon is pretty regular. We all sort of went off by ourselves to read our letters. Then Margaret and I traded. I hoped Stephanie would offer to show us hers, too, but she didn't. So we didn't push.

You don't push, not if you want your kids to trust you. Besides, my son and daughter have always had something special between them. He's a good foot taller than she is, but she always looked out for her "baby brother" in school. He never minded that she was the bright one, the leader. Not till he decided not to go to college, and he overheard one of the family saying that Stephanie should have been the boy. So our Bear joined up, not waiting for the draft or anything. I expected Stephanie to throw a fit—Margaret certainly did, but all my girl said was, "He needs to win at something of his own."

I wouldn't have expected her to understand what that means to a boy. Maybe she's growing up.

But it's still all I can do to keep a decent tongue in my head toward my brother-in-law with the big fat mouth.

On Election Day, it's a family tradition that everyone comes over to watch the returns on TV. There were going to be some hot words over the cold cuts, if things ran true to speed. And I couldn't see Steff sitting in the kitchen putting things on trays and talking girl talk with her aunts. Steff calls that sort of thing sexist. That's a new word she's got. Don't see why it bothers her. It's not like sometimes the women aren't talking the most interesting things.

For a while, I really thought we were going to make it through the evening without a fight. Stephanie came in, all rosy-faced and glowing from voting, then marching outside the poll all day. She'd left her protest signs in the garage, and she was wearing one of the good skirts and coats she took to school. When everyone said so, she laughed and went up to change into a workshirt and jeans.

"But you looked so pretty, just like a real college girl," her aunt told her.

"That was just window dressing," Stephanie said. "Can I help set the food out now? I'm famished."

She'd wolfed down about half a corned beef sandwich when the phone rang, and she flew up the stairs. "You're kidding. Massachusetts *already*? Oh wow! How's it look for Pennsylvania? I'm telling you, I think we're going to be lucky here, but I'm worried about the South . . ."

"You want another beer, Ron?" I asked my brother-in-law, who was turning red, pretending like he had swallowed something the wrong way and would choke if he didn't drink real fast. Personally, I think he voted for Wallace in the last election, but you can't pry the truth out of him about that with a crowbar.

We settled down to watch TV. Margaret and my sister Nance turned on the portable in the kitchen. I kind of hoped Stephanie would go in there, but she helped clear the table, then came in and sat beside me.

You could have knocked me over with a feather. Maybe the kids were right and people were sick of the bombings, the deaths, the feeling that Vietnam was going to hang around our necks till we choked on it. But state after state went to McGovern . . . "There goes Ohio! Straight on!" Stephanie shouted, raising a fist.

I don't know when all hell broke loose. One moment we were sitting watching John Chancellor cut to President Nixon's headquarters (and my daughter was doing this routine, like a Chatty Cathy doll, about Tricia Nixon). The next moment, she'd jumped up and was stamping one foot as she glared at her uncle.

"How *dare* you use that word?" she was saying to Ron, my brother-in-law. "They're *not* gooks. They're *Asians*. And it's their country, not ours, but we're destroying it for them. We've turned the kids into fugitives, the women into bar girls . . . and they all had fathers, too, till we killed them! What kind of a racist pig . . ."

"Who you calling a racist, little Miss Steff & Nonsense?" asked Ron. By then, he'd probably had at least two beers too many and way too many of my daughter's yells of "straight on." "Why, when I was in the war, there was this Nee-grow sergeant . . ."

"It's 'black'!" she snapped. "You call them *black*! How can you expect me to stay in the same house as this . . ."

She was out of the living room, and the front door slammed behind her before I could stop her.

"That little girl of yours is out of control," Ron told me. "That's what you get, sending her off to that snob school. OSU wasn't good enough, oh no. So what happens? She meets a bunch of radicals there and picks up all sorts of crazy ideas. Tell you, Joey, you better put a leash on that kid, or she'll get into real trouble."

I got up, and he shut up. Margaret came in from the kitchen. I shook my head at her: *everything under control.* I wanted to get a jacket or something. Stephanie had run out without her coat, and the evening was chilly.

"I'd teach her a good lesson, that's what I'd do," said Ron.

Damn! Hadn't I warned her, "I know you think it's funny calling your uncle Ronnie the Racist. But one of these days, it's going to slip out, and then there'll be hell to pay." But she'd said what I should have said. And that made me ashamed.

"She shouldn't have been rude to you," I said. "I'm going to tell her that. But you know how she feels about words like that. I don't much like them either. Besides, this is her house, too."

Ron was grumbling behind my back like an approaching thunderstorm, when I went into the front hall, took out a jacket from the closet, and went outside. Steffie was standing on the stoop, her face pressed against the cold brick. I put the jacket over her and closed my hands on her shoulders. They were trembling. "Don't rub your face against the brick, baby. You could cut yourself."

She turned around and hugged me. I could feel she was

crying with anger and trying hard not to. "I'm not going in there and apologizing," she told me.

"Not even for me?" I coaxed her. There'd been a time she'd do anything in the world for her old dad.

She tried to laugh and cry together, and sounded like the way she used to gurgle when she was a baby.

"I'll promise not to start any fights," she said. "But I won't promise to keep quiet if . . ."

"I told him you shouldn't have been rude to an elder and a guest . . ."

She hissed like the teenager she wasn't. Not anymore.

"I also told him this was your house and you had a right to have your wishes respected, too. Now, will you come in and behave like a lady?"

"It's *woman*, daddy," she told me.

I hugged her. "You know what I mean. Lady or woman, you're still my little girl. You're supposed to be for peace. Can you try to keep it in your own home?"

She looked up, respect in her eyes. "Ooh, that was a *nice* one," she told me.

"Then remember, tantrums don't win any arguments. Now, you go in. Maybe your mother needs help with the dishes."

"*He* ought to help," she muttered. "You do. It wouldn't hurt."

"No, it wouldn't." To my surprise, I agreed. "But if we wait for him to get off his butt, your mother's going to be stuck with all of them."

The gift of her obedience hit me in the face like a cold wind when you've had too much to drink. My eyes watered, and the lights up and down Outlook Avenue flickered. Everyone was watching the returns. Some of them had promised to drop in later. The Passells' younger boy had gone to school with Steff. He was the only boy on the street still in school, studying accounting. The Carlsons' middle son, who'd played varsity football, but always took time to coach our Bear, had left OSU and was in the Army. So was the oldest Bentfield, who'd been our paperboy. Fine young men, all of them. And the girls had turned out good, too, even Reenie, who'd got married too young.

Just a one-block street, but you had everything on it. Even a black family had moved in. Maybe I'd had my worries to start off with, but I was real proud we'd all greeted them like neighbors. On some streets when that happened, the kids dumped garbage on the lawn or TP'ed the house.

It was a nice street, a good block, and we'd all lived on it a long time. Nothing fancy, but solid. I wished my father could have seen my house. We'd come back since he'd lost everything in the Depression. But that's the way of it. Each generation does a little bit better than the last one and makes things a little easier for the ones next in line.

We've been five generations in Youngstown. I like to think our name counts for something. Now, this is sort of embarrassing. I don't go to church much, but I looked out over that street and *hoped*, that's a better word for it, that my kids would make that name even more respected. My daughter, the whatever-she-wanted-to-be. A lawyer, maybe. And my son. Who knew? Maybe he'd come home and go back to school, and then this Ambassador—I couldn't see my Bear as a diplomat, but . . .

"How many beers did *you* have?" I asked the sky, gave myself a mental shake, and went back in in time to watch President Nixon's concession speech. It wasn't, not really. You remember how close the race was against JFK. And the 1962 California election when he told the press, "You won't have Nixon to kick around any more."

I don't know. Man's a fighter, but he's not a good loser. I tell you, I don't know what a recount's going to do to this country just when we need a strong leader in place.

"Country's going to hell in a handbasket," Ron grumbled. "I'm going home. Hey, Nancy? You going to yak all night? C'mon!"

After he let, my wife and daughter came back into the living room. Margaret brought out a pot of coffee.

Stephanie sat down to watch McGovern's victory speech. She was holding her mother's hand.

"I admit I am distressed at this demand for a recount at just the time when our country needs to be united. But I am confident that the count will only reaffirm the judgment of the great American people as the bombing has gone on, pounding our hearts as well as a captive nation: it is enough!

"Now, I have heard it said," the man went on with shining eyes, "that I do not care for honor. Say, rather, that I earn my honor where it may be found. Not in throwing lives after lives away in a war we should never have entered, but in admitting that we have gone as far as we may, and that now it is time for our friends the South Vietnamese to take their role as an independent people, not a client state. Accordingly, my first act as Commander in Chief will be . . ." his voice broke, "to bring them home. Our sons and brothers. The young fathers and husbands of America. Home."

Tears were pouring down the women's faces. I walked over to Margaret. All the years we've been married, she's never been one to show affection in front of the kids. Now she leaned her head against me. "Our boy's coming home!"

Stephanie's face glowed like the pictures of kids holding candles in church or the big protest marches. She could have been at McGovern headquarters; that school of hers has enough pull to put her that high, but she'd chosen to come home instead.

I put a hand on her hair. It was almost as silky as it had been when she was in diapers. Again, my hand curved around her head. It was so warm, just like when she'd been little. "Baby, it looks like you and your friends have won. I just hope you're right."

* * *

Something woke me early that morning. Not the house. Margaret's regular breathing was as always, and I could sense the presence of Stephanie, a now-unfamiliar blessing. I went downstairs, ran some water in the sink, and washed off the serving dishes Margaret had set to soak overnight. Nice surprise for her when she got up.

Of course, I wasn't surprised when the phone rang.

"Hey, Al," I greeted him. Drunk again. "What's the hurry? It's only six months, not five years between calls this time."

"How d'you like it, Joe?" he demanded. "Those little bastards pulled it off. They don't want to go, so, by God, they stop the war. Can you believe it? Not like us, was it. I tell you, ol' buddy, we were suckers. Go where we were told, hup two three four, following orders like goddamn fools, and these kids change the rules on us and get away with it."

Maybe it would be better. Margaret and Steff had held hands and cried for joy. I had to believe it was better, that I wasn't just bitching because other men's sons wouldn't have to go through what I had. I started to talk Al down like I had in Korea, but my heart wasn't in it.

The sky was gray. All the houses on Outlook were dark. Soon it would be dawn and the streetlights would go out, regular as an army camp.

But what were those lights going on? I levered up from my chair—damn, my bones were creaking—and peered out. Lights on at Bentfield's? And, oh my God, Johnny Bentfield . . . no. Oh no. *Not my son, thank God!* Dammit, what kind of a man was I to thank God like that? Sometimes I make myself want to puke.

"Al!" I broke into his ramblings. "I gotta hang up *now*. Something's going on on the street."

"Probably a bunch of stoned kids, celebrating the new age. Well, they're welcome to it. Let 'em come running to me when it blows up in their faces. I'll laugh."

"Yeah, Al. Sure. But I gotta go."

Moving more quietly than I had since Korea, I slipped

upstairs and slid open drawers for undershorts, slacks, a sports shirt. Very cautiously, listening to see if they'd wake up, I dressed in the bathroom, then left the house, moving as cautiously as if I were scouting out my own neighborhood. I sneaked over to Bentfield's and peered in the window. At least they didn't have a dog. If what I feared was true, they'd have more on their minds than listening for prowlers. And if I were wrong, please God, if I were wrong, they were good enough friends I could always make up something.

But they were in robes in the living room. Alma Bentfield sat hunched over, hands over her face, while Stan came in, gray-faced, with coffee. The two little girls clutched each other, too sleepy to feel yet how badly they were going to hurt.

God *damn*! Just a little longer, and we'd have brought Johnny home safe. Someone must have called from Vietnam. Unauthorized. Don't ask me how.

I slipped out of their yard and back home.

"What's wrong?" Margaret's voice was sharp and came from outside Stephanie's room. She must have heard what she thought was a prowler, found me gone, and run to see if our daughter needed help.

"Better get dressed," I told her. "There's a light on at Bentfield's. I've had a crazy feeling. I went over and looked. It's about as bad as it can get."

My wife's face twisted, and she clenched her hands.

"I'll wake Steff, too," she said. "She's grown up enough to help out."

I went upstairs to change into a suit. It was almost time to get dressed for work anyhow. But long after I should have left, I sat in the kitchen drinking coffee. Margaret was cooking something. A casserole to take over, maybe. A knife fell into the metal sink. We both jumped and she spilled the milk she was pouring.

"Shit!"

In twenty-five years of marriage, I don't think I'd ever heard her cuss like that.

She mopped up, and I poured myself another cup. I sat staring at the birds and butterflies on the wallpaper mural she took such care of. Different from birds in Southeast Asia, that was for sure: nice tame birds and pale colors. They call it a green hell there.

"It's time to go," she reminded me. I picked up the phone to call my office and tell my secretary I wouldn't be in just yet.

"Hope you're feeling all right," Mary-Lynn wished me, almost laughing.

"I'm fine," I almost snapped. No point taking it out on her. She'd gone to high school with my kids. I remember how old I felt the day I interviewed her—and found out that her mother had been my secretary when I'd started out in practice.

"That's good." She was almost singing. Guess she was relieved too about how the vote had gone. Her husband—the first one was no damn good, but this guy seems to be treating her okay—would be coming home. Vet or no vet, he damn well better be good to her. She's a nice kid, and besides, big as he is, I'll beat the crap out of him.

I drank my coffee and looked out at the street till the olive-drab Army car I was expecting pulled up outside Bentfield's and the long-legged uniformed men strode up the neat walk to the front door. It opened, so reluctantly. All over the street, doors opened, and the women started coming out. Each one carried a covered bowl or baking dish.

Margaret kissed me on the cheek. Her lips were cold. Then she and Stephanie went out. My daughter carried the casserole. She had on her good clothes again and lipstick the color of bubble gum. It looked fake against her pale face, and I wanted to tell her to wipe it off, but I didn't. Her legs, under the short, dark skirt, looked like a little girl's, heading into the doctor's office to get a shot.

It was Johnny Bentfield who'd gotten shot.

My womenfolk went to Bentfield's and the door shut behind them.

All down the street, cars pulled out of the driveways like we were escaping.

When I got home that night, Steffie was in her jeans again, sitting in the living room.

"You shouldn't sit in the dark." I switched on some lights.

"Mom's upstairs with a headache. Took two Fiorinal." Margaret never took more than one.

I headed for the liquor cabinet and pulled out the Scotch.

"I'll do that," said my daughter. She mixed me a double the way I like them. To my surprise, she poured a stiff one for herself.

"I don't know, kitten," I began.

"I'm legal," she said flatly. "And I was there. You weren't. God!" She sat down too fast and lifted her glass. But she knows better than to belt down good Scotch.

"You did the right thing," I praised her. She'd done a good job, the sort of thing nice women like the ones on our street do without even thinking about it.

She wrapped her arms about her shoulders and hunched in. In her jeans and workshirt, she looked like a veteran of some army I'd never seen before. A vet who'd lost a buddy.

Finally, she looked up. The big brown eyes under their floppy bangs held my attention. "They brought her a flag. It was for John, they said. She didn't want to take it, but they put it in her hands. Her knees caved in, but she had to take the flag. We all sat around her. All day. Even after the soldiers left. They had other houses to visit. God *damn*!"

"Don't swear, baby. It's not nice."

"Wasn't nice to be there. Or to have to be there. What if . . ."

"Don't think about it!"

What kind of a father was I, leaving her alone like that?

But I couldn't help it. I got up and went outside to check on the garage door. Saw a neighbor.

"You hear about Bentfield?" he asked. Carefully, he bent and broke a dead branch off the hedge that divides our property.

I nodded. "My daughter's pretty shook up."

"It's worse than that. Stan told me, and I'm not telling the family. It wasn't VC that got his boy. 'Friendly fire,' they call it. He was stationed in front of the regular troops and, well, someone screwed up."

That's what happens when you cut and run. You get stuck facing something even worse. I had to go in and face Steffie like nothing had happened. She wasn't crying, at least, but she'd turned the lights off again.

"You want dinner? Mom said to heat stuff up."

I shook my head.

"Me neither."

"Let's not tell her we skipped dinner. She'd get mad."

We sat in the dark for a long time. After a while, the house got chilly, and it was time to go to bed.

Well, Nixon had his recount. It was close. Even closer than when he'd lost against Kennedy. I don't know, if I'd have thought he'd be such a bad loser, maybe I wouldn't have voted for him the first time. And the grins on the faces of those guys who look like Ho Chi Minh's grandsons at the UN made me want to wipe them out with my fist.

"It's face, y'know," Al said. After all these years, he'd finally made it to Youngstown on a business trip. Some of us got together at his Holiday Inn. These days, Al sells steel pipe. Frankly, I think he drinks through them—the gut he's got on him now! "Now that we're pulling out, they don't respect us. Not that they ever did, all that much. Talk about yellow . . . I know who's yellow, those little yellow . . ."

"Al." Father Klein picked his beer bottle out of his hand. "You've had enough. We've all had enough."

Al lurched onto his feet, his face red. Peanuts scattered across the table. I swept them back into the bowl. Didn't think Al would take on Father Klein. He was wearing his collar, for one thing. For another, he'd always been able to punch out anyone in our outfit.

"I wanted us to win," Al said. The fight drained out of him. "You know what happens when you retreat. Remember what we'd have got if they'd caught us in Korea? Tiger cages and bamboo under our fingernails. This isn't going to be a retreat. It's a goddamned rout. Who's holding the fort while everyone's pulling out? You mark my words, it's going to be a bloodbath."

"It's okay, Al," Father Klein said. "Joey and I'll walk you back to your room and you can stick your head in the john."

Pro-war or peacenik, we all went sort of crazy that spring. The atlas from our *Britannica* fell open at the maps of Southeast Asia as I showed Margaret just where our men were pulling back from.

"It's so green. Can't they just jump out?" Our dining room is white and gold: formal, Margaret calls it. If she likes it, fine, I'm happy. It seemed weird to be talking about weapons and jungles as we sat at a table covered by a cloth, eating off real silver.

"McGovern won't let us burn off the jungle. It's a no-no. Like DDT. Damn! It's all tunnels underneath. The VC can pop out of a tunnel, strike from behind, then disappear. Or hide in a village. You can't tell VC from rice farmers. And there's no good aerial cover."

"I don't want to talk about this at dinner," she said, and closed the atlas. She didn't ever want to talk about it. Well, she wasn't a vet. God forbid we ever use our women like that, though those nurses . . . you've really got to hand it to them. They've got guts. Day after day, nurses flew out with their patients. The big, silent planes flew out too, with the flags and the coffins. But the news wasn't showing them much anymore.

McGovern called it peace with honor. Withdrawal with honor, someone had tried to call it at a press conference; and all the reporters had cracked up. They'd had to fade to black real fast. Besides, you couldn't say that around the kids. McGovern still had them in the palm of his hand. They had a lot of influence, and they wanted our boys out. McGovern always had a bunch of them following him around, as interns or admirers or something. They were beginning to look a little frantic.

It was Father Klein who called it the long defeat. We were fighting to lose. It reminded me of something. Once I had to help the Bear with his history homework, and I read this thing about a Children's Crusade. They wanted to do what their elders couldn't—free the Holy Land, miracles, that sort of thing. So they left home and went on Crusade. And none of 'em ever made it back.

Every time the phone rang, I dreaded it. Sometimes it was Steff. She'd turned expert, like all the kids. We talked over the withdrawal, and she said the exotic names in tones I hadn't heard for years. Sometimes it was relief operations. Everyone wanted a check. Once it was Steff's school—some lady from development assuring us that no, the school wasn't planning to close down as it had in 1970 so everyone could go do relief work. Oddly enough, I don't think I'd have minded if it had. Let the college kids do their share. But while she had me on the phone, could she possibly convince me to donate . . .

Yeah, sure.

Al never called. After a while that sort of worried me, so I picked up the phone one evening at a decent hour and called him. Got his Mrs. and the cold shoulder, too, till I explained. Al was resting, she said. He'd been working too hard lately. No, he couldn't come to the phone.

Drying out, I thought. Not all the casualties of a war happen in combat.

Used to be, letters from the Bear were a surprise—a treat to top off a good deal or a reward to make up for a lousy one. Now, I started calling home about the time the mail usually came. "Any news?" I'd ask. Usually, there wasn't. If there was, Margaret would read Bear's letters to me. Steffie said he was still writing her, but she didn't offer.

Don't know when he had time. He said he was helping out when he was off-duty in one of the orphanages. Run by French nuns. Didn't know he'd learned some French, too. Maybe he wouldn't mind if his dad stuck his nose into his business when he came back and suggested going to college on a GI bill. There *had* to be a GI bill or something, didn't there? I mean, we owe those boys a lot.

Well, he always had been good with kids. He sent us one snapshot. There he was, all spit and polish, with these cute little round-faced kids with their bright eyes crawling all over him, scuffing up those patent shoes.

At least he got to keep clean and dry. I remembered how your feet felt like they'd rot off if you couldn't get them out of those stinking boots. In the jungle, you get mold on everything, it's so damp. I didn't like it when the Bear would complain that he had it soft, compared to most of the men. I was scared he'd try to transfer out. But I guess someone talked to him, and he thought of what he owed to his mom and sister, because after a while, he didn't talk about that anymore.

And meanwhile, those goddamn VC were getting closer to Saigon. The whole fucking—sorry, I never swear like that, must be thinking back to my army days—country was falling apart. Hated to admit it, but Al was right. As long as we came on like Curtis LeMay and threatened, at least, to bomb 'em back to the Stone Age, they'd at least respected what we could do to them if we really set our minds to it. Now, "paper tiger" was the kindest name they had for us.

President McGovern began to look haunted. He'd be a one-term president, that was for sure. And when he came down with cardiac arrhythmia, some of us wondered if he'd even manage that. The kids who surrounded his staff looked pretty grim, too. Like the kids who get caught stealing cars and suddenly realize that things are not going to be much fun anymore.

The anchormen on the evening news sounded like preachers at a funeral. I'm not making this up; it happened at Da Nang. You saw a plane ready for takeoff. Three hundred people crowded in, trampling on women and children, they were so panicky. Then the crew wanted to close the doors and get out of there, but the people wouldn't get off the runway, clear the stairs. They pulled some off the wheels and took off anyway. And you could see little black specks as people fell off where they'd hung on to the rear stairway.

Did McGovern say anything? Sure. "We must put the past behind us. Tragic as these days are, they are the final throes of a war we never should have entered. In the hard days to come, I call upon the American people to emulate the discipline and courage of our fine servicemen who are withdrawing in good order from Vietnam."

I'd of spat, but Margaret was watching the news with me. We couldn't *not* watch. Funny, neither of us had ever liked horror films, but we had to watch the news.

Some people waded into the sea, the mothers holding their babies over their heads. They overloaded fishing boats, and the Navy found them floating. Or maybe the boats hadn't overloaded. Those people mostly hadn't much, but it wouldn't have been hard to take what they had, hit them on the head, and throw them overboard.

Refugees were flooding Saigon. The Bear's French orphanage was mobbed, and the grounds of all the embassies were full. Would the VC respect the embassies? How could they? Human life means nothing to them, or else they wouldn't treat their own people the way they do. And Cambodia's even worse, no matter what Steffie's poli-sci profs say.

In a letter I didn't show my wife, Barry told me he could hear the cluster bombs drop. The North Viets were at Xuanloc, thirty-five miles northwest of Saigon, on the way to Bien Hoa airfield, heading south, always heading south.

"If our allies had fought as well as they did at Xuanloc, maybe we wouldn't be in this fix, Dad," Barry wrote me. "It doesn't look good. Don't tell Mom. But the Navy's got ships standing offshore in the Gulf of Thailand and a fleet of choppers to fly us out to them. I hope . . ."

I crumpled the letter in my hand. Later, I smoothed it out and made myself read it, though. My son was out in that green hell, and I was scared to read his letter? That wasn't how I'd want to greet him when the choppers finally brought him out. He'd be one of the last to leave, I knew that. Probably pushing the ambassador ahead of him.

I wrote I was proud of him. I didn't say the half of what I meant. I don't know if he got the letter.

Then one morning Mary-Lynn met me at the door of my office, and she'd been crying.

She wouldn't let me inside. "Mrs. Black called. You have to go home, she says. Right away. Oh, Mr. Black, I'm so sorry!" She wiped at her nose. I was in shock. I pulled my handkerchief from my suit jacket and handed it to her.

She put her hands out as if I was going to pass out. "There's a . . . there's a *car* out there . . ."

"Not . . ." I couldn't say the word. It would make it real. My boy. Never coming home? I couldn't make myself believe it.

"They've got a car there and Marines—oh, your wife says please, please come straight home . . ."

The spring sun hit my shoulders like something I'd never felt before. What right did the sun have to shine here? The trees in Crandall Park were fresh and green, and the gardens at the big corner house where they always spent a mint on flowers looked like something out of the first day of the world. How did they dare? My boy had been shot. Other men's sons had been shot in a green hell they should have burnt down to ash.

A voice broke in on the radio.

". . . the American Embassy has closed its gates, and the Ambassador . . . Ambassador Bunker has refused evacuation . . ."

He'd have been there, my son. Firing into the enemy, not wanting to fire, I knew that, but there'd be a wall of Marines between the VC and the panicked crowd and the diplomats they had sworn to protect. . . .

I had people to protect too. I put my foot hard on the gas, peeled round a slowpoke station wagon with three kids and their mom in it, and roared up Fifth Avenue.

". . . We interrupt this program . . . there is a rumor that Ambassador Bunker has been shot. . . . We repeat, this is a rumor, no one has seen his body . . ."

Sweet suffering Christ! Damn that red light, no one was around, so it wouldn't matter if I crashed it. Didn't want to smear myself all over the landscape before I got home; Margaret would never forgive me if I got myself killed coming home to her now, of all times.

*God*damn siren! I thought of giving the cop a run for his money, but you don't do that in Youngstown. Not ever, and especially not if you're a lawyer.

The man who got out of the car recognized me. "Hey, Counselor, what you think you're doing? You were going seventy and you crashed that light . . ." He sniffed at my breath, then pulled out his pad. "You know better than that. Now I wish I could let you off with a warning . . ."

A fist was squeezing my throat. Finally, it let up long enough for me to breathe. "It's my boy . . ." I said. Then I laid my head down on the steering wheel.

A hand came in over my shoulder and took the keys. "I'm driving you home. The way you're driving, you could get yourself . . . Come on, Counselor."

I made him let me off up the street. No telling what Margaret would have thought if she'd seen a cop car roll up to the door. The Marine car was in the drive. The men saw me get out of the car and followed me. I made it up the front walk, feeling like I was walking off a three-day binge. Toni Carlson opened the door. She was crying, but

Margaret wasn't. Sure enough, the living room and kitchen were full of women with their covered dishes.

"I called Steffie's school," Margaret said before I could even get to her. She had Barry's service photo out like they do in the newspapers. His face grinned under his hat. God, he was a good-looking boy. "Her plane gets in this afternoon."

"I'm going to pick her up," said a voice from behind me.

"Sir," began one of the Marines. A fine young man. I had . . . I have . . . a son like him.

He shook my hand and bravely said the things they're supposed to say. "Sir, the President of the United States and the Secretary of Defense have asked me to inform you that your son . . ." The boy's voice faltered, and he went on in his own words.

Missing. Presumed dead. My son was . . . is . . . a hero. But presumed dead. After Ambassador Bunker died (that wasn't supposed to get out yet, but he supposed I had a right to know), the surviving Marines were supposed to withdraw. But Barry gave his seat to a local woman and a child.

"Probably knew them from the orphanage," I muttered.

"No doubt, sir," said the Marine. It wasn't his business to comment. He'd be glad to get out, even if he had more families' hearts to break that day. Lord, I wished I could.

At least he didn't have a damn flag. As long as you don't get the flag, you can still hope.

Her school sent Steffie home, the way these schools do when there's been a death in the family. Pinkos they may be, but I've got to admit each of her professors and the college president wrote us nice letters. Take as much time as you need before coming back to class, they told Steff. Better than she got from some of her friends. Once or twice, when she thought I wasn't looking, I saw her throw out letters. And I heard her shouting on the phone at someone, then hang up with a bang. All she ever said was, "You never know who's really your friend."

I thought she'd do better to stick out the term, but she decided to take the semester off. Seeing how Margaret brightened at that news, I didn't insist she go back. And when my wife threw a major fit and screamed, "I can't bear to lose *both* the men in our family!" at the dinner table and practically *ordered* me to get an EKG, I kept the appointment with our doctor that she'd made.

Oddly enough, now that the worst had happened, I slept like a baby right through the next time the phone rang at 3:00 A.M.

Steffie came into our room. She spoke to Margaret. "It's from Frankfurt. West Germany."

Why would she be getting a call from West Germany of all places?

Margaret got up and threw on a robe. "It's in, then?"

My daughter nodded. I stared at both women. Beyond family resemblance, their faces wore the same expression: guilt, fear, and a weird kind of anticipation under the sorrow that had put circles under their eyes.

Like the damn fool husbands on TV, I waited for my womenfolk to explain what was going on. It didn't much matter. After all, when your country's lost a war and you've lost a son, what else can happen?

"We have to Talk," Margaret said in *that* tone of voice. "I'll make us some coffee."

So at three in the morning, we sat down to a family conference. Margaret poured coffee. To my surprise, she looked imploringly at Steffie.

"The call from Frankfurt came through on my line," she said.

That stupid Princess phone!

"That's where they evacuate the refugees and process them."

My hand closed on the spoon till it hurt. How did that rate a transatlantic phone call?

Stephanie took a deep, deep breath and drew herself

up. For a moment, I thought I could see her brother, making up his mind at the Embassy to give up his place to a woman and a child.

Our eyes met. She'd been thinking of Barry too.

"You know that woman and kid Barry pushed onto the helicopter in his place?"

"The ones he knew from the orphanage?"

"Where'd you get that idea?" Margaret broke in.

"Mom, he *did* meet Nguyen at the orphanage."

"Now wait a damn minute, both of you. Maybe it's too early, but no one's making sense!"

Margaret set down her coffee cup. "Joe, please listen."

"Dad, about a year ago, Barry wrote me. He'd met a girl who worked at the French Embassy. She's from Saigon, and her name is Nguyen."

I held up a hand. I wanted to be stupid. I wanted to be Ward Cleaver and have this episode end. Margaret would switch off the TV set, the show would be over, we could all go back to bed, and none of this, *none* of the whole past miserable year would have happened.

So my boy had sacrificed himself for a friend. . . .

"She's his *wife*, Daddy. And the child . . ."

When you're on the front lines and you get hit bad, it doesn't hurt at first. You go into shock.

"You knew about this?" I asked Margaret. She looked down, ashamed.

"And didn't tell me?" Both women looked down.

"My son *married*—how do we know it's true?—he says he *married* this goddamn gook! Her people *killed* him, and you have the nerve to say . . ."

"If you say that word, I'll never speak to you again!" Stephanie was on her feet, her big flannel nightgown billowing in flowers and hearts about her. "Nguyen's not a bar girl. Barry said she's a lady. She worked at the French Embassy. She speaks French and Vietnamese . . . some English."

"They seem to have communicated just fine without it!" I snapped, hating myself.

They'd hidden this from me! Barry had written to Stephanie, and all those calls when she'd said, "I need to talk to Mom," they were talking about this unknown girl. This gook girl. Who my son had planned to bring home. I could just see Ronnie the Racist's face.

They'd hidden this from me.

"Oh Mom, I'm making such a mess of this!" Steffie cried. "I didn't really believe he'd take it like this . . ."

"Give him some time, darling," said my wife. "We were caught by surprise, too."

"*You* give him some time," my daughter burst into tears. "The only grandkid he may ever have, and all he can think of is to ask, 'Are they really married?' and call the mother a gook and a bar girl! I haven't got time for this! I have to pack and go to Washington to meet Nguyen, and then I have to go . . ."

I reached up and grasped my daughter's wrist.

"Just where do you think you're going?"

That little bit of a thing faced me down. "I'm joining the Red Cross relief effort." She laughed, shakily. "I wish I'd listened to you and become a nurse after all. It's a hell of a lot more useful than a poli-sci major for what I need to do. We're going over there."

"That hellhole's already swallowed one of my kids!"

"That's right. So I'm going over there to look for him."

I shook my head at her. Just one small girl in the middle of a war zone. What did she think she could do?

"Daddy, you know I've *always* looked after my brother. No matter how big he got. Except with this . . . this mess about the war. I did what I thought was right, and see how it worked out." She wiped at her eyes.

"Somehow, I have to make up for that. All of us do. So I'm going to look for him. And if I . . . when I find him . . . so help me, I am going to beat the crap out of him for scaring us this way!" She was sobbing noisily now, and when I held out my arms, she flung herself into them.

"Oh Daddy, I was wrong, it all went wrong and it got so fucked up!"

"Don't use words like that," I whispered, kissing my girl's hair. "Not in front of your mother."

"It's all right," said Margaret. "I feel the same way."

"Unless I find him, Nguyen and the little boy are all we've got of Barry. And we're all *they've* got. But all you can do is call them bad words and . . . and . . ."

I patted her back and met my wife's eyes. She nodded, and I knew we'd be having guests in the house. No, scratch that. We'd be having new family members come to live here. And if my sister's husband even *thought* of opening his big fat mouth, I'd shut it for him the way I'd wanted to for the past thirty years.

Stephanie pulled out of my arms and pushed her bangs out of her eyes. I sighed and picked my words. If I said things wrong, I was scared I'd lose her.

"We've been in this town for five generations," I began slowly. "I think our family has enough of a reputation so people will welcome . . . what did you say her name was?"

"Nguyen," Margaret whispered. Her eyes were very bright. "I'll brush up on my French." She used to teach it before we got married. "And the little boy—our grandson—is Barry, Jr. I can't imagine how that sounds in a Vietnamese accent, can you?"

A tiny woman in those floaty things Vietnamese women wore. A little lady. My son's wife . . . or widow. And one of those cute little black-eyed kids, unless he looked like Bear. Family. Just let anyone *dare* say anything.

"We can put them in Barry's room," I stammered. "I suppose."

"Nguyen can have mine," said Steffie. "I won't need it. Oh, Daddy, I was wrong about so many things. But I was right about you after all."

She kissed me, then ran upstairs, a whirlwind in a flowered nightgown. I could hear closets and drawers protesting and paper ripping.

"I wish she'd been right about all of them," I told Margaret. She took my hand.

"I'm going with Stephanie to pick up . . . Nguyen," my wife informed me.

It would get easier, I sensed, for both of us to think of her and the boy as family once we met them. My son's wife. My son's son. This wasn't how I'd thought that would be.

In a few minutes, once the shock wore off, I supposed I'd get to see the pictures. I knew there had to be pictures. But you don't live with a woman for this many years without knowing when she has more to say. And having a pretty good idea of what it is—most of the time.

This time, though, my guess was right. "Joe, I want you to come with us to Washington so we can all meet as a family. Nguyen must be terrified. She's lost everything and, and everyone."

Her voice trembled, but she forced it to calm. "It would mean a lot to her. Steff says the Vietnamese are Confucian. If the head of our family were there to greet her, she'd *know* she was welcome, she and the little one."

A smile flickered across her face. "I wonder where we can get a crib," she mused. "All our friends' children are grown and haven't started having babies yet. We'll be the first to have a grandchild."

I bent over and hugged her. "Did you make a third plane reservation?"

She smiled at me. "What do you think?"

"I'll carry your suitcase downstairs for you, baby," I told my daughter.

"Oh, Dad, you know I'll have to lug my own stuff once I go overseas . . ."

"As long as you're in *my house*, young lady—"

"It's on my bed." I went into her room to get it. She'd taken a cheap plaid fabric thing, not one of the good, big Samsonite cases she'd gotten for high school graduation. Her room wasn't just clean: it was sterile. She'd even torn down her posters and hung the crewelwork back up. I wondered what this strange new daughter-in-law of mine would make of the pretty blue and lilac room.

My foot sent something spinning and rolling. I bent to retrieve the thing, which promptly jagged my finger. One of Stephanie's protest buttons, hurled away as if in despair, poor girl. "Suppose they gave a war and nobody came?" it asked.

Suppose they did? It had never happened yet.

Suppose, instead, they gave a peace? That hadn't worked, either.

But I can always hope, can't I?

After all, I have a grandson to look out for.

1972

Watergate, the scandal that drove Richard Nixon from office, was such a major event that it deserves its own story—and, given the nature of this book, the story is obvious: what if the details of the break-in and cover-up had surfaced *before* the 1972 election?

Brian Thomsen, Hugo-nominated editor of Warner Books, offers an answer in this, his first science fiction story.

Paper Trail

by Brian Thomsen

The President looked out over the White House lawn and was troubled. Conspiracy and coverups had been all, and platforms, track records, and promises had become secondary.

Yet, despite it all, he had won the election and he was the President of the United States.

He hoped that history would be kind to him.

Washington Post
June 17, 1972
PHONE REPORT
TIME LOGGED: 0500
TO: Harry M. Rosenfield (Metropolitan Editor for the *Washington Post*)

FROM: Alfred E. Lewis (Reporter for the *Washington Post*, Police Beat)

At 2:30 A.M. five men dressed in business suits and all wearing Playtex rubber surgical gloves were arrested in a burglary at Democratic headquarters in the Watergate office-apartment-hotel complex. The men in question were carrying sophisticated photographic equipment and electronic gear. The men apparently knew their way around. The suspects are scheduled to appear in court this afternoon for a preliminary hearing.

Washington Post
Memo from the desk of Barry Sussman (City editor)

Bob Woodward called 0900. Assigned to cover break-in at the Democratic National Committee headquarters.

Washington Post
1830
Story submitted to Barry Sussman for Sunday edition June 18, 1972 by Bob Woodward
Byline to read Alfred E. Lewis

Five men, one of whom is said to be a former employee of the Central Intelligence Agency, were arrested at 2:30 A.M. yesterday in what authorities described as an elaborate plot to bug the offices of the Democratic National Committee.

There was no immediate explanation as to why the five suspects would want to bug the Democratic National Committee offices, or whether or not they were working for any other individuals or organizations.

Washington Post
1845
Story submitted to Barry Sussman for Sunday edition June 18, 1972 by Carl Bernstein
(to be used as uncredited sidebar)

The five suspects were identified as James W. McCord, Jr., Bernard L. Barker, Frank A. Sturgis, Virgilio R. Gonzalez and Eugenio R. Martinez.

Barker, Sturgis, Gonzalez, and Martinez, all from Miami, Florida, had previously been involved in anti-Castro activities and were alleged to also have CIA connections. Sturgis, an American soldier of fortune and a non-Cuban, is reported to have been recruiting militant Cubans earlier this year to demonstrate at the Democratic National Convention.

Associated Press Wire Service
June 18, 1972

ONE OF THE SUSPECTS IN YESTERDAY'S ALLEGED BREAK-IN AT DEMOCRATIC NATIONAL COMMITTEE HEADQUARTERS HAS BEEN IDENTIFIED AS JAMES W. MCCORD, JR., THE SECURITY COORDINATOR OF THE COMMITTEE TO RE-ELECT THE PRESIDENT

JOHN MITCHELL, THE FORMER U.S. ATTORNEY GENERAL AND THE PRESIDENT'S CAMPAIGN MANAGER, ISSUED A STATEMENT: "THE PERSON INVOLVED IS THE PROPRIETOR OF A PRIVATE SECURITY AGENCY WHO WAS EMPLOYED BY OUR COMMITTEE MONTHS AGO TO ASSIST WITH THE INSTALLATION OF OUR SECURITY SYSTEM. WE WANT TO EMPHASIZE THAT THIS MAN AND THE OTHER PEOPLE INVOLVED WERE NOT OPERATING ON EITHER OUR BEHALF OR WITH OUR CONSENT. THERE IS NO PLACE IN OUR CAMPAIGN OR IN THE ELECTORAL PROCESS FOR THIS TYPE OF ACTIVITY, AND WE WILL NOT PERMIT OR CONDONE IT."

Washington Post
June 19, 1972
Memo

TO: Benjamin C. Bradlee (Executive Editor)
FROM: Howard Simmons (Managing Editor)
RE: Bob Woodward and Carl Bernstein

The following story was handed to me by Barry Sussman for inclusion in tomorrow's early edition:

WHITE HOUSE CONSULTANT
LINKED TO BUGGING SUSPECTS
by Carl Bernstein and Bob Woodward

E. Howard Hunt, a consultant working for the Special Counsel to the President, Charles W. Colson, has been linked to the recent break-in at the Democratic National Committee headquarters.

Hunt, a member of the CIA from 1949 to 1970, now employed as a writer for the Washington public relations firm Robert R. Mullen and Company, is believed to be the "Dear Friend Mr. Howard," and "Dear Mr. H.H." listed in the correspondence and address books of the break-in suspects.

A White House source verified Hunt's work as a consultant on the declassification of the Pentagon Papers, but denied any connection between him and the break-in and moreover continued, "I am convinced that neither Mr. Colson nor anyone else at the White House had any knowledge of, or participation in, this deplorable incident."

Hunt's response to the question of why his name and phone number were in the alleged perpetrators' address book was: "Good God! In view of the fact that the matter is under adjudication, I have no comment."

What do you think?

Washington Post
June 19, 1972
Memo

TO: Howard Simmons
FROM: Benjamin Bradlee
RE: Woodstein

This is the last straw and an opportunity to kill two birds with one stone. I admire tenacity, drive, and pride but not at the expense of good journalism. The story entitled WHITE HOUSE CONSULTANT LINKED TO BUGGING SUSPECTS is a perfect of example of everything that is wrong with the current crop of young turk reporters. First, both reporters neglect to fully identify one of the burglars, causing us to once again get scooped by AP—then they try, through hyperbole and manufactured anonymous sources (Deep Throat indeed), to draw some absurd connection between a third-rate burglary attempt and the White House, adding insult to injury. I wish reporters today would report the news rather than make it up out of allegations, speculations, and second-rate bullshit.

Woodward has been a prima donna since he started here nine months ago. Somebody is going to have to teach that boy that being a reporter is more than just showing up at the right garden parties and calling a few close friends for tips.

And Bernstein may have been a boy wonder at one time but now he's just a pain in the ass. Ever since his run-in with the cops at that anti-Nixon rally at the Watergate last year, that long-haired hippie freak has been trying to bring down the current administration. Sometimes you can't tell whether he wants to be a reporter or a revolutionary or a rock critic. The *Washington Post* is not *Rolling Stone*, and he is definitely not Hunter S. What's-his-name.

Give these two their walking papers.

Alfred Lewis can take care of any necessary follow-up on this Watergate thing.

THE WHITE HOUSE
July 2, 1972

CONFIDENTIAL MEMO
TO: John D. Ehrlichman, Assistant to the President for Domestic Affairs
FROM: Kenneth W. Clawson, Deputy Director of Communications

My contacts from my tenure at the *Washington Post* mentioned that those two reporters who were fired last month, Woodward and Bernstein, have continued their investigations into the Watergate break-in. Somehow they've made the connection between Hunt and McCord, and the check that was paid to Bittman to take their case. If they make the connection between the check and Dahlberg and the Committee to Re-elect, they can establish a paper trail leading directly to the White House.

THE WHITE HOUSE
July 3, 1972
CONFIDENTIAL MEMO
TO: G. Gordon Liddy
FROM: John D. Ehrlichman

I think that it is about time that we imposed a deadline on the Bernstein-Woodward research

Washington Post
July 10, 1972
(Page 12)
FORMER WASHINGTON POST REPORTER KILLED IN HIT-AND-RUN ACCIDENT

Carl Bernstein, who until last month had been a reporter on this newspaper, was killed yesterday in a hit-and-run accident outside the Library of Congress. Bernstein was twenty-eight, and had worked for the *Post* for twelve years.

According to Bob Woodward, who was with Bernstein

at the time of his death and had barely escaped the oncoming vehicle himself, "The driver seemed hell-bent on running us over . . . swerving into the oncoming lane in pursuit of us."

Bernstein was pronounced dead at the scene.

Police investigators claim to have several leads but are quick to point out that most hit-and-run drivers are never identified.

Washington Post
July 11, 1972
(Headline)
GENERAL ALEXANDER HAIG DISPATCHED TO PARIS FOR THE DURATION OF THE PEACE TALKS

THE WHITE HOUSE
July 12, 1972
TO: John Ehrlichman
FROM: G. Gordon Liddy

With Bernstein's unfortunate accident, and Woodward neutralized without his "highly-placed White House source," I feel that it is safe to close the folder on the public's interest in Watergate.

August 1, 1972
TO: Mr. Leonard Wexler, Executive Editor of the *New York Post.*
FROM: Admiral Harris Casey, U.S. Navy, retired.
RE: Bob Woodward

Please grant Mr. Woodward the consideration of an interview. I can attest to his abilities as a reporter from his days as a member of the Navy officer corps (we also share the same alma mater, Yale). He has an unusual story that, in his words, was too hot for the *Washington Post* to handle.

New York Post
August 7, 1972
(Headline)
WHITE HOUSE CONSULTANT LINKED TO WATERGATE BURGLARS
(Page 3 sidebar)
HIT-AND-RUN LINKED TO THE CRP

The sedan that killed former *Washington Post* reporter Carl Bernstein was paid for by a check from the Committee to Re-elect the President.

Records indicate that the car was registered to a Will Gordon, and paid for by a check from the CRP.

Bob Woodward, who was with Mr. Bernstein at the time of the accident, traced the sedan to its rental agency by means of its license plate number.

New York Post
August 8, 1972
(Headline)
CRP LINKED TO WATERGATE BREAK-IN AND REPORTER HIT-AND-RUN
by Bob Woodward
(Page 2)

Kenneth H. Dahlberg, Midwest Finance Chairman for the Committee to Re-elect the President, has come forward to the *New York Post* to admit that checks from his office were issued to Howard Hunt to pay the lawyer for the Watergate burglars, and to G. Gordon Liddy (Finance Counsel, CRP), to rent, under the name Will Gordon, the car that is alleged to have run down former *Washington Post* reporter Carl Bernstein.

Dahlberg indicated that the checks were drawn from a large slush fund that was designated for unnamed special projects of the CRP, alleged to amount to millions of dollars in cash.

When asked why he came forward, Dahlberg only replied that the line had to be drawn somewhere, and he wished that it had been drawn prior to Mr. Bernstein's death.

New York Post
August 9, 1972
(Headline)
WHITE HOUSE AIDE INDICTED IN CONNECTION TO HIT-AND-RUN MURDER
(Page 2)

White House aide G. Gordon Liddy has been indicted in connection with the hit-and-run murder of former *Washington Post* reporter Carl Bernstein.
CRP DIRECTOR AND PRESIDENTIAL AIDE SUBPOENAED
CRP Campaign Director Clark MacGregor and Assistant to the President for Domestic Affairs John D. Ehrlichman have been subpoenaed in connection with the joint investigation into the burglary of Democratic headquarters and the murder of Carl Bernstein.
CRP AUDIT ORDERED

Washington Post
August 16, 1972
(Headline)
EHRLICHMAN INDICTED IN CONNECTION TO LIDDY CASE

New York Post
August 16, 1972
(Headline)
EHRLICHMAN AND LIDDY CHARGED WITH CONSPIRACY
DIRTY TRICKS SLUSH FUND CONNECTED TO BURGLARY AND HOMICIDE

Village Voice
August 17, 1972

(Cover Story)
WHITE HOUSE RACKED WITH CONSPIRACIES AT HOME AND ABROAD
- U.S. IMPERIALISM KEEPS CONFLICT ALIVE IN VIETNAM
- REPUBLICAN DOLLARS BUY INEPT BURGLARS AND COLD-BLOODED KILLERS
- *WASHINGTON POST* PURPOSELY BURIED EARLIEST EVIDENCE OF CRP DECEIT

Washington Post
August 23, 1972
(Headline)
PRESIDENT RICHARD NIXON NOMINATED BY REPUBLICANS FOR A SECOND TERM

Washington Post
August 29, 1972
(Headline)
PRESIDENT PLEDGES SUPPORT OF AUDIT
(Page 1)

In his first press conference since securing the Republican nomination, the President pledged his support of the upcoming audit of the CRP while attesting that as he understood it numerous campaign fund violations may have existed on both sides.

When questioned on the murder of Carl Bernstein, Press Secretary Ronald Ziegler terminated the press conference. Later a formal White House statement was issued, pledging the President's support in the investigation into the alleged murder of Bernstein, while mourning the loss of such a distinguished member of the press.

Associated Press Wire Service
September 4, 1972

LABOR DAY WEEKEND POLL INDICATES A LOSS OF SUPPORT FOR THE PRESIDENT. THOUGH VAST MA-

JORITY BELIEVES HIM INNOCENT OF ANY CONNECTION TO BREAK-IN OR HIT-AND-RUN, MOST ADMIT TO A CERTAIN LOSS OF FAITH IN THE INTEGRITY OF THOSE MEN WHO HAD BEEN APPOINTED BY HIM.

Washington Star-News
September 23, 1972
(Headline)
CRP AUDIT YIELDS DISCLOSURES OF DIRTY TRICKS AND "MISC. PAYMENTS"
WHITE HOUSE CHIEF OF STAFF HALDEMAN LINKED TO FUND

Chicago Tribune
September 25, 1972
(Headline)
SLUSH FUND DISPOSITIONS TRACED TO WHITE HOUSE ... BUT HOW FAR FROM THE OVAL OFFICE? DID NIXON KNOW?

San Francisco Chronicle
September 25, 1972
(Headline)
PRESIDENT'S RIGHT HAND HALDEMAN INDICTED IN SLUSH FUND SCANDAL
DID THE PRESIDENT KNOW WHAT HIS RIGHT HAND WAS DOING?

Dallas Morning News
September 25, 1972
(Headline)
IS THE ROAD TO RE-ELECTION STAINED WITH BLOOD?

Associated Press Wire Service
October 15, 1972
COLUMBUS DAY GANNET POLL CLOUDS NIXON'S RE-ELECTION HOPES

(Americans forgive mismanagement in war . . . but not when it leads to murder on Washington streets)

Chicago Sun-Times
(Headline)
WILL HIT-AND-RUN SLUSH FUND BE NIXON'S CHAPPAQUIDDICK?

New York Times
November 1, 1972
SIGNET BOOK ON CRP AUDIT BECOMES INSTANT BESTSELLER

In the end it had all been a media circus. Tabloid TV interviews, instant book bestsellers, and scandal galore.

The American people had been cheated. A fair election had been impossible. An incumbent President in such a situation should have stepped down. That would have been the honorable thing to do . . . but then again an honorable man would never have found himself in this situation.

The President sighed and returned to his desk in the often-coveted Oval Office. A new term had just begun, and it was time to get down to work. He'd been the least disliked of the candidates, and it had been years since a Democrat had been elected president.

Everything else was now in the past, and he knew he would be starting from scratch. The first thing he had to do was to keep as many of his campaign promises as possible. With a Democratic majority in both the House and the Senate, he might be able to make a difference . . . but first, President George McGovern would bring our boys home from Vietnam.

1976

To some of our younger readers, Jimmy Carter is the only Democratic president to serve within their lifetime, or at least within their memory. He was also the first president to face a hostage crisis in the Middle East, and in the end it was that crisis that probably cost him his job.

Could the crisis have been solved? Alexis Gilliland, Campbell winner, author of *Wizenbeak* and *The Shadow Shaia*, and longtime Washington bureaucrat, explores the manner in which Gerald Ford, Carter's defeated opponent, might have attacked it.

Demarche to Iran

by Alexis A. Gilliland

Chapter 1.
The Election

Naked, President Gerald Ford lay on the table and screamed. The masseur grunted and repeated the stroke a little less forcefully. "You politicians sure manage to tie yourselves into knots, Mr. President. What brought *this* on?"

A faint groan. "What do you mean?"

The masseur rubbed a little fresh oil on his hands and began going down the long muscles on each side of the spine. "What were you doing when your back seized up on you?"

"Uh, well . . . I had just decided to put Watergate behind us forever by giving Nixon a full pardon for everything."

"And then it hit you? Your gluteus maximus has more political savvy than your cerebral cortex and cerebellum put together, Mr. President."

"I don't know what muscles you're talking about, Darko."

"Forget the muscles, Mr. President. Speaking as a masseur, Nixon is a pain in the ass to the whole country, and to *really* put him, and Watergate, behind you, the cramp he caused needs to be worked out."

"Oh, oh, oh . . . that feels much better. Yes. Oh my. How would you work the cramp out of the country?"

"When you have a cramp, the brain has to know where it hurts so it can relax each individual muscle around the cramping muscle before it can finally ease the cramping muscle itself. A blanket pardon is fine for Mr. Nixon, but the country will stay cramped and hurting for a long time. What you do is have the Justice Department draw up a bill of particulars, everything they know, everything they can find, everything they can think of, and then, then you pardon Nixon for the whole list." The masseur began working on the back of Ford's arms. "And publish the list."

"His enemies will say he was guilty of everything on that list, even if he wasn't."

"So let them. He's pardoned. If it makes them feel better isn't that good for the country?"

"I suppose so. They feel better, the country feels better, that would make it easier to get reelected president."

You mean elected, thought the masseur, rubbing oil on his hands, but he said nothing.

"All right," said Gerald Ford decisively. "That's what I'll do, then."

* * *

On the second Tuesday of November, 1976, President Gerald Ford defeated the Democratic challenger, Jimmy Carter, when Illinois shifted from Democratic to Republican after the second recount.

Chapter 2.
The Crisis

Much of the world does not run in synchronicity with American Presidential elections, and the Shah of Iran, Mohammad Reza Pahlavi, after many years of refusing to listen to the truth, fell as he was bound to. Correctness of action, of judgment, of timing, might have sustained him a little longer, but error was rooted in the Shah's personality and bore fruit in his institutional shadow. And while the Ford Administration did not offer the same advice that an alternate Carter Administration might have offered, the advice that it did offer was equally disregarded. Systematically making his own mistakes, while blaming his advisors for not telling him the truth he refused to hear, the Shah lost his grip on the Peacock Throne and went into exile on January 16, 1979. The interim regime of his successor, Prime Minister Shapur Bakhtiar, fell six weeks later, after the Shah's Imperial Guard was destroyed in fierce fighting. An Islamic Republic was formed as the Shi'ite religious leader Ayatollah Ruholla Khomeini took power after defeating the secular elements of the Iranian revolution in a series of violent clashes.

Not a well man, even before his fall from power, Shah Pahlavi came to New York for medical treatment. The Iranian government requested that he be returned to Teheran to stand trial for crimes against the Iranian people. The United States, perhaps mindful of a debt of honor owed its former ally, declined to accede to that request. On November 4, 1979, militant Iranian students seized the American Embassy in Iran and took ninety people hostage, including sixty-three Americans, and demanded that the Shah be returned.

The mood in the Oval Office was somber that evening. "What do we do now?" asked President Gerald Ford.

"Maybe we can cut a deal with Khomeini to get the hostages back," suggested Richard Cheney, White House Chief of Staff.

Secretary of State Henry Kissinger shook his head. "I don't think so, Richard. Khomeini let the students take our people in the first place. What he is doing is pretending that his government is not responsible so he can reap the benefits of this illegal and outrageous act. Besides, what sort of a deal could we make?"

"We could give him the Shah," suggested Ford.

"No, no," demurred Kissinger, shaking his head. "America has pretensions to greatness that would be destroyed forever by such a craven act."

"Well, then, what about going in and getting our people out?"

Admiral Morrisy, Head of the Joint Chiefs of Staff, coughed into his hand. "We don't have the capability to do that, Mr. President. Teheran is a hell of a long ways from anywhere we could jump off from. Perhaps you ought to try diplomacy."

"Don't look at me," said Kissinger indignantly. "There are also limits to what can be achieved with diplomacy."

President Ford rubbed his head. "Well, we have to do something, Henry," he said at last. "Suppose we . . . suppose we threaten. . . ?"

"Threaten what?" asked Kissinger.

"Threaten to rescue the hostages if they don't give them back?"

"Well, forget about military action, Mr. President," said Admiral Morrisy. "What you want to do just isn't feasible."

Henry Kissinger shrugged. "We will explore our diplomatic options, Mr. President, but I must tell you that I am not hopeful for any favorable outcome."

"We can seize Iranian bank accounts," suggested Cheney. "That will hit them where it hurts."

A long sigh. "My back is killing me," said Ford. "We'll seize the bank accounts unless we can think of something better to do, I guess. Suppose we break for supper and meet back here at ten-thirty to see if anything turned up?"

Morrisy checked his watch. "2230 hours will be fine," he agreed, and the meeting adjourned.

"You've had much worse, Mr. President," said the masseur. "Much worse. This will come out pretty easy if we just work around the knots. What all was bothering you?"

"Our embassy in Teheran," replied Ford. "Those damned students took our people hostage and what am I going to do about it?"

"Use diplomacy, of course. What are diplomats for except to rescue other diplomats in trouble?"

"Ah, Darko. Kissinger says he isn't hopeful about diplomacy."

The masseur rubbed fresh oil on his hands. "Kissinger, hah! He's thinking about the Russians, about the big picture, about the whole world, and he's thinking so hard that he can't see the obvious answer."

President Ford rolled over on his back and the masseur began working on the scalp and facial muscles. "What obvious answer?"

"Well look, the students have our people, right? But Khomeini says it isn't the government, and he can't control the students. That's what he says. So what do we do? We make the government *want* to give our people back."

"We're going to seize Iranian bank accounts. Maybe that will do it."

"That, Mr. President, is a dumb idea. Capitalistic, but dumb. You want to deal with religious fanatics by threatening money that isn't even theirs? No!" Skilled hands snapped the head back and forth, loosening the neck muscles. "What any leader hates is uncertainty. So you use diplomacy to make Khomeini uncertain."

A long sigh. "That feels good, yes. But Kissinger is not optimistic about diplomacy. What can we do?"

"Make threats. Bare your teeth and growl. Let them worry about what you might do, and weigh it against the fun they are having holding our people hostage."

"Oh, come on, Darko. What threats can we make?"

The masseur cracked his knuckles. "Why not call in the Iranian Ambassador and tell him that if the hostages are not released within forty-eight hours, we will sever diplomatic relations with Iran?"

"What?" Gerald Ford laughed. "The students have already severed diplomatic relations for us."

"You Americans have no sense of history," said the masseur. "Mr. President, when my countryman Gavrilo Princeps shot the Archduke Franz Ferdinand, the Austrians made demands on Serbia, outrageous demands, which they enforced by a demarche with a time limit."

"What's a demarche, Darko?"

"The threat to break off diplomatic relations. Tell the Iranian Ambassador *that* tomorrow and see what he says." The masseur wiped his hands off on the towel. "He, I bet, will know that a demarche with a time limit is serious business."

"You think so? Why should he?"

Because that is how World War I got started, thought the masseur, which he will remember even if you do not. "Because it is his business to know these things, Mr. President."

A sigh. "What if it doesn't work?"

"Then you break off diplomatic relations and think of something else," was the reply. "Would you be any the worse off?"

Gerald Ford sat up and swung his feet over the edge of the table. "I suppose not," he said doubtfully. "I'll ask Henry what he thinks."

"It's the way to go," said the masseur. "I was right about pardoning Nixon, wasn't I?"

* * *

Henry Kissinger studied the coffee cup he was holding in his hands as if it might reveal some arcane knowledge. "From a public relations point of view it makes sense, Mr. President. It shows that we are taking the matter seriously, which should please the American people and satisfy our critics for a while. But think ahead. What will we do when the deadline passes and our embassy staff has not been returned?"

"For openers," said Cheney, "we could seize the Iranian assets which we are right now in the process of freezing."

"That won't do us much," replied Ford, slumping into his high-backed leather chair. "Ayatollahs and mullahs don't think the same way as bankers and capitalists."

Admiral Morrisy looked up. "Besides that, you can't actually seize foreign assets without a formal declaration of war. And after Vietnam we don't want to declare *another* war, do we?"

"We never declared war in Vietnam," said Kissinger. "For what seemed to be good and sufficient reasons at the time. That, maybe, was a mistake. If we had, Jane Fonda would have been a traitor *de jure* as well as *de facto*."

"You aren't thinking about declaring war, are you Henry?" asked Donald Rumsfeld, the Secretary of Defense. "It might lose us the election in 1980."

I'm not eligible to run in 1980, thought Ford complacently. "Wait a minute, Don," he said. "Henry is always telling us how the threat is worse than its execution, right? So we issue this demarche with a time limit and what we do while we're waiting is make faces. You know, bare our teeth and growl."

"The technical term is saber-rattling," said Kissinger, polishing his glasses with his handkerchief. "The problem is that once you begin, it becomes very difficult to back off. And Iran is one of the most, if not *the* most, important American allies in the region. We don't want to go to war with the Iranians, Mr. President. Despite the Ayatollah, they are our friends."

"Well, there are friends and then there are friends,"

conceded Ford. "The worst enemy you can have is the Republican standing against you in the primary. You can lose to a Democrat and still keep control of the party, but a challenge from inside, from a friend, a former friend anyway, is deadly. If nobody has any better ideas, we ought to go for it."

"Mr. President," protested Kissinger. "Geopolitically, Iran is our bulwark of defense against Russia in the Persian Gulf. It cannot, it can NOT be in America's interest to go to war with Iran."

"It isn't the Russians holding our people hostage, Henry. And besides, we aren't going to war with anybody. We're only going to break diplomatic relations with the creeps who kidnapped our diplomats."

"You are taking the first steps to war, Mr. President." Kissinger folded his handkerchief and slipped it back in his jacket pocket. "The first steps on a steep and slippery slope. I urge you, do not do this thing."

A sigh. "Worried about the elections in 1980, Henry? I thought you were my foreign policy guy." President Ford shook his head. "I want our people back, okay?"

"Freezing the Iranian bank accounts will do it," said Cheney.

"I hope so, Dick," said Gerald Ford. "I really do. But it isn't the way to bet. Henry, have you got any other ideas?"

The Secretary of State slumped back in his chair and shook his head.

"Then let's go for it."

Rumsfeld looked up with a start. "Go for what?"

"The demarche with a time limit," said Kissinger despondently. "Only if you want to rattle American sabers, maybe we should give Teheran another day. To let them think about it, Mr. President, seventy-two hours instead of only forty-eight."

Ford nodded. "That will do," he agreed. "Dick, have the Iranian Ambassador in here tomorrow morning, eleven-ish, and I'll tell him. And set up a press conference immediately afterwards." He looked at his watch. "My God, how did it get so late?"

"Time flies when you're having fun," said Kissinger.

In Teheran the Ayatollah Khomeini met with his council of advisors. "The threat is ludicrous," he said. "To break diplomatic relations with the Great Satan is a consummation devoutly to be desired. Why should we move the breadth of a hair for such frivolous posturing?"

President Aboulhassan Bani-Sadr shook his head. "The Ambassador was quite worried."

Khomeini smiled coldly. "The Ambassador is less devout than one might wish. These things may very properly be left in the hands of Allah, who will ensure a just and merciful outcome for the faithful."

"Quite so, Ayatollah. Nevertheless, the Ambassador has made a study of European history, and the American threat, which is also not a threat, takes the form of what he called 'a demarche with a time limit.' You smile. What does it matter how such a stupid threat is called? What matters is what the Americans think they are doing, and in European history, which is also American history, the first World War began when Austria issued demands against Serbia enforced by this very same demarche with a time limit."

"Ah, indeed." The Ayatollah stroked his beard. "Then you think the Americans, who showed themselves so lacking moral fiber in Vietnam, have sufficient will, sufficient spirit to begin a war with us? They will surely be defeated, and in their heart of hearts they must know it."

"In time their defeat is inevitable," agreed General Mohammed Suliman, "but they have maneuvered things so that it will be very hard for their President Ford, who is not the most astute of politicians, to avoid a formal declaration of war unless we return the American embassy staff."

"Huh," grunted the Ayatollah. "Then let the fool sit with his feet to the fire if it pleases him."

Suliman smiled ingratiatingly. "In Ford's press conference a reporter asked him how such a war would be fought, and would the much-hated draft be resumed? Our enemy, Satan, hardly deserving of the title 'Great,' replied that he thought the question was premature, but later opined that a naval blockade would be sufficient for the foreseeable future."

"Indeed?" asked Bani-Sadr. "Is that what might we expect the Americans to do if they actually screw up their courage to declare a war they cannot win?"

"A naval blockade, seizing our supertankers on the high seas, perhaps the occupation of some of our small, offshore islands." Suliman paused in contemplation. "From which they might broadcast lies and propaganda hateful to the ears of the faithful, and the debased sounds of western music, so popular among our secular and misguided youth." He smiled. "Nothing serious."

"Such a contest of wills we can endure forever," Khomeini declared flatly. "The Americans will lose heart and go home eventually, or when they elect a new president, which they do about as often as they change their shirts, but in the meantime we will have a jihad to unite and purify the Iranian people."

"Allah is Great," murmured Rafsanjani at the end of the table. "And there is no God but Allah. America, the Great Satan, is a naval power, a loathsome sea beast, while Iran is a land power with valiant soldiers, heroic men of the faith. Think well: Do you imagine that in such a mismatched war where the unbelievers have, for instance, occupied Kharg Island, that we could sustain a jihad when we are powerless to cross the water and drive them from our sacred Iranian soil?"

"We can sustain the jihad," replied Khomeini with calm certainty. "And in time the unbelievers will be driven into the sea from whence they came."

"Truly hast thou spoken," said Rafsanjani, his eyes downcast. "But 'in time' could be years, two or three or even five or seven. And we have long endured historic disputes with our neighbors, such as Iraq, which might become troublesome."

"The Iraqi President, Saddam Hussein, is an evil hypocrite," Khomeini conceded. "Nevertheless, even he would hesitate to inject himself into the wrong side of a Holy War." A slow frown settled on the Ayatollah's face. "At least, he would hesitate for a long time." He sat pondering the matter. "Tonight I shall go on television to expound upon the jihad, instructing our people regarding their duties to Allah and the Fatherland."

Gerald Ford sat gazing at the flood of papers on his desk with a kind of glassy-eyed stare. "I have to read all of this?" he asked plaintively.

The Secretary of State nodded. "If crises were more fun, we might have them more often, Mr. President."

"Shit." Ford stirred the papers with one hand. "Henry, what's important here?" A sigh. "I know, I know. It's *all* important. But what's *really* important?"

Kissinger shrugged and pulled out a paper. "Let's take matters in order of their importance and work down, then. This is a transcript of a speech made by the Ayatollah Khomeini last night. What he says, about the virtues of the Holy War and the Islamic duty to wage the jihad, and his generally militant tone, are important. Equally important, in my judgment, is what he doesn't say. He does not mention the hostages, and while he denounces the United States as the Great Satan, he does not attack you, personally."

The President picked up the transcript and began scanning it. "Oh," he said at last. "Oh my. Henry, the man wants a Holy War. He really does."

"Actually, in the absence of specifics, I find the message rather encouraging." Kissinger smiled. "Also encouraging is that he hasn't given the speech to the press. At least the American press. Remember, there are still two more days before our deadline has passed, so what this diatribe really is, is a bluff, the Ayatollah trying to intimidate us, to scare us off."

"The media will report on it, though," said Ford. "It's news. And then the sons of bitches will ask me about it in the Rose Garden this afternoon. What can I tell them?"

A shrug and a slow shake of the head. "Tell them that the Ayatollah is speaking as a teacher of religion and not as the leader of his country," replied Kissinger at last.

"He's talking about the jihad," protested the President. "The old fart is talking Holy War! I don't want a war with Iran! What am I going to tell the damned press?"

"Tell them that a Holy War is impossible," said Kissinger at last. "America is a secular state, and at sea the Iranians are too weak to challenge us. Now this next item, the sailing orders for the Seventh Fleet, sort of emphasizes the point."

Policy is often made by accident, since in many cases the policy maker does not know what it is until he has spoken the words defining it; a case of where the mouth leads, the mind must follow.

In the Rose Garden, President Gerald Ford was asked if the U.S. and Iran were heading toward a Holy War. He replied: "A Holy War is impossible. America is a secular state and the Iranians don't have . . ." he paused, trying to think of *sea power*, and failing, ". . . nuclear weapons!"

"Mr. President, does that mean that you would use atomic weapons in a war against Iran?"

Ford blinked and smiled. "Whatever it takes," he replied. And then modified his statement. "To get our hostages back, of course."

Within the next twenty-four hours, that statement provoked strong diplomatic protests from Russia and China, a demonstration of more than a million people in London, a demonstration of more than a million and a half in Tokyo, and the burning of the U.S. Embassies in Pakistan, Syria, and Iraq.

* * *

After the prayer, the Ayatollah Khomeini turned to his advisors. "Alas, my friends, this infidel swine, the thrice-cursed Ford, says that we are impotent to wage jihad without nuclear weapons. Advise me."

"The world condemns the barbarity of the Great Satan," said Hojotollah al-Maleki. "They condemn it universally, even in Zionist-occupied Palestine."

"Quite so," agreed Khomeini. "And of all the nations who are praying for Iran, how many have offered to stand by us, to give us material aid?"

"None," said the Hojotollah, "but it may be too soon."

"Thank you, al-Maleki. We must depend upon Allah and ourselves in this matter, and that is as it should be. Yes?"

"There is an element of truth in the Great Satan's sneering gibe," replied Bani-Sadr. "To lead the faithful into battle against a foe armed as the Americans are known to be armed invites unrecompensed martyrdom. How would it profit the Shi'ite to be destroyed if it were the Sunni who should reap the benefits of our sacrifice?"

"A craven view!" said Rafsanjani, slapping the table for emphasis. "The Americans will not use nuclear weapons. Their threat to use nuclear weapons is a palpable bluff, and since we are still in the talking period of the evil deadline which they imposed, we ought to match them bluff for bluff and lie for lie."

Khomeini smiled his agreement. "Well said, thou good and pious servant of Allah. And what sort of bluff would you suggest that we make to unman these frivolous and secular Americans?"

"Tell them the truth," Rafsanjani replied. "That God will deliver, or already has, if you prefer, delivered nuclear weapons into our hands. They will quail before our imagined might, and the invincible might of Allah."

"How say you, General Suliman?"

"May it please your Holiness, it seems to me that the Americans cannot now back down. We have seized their nest-of-vipers embassy, and they have responded gravely and with considerable dignity in the face of this provocation, ostensibly delivered by our radical students. If we pile mendacity upon mendacity, claiming to have nuclear weapons when we do not, claiming that our students are out of control when they are not, the time will surely come when we must face them on a most evil and unsatisfactory battlefield."

"In jihad, all battlefields are glorious," said the Ayatollah softly. "In what manner do you find the prospective jihad evil or unsatisfactory?"

General Mohammed Suliman composed his hands in an attitude of prayer. "Allah is merciful," he said. "Nevertheless, our army is supplied with American aircraft, with American weapons. Who will replace our losses of material in a war longer than a few weeks? Allah is great. Nevertheless, the American Seventh Fleet will be at the Strait of Hormuz three days hence. We can lay mines to annoy them, but oppose them we cannot. There is no God but Allah. Nevertheless, if the Americans declare war, no Iranian ship or boat will be able to venture out upon the waters of our own Persian Gulf without being destroyed. A Holy War should end in glorious victory. Such a conflict as this is likely to be, protracted, interminable, indecisive, should if possible be avoided."

"Then let the Americans give us the Shah," said Khomeini mildly. "We ask for nothing more than simple justice. Thank you for your pious and well-intentioned opinions, General." He turned to Rafsanjani. "The Great Satan has been most circumspect in making his threats against us. Even today, it is not manifestly clear that the American dogs would do more than sever the diplomatic relations between our two countries. In these circumstances, how ought we to deliver the threat, nay, the promise, that when the jihad rises like a great scorching wind, Allah will deliver nuclear weapons into our hands?"

"In the square before the American Embassy," replied Rafsanjani. "To the tumultuous approval of the Iranian people, before the television cameras, so that all the world can see our firm resolution in the face of American provocation."

"Ah, indeed?" murmured the President.

Khomeini nodded. "You have doubts, Bani-Sadr?"

"Yes, Ayatollah. How can Rafsanjani know what the response of our people will be to this new, mendacious, and dangerous proposal of his?"

The Ayatollah stroked his beard reflectively. "He has faith in Allah and in the Iranian people, as should we all. Nevertheless, I can see your point; that it would be better to rehearse the announcement before letting the television show the world something unseemly. Rafsanjani?"

"God is great, Ayatollah Khomeini."

"This afternoon go with my blessing to deliver your prepared remarks, off-camera, to the students before the embassy. If it is well received, have our people gather together a great crowd before sundown and deliver it to them and to all the world. Thus shall we defy the Great Satan, humiliating him with the might of Allah."

Rafsanjani stood on the speaker's podium addressing the faithful in the late afternoon sunlight. The speech was going better than he had imagined, and the full-throated chant of "Ji-had! Ji-had! Ji-had!" echoed through the square. "O my brothers," he declared with unfeigned fervor. "There are some among us who are weak in faith, some among us who doubt the might of Allah, some among us who say that because the Great Satan has nuclear weapons and we do not, that we cannot prevail against him in a Holy War. Know you then, that when the Jihad comes upon us like the fierce desert wind, Allah, blessed be His Name, will deliver nuclear weapons into our hands so that we may smite the Great Satan and destroy him utterly! The Americans and their hateful technology shall not prevail against the True Faith!" He raised his arms. "JI-HAD!"

The mob gave it back to him, "Ji-had!" but with less

enthusiasm than before, as if they were trying to think over what they had been told.

Again Rafsanjani raised his arms and cried "JI-HAD!"

And again the mob gave it back to him, "Ji-had!" but from the back of the crowd came a counter-cry, feeble but clear. "No nukes."

Rafsanjani looked annoyed. Maybe it had been a mistake to rehearse this, to have given the leftists a chance to organize a response. Nevertheless, he was the master of the many-headed beast standing before him, and he began to work it up, "Ji-had, Ji-had, Ji-had!" Starting soft and slow like a small earthquake Rafsanjani pumped it up to a crescendo that would topple governments.

In the back of the great crowd two or three hundred men pulled together in a cluster were shouting "No nukes! No nukes! No nukes!"—timing themselves so that they made themselves heard in the pauses between the mighty chant of "Ji-had." Rafsanjani scowled at their temerity, and picked up the tempo to drown them out.

The little cluster of men in opposition drew closer together and began to push their way toward the speaker's podium. They were shouting, but they couldn't be heard over the thunderous chant of "JI-HAD! JI-HAD! JI-HAD!" On the other hand, nobody was opposing them. The little group was pushing its way through a hostile mob hundreds of times bigger like a knife through warm butter.

It never occurred to Rafsanjani that he was in any danger, or if it did, he never attempted to run, to seek safety. The cluster of men reached the platform and dragged him from it, and strangled him with his own turban, live, before the eyes of the world.

"Run the tape again," said Khomeini. "From the point where the first 'no nukes' was heard." They sat in silence and for the seventh time watched the little group push unopposed through the great mob to pull down Rafsanjani. Allah is merciful, thought the Ayatollah. It was in my mind to speak in Rafsanjani's place today, to lend my own authority to the doctrine which he so ably expounded. Could those godless men have taken me as they did Rafsanjani? "That will do," he said at the end of the tape. "General Suliman, we have about eight hours left before the expiration of the American demarche. Do you think that we ought to hand over the nest full of spies and traitors we seized in the American Embassy?"

"Allah is merciful," replied the General. "And to free the American Embassy would also be an act of mercy. Such an act would also appear to coincide with the best interests of Iran."

"The secular interests, in any event," said Hojotollah al-Maleki, dourly. "If we persevere, Allah will surely put nuclear weapons in the hands of the faithful."

Khomeini raised his eyebrows. "Ah, al-Maleki. If you found yourself holding a nuclear bomb, could you tell whether it was God or Satan that gave it to you?"

"God, of course," replied the mullah. "I would have nothing to do with Satan."

A soft chuckle. "To be sure. But Satan might have something to do with *you*."

"They might not declare war, the Americans," said the Hojotollah, changing the subject.

Khomeini nodded regretfully. "True, they might not, al-Maleki. But we are presently inclined to agree with President Bani-Sadr and General Suliman that most probably they will. And it is also necessary to meditate upon the death of the noble Rafsanjani." He sat stroking his beard with his right hand. In time we shall find a Holy War to temper the spirit of the Iranian people, he thought, but not now, not with the Americans thus provoked. The outcome is too uncertain.

"Do you wish to call the students holding the American Embassy and tell them to set the prisoners free?" asked Bani-Sadr.

A long sigh. "No," said Khomeini. "Such is not my wish, but let it fall as Allah wills. Call them and I shall so order the matter."

* * *

Although the hostages were returned four days after they were seized, President Gerald Ford was severely criticized for his ham-handed handling of the Iranian hostage crisis. The general consensus was that he threatened to use nuclear weapons against a non-nuclear and friendly power, who was thereby alienated from the American cause forever. This was regarded as a defeat for American diplomacy, as serious as the loss of Vietnam had been for American arms, and the most serious of many blunders committed by President Ford during his term of office.

1984

Ronald Reagan won an overwhelming victory over Walter Mondale in 1984. It was the first time in more than half a century that the word "liberal" was used as a purgative in a national election.

But when the dust had cleared, Reagan rarely pushed for any of the right-wing social programs his supporters wanted, and Mondale, had he won, would have had very little choice other than to continue pouring money into a defense department that had less than a thirty-day supply of ammunition when Reagan first took office. So would there really have been much of a difference if Mondale had won?

Lawrence Person, who burst upon the science fiction scene during the past year with a flurry of fine short stories, thinks so—and in this story, he shows you exactly where that difference would be most strongly felt.

Huddled Masses

by Lawrence Person

"U.S. troops in Mexico skirmished briefly with Mendarist rebels near Tierra Blanca, a town in the Veracruz province—"

"Jesus, do you have to listen to that shit, man?"

"Shut up, my brother's down there."

"—were repulsed with only three American casualties. There was also minor fighting in the Chihuahua province between CMLA rebels and Mexican Army troops, just eighty miles from the U.S. border, but no American units were involved. In a related story, special presidential envoy Hodding Carter reported no progress in the ongoing peace talks in Guatemala City, now entering their third week. Mr. Carter once again charged Guatemala with arming the Mexican rebels, but the Reyes government has consistently denied the allegations. Mr. Carter also said that no progress had been made on the issue of Cuban combat troops in Guatemala and El Salvador.

"In North Korea, President Kim Il Sung demanded that his country be made a co-sponsor of next year's Olympic games in Seoul—"

"There, the important stuff's over. Why don't you put on KLOL or something?"

"Because I've only got AM. Besides, I like to keep up with what's going on."

"Aw man, it's just the same old shit, day after day. Just a bunch of people you don't know killing each other for no goddamn reason."

"Yeah, but a lot of that stuff affects us, sooner or later. Just look at . . . aw, shit."

Brian Hester eased his foot off the gas pedal as he saw the solid gridlock of traffic in front of him on I-45. If they were lucky it was just another wreck, but Brian suspected it extended all the way to 610.

"—Jones Industrial Average dropped to 1380 in a broad-based sell-off in reaction to President Mondale's imposition of additional wage and price controls—"

Hector Rodriguez took a look at the traffic snarl in front of him and blew air from his lips. "Aw, *man*, not again."

Brian laughed. "You sound like you're surprised."

"Disappointed, more like. I thought we might get to work on time for once."

"Dream on."

"In local news, unemployment for the Houston metropol-

itan area reached 21.8 percent, two points below the national average—"

"Just what I needed to hear," said Brian, turning off the radio with a snap.

"What do you care, man, you've got a job."

"Yeah, but that doesn't mean I like it."

"Aw, come on, I know you like it. You get off on beating us Mexicans, I seen it."

Brian was silent as he slowed the car to a crawl. I-45 looked like a parking lot, and there didn't appear to be any end to the jam in sight. Brian cut off the truck's air conditioner and rolled down the window. Rodriguez followed suit. It was an '81 Dodge Ram with an extended payload bay and it tended to stall in traffic if the air conditioner was on. The pungent smell of exhaust fumes filled the cab.

"It's . . . I don't know, it's just not . . . it just doesn't feel right anymore. I mean, it's not like we're doing any good or anything."

"Hey, lighten up. It's just a job, man. Don't let it get you down."

"I don't know. I've been looking through the classifieds, but there's damn little I'm qualified for. Maybe HPD."

"Aw man, talk about your chickenshit jobs. Guess you're tired of just beatin' up Mexicans and you want to kill some, huh?"

"I don't know, I was thinking that real police work might be better."

"Well you're wrong on that. I got a cousin who's in there and he has to put up with a lot more bullshit than we do. Plus the pay sucks."

"Yeah, I was just thinking."

"Thinking? Man, don't you know that shit's bad for you? Besides, with Peggy pregnant you shouldn't be thinking about switching jobs."

Brian shrugged. "Yeah, I guess you're right."

There were a few moments of silence as the car crawled along.

"Now that you're through listening to the news, can I turn on some music?"

"Sure."

Rodriguez turned the radio on.

"—orts news, the Astros beat Cincinnati 4–0 last night to complete a sweep of the Reds. Nolan Ryan pitched a two-hit shutout to go 7 and 1 on the year, and José Cruz hit a two-run homer in the 6th—"

"All right José!"

"—to provide the winning run. In other scores around the league—"

"Fuck that shit, man," said Hector, spinning the dial. He made a face as he heard snatches of country music between the static, and finally settled on a station where they were playing an old Madonna song.

"Like a Vir-gin." Rodriguez sang along in an absolutely putrid, off-key duet with the radio, *"like a vir-ER-er-er-gin."*

Brian laughed and shook his head. As they topped the next rise they could see the flashing lights of a police car about a mile in front of them.

"*Very fiirst tiime*, c'mon man, sing along!"

Brian laughed again, then flicked on his signal to merge into the right lane.

"Stop off for some tacos, Rodriguez?"

"Yeah, got some fish tacos off your wife."

"In your dreams."

"It was some nasty stuff, man. You ought to do something about those scabs."

INS Director Billy Foreman smiled and shook his head, checking off something on his clipboard. "Better be careful, or I'll kick your ass all the way back to Corpus."

"Hey, I told you I don't go in for that S & M stuff. Maybe you should get your dog for that. And hey, that's the reason we were late. My dog had chapped lips. Had to take him to the vet."

"OK, now that Hester and Taco Breath are here we

can begin. First off, for this morning's lovely and diverting entertainment we've got an open-air squatters' market a few blocks off Highway 59. We've received a couple of complaints from local residents—"

"Yeah, like they're driving down those high property values," said Parker, and the rest chuckled.

"Yeah, it's such a *lovely* place," said Foreman. "Anyway, they say it's swarming with illegals, mostly Mex. We've got a couple of the buses scheduled to get there at eleven, so we'll hit them around ten-thirty. Hester, you and Parker are going sweep in from the north, while Rodriguez and Getz are going to come in from the south. There's a big barbed-wire fence to the east, and Kelley and I will be off to the west with Washington and Harmel in reserve. I'm sure we'll lose a few of them, but there's more than enough to go around. You know the procedure, kick everyone with plastic or green. Also, new rules from Regional. Anyone that can speak English, I mean more than a sentence worth, kick them too."

That got a rise out of them. Jack Harmel was the first to make his voice heard over the roar. "That means we're going to lose every illegal that's been here more than two or three months."

"Probably so, and I don't like it any more than you. But my hands are tied—this is straight from Regional. Most of the Region 3 centers are already near capacity, and thanks to our close personal friend Judge William Wayne Justice, if any center exceeds its 'judicially mandated maximum' *everyone* there gets kicked."

"Shit, just what we need," said Parker.

"Like I said, I don't like this any more than you. OK, that should take us up through to lunch, and this afternoon we play 'raid the construction site' out near Katy. There's a sheet with the details in your slots.

"One final thing you might be happy to hear before we get going. We had the second highest urban seizure rate in the country last month, right behind San Diego. What can I say, guys—you're doing a great job, at least given the circumstances."

"We getting any reinforcements anytime soon?" asked Getz.

Foreman shrugged. "Can't say for sure right now. Christ knows we could use them, but there's nothing definite yet. The boys in the Valley have been getting all the new manpower Washington throws our way, and they've got their hands full just trying to stem the refugee tide at the border. I can't argue with that, especially since putting a dent in border crossings would make our job a lot easier, but what it means right now is that all Urban's getting is crumbs.

"Trust me, when I find out you'll be the first to know. Right now I'd just settle for a couple more processing clerks so we could get the ones we *are* catching out of the centers faster. Alright kids, let's go stick our fingers in the dike. Oh yeah, and speaking of our pal Judge Justice, there's one last thing I'm sure you'll all be absolutely *thrilled* to hear. Today's *Chronicle* has a story about Judge Powell's retirement, and guess who's on Mondale's short list to replace him?"

"Motherfu—"

"Yeah, Getz, I love it too. All right folks, meet you at the site in thirty."

"—so then I'm up to my waist in mud, holding this huge, steaming pot that keeps burning my arms as I move, and Major Freely keeps yelling 'C'mon dogboy, where's that fucking chili?'" Parker laughed and shook his head. "God, I hated Fort Polk."

"Do you miss it?"

"What, Fort Polk?"

"No, the Army."

"Hell no," he said, then added a few seconds later: "Well, sometimes. There wasn't as much paperwork, at least if you were a grunt. And Germany was great. Really, really great beer. I mean, it's hard for me to drink American beer now 'cause it all tastes like piss, you know? But hell, other than that I'm glad to be out. Didn't really feel that way when we were demobilized, but I'm glad to be out now. Still miss the money, though. Another year in the Army and I could have gone to med school."

"This must be the place," said Brian, eyeing the open-air market as he drove by. There were at least two hundred people wandering around the makeshift stalls, and not a black or Anglo face in sight.

"Better check in with Billy," said Brian. Parker nodded and lifted the walkie-talkie from the seat beside him.

"Parker to Foreman, come in, over," he said, then removed his finger from the transmit button. He waited several seconds while the radio crackled with static.

"Parker to Foreman, come in, over."

"Foreman here. You guys in place, over?"

"Getting there. We're pulling up behind the warehouse now. Everyone else ready, over?"

"We're still waiting for Washington and Harmel, over."

"Well, we're pretty much in place. Give us a holler when they arrive, over."

"Will do. Hang loose, guys. Over and out." Parker set the walkie-talkie down in the seat, a faint hiss of static still coming over the open channel. Brian eased the truck to a stop near an overflowing dumpster in back of the warehouse, then killed the engine.

There was a moment of silence.

"So anyway, no, I don't really miss it," said Parker in the stillness. "Your brother's in the Army, isn't he?"

"Yeah, he's with the 82nd Airborne in Mexico now."

"Now there's something I'm not sorry to have missed. I've got a friend of mine who's still in, a tank driver with the 1st Cavalry at Fort Hood. When they crossed the border he said it took *six hours* to clear refugees off the bridge at Nuevo Laredo. Six hours. He also says that the Mendarists are starting to use Russian anti-tank weapons.

"I mean, I don't want to get you worried about your

brother, or anything. But Mark, the tank guy I know, says that things were starting to get pretty nasty down there."

Brian sighed. "Yeah, that's what I heard too. My mother's, like, half-crazy with him down there. I mean, she'd already started getting real religious after my father died, but it's gotten a lot worse. Every time I visit her she wants me to get down on my knees and 'pray for Tom.' We got a letter from him last week, but that only made her worse. He said things were getting pretty hairy, but couldn't give any details. He said—"

"Foreman to Parker, come in."

Parker picked up the walkie-talkie. "Parker here, over."

"All right boys, Washington and Harmel just arrived, so it's showtime. Everyone in position, over?"

"Parker and Hester in position, over."

"Getz and Rodriguez in position, over."

A few seconds later: "Harmel and Washington in position, over."

"OK, everyone move in five minutes. Rodriguez, you make the finger. Over and out."

Parker put the walkie-talkie down and unlocked his door. "You heard the man."

"Yeah," said Brian. He got out of the truck and locked the door behind him. Other than the sound of a barking dog and distant traffic it was almost silent, the reek of overripe garbage mixing with the smell of exhaust fumes. Both of them checked their weapons (Brian had a Colt .45, Parker a NATO-issue 9 mm.), then flicked the safeties off.

There was a moment of silence.

"I'll cover, you grab," said Brian.

"Fine by me."

They made their way around the dumpster to the side of the warehouse. As they neared the market the smell of garbage faded and was replaced with that of cooking tamales, and what passed for urban silence was replaced with a low babble of Spanish voices.

Once they got closer they moved into the shadow of

the warehouse and hugged the wall, keeping out of sight. They stopped entirely at the corner, and Brian eased forward just a little to get a better look.

It was pretty much as he expected, a haphazard arrangement of makeshift stalls, with fruit crates and cardboard boxes serving as impromptu tables. The most crowded stall was the one near the center where a heavyset Mexican woman and her family were selling tamales off a real vending cart. The rest of the vendors were selling everything from hubcaps to cookware, most of it in poor shape, and a few were selling what looked like just plain junk. The patrons were all Hispanic, and several refugee families, looking thin and haggard, wandering listlessly from table to table in threadbare clothing. The rest were overwhelmingly male, most wearing the illegal alien uniform of choice, tattered blue jeans and worn, long-sleeved, button-down shirts with checkerboard patterns.

Brian checked his watch. It was time.

As he lowered his hand to his holster he saw Rodriguez and Getz run out from the shadow of the opposite building, blocking the front exit.

"Freeze! INS!" yelled Rodriguez, holding his ID up above his head in one hand and leveling his gun with the other. Rodriguez yelled "INS" one more time, then shouted something in Spanish so rapid that Brian couldn't even pick out individual words.

Instantly, the entire market erupted in chaos. Though the ones closest to Rodriguez froze, the rest tried to scatter, a few women screaming as their goods were overturned by would-be escapees. Brian moved into the open as he drew his gun, Parker right behind. The illegals who had been making for the warehouse alley froze and put their hands in the air.

All, that is, except for three men off to Brian's left, who immediately broke away from him toward the center of the market, one of them hastily stuffing a plastic baggie into his jacket.

Oh shit, thought Brian, then he yelled for them to stop as he took off after them.

The three glanced back at him briefly, then burst away from him in different directions, dodging into the already panic-stricken crowd. Brian kept track of the one with the baggie and doggedly ran after him.

The Mexican glanced back at him again, his eyes wild, then put on a extra burst of speed, lunging through the nearest stall and sending a battered TV tray loaded with stacks of Spanish-language pornography and photonovels crashing to the ground.

The Mexican finally ran out of room to run as he came to the chain-link fence at the back of the lot. He took a running jump and started climbing it like a madman. Brian reached him before he got to the top and grabbed the Mexican's right work boot with his free hand, keeping the gun trained on the ground with the other.

The Mexican reached into his pocket, and for a moment Brian thought he was going to ditch the dope on the other side of the fence.

Then he saw the switchblade.

Brian started to bring the gun up but the Mexican was already lunging at him. Brian pulled his head back just as the Mexican swung at his face, and the blade slashed air inches away from his face, then carved a six-inch-long gash in his left forearm.

Brian fired his gun as the two of them hit the ground, and felt warm liquid gushing all over his hand.

The Mexican screamed as he jerked away, his free hand clutching the wound in his side. Then he brought the knife up again and Brian fired two more shots, the first hitting the Mexican in the chest and the second in his right shoulder. The Mexican dropped the knife as he staggered back against the fence. He started to slide down, then stopped as his right hand gripped the chain links, and for a few seconds he tried to pull himself back up, making sick wheezing sounds all the time. Finally, his fingers unclenched and he slid heavily to the ground.

Brain grabbed at his wound as Foreman and Parker came running up to him.

"Shit, what the hell happened?" asked Parker.

"He was holding," said Brian as Parker kneeled to look at his wound. "I tried to grab him and he pulled a knife on me."

Parker glanced at the gash only a second, then stood up. "Put some pressure on it and see if you can slow the bleeding. I'll get the kit," he said, and then was off and running like a shot.

Foreman pulled a red bandanna out of his back pocket and tried to bind up the wound. It was soaked clear through in a matter of seconds.

"Goddamn it," he said under his breath. *"Parker! Hurry up!"* Foreman applied pressure to the upper part of Brian's arm. "How's it feel?"

"Bad, but not as bad as it looks."

Parker came running up with the med kit and almost instantly got to work on the cut, letting his army medic instincts take over.

"I've seen worse," he said at last, then was busy wrapping the gauze around Brian's arm and taping it in place. "You're gonna have to see a doctor right away, but you shouldn't be in danger of losing it or anything."

Foreman let go of the arm and walked over to search the body. He pulled a small plastic baggie out of the Mexican's jacket pocket.

"Is this all he was carrying? Shit, half of it's nothing but stems," said Foreman, turning the bag over in his hands and watching the marijuana leaves tumble around inside. He shook his head. "The crazy fucker got himself killed because he was carrying half a lid of bad Mexican grass."

"Your arm feel OK?" asked Foreman.

Brian laughed. " 'Course it feels OK, I'm still higher than a kite."

The two of them were sitting out on the patio at Good

Company, eating a late lunch. There had been two gunshots and a heart attack ahead of them at Herman and they'd waited almost an hour before seeing a doctor, a small Filipino man named Ortio who said less than twenty words to Brian through the entire procedure. "Deep but clean. Easy fix." It took more time for them to fill out the forms and check out than it took the doctor to sew him up.

Foreman finished up the last of his burger while Brian struggled to cut his enchiladas with a fork. "Need any help with that?"

"I can handle it myself, mother," said Brian, taking another bite.

"OK, just checking. Listen, I'm sure it'll be no problem to get you the rest of the week off with sick leave, and then we can get you to ride a desk for a couple of weeks till your arm's healed."

"Aw, c'mon Billy, you know I hate paperwork. I'm sure I'll be fine by next week."

"Bullshit, Brian. I'm not going to have anyone out in the field that's less than a hundred percent. And c'mon, you deserve the rest, you've been doing a hell of a job lately."

Bran shrugged and took another bite of enchiladas, then wiped his mouth with a napkin. "I don't know, Billy. I just . . ." He shrugged again. "I don't know, I've been thinking about looking for something else."

"Why? Is it this thing today? I mean yeah, I'm sure it has to be pretty damn rough on you, but it's not—"

"No, it's not that. It's just, well, I don't feel like I'm doing any good. I mean, what the hell are we doing, anyway? We're catching maybe five percent of the illegals that get through, maybe less, and after we send them back they just cross the border and try again."

Foreman nodded. "No argument with you there. We're not doing nearly as much as we should, but we're doing as much as we can with the budget we've got. And having three re-orgs in the past two years hasn't helped much either. But we've got to do something, because it looks like things are only going to get worse.

"I mean, when the contras were fighting, we got Nicaraguan refugees. Then when Nicaragua invaded Honduras we got Hondurans, and when the revolutions in El Salvador and Guatemala got underway we started getting Salvadorans and Guatemalans. And now that we've got a civil war in Mexico going on, we're going to get more Mexicans. But the thing is, there are a hell of a lot more people in Mexico than in all the rest of Central America combined.

"Brian, when I joined the force back in '82, we had one, maybe two million illegals coming over the border every year. A lot of people bitched about it and most of the illegals got through despite what we did, but it wasn't a crisis or anything. Now we've got a *million* illegals streaming over the border *every month*, and I read somewhere, I think it was *Time*, that this guy was predicting that if the war gets worse we'll have *two million* every month. Think about it, Brian, the entire population of Houston coming over the border every month."

"Yeah, I know, but I can't help thinking I would do the same thing if I was in their shoes. I mean, when they were just coming over here for jobs that was one thing, but if there was a war going in my backyard I sure as hell wouldn't stick around, I'd do what they're doing, and get my family someplace safe."

"But war or not, there's only so many jobs to go around. Hell, I've got a stepbrother who can barely make a living as a construction worker because there are so many wetbacks out there willing to work for two bucks an hour." Foreman sighed and looked around, then leaned closer to Brian.

"Listen, keep this under your hat," said Foreman, speaking softly. "It's not official yet. But there's word we're going to get two new subgroups in the next month or so, and I put in your name to head one of them."

"A promotion?"

Foreman nodded. "And a raise. It won't be a whole lot, about a hundred dollars more a month, but every bit helps, right? But anyway, yeah, I'd really like you to stay on Brian, 'cause I need all the help I can get."

Brian put down his fork and wiped his lips with his napkin, then crumpled it into a ball and dropped it onto his plate. "I don't know what to say. I mean, it sounds pretty good, but I'll have to give it some thought."

"Hey, no problem. Take your time. You didn't have something else already lined up, did you?"

"No, not really. In fact, I wasn't planning on doing anything till after the baby comes anyway."

"OK then. If it sounds good to you, why don't you wait out the rest of the year and see how you like it. Fair enough?"

Brian thought a minute, then nodded. "Fair enough." They shook on it.

As they were walking back to Foreman's El Dorado, they saw a group of Hispanics in work clothes on the other side of the street. Foreman tapped Brian lightly on the side.

"Bet you five bucks they're illegals," he said quietly.

Brian shook his head. "No bet."

1988

George Bush soundly defeated Michael Dukakis in the 1988 election.

Or did he?

Trust Robert Sheckley, author of *Dimension of Miracles*, *Mindswap*, and *Untouched by Human Hands*, and probably the finest humorist in the history of the field, to provide an answer which is both uniquely science-fictional and uniquely Sheckleyesque.

Dukakis and the Aliens

by Robert Sheckley

Dukakis had always known that first day in the White House was going to be weird. But he could never have guessed how weird. The strangeness began as soon as he was alone in the Oval Office. He sat down in the big presidential command chair and closed his eyes, just for a moment, to dream again the dream that had come true—himself, President, sitting in the Oval Office, the highest office on the planet, and almost certainly the whole solar system with all its asteroids and comets. . . .

"Mr. President, sir?"

Dukakis's eyes snapped open. He hadn't even heard anyone come in. Rubber-soled shoes, he supposed. But he hadn't even heard the door open. He'd left word everyone was to leave him alone until he called for them. And now here was this guy, early thirties, balding, leaning anxiously over him. The guy's dark hair was cut short and parted on the left. He wore a dark blue suit. There was a small white flower in his buttonhole.

"Yes, what is it?" Dukakis asked. "Who are you?"

"I'm Watkins, sir," the man said. "One of your new Secret Service guards."

"Yes, Watkins, what can I do for you?"

"Sir, there are certain matters of state secrecy that we members of the presidential bodyguard are sworn to divulge to the new president as soon as he is physically inside the Oval Office."

"Must that be right now?" Dukakis asked, rubbing his eyes.

"You can understand our hurry, Mr. President. There are matters of highest importance of which the public is not really informed. Not even the inner circle of advisors and experts knows everything, and certainly not all the details. The only person who knows it all is the president. He is the final arbiter, the place where the buck stops, the man who has to at last decide what should be done."

"Done about what?" Dukakis asked.

"That is for you to decide, sir, after I have divulged to you what is arguably the biggest secret of this or any administration in the past or even into the foreseeable future."

Dukakis laughed. "What is it? Are you going to introduce me to little green aliens?"

Watkins paled visibly. "Has someone already gotten to you?"

"What are you talking about?" Dukakis said. "I was making a joke."

"The aliens are no joke," Watkins said. "Come with me, sir, and I'll take you to them."

"I beg your pardon?"

"The aliens, sir. I'm taking you now to meet them."

"Not now," Dukakis said. "I'm really not up for aliens.

And I'm supposed to meet the President of Nigeria in fifteen minutes."

Watkins made an expression of concern. "I had hoped, sir, that we could do this expeditiously."

"What about next Tuesday, between ten and eleven, for the aliens?" Dukakis asked.

"I'm afraid that won't be soon enough for them," Watkins said.

Dukakis laughed, then noticed that Watkins was not laughing. Dukakis's face resumed its familiar lugubrious non-smiling lines. He asked, jokingly, but in a tone that one could take seriously, too, if one wanted to, "What do *we* care what will or will not be soon enough for them?"

"I'm afraid we care very much," Watkins said. "This is a matter of the utmost urgency. Please come with me, Mr. President. There are some people you need to meet. I suppose 'people' is the correct word."

Dukakis stirred uneasily. This first Secret Service briefing wasn't going the way he had anticipated. Why hadn't anyone told him about this alien thing? He felt out of his depth.

"I'd like to call in my advisors," Dukakis said.

"We'd prefer you didn't." Watkins said. "Not yet. You can consult with them after you've learned about the alien matter. But not before. You must be briefed first so that you can decide how much to tell your advisors."

"I don't understand what it is I'm being briefed on," Dukakis said.

"You will very shortly," Watkins said. "If we may just proceed . . ."

The Secret Service man seemed to be familiar with the Oval Office. He walked to a tall closet and unlocked it with a key from his pocket. Dukakis looked in over his shoulder. There was a long row of suits hanging on a rack. Watkins pushed them aside, revealing, behind them, the open-framed ironwork of a small elevator.

"I didn't know this was here," Dukakis said.

Watkins smiled. "You weren't supposed to. Not until now."

Watkins opened the gate. Dukakis walked into the elevator. Watkins came in behind him and closed the gate. Dukakis went to the switchboard. There were four floors listed.

"Which one should I press?" Dukakis asked.

"None of them," Watkins said. "These just go to the parking garages under the White House."

"Where are we going?"

"You'll see." Using a Swiss Army knife, Watkins pried at the panel. It came loose. Behind it was a single red button caged in a wire holder. Watkins took off the wire container.

"Now you can press it," he said to Dukakis.

Dukakis pressed the red button. There was a soft hum of machinery. The elevator began to move down, then sideways. It picked up speed alarmingly.

"What's powering this thing?" Dukakis asked.

"Tesla coil," Watkins said.

"Never heard of it," Dukakis said.

"The full technology has never been released to the public."

"Why not, if it's so good?"

"That's part of what we'll be explaining to you, sir."

"Where are we going?" Dukakis asked.

"To the secret installation under Dulces, New Mexico."

"New Mexico? But that's thousands of miles away!"

"Two thousand and seven miles from Washington, to be exact. But magnetic induction travel like we're doing is very rapid."

"You said the secret base?"

"Yes, sir."

"I didn't know we had any secret base there."

"We don't, strictly speaking. We have an air force base. The aliens, however, have a secret base under ours."

"Underneath? You mean under the ground?"

"Yes, sir. There are nine underground levels to it."

"That's a big underground city," Dukakis said.

"Yes, it is, sir."

Watkins felt along the wall of the elevator, pressed two small buttons. Cushioned seats unfolded into existence. A secret bar opened from the wall.

"You've got everything in here!" Dukakis said admiringly.

"Even a fax machine. Though we're traveling so fast as to make use of one unnecessary."

Dukakis made himself comfortable. Watkins opened one of the floor panels and took out lunch. Dukakis thought the turkey sandwiches were a little dry, but they were pretty tasty; real turkey breast, not that pressed stuff. A bottle of High Sierra Beer washed it down nicely. Whoever stocked this place knew his beer, Dukakis decided.

There were current newspapers in a little rack. Dukakis read for a while, then tried to figure out the rate of speed they were traveling at. But he couldn't work it out. Looking at his watch, he saw they had been in the elevator for almost two hours.

He looked at Watkins. Watkins, seated opposite him, had his hands clasped behind his neck and was rocking gently back and forth.

Dukakis was not amused by the whole situation. But he had begun to wonder if this might be some sort of plot. He thought about old political rivalries. He thought about the Soviets, and the Mafia. Was someone out to get him? Was he being paranoid? Where did paranoia end and prudence begin?

At last the elevator came to a stop. Watkins opened the door.

Outside there was a long corridor.

"Now we walk," Watkins said. "I'm sorry about that, but this part of the transportation system hasn't been completed yet. I don't need to tell you who's behind the delay."

Dukakis didn't know what Watkins was talking about but decided not to ask. "Where are we?" he asked.

"Dulces, New Mexico. Underneath it, I mean. In the topmost level of the alien underground base."

"But what are we here for?"

"They need to know your decision, Mr. President."

"On what?"

"Well, sir, that's what the briefing will be all about."

They walked down a tunnel-like corridor. It had curving sides, and there were lights recessed into the ceiling. The walls seemed to be made of polished aluminum. There was a soft hum, as of machinery somewhere behind the walls.

Dukakis was getting a little more nervous now. He knew he shouldn't have come out here without a bodyguard. And he ought to have checked up on Watkins before following him blindly like this, all the way to New Mexico. If only he'd had a day or two in office to accustom himself to command! He hoped he didn't end up paying for being too easygoing.

They continued down the long tubular hallway with the little lights spaced at three-foot intervals in the ceiling. Neither was saying anything.

After a while Dukakis could see a door at the end of the hall. There was a guard standing in front of it. The guard was very tall, and he was dressed in a dark blue uniform with crimson and gold epaulets. Dukakis made a mental note to find out what branch of the service the guard belonged to. His uniform was not familiar. Dukakis noted also that the man's face was a featureless blank.

"Who is that guy?" Dukakis asked in a whisper.

"Oh, he's one of the Synthetics," Watkins said. "Don't worry, he's on our side."

They stopped in front of the guard.

"May we pass?" Watkins asked.

"Just a minute," the guard said. He was holding an odd-shaped handgun with a flaring bell-shaped muzzle. "Papers, please."

Watkins took two plastic-enclosed folders from one of his inside pockets and handed them to the guard.

The guard glanced at them, nodded. "Now I must perform the physical inspection."

"Certainly not!" Watkins said. "Not on him. He's the President!"

"I have my orders," the guard said. "You know what they say: in the Goblin Universe, anyone can wear anyone's face."

"But this place is fully shielded against intrusion."

"That's what they thought at Ada, Oklahoma," the guard said.

"Oh," Watkins said. "I had forgotten."

"Please, sir, don't make me use force."

"Oh, very well." Watkins turned to Dukakis. "It's just a formality, sir. He needs to look up your nostrils with a little instrument."

"I don't entirely understand—" Dukakis gasped as the guard seized him, pulled him forward. It seemed best not to resist. The guard tilted Dukakis's head back with one hand and shone a small light up his nostrils with the other. He peered into both nostrils, then turned off his light and released Dukakis.

"You may proceed," the guard said.

Dukakis was still stunned. Watkins pulled him down the corridor. The two men walked along in silence for a while, until the guard was out of sight.

"What was that all about?" Dukakis asked.

"He was looking for implants, sir," Watkins said.

"What are implants?"

"Controlling devices put directly into the brain. They insert them up the nostril, sir, into an area near the optic nerve. Implanted subjects have no control over their actions."

Dukakis frowned. "I do not believe the nostril connects directly with the optic nerve area."

"I realize that, sir. They have to drill a tiny laser hole and then put in the insert."

"Who is this 'They'? Who does this?"

"We're not entirely sure," Watkins said. "At first we thought it was the Zeta Reticulis Grays, but now we're not. We suspect the implanting to be the work of advance elements of reptiloids from Draco. There's still a chance it's being done by the Grays, however, since no one has seen a reptiloid on Earth and lived to report it."

"Who are these Grays?" Dukakis asked.

Watkins smiled ironically. "We used to think they were our friends. Now some us are having second thoughts about working with them. But please don't tell them I said so." Watkins glanced at his watch. "Damn! We're really late! And there's miles of corridor ahead. But I think there's a shortcut around here somewhere. . . ."

Watkins felt along the wall, found a place, pushed it. A section of the wall slid out, revealing another, smaller passageway.

It was dark inside. Dukakis looked at Watkins questioningly. "Please don't balk now," Watkins said. "We simply have to do it." Dukakis grimaced, shrugged, and followed Watkins into the hole.

They walked along in the dark for a while. Then the corridor widened out and there were low lights set into the walls. By this dim glow Dukakis could make out that they were in a large room furnished with big vats, bathtubs, and stone tables.

"What sort of place is this?" Dukakis asked.

"Well, it's a sort of workshop," Watkins said. "I'm sorry I have to bring you through here, sir, but we *are* in a hurry."

As Dukakis's eyes became accustomed to the darkness, he saw there were hooks set into the low stone ceiling. From those hooks hung chunks of meat, still dripping with blood. Dukakis could see coils of entrails hanging over several hooks. Some of the chunks of meat were entire torsos, thighs, hams, buttocks. All or most of them appeared to be human. As he became aware of this, the Durank, rotting smell of the meat rose up and assailed his nostrils.

"Ugh!" cried Dukakis.

"I'm sorry, sir," Watkins said, handing the president a handkerchief that had been impregnated with a strong perfume.

"Those dripping things hanging from the hooks . . ."

"I know, sir. It doesn't look good. I'm sorry we had to come this way."

They came to a row of white porcelain bathtubs. Each was filled with what seemed to be a noisome and horrific experiment. In one, there was a headless male torso, and from the region of its stomach a hand was growing. The other tubs contained similar necrotic apparitions.

"Gawk," Dukakis said, retching.

Watkins shook his head and in a grim voice said, "It is what comes of aliens using the Earth as a dumping ground for genetic engineering projects from all over the galaxy for all these years. We've complained about it, sir."

Farther on they passed a big vat seven feet deep, ten yards long by five yards wide. In it were hunks of meat, both animal and human—haunches, shoulders, hands. Splashing around among the hunks of meat were small gray men. They seemed to be having a good time. They were playing a sort of volleyball with human heads.

Dukakis mastered himself. "Who is responsible for this atrocity?"

Watkins said grimly, "It seems to be the work of the Short Grays of Zeta Reticuli. The other Grays, the tall ones, rely on glandular secretions and follow a much less messy procedure. It's those damned Short Grays who like to bathe in the stuff, even though it is isn't strictly necessary for their survival."

"It's not?" Dukakis said.

"No, sir. They could take care of their bodily needs much more quietly by a mincing of human and animal parts painted onto their vital organs with a fine-haired brush. But no, they insist on bathing with the human parts."

"But why?" Dukakis asked.

"They give many reasons, but the chief thing seems to be to serve their perverted sense of humor."

"You mean they find this sort of thing funny?" Dukakis asked.

"Yes, sir. I'm afraid so. They start giggling as soon as they get into the vat. When they push the first floating parts aside, they begin to get their first bursts of hysterical laughter."

"But that's horrible!"

"It is a sure sign of their alienness," Watkins said. "Aliens don't have much regard for things that are sacred to us humans, like our bodies."

Dukakis and Watkins walked on and at last came out of the dark passageway and into a brightly lit area.

Dukakis thought it looked quite like an immense airplane hangar at night. It was lit brilliantly. Several 747s were parked in corners of the hangar. Big as they were, they were dwarfed by the size of the structure itself.

An open-sided bus came out of a passageway and speeded toward Dukakis and Watkins. At the last moment it skidded to a halt. A door opened in the bus. A man came out, and said to Watkins, "Is that the new president there?"

"Yes, Budkins," Watkins said. "He's here."

"We need to confer with him at Central Planning at once."

"I'm afraid there's no time for that," Watkins said. "He's seen the feeding vats. I think I'd better get him back to Washington immediately."

"Couldn't he just come to the meeting and tell us what he thinks about Evacuation Plan Craven B?"

"My dear fellow," Watkins said, "he's only just learned about the alien conspiracy. There's been no time to brief him on the evacuation plan."

"Even a snap judgment would be useful."

"Out of the question," Watkins said.

"No, wait a moment," Dukakis said. "I want to hear this. What *is* the evacuation plan, Mr. Budkins?"

Budkins said, "The proposition, Mr. President, was that in the event of attack and takeover of America by aliens, all male government officials from the level of GSC 04 and higher would be led to the secret spaceships and taken to our secret Mars colony."

"What about their families?" Dukakis asked.

"No time for that, sir. Sometimes it's better to begin again. On Mars the male government personnel would begin a program of breeding, using for that purpose the bodies of secretarial female personnel who would be transported to Mars for that purpose."

"I'm not sure what I think of that," Dukakis said. "Government officials should stick to their posts, even if the ship is sinking."

At that moment a diminutive figure with a bald head, standing about three and a half feet high, wearing a black uniform with silver markings, and carrying on his back a small backpack, stepped out of the wall, crossed the corridor and stepped into the wall on the opposite side, disappearing into (or perhaps behind) it.

"What was that?" Dukakis asked, startled.

"I didn't get a good look," Watkins said, "but I think it was one of the Very Short Grays from Belletrix. What they call the Small Men from Belletrix."

"But he walked through the walls!"

"Yes, sir. It was made possible by that special backpack you might have noticed he was wearing. I sure wish we could get our hands on a couple of those things."

"What could you do with them?"

"They'd enable us to search the aliens out and find out for ourselves just what they're up to. It's very confusing not knowing for sure."

At that moment Dukakis suddenly had had enough. "I gotta get out of here," he said. He looked at the Watkins and Butkins. Their faces were pale, fanatical, inhuman. Butkins raised a hand in which there was something white and soft and ugly. Dukakis turned and ran. He heard a splintering explosion behind him. He continued running, turned a corner, and found a branching of the ways. He chose the left branch and continued down the polished steel tube.

Ten minutes later they had Dukakis cornered. He turned to face them. Suddenly a smile broke out across his glum face. He raised one hand. In it was a Wand of Power.

"My God!" cried Watkins. "Where did he get that?"

"More to the point," Budkins said, "who is he, really?"

"No time to find out," Watkins said. "Have you got your laser cane?"

"Of course." Budkins took the small rod out of his right-hand jacket pocket. Pressing the expansion stud, he caused the rod to extend to its full three feet. Watkins had done the same.

"Ready?" Watkins asked.

"Ready!" Budkins said.

"Then let's fire!"

Caught in the intersecting laser beams, the figure of Dukakis leaped and kicked, transfixed by the twin beams like a bug on a pin. He struggled and writhed, but he did not fall. His face changed, lengthened, whitened, became unfamiliar. His hands grew, changed color from hairy brown to glassy green. Those hands grasped the twin laser beams, and their touch seemed to render the energy beams palpable. Dukakis's hands twisted, and the laser beams fell apart like shattered glowing glass-strands. Dukakis straightened and turned toward Watkins and Budkins, his body hunched over in a posture of aggression. He started toward them and they cowered back. Budkins dropped his laser rod and pulled out a .45. He fired, and the slug recoiled from Dukakis's chest. Laughing horribly, Dukakis reached out with his terrible hooked hands. . . .

And at that moment Watkins pulled out a strange-looking handgun. He squeezed the firing stud. A white light shot out, touched Dukakis, and instantly covered him with coruscating energy. Dukakis screamed as his body fluids boiled off. His body moisture boiled away, and the paper-dry nerves and flesh flared up briefly and died away. A few wisps of black ash floated to the floor.

"Are you all right?" Watkins asked.

"Yes, I think so," Budkins said. "But who or what *was* that?"

"Something or someone we hadn't anticipated," Watkins said.

"A new player in the Earth game?" Budkins asked.

"Yes," said Watkins. "There always was the possibility that the Teal Greens of Aldebaran, who have hitherto showed no interest in Earth, would take a hand."

"As if we didn't have enough problems," Watkins said. "Now the Teal Greens!"

"But I think we can still do something about it," Budkins said. "You must contact the Master Programmer at once. Tell her it's essential she take a couple of months off the Earth Main Sequence Time Clock and reset for a Bush victory."

Watkins wasn't sure. "You know how she hates to redo human history. You know what she says: too many anomalies spoil the construct."

"She's got to do it," Budkins said. "The time-line of the Bush presidency is now the only available one that doesn't have the Teal Greens taking over. It'll give us a breathing-space to mount a defense against them."

"All right," Watkins said. "I'll do it. But you know the time-line forecast: with Bush we get the Kuwait invasion and the Persian Gulf War."

"I know," Budkins said, "but what can we do? It's either that or the Teal Greens."

"All right." He went to the door, then turned. "What do you want us to do about Dukakis in this new time-line?"

"Don't worry about him. It's Bush we have to worry about now."